William George Hawkins

Life of John H.W. Hawkins

William George Hawkins

Life of John H.W. Hawkins

ISBN/EAN: 9783337333195

Printed in Europe, USA, Canada, Australia, Japan

Cover: Foto ©Raphael Reischuk / pixelio.de

More available books at **www.hansebooks.com**

OF

JOHN H. W. HAWKINS.

COMPILED BY HIS SON,

REV. WILLIAM GEORGE HAWKINS, A.M.

"The noble self conqueror, the earnest, generous friend of the inebriate, the consistent, devoted advocate of the temperance reform in all its stages of development, and the kind, sympathising brother, ready to aid by voice and act every form of suffering humanity."

SIXTH THOUSAND.

BOSTON:
PUBLISHED BY. BRIGGS AND RICHARDS,
456 WASHINGTON STREET, COR. ESSEX.

NEW YORK:
SHELDON, BLAKEMAN & CO.
1862.

LITHOTYPED BY COWLES AND COMPANY,
17 WASHINGTON ST., BOSTON.

Printed by Geo. C. Rand and Avery.

To

MY GRANDMOTHER,

WHOSE PRAYERS, UNINTERMITTED FOR MORE THAN FORTY
YEARS, HAVE, UNDER GOD, SAVED A SON, AND GIVEN
TO HER NATIVE COUNTRY A PHILANTHROPIST,
WHOSE MULTIPLIED DEEDS OF LOVE
ARE EVERYWHERE TO BE SEEN, AND WHICH ARE HERE
BUT IMPERFECTLY RECORDED,

This Volume

IS AFFECTIONATELY DEDICATED

PREFACE.

THE compiler of this volume has endeavored to obey the command taught him in his youth, "Honor thy father," etc., etc. He has, therefore, turned aside for a brief period from his professional duties, to gather up some memorials of him whose life is here but imperfectly delineated. It has indeed been a labor of love; how faithfully and judiciously performed must be left for others to say. The writer has sought to avoid multiplying his own words, preferring that the subject of this memoir and his friends should tell their own story. His chief solicitude has been to do justice to a loved and honored parent, and to the Great Reform, with which he was so closely identified. It was found possible to incorporate but a small part of his correspondence and other documents within the compass of four hundred pages, but enough, it is hoped, fully to illustrate his character and services. It is believed that there is not a denomination of Christians in the land unblessed by this reform. If it has thus been the instrument in the smallest degree of advancing the Redeemer's kingdom, it should receive the cordial support of every earnest and sincere laborer in the cause of truth and righteousness.

A perusal of this volume will show that a large part of Mr. Hawkins' life was devoted to the interests of Massachusetts; how much good he effected, eternity only can unfold. He canvassed this State more thoroughly than any other. She was the first to recognize in him a reformer whose influence was likely to be great in the land; he therefore loved her, and adopted her as his home. He has frequently, upon public occasions, expressed the wish to end his labors here, and here to be buried. Will not Massachusetts, therefore, on some fitting occasion, indicate an appropriate spot to which his remains may be removed, and erect over them some humble memorial of his deeds?

The great dignity and importance of this reform is seen by a glance at that bright galaxy of divines, statesmen, physicians, and philanthropists, who have at different periods given to the subject their thoughts and prayers and labors. They are fixed in their elevated positions, and the radiance of their beams shall yet lighten all the land. Our heart has been gladdened as we have from time to time noted them down, somewhat in their chronological order: Rush, Porter, Armstrong, Humphrey, Edwards, Swan, Bonney, Dexter, Chapin, Beecher, Nott, Kittredge, Hewett, Stuart, Tucker, Fisk, Sewell, Warren, Woods,

Hunt, Walworth, Sargent, Delavan, Keener, Pierpont, Grant, Jewett, Barclay, Sigourney, McIllvaine, Hitchcock, Potter, Tyng, Marsh, O'Neale, Cocke, Beaman, Chipman, Gough, Riley, Kellogg, Cary, Dow, and Arthur.

The compiler expresses his thanks to the many friends of his father who so promptly responded, from various parts of the country, to his circular, and to the Rev. Dr. Marsh, and other friends, for valuable files of public journals. In a life so active as was Mr. Hawkins', many incidents will be found scattered through the country in files of newspapers, and in the memories of the living; any information of that character, communicated to the compiler, at No. 11 Cornhill, Boston, will be gratefully received.

W. G H.

Boston, January 26th, 1859.

CONTENTS.

CHAPTER I.

CHAPTER II.

CHAPTER III.

CHAPTER IV.

CHAPTER VII.

CHAPTER VIII.

CHAPTER IX.

CHAPTER X.

CHAPTER XI.

CHAPTER XII.

CHAPTER XIII.

CHAPTER XIV.

CHAPTER XV.

CHAPTER XVI.

CHAPTER XIX.

CHAPTER XX.

CHAPTER XXI.

JOHN H. W. HAWKINS.

CHAPTER I.

"Let not ambition mock their useful toil,
Their homely joys, and destiny obscure;
Nor grandeur hear with a disdainful smile
The short and simple annals of the poor."

IT was in the month of August, 1858, that the writer of these pages was passing along Fells Street, on Fell's Point, in the city of Baltimore, in company with John Henry Willis Hawkins. The father and son were returning from a day's fishing excursion, planned, it is believed, wholly for the son's recreation. As they approached a bend in the street, Mr. Hawkins stopped, and pointing across the way, said, " Do you see those dilapidated buildings? Just on that spot once stood the dwelling in which your grandfather lived and died, and where I was born." Fell's Point is one of those projections into the harbor of Baltimore where the water is deepest, and ships of the largest size may approach. Stretching from this street are numerous long wharves, where busy mariners pass and repass in crowds. " No wonder, then," it was replied, " you

1

are so fond of the water and the finny tribe, and that you are so expert a swimmer, since you passed your boyhood so near the harbor."

A brief genealogy of the Hawkins family has been preserved, from which we make a few extracts. William Hawkins, the uncle of John H. W. Hawkins, arrived in Baltimore, from England, on the 14th of October, 1773, with his father, John Hawkins, who had a family of ten children.* His grandfather's name was James, the son of Charles Hawkins, of Exeter, England; the latter was killed in 1704, at the head of a regiment of which he was colonel, at the taking of Gibraltar. The military life seems to have possessed considerable attraction for several of the descendants after their emigration to this country.

Of the ten children of John Hawkins, the grandfather of John H. W. Hawkins, nine were sons. John, his father, was the sixth, and was born in 1764. He, with several of his brothers, settled in the city of Baltimore; the others, fonder of adventure, emigrated to the Western States, and there engaged in business, where, it will be seen, the subject of this memoir found them in after years. In 1800, his father was pursuing a

---

* William Hawkins,   born 1754, died 1818.
  James Hawkins,   "   1756.
  Robert Hawkins,   "   1758, "   1769.
  Jane Hawkins,   "   1760, "   1802.
  Thomas Hawkins,   "   1762, "   1816.
  JOHN HAWKINS,   "   1764, "   1811.
  Archibald Hawkins,   "   1766, "   1851.
  Isaac Hawkins,   "   1768, "   1795.   .
  Robert Hawkins,   "   1770, "   1800.
  Samuel Hawkins,   "   1772, "   1773.

Susannah Brown Hawkins, the mother of the above, was born in 1736, and died 1772, aged 36.

thriving business as a merchant tailor, on Fleet Street, Fell's Point, in the city of Baltimore.

His mother, Elizabeth Dorsey, was respectably connected; the name of Dorsey being known in the early annals of Maryland in connection with many noble virtues and praiseworthy deeds. Both father and mother were professors of religion, and were well known among the Methodist preachers of that early day as exemplary Christians, and possessed of those expansive charities which made the dwelling of " Brother John Hawkins," the place of common resort for the preachers. There religious meetings were held, and many earnest prayers offered that these pious parents might bring up their numerous and increasing offspring in the love and service of their Maker.

To John and Elizabeth Hawkins, were born ten children; viz., Ruth, John Henry Willis, William (died from home), Nicholas (drowned), Frances, Elizabeth, William, Ellen, Archibald, and Ann. John Henry Willis was born Sept. 28, 1797. His father died June 3, 1811, when this, his second child, was in his fourteenth year, and the education of his children was immediately placed under the direction of their uncle, William Hawkins; all, except John, received an excellent education. The teacher under whom they had been placed several years before their father's death, was the celebrated Alexander McCaine; a gentleman well fitted, intellectually, for his business, but a most rigid disciplinarian. The other children seem to have experienced but little inconvenience, however, from this trait in his character, or, if they did, but little complaint was made; but the restless, active spirit of John would at times rebel against the rigid restraint under which

he was placed.   Mr. McCaine was a man of powerful
frame, and stentorian lungs, and woe to the youth who
felt the weight of his massive hand.   Being considered
the rogue, and possibly the dunce of the school, John
was often the subject of chastisement; sometimes,
probably, beyond his deserts.   But a resolute will and
great power of endurance enabled him to bear up under it.   At times, however, he would become so terrified at the threats of his teacher as to be rendered
wholly incapable of efficient study.   In a letter from
his sister Frances, speaking of his school days, she remarks :   * " His great difficulty with his teacher, Mr.
McCaine, arose from his daring, brave, and restless
spirit, which prevented him from applying himself to
his studies, thereby bringing censure on himself from
his teacher.   He was a great favorite at school, always
ready to defend and protect the helpless."

It would be doing injustice to the memory of Rev.
Mr. McCaine to omit making mention of a pleasing
incident that occurred in after years.   In a tour which
Mr. Hawkins made through the Southern States, he
was invited by Mr. McCaine, then pastor of a church
in one of the largest of the Southern cities, to lecture to
his congregation.   The assembly was a large one, and
the venerable preacher, on introducing Mr. Hawkins
to the audience, placed his hand upon his head and referred in most touching terms to their early relation as
teacher and pupil, — to the wonderful changes that
time had wrought in their histories, and the gratification which the present meeting afforded him.   The incident added much interest to the services, and many
were deeply affected.

* Mrs. Schaeffer's letter, dated Oct 6, 1858.

Frequent complaints of his ungovernable spirit coming from his teacher to his mother and uncle, after due consultation it was determined to apprentice John to Mr. Joseph Coxe, of Baltimore, to learn the trade of a hatter. Aware of the restless disposition of the youth, due care was taken that the master selected for him should be a man who could maintain perfect subordination among his apprentices. The young apprentice entered heartily into the business, and became a most expert artisan. His fellow-workmen assert that few men could accomplish tasks equal to him. The apprentices at this establishment were, in the estimation of their master, well cared for; all were required to be in bed at nine o'clock, and the hour for instruction in the schoolroom was rigidly observed; industry was the law of the establishment, and no drones were retained a moment. Mr. Coxe was a man of iron will, and not insensible to the duties which he owed to his apprentices.

There was, however, one fatal custom prevailing in that day, which was the source of untold woes to the youth under his charge. Stimulating liquors were daily dispensed to his apprentices and journeymen, under the erroneous belief that they tended to increase their vigor and activity. The use of liquors in the shop only led to the continued use of them when the labors of the day were over. Thus many were led imperceptibly to form habits of inebriety, which were never broken up. Of this period of his life, Mr. Hawkins thus speaks in one of his public addresses: —

" I was born of respectable parents, and was educated by a minister, and then bound out to the hatting business, in as per-

1*

fect a grog-shop as ever existed. A few days before I left Baltimore, I found the old books of my master; there were the names of sixty men upon them, and we could recollect but one who did not go to a drunkard's grave. Another hatter says it was just so on his books. At one time there were twelve of us as apprentices; eight of the twelve have died drunkards, one is in the almshouse of Baltimore, one is keeping a tavern in Baltimore, and here am I."

CHAPTER II.

"Then a soldier, * * *
Jealous in honor, sudden and quick in quarrel,
Seeking the bubble reputation
Even in the cannon's mouth."

IT will be remembered that the subject of this memoir was apprenticed to Mr. Coxe some time during the year 1811, when he was in his fourteenth year. Shortly after, in 1812–13–14, the country became convulsed from one end to the other by the battles, both by sea and land, in the war with Great Britain. Thrilling accounts of those scenes and occurrences were published, and read with avidity, particularly by the youth of the country. The surrender of Hull, the capture of the Alert, the attack on Queenstown, the siege of Fort Meigs, the battle on Lake Erie and the success of Perry, the capture of the Peacock by the Hornet, the killing of Tecumseh, the exciting events of the Indian war in the West, and, finally, the capture and burning of Washington, and the approach of the British naval forces on Baltimore by way of Chesapeake Bay, — all these events furnished to the apprentices at Mr. Coxe's material for many a brave speech, and inspired them, doubtless, with the resolution, young as they were, to lay down their lives in their country's behalf, should opportunity offer and the cause demand it.

It was under this state of feverish excitement that the announcement of the landing at North Point or

(7)

six thousand British soldiers, under the command of General Ross, fell like a thunder-clap upon the citizens of Baltimore. There was hurrying to and fro in her streets, and parents were busily employed in sending their children into the country, away from the impending danger. Mr. Coxe made immediate arrangements for sending his apprentices away from the city for their better security; but John Hawkins, that very month, September, but seventeen years of age, was not thus to be restrained in his liberty. Leaving the others, in company with a cousin he proceeded to the armory, secured a rifle, and joining the volunteer forces, three thousand two hundred strong, under the command of General Striker, he marched with them to North Point, fourteen miles distant. This was on Sunday, the 11th of September, 1814. What took place on the ensuing day, the 12th of September, is well known. The British forces were not only kept in check until the forts and batteries near the city were placed in a good state of defence, but great damage was done to their lines, and their commander was shot down, advancing at the head of his column, by two American youths. These youths, Wells and McComas, were members of a company of sharpshooters, riflemen, of which Dr. S. B. Martin, brother-in-law of Mr. Hawkins, was surgeon; being an actor in the scene, his account is both valuable and reliable.

This company had been sent in advance of the volunteers, to ascertain the position of the enemy and to report the condition of their forces. It was soon ascertained that they had deployed in the form of the letter V, and before they were aware of the danger they found themselves nearly surrounded. Most of them effected a safe retreat; Maj. Heath's horse was shot under him.

Early in the day the word had passed along the lines, " *Remember, boys, General Ross rides a white horse to-day !* " The two young men had declared, that morning, their intention of selling their lives dearly. Instead of retreating with their comrades, they penetrated the British advanced forces, and discovering General Ross mounted on his white charger, they aimed the fatal shots. The enemy was thrown into confusion, and some moments were consumed in preparing a litter for the removal of their general, weltering in his blood.

Dr. Martin, a few days after the battle, rode down to North Point, to the residence of Mr. Gorsuch, at whose house General Ross and his officers had breakfasted on the morning of the twelfth, and learned from him the following facts. On their departure for the field of battle Mr. Gorsuch asked the General if he should prepare supper for them upon their return. " No," said he; " I shall sup in Baltimore to-night, or in hell! " It is believed that this account bears upon its face much stronger evidence of authenticity than any of the other numerous versions that have hitherto been published.

General Ross was killed in a slight skirmish with the rifle company a few moments before the battle commenced. The volunteer forces were soon engaged. John Hawkins was in the front of the battle; several of his companions in arms fell at his side, and a ball pierced his hat. So near was he that he distinctly saw the action which deprived not only the British general but the two brave young Americans, Wells and Mc-Comas, of their lives; — they were immediately shot. The engagement lasted one hour and twenty minutes.

The killed and wounded of the Americans amounted
to one hundred and three, among whom, says S. G.
Goodrich, were many of the first citizens of Baltimore.

The young apprentice and his youthful comrade
returned to their homes in the evening of that ever-
memorable day. His mother and sisters were, as would
naturally be expected, alarmed and anxious as to his
fate, knowing as they well did his impetuous temperament; and his mother had been often to the door
and looked up the street for her son and nephew, and
when at last she saw them coming she hastened to
meet them, exclaiming, "Why, my son, could you be
so venturesome?" "My dear mother," he replied,
"you should be thankful that I am alive." On enter-

ing the house they could scarcely be recognized by the members of the family, their faces were so covered with sweat and powder and dust. 'They were themselves in a high state of excitement, not knowing what was to befall their homes on the morrow. They went to bed in a room called the "band-room," in which religious meetings had been held. His sister Ellen could with difficulty convince herself of his safety; after they had retired she went to their bedside and placed her hand upon his breast; the heavy throbbing of his heart alone assured her that he was indeed safe.

This demonstration of the enemy resulted in their entire discomfiture, and on the 14th of September, when night came on, they silently withdrew and re-embarked. A record of these transactions was carefully preserved in the family, by Rev. John Baxley,[*] who married Mrs. Hawkins the same year, she having remained a widow from June 3, 1811. Mr. Baxley, in his private journal, says: —

Sunday, 11th September, 1814. — The British fleet are in sight of this city (Baltimore), about fifteen miles distant, at the mouth of the river Patapsco, at North Point, in number about thirty-five sail. In the course of the day the most of the ships worked inside of North Point, and appeared to be making preparations to land their troops. This has been a day of great alarm, and to some of terror and dismay. In the morning of this day I felt my heart comfortably engaged in devo-

---

[*] Rev. John Baxley was a local preacher of the Methodist church, a man of a highly cultivated mind, and in the early days of his ministry was extensively known as an able and efficient preacher. Thousands have been instructed, blessed, and saved, under his thrilling appeals; his sermons were always methodically arranged and fertile in appropriate illustrations. He died in 1849.

tion, but in the afternoon found my mind very much taken up with the events taking place, and with what may be expected to follow, yet feel a confidence that God will mercifully spare the city, and save the inhabitants from destruction.

Monday, 12th.—Through the course of this day experienced considerable exercise of mind, and spent several hours in viewing the enemy's ships, to the number of sixteen sail, come up the river, and take their positions near Fort McHenry, evidencing their intentions to make an attack. In the afternoon, while viewing the approach of the hostile fleet, distinctly heard the firing of artillery and musketry on land, about two o'clock, and in the evening learned that there had been an engagement between the enemy and part of our troops on Patapsco Neck, which lasted more than an hour, when our troops received orders to retreat, which it is said they did in good order, and reached the lines or entrenchments a little after sunset; many greatly fatigued and exhausted; *among them my wife's son* * *and nephew.* Some lives have been lost on both sides, without doubt. I feel myself exercised about my family, and should have been better satisfied if they had been in the country; yet feel a degree of confidence that we shall be preserved.

Tuesday, 13th.—At about seven o'clock the enemy commenced bombarding Fort McHenry, which continued with some little intermission till after eleven o'clock at night. The weather has been cold and wet, and every thing seemed to favor the enemy's operations; wind, tide, darkness, and rain, were in their favor. Under cover of the darkness they succeeded in getting past the fort, up the south branch of the Patapsco, with a number of barges, said to contain about twelve hundred and fifty picked men, with a view, no doubt, to attempt storming the fort on the land side. Thinking their object in some measure obtained, they are said to have cheered, and then commenced firing rockets and shells. Our batteries up the river (which they had not observed), and Fort McHenry, immediately opened a most

---

* John H. W. Hawkins.

tremendous and destructive fire on them, which compelled a retreat and it is supposed they must have lost a great number of men.*

Such a terrible roar of cannon and mortars I never heard before, and never wish to hear again. I was awakened out of sleep by its commencement about one o'clock in the morning of Wednesday the 14th. I at first felt much alarm, until fairly awake, and enabled to ascertain what was the real state of things. I was at first apprehensive that the enemy had succeeded in effecting a landing, and were entering the city. Under this impression I waked up all my family, and had them ready to fly, in the event of the city being set on fire by the enemy; great alarm and distress were excited among

* West of Fort McHenry were the concealed batteries, which checked the approach of the enemy, and which effected such destruction of their barges, spoken of in the diary of Baxley.

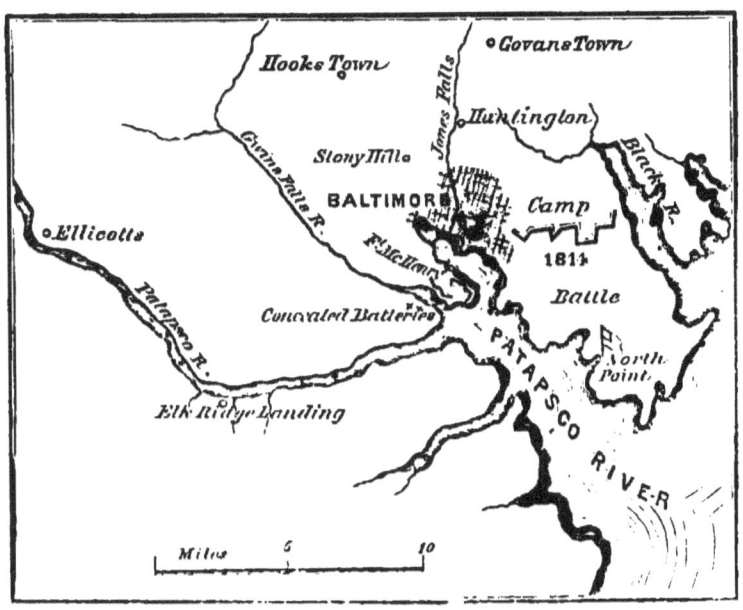

the women and children, and terror and consternation seemed to fill every mind for a time. But it was soon ascertained, that having failed in their attempt to effect a landing, they had given the signal for retreat, and although they continued to throw shells at intervals until seven o'clock on Wednesday morning, *the army* had *retreated* to North Point, and had commenced reëmbarking; and about nine o'clock the shipping that bombarded Fort McHenry were all under way, standing down the river to join the fleet at North Point. Surely the hand of the Lord was manifested in our deliverance from our enemies; for in my opinion they could have taken the city had they followed up the success they obtained at North Point; but it would appear as if the Lord had intimidated them with fear. I visited Fort McHenry with coffee and some other refreshments, about eight o'clock, and found that the warm coffee was greatly reviving to the men, who had been standing in the mud and wet for a number of hours."*

* Rev. Mr. Baxley had several relations among the volunteer forces inside the fort.

CHAPTER III.

Religion, therefore, is a necessary and indispensable element in any great human character. There is no living without it. Religion is the tie that connects man with his Creator, and holds him to his throne. If that tie be all sundered, all broken he floats away, a worthless atom in the universe; its proper attraction all gone, its destiny thwarted, and its whole future nothing but darkness, desolation, and death. — WEBSTER.

IN the year 1815, immediately after the war, an event occurred in the life of the subject of this memoir, which was to affect his whole future destiny.

In an extensive religious awakening in his native city, in which thousands were brought from darkness to light, the young apprentice was led to reflect upon his past life, and became thoroughly converted to the love and service of his Maker. The entireness of his renewal, and the earnestness of his devotion to his Maker, were immediately evinced, by actively engaging in the work of instructing and reclaiming others. He made no delay in connecting himself with the Methodist Episcopal Church, and in endeavoring to walk in all the commandments and ordinances of the Lord blameless. His pious mother has often remarked, that he was spoken of by others as the most exemplary and devout young man in the community. He assumed the straight-breasted coat and standing collar, the prevailing custom of his Methodist brethren in that day, and he was subjected on this account to no little annoyance. He often referred, in after years, to the criti-

(15)

cisms passed upon him by his fellow apprentices who met him on his way to church.

His first work was to establish a Sabbath school for boys on Fell's Point, the first ever opened in the city of Baltimore. It is true, some maiden ladies had commenced Sunday-school instruction for girls, but his was the first effort to bring young men under its benign influences. So little interest was felt in the importance of these schools, that he found it impossible to procure the reading of his notices, for the organizing of the schools, by the clergy from their pulpits. He persevered, however, and a large number were gathered. Great difficulty was experienced in obtaining teachers, most of the labor of instruction falling upon himself. His exertions were unremitted until the close of his apprenticeship and his departure to the Western country. Much good, however, followed from these efforts, and more than one Methodist clergyman attributes his first religious impressions to the influence of this school. The last address delivered on earth by Mr. Hawkins, was before a Sabbath school in Pequea, Pa., in which he gave an account of the establishment of Sunday schools, and the incidents connected with his own early efforts in Baltimore. He related one incident which is well worth recording. On his late visit to Baltimore, in August, 1858, an individual came up to him and cordially grasping him by the hand, asked if he did not remember him; he replied that he was sorry to say that he did not. The individual then gave him his name, adding, " I was one of the youths whom you induced to join the first Sabbath school in Baltimore, and my best and earliest impressions were obtained from you. I have in my possession the Psalter and spelling-book you then gave me; I shall prize them very highly, and when I am dead shall bequeath them to my oldest son."

During this period of his efforts in the Sunday-school cause, he became interested in a very aged African, who had been thoroughly converted to God, but could not read his Bible, and expressed a longing desire to "Massa John," as he called him, to read one chapter, if no more, in that precious volume, before he died. Mr. Hawkins undertook the task, and for that purpose met the aged disciple two nights in every week, for a whole year. He began in ignorance of a

single letter ; but his instructor was not to be discouraged.   Procuring a board, he covered it with sand, and commenced by teaching him to form letters, then words, and then sentences, with his finger.   At the end of the year he had the pleasure of hearing his pupil read the first verse of the third chapter of the first epistle of John : " Behold, what manner of love the Father hath bestowed upon us that we should be called the sons of God," etc.   When the old man got through the verse, raising his eyes and hands to heaven he exclaimed, " Bless de Lord! bless de Lord!   Now is thy servant ready to depart."   "But," said his teacher, "this is only the first verse ; I intend you shall read the whole chapter ; " and he continued his efforts until the object was accomplished, to the infinite joy and spiritual benefit of this pious servant of God.

Whatever difficulties the subject of this narrative had with his employer previous to his conversion, he never afterwards had any cause for complaint; he was a pattern of industry, and was acknowledged to be the most skillful of his apprentices.   At the age of twenty-one he was considered thoroughly acquainted with every department of the business of manufacturing hats.   He often remarked that during the whole seven years of his apprenticeship he lost but three days ; two when at the funeral of a brother who had died in the country while on a visit, and the other at the battle of North Point.   On the day of his coming of age there was due to him from his master, twenty-five dollars for extra work.   Twenty dollars of this sum he immediately expended in books for his Sabbath school, and five dollars he reserved for the purchase of firewood to keep the school in operation during the winter season.

We turn now to an entirely new chapter in the life of Mr. Hawkins. Rejoicing in his freedom, emancipated as he believed from an irksome servitude, he determined for a brief period to enjoy life, and then, with the wide world before him, to seek his fortune, independent of others' aid. He was free in the latter part of the year 1818.* His first letters of which we can obtain any trace commence in this year. His mother had numerous relatives residing in the State of Maryland, engaged in agricultural pursuits, some of them in Howard county, and in the immediate neighborhood of Lisbon. He was invited, it would seem, to spend the first Christmas of his freedom with them. He thus writes : —

LISBON, HOWARD Co., Dec. 31, 1818.

DEAR MOTHER, — I take this opportunity to inform you that I am well, and trust you are also. I have had the *greatest Christmas* this year that I have ever enjoyed in all my life before. I have been visiting every day since my arrival here. On Christmas day I heard the Rev. Henry Welch preach a Baptist sermon. I had to receive my portion, for he tore the Arminians to pieces with much severity. He said they were all as blind as bats. I dined this day at Uncle John Welch's, where the sermon was preached. On Tuesday I heard Brother Robert Hood preach the funeral sermon of Debby Dorsey. To-day I sat down to a great dinner given at Catharine Warfield's. On Saturday I heard Brother Machelfresh preach a very good discourse, from which I received much good. On

---

* His brother William, twelve years of age at the time, writes to a cousin in Richmond, Va., under date of November 6, conveying the pleasing intelligence, as something recent. He says, "John and Fletcher (his brother-in-law) *are free,* and are now at home ;" and in January following, writes again, "Brother John has gone to the country."

Wednesday morning I went over to Aunt N—— W——'s, where I was received with great pleasure, and was treated as her son, and by her children as a brother.

My mind, dear mother, is very uneasy about dear sister Ruthy. Let me know how you all are, but particularly Ruthy, for you know I left her very sick. As for myself, I am enjoying my visit much, and am as happy as if I was placed upon a king's throne; my relatives everywhere have treated me with the utmost kindness and politeness. I have seen a great many pretty girls here, and have actually picked out one, worth about fifteen or sixteen hundred dollars; now this is a fact. I don't know that I shall ever come down to you again; but at all events, you may expect me down about the last of January; you need not expect to touch me before. To-morrow morning I expect to start on a visit to Newmarket, and to Frederick; we design returning in a week or two. I have no more at present to write; but give my love to papa, particularly to friend Dr. George B. Schaeffer, Rev. John Daly, *and* Miss Julia.* Tell Fletcher to pay up my meeting-fees at the Hatter's Society, or I shall be under a fine, and I will pay him on my return.

Nothing more, only beseeching you to write me and let me know how Ruth and all the family are; don't fail.

I remain, with love to all,

Your affectionate son until death,

John H. W. Hawkins.

P. S.—Here is room for you all to criticize; the poor pen should bear the blame, for it won't do as I want it, it is so stubborn.

The visit over, we presume he returned to Baltimore

* Who this "Miss Julia" was cannot be ascertained; the remark may have been a ruse to keep them in the dark as to one Miss Rachel Thompson, to whom he was in reality attentive.

about the last of January or first of February, 1819.
He found business of all kinds very much depressed,
and after seeking in vain for employment, he determined to seek his fortune in the Great West; his great
love of adventure acting also as a powerful stimu-
lant.

CHAPTER IV.

"I hail thee, Valley of the West,
    For what thou yet shalt be!
I hail thee for the hopes that rest
    Upon thy destiny!
To me, in all thy youthful pride,
Thou art a land of cares untried,
    Of untold hopes and fears."

In April (30th), 1819, his father-in-law,* writing to a nephew in Richmond, Va., thus adverts to the pressure of the times: —

Business is very dull here, and great distress is felt for the want of money, and we have had several failures, and it is likely that we shall have more. John Hawkins has gone to Pittsburg; he wrote under date of 16th April that he was well, and much pleased with the place, and had obtained employment at two dollars per day.

In a letter dated June 4th, same year, he says: —

We have had bad times here in business, but hope to see better days. Only one bank out of the *ten* here has got into difficulties; that is to say, the City Bank; but report makes things much worse than they are in reality; yet they are bad enough.

It was under these circumstances that John Hawk-

---

* Rev. Mr. Baxley was at this time first book-keeper in the Marine Bank of Baltimore.

(22)

ins, almost penniless, decided to leave his native city, and relations to whom he was most tenderly attached, and seek his fortune in those Western States of whose great enterprise and rapid growth he had heard so much. The letter alluded to above, of April 16th, nas not been preserved; but we have a brief journal which he kept on his journey out, detailing his adventures, etc. It is entitled, " A Journal of John H. W. Hawkins, from Baltimore through the Western States, commencing April 6th, 1819, and ending April 30th, 1821."

April 6, 8 *o'clock.* — I left Baltimore *on foot,* and arrived in Lisbon, twenty-six miles, at four o'clock, P.M.

Remaining here two days to see the relatives whom he had left in February, recurring with delight to his former visit, and inquiring particularly, without doubt, about the young lady "worth about fifteen or sixteen hundred dollars," and filling their minds with large ideas of his intended journey and sight-seeing, he departs on Thursday, the 8th.

Left Lisbon in the stage, and arrived in Frederick; left same day and went to Middletown, where I remained for the night.

Friday, 9th. — Left Middletown, and arrived in Hagerstown, at which place I endeavored to obtain work, but found it impossible. I remained until Monday morning. I found the people here very kind and accommodating; they treated me with the utmost politeness.

Monday Morning, April, 12th. — I left Hagerstown at one o'clock in the stage for Cumberland; arrived there the next day, then took passage in the stage for Uniontown. This evening the tire came off the wheel; we still kept on for nine miles; the spokes by that time were not more than eight inches long. Stopping long enough to get a wagon-wheel, we pro-

ceeded on our journey; travelling all night, found ourselves at
a little before sunrise in Uniontown. I here took passage in
the stage for Brownsville, which is twelve miles from Uniontown. I here took passage in a boat down the Monongahela,
for Pittsburg; but the boat went so slow that I left her, got on
the shore, and went on foot for Pittsburg, and arrived there
the next day, Thursday. Here I got work at Mr. Edward
Patchell's; I finished hats for him awhile and then went to
making them. I boarded in this place with Mr. John Win-
kight, at three dollars and a half per week. I am pleased with
this place but not with the people; they are not sociable in the
least. The Methodists are very proud; much more so than
they are in Baltimore. This is quite a large place for a country town; the streets are very well paved, and the houses are
of brick, and mostly two and three stories. While near Cumberland I had the pleasure of viewing the spot where General
Braddock had his fort erected and defended the town of Cumberland. I saw also the remains of the fort erected by General Washington.

Fort Necessity was erected by Washington, as it is
well known, in May or June, 1754. It was in this
place that he defended himself with so much bravery
against the French and the Indians, nearly fifteen hundred in number, led on by M. de Villiers. After an ob-
stinate resistance of ten hours, he agreed to a capitula-
tion, by the terms of which he was allowed to return
unmolested to Virginia. The remains of Fort Necessity are still to be seen near the national road from
Cumberland to Wheeling, in the south-eastern part of
Fayette County, Pennsylvania.* It was along this
route that Mr. Hawkins proceeded on his journey to
the West. The picturesque character of the scenery

* See Marcius Wilson's History of the United States, p. 177

in this part of Pennsylvania, rising, as it does often-times, into the truly grand and sublime, arrested the traveller's attention, fond, as he evidently was, of the beauties of nature. "This, certainly," he remarks in his journal, "is a very beautiful country."

He remained in Pittsburgh only six or eight weeks, working the while at his trade; but either from want of employment, or from love of adventure, he left there some days before the 14th of June. He makes mention in his journal of having been from the 14th of June to the 7th of July, in going down the Ohio river from Steubenville to Cincinnati. He also remarks on the time consumed in making the voyage as being very long, owing to the low state of the water, and adds that, generally, with high water, the passage was accomplished in seven or eight days.

He goes into a minute account of all the towns passed on both banks of the river, delaying long enough in each to ascertain the probable population, manufactures, and public buildings. To give all the details collected would unduly prolong this narrative. Some of the statistics given are strongly indicative of the habits of the people, and the extent to which intemperance and rum-shops prevailed. He says of Steubenville, Ohio, "It is handsomely situated on the right bank of the Ohio as you descend, and occupies, with its out lots, a very fine bottom of the river, rich, extensive, and well farmed. Its manufactures are as follows: one Woolen Factory, one Hot-air Foundry, one Paper Mill of three vats, one *Brewery*, one Steam Flour Mill, one Steam Cotton Factory, one Nail Factory, two Earthern Ware Factories, one Tobacco Factory. It has four preachers, six lawyers, five doctors, twenty-seven stores, *sixteen taverns*, two banks, one printing office, and many other professions too tedious to mention."

He indulges in the same minute description of Wellsburgh, Wheeling, Pultney, Marietta, Point Pleasant, Gallipolis, Guyandot, Greensburgh, Burrsburgh, Portsmouth, Adamsville, Manchester, Ohio; Maysville, Augusta, Newport, Kentucky; and Cincinnati. He reached Cincinnati on the 7th of June, 1819, wrote his mother a letter on the 9th of the same month, and on the 14th took his departure for Madison, in the State of Indiana. We give this letter, omitting but few sentences. It shows that up to this period he had maintained his integrity and sobriety of conduct, although, as he says, beset with many and " sore conflicts."

CINCINNATI, July 9, 1819.

DEAR MOTHER, — I take this first opportunity to inform you that I am well. I arrived at this place on the 7th instant, after a tedious journey from Steubenville, in consequence of the water being very low. I was from the 14th of June to the 7th of July coming from Steubenville. Many, in time of high water, come in seven or eight days. This is a beautiful place; it contains from three to four thousand houses, chiefly of brick, and about fourteen thousand inhabitants. I expect to commence work on Monday morning. At present I am boarding with Ezekiel Hall. I have seen a great number of my acquaintances since coming here. [He mentions the names of eight or ten of them.] I am happy to hear that sister Frances and George* are married. I hope they may live happily to-

---

* The George referred to here, was the Rev. George B. Schaeffer, a clergyman in the Protestant Episcopal Church, who was married to his sister Frances on the 25th of May, 1819. He was a faithful and earnest minister of the P. E. Church, but died early in life, a martyr to too se-

gether here, and in the end be crowned with everlasting life. I understand, also, that sister Ruth and ·Captain What-you-call-him * are to be married very soon. For my own part, I have little notion of getting married yet awhile. I hear very distressing news from Baltimore, about the times; however, I hope *the times* will be better before I get back, which will be, perhaps, in a year from this; it may be sooner.

I thank God, that I still feel myself a subject of his grace. I have had *sore conflicts* since I left home, but still, blessed be God, he is my friend and advocate, and I know he will not forsake me if I put my trust in him! He is "a friend that sticketh closer than a brother." I feel no disposition to leave him, for he has done great things for me, whereof I have cause to be exceeding glad; and should we never meet again 'in this world, I trust we may at the right hand of the Majesty on high. Thomas M—— wishes you to let his friends know that he and family have arrived here safely, and has as much work as he can do. My love to all the family, and to all who may inquire for me; nothing more at present. You will please write immediately, and direct your letter to the care of Ezekiel Hall, Main Street, Cincinnati. I will answer immediately.

I remain ever your affectionate son,
JOHN H. W. HAWKINS.

From his journal it appears that he made but a brief sojourn in Cincinnati; probably the employment not meeting his expectations, or not being permanent. He says : —

I left Cincinnati on the 14th of July, and arrived in Madi-

---

vere mental application. Mr. Hawkins became strongly attached to Mr. Schaeffer, and on his return from the West was married by him to Miss Rachel Thompson, of the city of Baltimore.

* This was, doubtless, an erroneous report. His sister Ruth was married shortly afterwards to Dr. Samuel B. Martin, at present a practising physician in the city of Baltimore

son, Indiana, on the 17th of same month, in which place I remained until the 23d of August, and then went over to Bedford, in Kentucky. In this place I went to work for Mr. Thompson, for whom I worked until the 8th of December, 1819. I was then compelled to cease work, in consequence of his having no *napping* on hand.

Judging from his letter to his mother, he went immediately to Madison, to spend his idle time with his relatives : —

BEDFORD, KY., Nov. 17, 1819.

DEAR MOTHER AND FATHER : — Your letter of the 6th of September came safe to hand last week, and it affords me much pleasure to hear of your good health. [The hard times at the East compelling many emigrations, he continues :] I am happy to announce to you the safe arrival of Mr. T——— R———, and family. I——— C——— and B——— Sands stopped in Limestone, nearly two hundred miles above Madison. I cannot express the joy and comfort I received in embracing these dear friends ; they are all pleased with Madison and the country. S——— H——— is particularly pleased with the trip. I have been working for a Mr. Thompson, in Bedford, eleven miles from Madison, ever since the 23d of August, and expect to work for him all winter. I get better wages than I got in Baltimore or anywhere else. Board is low ;— two dollars and a half per week. I shall soon be in want of some linen, but do not like to pay what they ask for it in this country. Linen that you can get in Baltimore for fifty cents, they ask one dollar and a half for here, and this is too extravagant. If you can possibly find an opportunity of sending me enough for the present, I will compensate you for it if I am ever privileged to see you again, which I hope I may next spring. Thank God that I am able to say that I am making some advancement in the divine life. I bless God that I do enjoy a peace of mind that the world knows nothing of. When I reflect upon the goodness and mercy of God which has been, and still is, manifested towards me, it fills me with astonishment, and compels me to say, Who am I, that God should be mindful of me, or that he should visit me. Glory to God; I am resolved, though earth and hell combine against me and endeavor to stop my progress heavenward, in him will I trust; for he has hitherto supported me in all my afflictions, and in all my troubles he has made a way for my escape. I am a great distance from you, and know not that I shall ever be permitted to see you again this side eternity. If this should be the case, my prayer is that we may meet in heaven, where we shall part no more. Oh, may you be able in that great day of accounts, when God the Great Judge shall call you to his bar, to say, " Here, Lord, are we, and all the children whom thou gavest us." Shall this be the case? oh, my soul, shall this be the case? God grant it, for the sake of Jesus Christ. O my dear parents, pray much for your dear children that are yet out of the ark of safety. Oh that God may hear our prayers for those who have come to the years of accountability, and may he lead those who are young by the right hand of his power in all the paths of virtue until he shall call them to himself.

You write that the fever* has been very bad. Archibald has since written me that it had abated, which I am glad to hear. I have nothing more at present to say. Give my love to all the dear families and to all who inquire after me, particularly my dear friend J—— K——.

I ever remain,
Your affectionate son,
JOHN H. W. HAWKINS.

N. B. — Direct your letters to Madison, Indiana.

---

* During the summer of 1819 the yellow fever made its appearance in Baltimore, and raged with such virulence that as many as a hundred and more deaths occurred weekly for some time. All who could leave the city fled at its approach.

3*

MADISON, INDIANA, Dec. 21, 1819.

DEAR FATHER AND MOTHER,—It is with much satisfaction that I write you a few lines. I am glad to inform you that I am well and in perfect health; you may know this when I tell you that I weigh one hundred and sixty pounds.

I do adore the Lord for my health and strength, but still more do I adore him for the visitations of his Holy Spirit. I can testify that God is mine and I am his, by a feeling sense of his love shed abroad in my soul. That little spark of his love that I enjoy in my soul, I would not exchange for the riches of the Indies, or for the king's throne; no, never, never will I give up my shield, never will I let go my hold.

> " I'll lift my hands, I'll lift my voice
> While I have strength to pray or praise,
> This work shall make my heart rejoice
> To spend the remnant of my days."

Since I left you, many, very many have been my troubles and afflictions, but out of them all the Lord hath delivered me. I am determined to go forward, until I shall lay down the cross and take up the crown of life eternal. God grant this to be our happy lots. You mentioned in your last letter that you had a great desire to come to this country; my advice to you is, if you can possibly make arrangements, come, for there never was such a country. Your relatives really desire that you should come. If you make up your mind to come, come when the river is high,—say, about April. Bring tea and coffee with you, for these are scarce articles here; coffee sells at fifty and sixty-two and a half cents per pound, tea at three dollars and fifty cents per pound.

I know not when I shall see Baltimore again; perhaps not before next fall; it may be not before a year from that time. I, like the rest of the human family, expect to *live another life,*

as soon *as circumstances will admit.** Give my love to all the family, and to uncle J—— R——. Tell him by all means to come into this great country. My love to Father Kingston†
and all who may inquire for me.

I remain ever,

Your affectionate son,

JOHN H. W. HAWKINS.

P. S. — Don't forget to send the linen, and I will be much indebted to you ; you can send it by Mr. R—— or some one else.   J. H. W. H.

The distress in commercial matters which had begun in the East now reached the West, crushing the young enterprise of the people, and producing great suffering among the emigrants who had fled to the Western States in search of employment and a more comfortable state of affairs. Another source of much misery was the drinking usages of society, not then, as now, confined to particular classes in the community; but all, of every rank, of every profession, with but few exceptions, were addicted to the moderate, if not extravagant, use of intoxicating drinks. Without the glass of whisky toddy the minister could not enter upon his duties, the lawyer was unfit to plead, the judge unable to render a decision, the schoolmaster to teach, the doctor to visit his patients, the laborer to perform his task, the housewife to enter upon the duties of the day. The commercial disasters of the times added to the catalogue by driving many in thoughtlessness to drown their sorrows in the intoxicating cup.

---

* One object he no doubt had in view, was the accumulation of means, in anticipation of marriage.

† This seems to have been a spiritual friend, to whom he had become attached after his conversion.

But little effort had been made to stay the ravages
of intemperance.   It is true that in 1813 a society had
been formed in Boston, "the object of which was the
suppression of the use of ardent spirits as a drink."*
It was even at this early day ascertained that more
money was expended for alcoholic stimulants than for
the school and pulpit, involving not only a waste of
material, but the ruin of thousands, the corruption of
public morality, and a slow but sure degradation of the
State.   But these evils had by no means reached their
climax.   The country was rapidly approaching an
alarming state of demoralization, of physical and mental suffering ; and, in 1833, the astounding fact was ascertained, that the infatuated appetite of the people for
intoxicating beverages. was hurrying thirty thousand
human beings annually into all the horrors of drunkenness.   In the West, distilleries were being erected in
every eligible locality, and the floodgates of moral and
social death were opened in every direction.

It was amid these increasing evils, with the waves
of ungodliness raging on every side, that the subject of
this memoir sought, in the Far West, away from home
and kindred, by the industry of his hands to make his
fortune, and to maintain his character as a professing
Christian.   Such was considered, among all classes, the
harmlessness of stimulating beverages, that. it is more
than probable, though there is no positive evidence of
the fact, that Mr. Hawkins was at this early day in the
habit of its moderate use, and, possibly, at times indulged immoderately.   It is not improbable that rumors
of his becoming unsteady had reached his parents, and

---

* See the volume lately issued in Boston entitled " When will the Day
Come ? " from which the above statements are derived.

to guard him against evil consequences, a letter had been written to him in which great concern was expressed both for his temporal and spiritual well-being.

His father-in-law, Rev. John Baxley, was a man of excellent judgment, and of large experience ; and a letter from him to his son-in-law would be likely to make an impression upon his mind; that letter has not been preserved, but one written about the same time to his cousin, exhibits the character of the advice he would be likely to give.

(REV. JOHN BAXLEY TO HIS NEPHEW.)

BALTIMORE, July 24, 1819.

MY DEAR NEPHEW, — Yours by Mr. R—— was duly received. In an interview with Mr. R—— this morning, he was much concerned to hear that you had suffered from painful exercises of mind. You should strive against giving way to depression of spirits, and endeavor to be cheerful. Do not let your thoughts dwell on gloomy subjects ; and, if possible, try to find a friend to whom you can freely open your mind, and let him know all your painful exercises. When you write to me again, tell me your doubts, and fears, and temptations, and every thing that gives you distress, and I will do my best to advise and comfort you. You should get acquainted with the preachers, and the old, experienced members of society ; their conversation and prayers, and their experience, will be of great use to you ; but, above all, go to the Lord Jesus Christ in prayer ; he was tempted in every point, even as we are, and he knoweth how to succor, and he will succor "them that are tempted." Read the Scriptures, and other good books, and meditate upon what you read, and also on what you hear from the pulpit. I send you with this letter a pocket Bible, a " Discipline," " The Christian Pattern," and two volumes of Wesley's Sermons ; take special care of the Sermons. Be sure to write us by every opportunity, and open your mind to me freely.

I remain, dear L——,

Your affectionate uncle,

· JOHN BAXLEY.

It was in reply to a letter giving him judicious advice similar to the above, that his son John replied :—

MADISON, Feb. 26, 1820.

DEAR FATHER,—Your letter of 21st January last, came safe to hand. Your letter afforded much satisfaction, as you feel interested for my temporal and spiritual welfare. My dear father, I assure you I feel much interested for myself. It is certain I am exposed to dangers on the right and left; but that God who delivered Daniel and his three servants from the fiery furnace, has delivered me; he has fought my battles, *and, so far,* brought me off conqueror. Is not this reason enough for me to trust in him? I *think* it is. Nothing, however, shall separate me from him; no, *not even the sufferings of the martyr ;* for the Lord is my strength and my salvation; if I perish, I am resolved to perish at the feet of my Saviour, pleading for mercy.

I feel indebted to you for your fatherly advice; certainly, you could not do me a greater favor, at present, than to forward me such wholesome food. Receive my sincere thanks, for it is the only reward I can offer you at present. *You know* the way; go on, and God will, in the end, take you to himself.

I must now give you some detail of the times in the West. There is general suffering among the people. I never witnessed *such* distressed families as I have seen in the past few months. Only reflect; it has now been *eleven months* since I left you, and I have done but five months' work; this, certainly, is discouraging. I must *leave* the country. If I could raise the money I would come on to Baltimore immediately. However, you may expect me in the spring or fall; at present I have no work to do, and have had none for two months past. *I hardly know what to do*, but this thing I will do, endeavor to keep in the favor of God. Pray that God may keep me, and protect me. Give my love to affectionate mother, brothers and sisters, and all my dear connections.

I remain your affectionate son,

JOHN H. W. HAWKINS.

This letter was written in February; it appears from his journal that he recommenced work for Mr. Thompson, in Bedford, Kentucky, on the 11th of March. Occupation seems to have entirely relieved his mind, and he consequently writes more cheerfully.

MADISON, July 11, 1820.

DEAR FATHER AND MOTHER, — Your affectionate letter of the 21st of June, came safely to hand. I was extremely glad to hear from you. It affords me great satisfaction to hear from you at any time. I am, you know, at a great distance from you, and stand almost alone in the world. But blessed be God, he supports and protects me in every trying circumstance. I have just recovered from a very severe attack of the bilious fever, which reduced me very much. I have great cause to thank the Lord for his goodness in supporting me under my afflictions, and bringing me again to health; he has done much for me, whereof I have cause to be exceeding glad.

I have as much work as I can do all the summer. The times are much better here than they are at the East. I shall continue here as long as I can get any work to do. I hope you will come out yourself if you possibly can.

It gives me much pleasure to hear that W —— has a situation in so respectable a house; I hope he may do well. Let him remember his Creator in the days of his youth. That God may bless you, and all the family, is the sincere prayer of

Your dear son,

JOHN H. W. HAWKINS.

Here his letters cease, and but little is said in his journal, except that he was again thrown out of employment in the month of November, 1820, and remained in this unpleasant position until nearly all his money was expended; and what was worse, with bad habits contracted and evil associations formed. He had squandered all he had earned, and was reduced, without doubt, to much misery and wretchedness. His journal received less attention; the entries upon it becoming briefer, and the handwriting less neat and correct. Under date of April 7, 1821, we find this entry: "I left Bedford for Madison this day." Again: "Madison, Tuesday, April 10th, 1821, left Madison for Bedford in company with Mr. Gibson and Mr. Vail. We walked this day forty-five miles. We left North Ferry 11th April, and reached Cincinnati April 12, thirty-two miles. I left Cincinnati in the Wheeling packet, Mr. Knights, captain, which I thought most expedient, and about the same expense as travelling on foot."

CHAPTER V

"Light-winged hopes, that come when bid,
And rainbow joys that end in weeping,
And passions among pure thoughts hid,
Like serpents under flow'rets sleeping."

"Oh, who, when fading of itself away,
Would cloud the sunshine of his little day?
Now is the May of life. Careering round,
Joy wings his feet, Joy lifts him from the ground."

POSSESSED, as the subject of this memoir was, of a happy temperament and an uncommon love of novelty, he, without doubt, found enough in those Western wilds, and on the waters of the Ohio, to render the passage full of pleasing incident. Nothing seems to have escaped his watchful eye; and his retentive memory enabled him to relate in after years, in a most vivid and lifelike manner, the events and incidents of his Western tour. His journal continues:—

Friday, April 13*th.*—We arrived at Maysville at four o'clock in the morning, and left there the same morning at eleven o'clock.

Saturday, 14*th.*—We reached Portsmouth at seven o'clock in the morning, and stopped a few moments to receive some wood on board, and then set sail at fifteen minutes past eight. This morning we passed the fast-sailing steamboats Robert Thompson and Courier; at night passed the Velocipede, all bound to the Falls of the Ohio.

Sunday Morning, 15*th.*—Stopped at Mr. Vantumes, to re-

4   (37)

ceive wood, and then proceeded on our journey. Stopped also
at Point Pleasant, at the mouth of the Kanawha, to discharge
part of the cargo, which did not detain us long. This is a considerable river of Virginia, navigable about two hundred miles
with keel boats; with steam eighty or ninety miles.

Monday Morning, April 16*th.* — We continued our journey
with considerable speed against wind and current; this evening we passed two keel-boats with forty-two missionaries,
bound two hundred and fifty miles up the Mississippi, and one
hundred and fifty up the Missouri, to the Osage village of
Indians. May the Lord preserve them and bless their labors.

Tuesday Morning, 17*th.* — Continued our journey; the
weather very disagreeable, raining hard; we stopped to receive
some wood, which detained us about an hour and a half; commenced snowing fast this morning and lasted until eleven at
night.

Wednesday, 18*th.* — We arrived at Wheeling at five o'clock,
at which place I remained but a few hours.

Little did he think at that time that in a few years
he was to make this place his home, and then, after
years of sadness and degradation, to revisit it as the
Apostle of Temperance, awakening associations of the
most touching character in the minds of many who
knew him in former days.

In the evening stopped at John Dagg's; here passed the
night; it is twenty-five miles from Wheeling.

Thursday, 19*th.* — I arrived in Washington, Pa., in the
morning, in which place I saw Uncle Charles Hawkins and
Aunt Orr, who received me with much friendship and affection.
In this place I heard the Reverend Mr. Brown, a celebrated
Presbyterian clergyman.

Easter Monday, April 23. — Left Washington and arrived
at Mr. Johnston's, thirty miles distant, on foot, and remained
for the night.

Arrived at Smithfield, Tuesday morning, April 24th.

25th. — Left Johnstown and arrived at Wentling's, thirty-three miles. Wednesday, four A.M., left Wentling's, and passed the ruins of Washington's station (Fort Necessity), and arrived at Alexander Sandford's, Cumberland, Md., where we remained for the night; forty miles. This day, at twenty-five minutes after three, arrived on the top of Mount Savage; all well.

Thursday, April 26th. — We left Cumberland at four o'clock in the morning. This day at twelve M., we arrived at the top of Polished Mountain, very much worn out, but still kept up our spirits; reached Rubery's Tavern, where we remained for the night. This evening we passed eight Cherokee Indians, returning from Washington; they were all chiefs of the Cherokee nation; walked this day thirty miles.

Friday, April 27. — Passed Hancock, leaving Rubery's station at fifteen minutes after six, reached the top of Sideling Hill and arrived in the evening at Kilpatrick's, thirty miles, where we remained for the night.

Here the journal is so badly written as to be scarcely legible.

Saturday, April 28. — Left Kilpatrick's at three A.M., commonly called the Boggy Springs, and arrived at Deer Stand, where we remained for the night; forty miles.

Sunday, April 29th, 1821. — I arrived at cousin N. Warfield's, with whom I remained till Monday, April 30th.

He had now arrived within thirty miles of his home, Baltimore, penniless and forlorn.

In the dusk of the evening, in the month of May, 1821, an individual might have been seen stealing his way along the outskirts of the city. He has passed through by-ways until he reaches a residence near the corner of Calvert Street and Lovely Lane. As he approaches the front of the house, a crowd of joyous girls who are playing there open their ring to let the stranger pass; his face is haggard, and he walks wearily as one worn by travel; perhaps he is a beggar, with whom they fear to come into too close contact. He passes in by the back entrance, and inquires of the servants for one whom in former days he loved to call " Mother." A single glance sufficed for mother and son to recognize each other.

Of this event in his life he thus speaks in an address delivered in Faneuil Hall, Boston, in April, 1841: —

When twenty-two years of age, in 1818, I went to the West. As soon as I was away from paternal care I gave way; all went by the board, and my sufferings commenced. For six months I had no shoes, and only one shirt and one pair of pantaloons. Then I was a vagabond indeed. But I returned, ragged and bloated, to my mother's home. When I got to the edge of the town I was ashamed even to walk on the ground of my nativity. In the dusk of the evening I crept along to my mother's, and was soon dressed up decently. My mother only said, " John, I am afraid you are bloated." I then drank nothing for a while.

His sister, Mrs. Frances McC. Schaeffer, in a letter to the writer says: " I was at home on a visit when he returned, and never shall I forget his appearance; he was truly the prodigal son; he immediately reformed, went back to the church, and joined the prayer and class meetings." Finding no employment in Baltimore, he went immediately to Westminster, Md., where he had heard of an opening. From that place he wrote as follows: —

WESTMINSTER, June 12, 1821.

DEAR FATHER AND MOTHER, — It affords me much satisfaction to write you a few lines, informing you that I am well and very much pleased with the place. Its situation is very beautiful, well watered, and extremely healthy. The people in the place are nearly all Germans, but appear kind. I am at work for Mr. Nicholas Leman, who is a German; I board with him. I have become acquainted with Mrs. D.'s family; they treat me with as much respect as if I was her son. I visit them almost every evening. I have also become acquainted with two old ladies here, who knew my father and grandfather in Ireland.* Grandfather John Hawkins lived near their father's farm. I have as much work as I can do, and tolerable wages; boarding at two dollars per week.

I have joined society here, and we have had delightful times; we have prayer meeting once a week, preaching every other Sunday, class meeting every Sunday at Sister D.'s. Since coming here they have given me full charge of the Sunday school.

I shall write again on Monday next, by Brother Reese, my class-leader. I wish you to send me without fail the books † Ruthy has of mine in her case, for the use of the Sunday school; they consist of a parcel of Testaments, Psalters, spelling-books, and New York Primers. If you cannot send them by Mr. Leman, have them ready for Mr. Reese next Monday. I expect to be down on the Fourth of July. My expenses from Baltimore to this place were only six and one-fourth cents; that is cheap traveling.

Give my love to all the family, to Dr. Martin, and to all who may inquire after me. Remember the books, please.

I remain, very affectionately, yours,
JOHN H. W. HAWKINS.

* Several members of the Hawkins family emigrated from England to Ireland in the eighteenth century.

† These were the books which he had purchased when an apprentice for the Sunday school on Fell's Point, Baltimore, and which had been carefully laid away on his departure for the West.

4*

Feeling a little impatient at not receiving the books by Mr. Leman, he writes again on the 18th.

WESTMINSTER, FREDERICK Co., MD., June 18th, 1821.

DEAR MOTHER, — It affords me much satisfaction to hear from you at any time and by any source.

In the letter I wrote last week, I requested you to send me the books that are in Ruthy's bookcase.· Probably you have not the key ; if you have not, I wish you to get them out by some means, and send them to me by Mr. Reese, as we are in want of them for the Sunday school, as we are out of books. The gentleman who will hand you this is Brother Andrew Reese, my class-leader, one of the best of men.

Do not fail to send the books. You will please send me a box of wafers. Give my love to all.

You may expect me down on a visit on the 3d of July.

I remain, as ever, your affectionate son,

J. H. W. HAWKINS.

On returning to the city of Baltimore, in July, 1821, Mr. Hawkins found business in much better condition, and obtained regular employment at the hat factory of Messrs. Lamson and Clapp. On January 23, 1822, he went to Annapolis, Md., where he remained at work until May 30, 1822, when he returned to Baltimore and recommenced work for Messrs. Lamson and Clapp.

CHAPTER VI.

"Across the threshold led,
And every tear kissed off as soon as shed,
His house she enters, there to be a light
Shining within when all without is night;
A guardian angel o'er his life presiding,
Doubling his pleasure, and his cares dividing."

LIVING at home, under the eye of his mother, and having permanent occupation, Mr. Hawkins' deportment at this time was creditable to his family, and he was himself regarded as an honor to the church to which he belonged. His Sundays were spent at church and in the Sunday school, to which he was devotedly attached. The favorable influence which he exerted upon the young men of his acquaintance was a subject of frequent remark. His relatives, in whose society he loved to be, were occupying influential positions in society and in the church, and he had thereby many safeguards thrown around him. Besides, he had renewed his acquaintance with a most amiable and pious young lady, Miss Rachel Thompson, daughter of Joseph Thompson, Esq., of Baltimore, whom he had frequently met before his first visit to the West, and whom he had never forgotten.

The union of these persons, both of them about the same age, was regarded by parents and friends as most auspicious for their future welfare. They were members of the same church, and equally anxious to be

(43)

useful members of society; and their attachment was of the most tender and affectionate kind. They were married on Christmas-day, December the 25th, 1822, by the Rev. George B. Schaeffer, brother-in-law of the bridegroom.

For a number of years their married life seemed to glide happily on with little of incident to mark its progress. He was faithful to his business, and the weekly fruits of his industry afforded ample support. Remaining with his mother until their first child was a few months old, they commenced housekeeping in September, 1824. Their first and only son, William George, was born October 22d, 1823; their first daughter, Elizabeth Dorsey, was born July 6th, 1825; the second, Hannah Woolsey, on June 15th, 1827.

During all these years, up to 1828, Mr. Hawkins enjoyed almost uninterrupted domestic comfort. In conformity with the customs of society at that day, there is little doubt that he indulged moderately in the use of stimulating beverages, but he was careful not to run into excess; or, if he did, his sense of self-respect led him to keep the fact from the knowledge of his family and friends. It was not until years after, that the demon of the still acquired such power over him as to rob him of all self-respect, and reduce him and his family to wretchedness almost insupportable. Had he lived in this day, with habits such as his then were, he might have been classed as a genteel, moderate drinker, having too much politeness not to furnish the visitors at his house with a social glass, or to refuse one when proffered in return.

An intimate friend and fellow-laborer who knew him well at the period referred to, and who has since reached a high position in his native State,— Hon. Joshua Vansant, of Baltimore, — says of him, that a more delightful companion than John Hawkins he never had, and although many years acquainted with him after his first marriage, he never once saw him under the influence of liquor in a manner to excite any unpleasant feelings in others. Of an exceedingly social nature, his company was much sought for by his fellow-craftsmen, and many a pleasant story enlivened their evening gatherings. He was fond of a good joke, and possessing an exceedingly retentive memory he was never at a loss for entertaining topics of conversation.

Although doing well at his business as a journeyman, he determined, with the assistance of his wife's relatives and at their solicitation, to remove to Wheeling, Va., and commence the business of manufacturing hats on a large scale. Having so decided, he arranged his affairs in Baltimore, employed a large Western freight wagon, drawn by six horses and covered with canvas, and having packed his household effects in its ample enclosure, sent it off in advance, late in April, 1828, and followed with his wife and three little ones, making the journey part of the way by stages, and when the weather and roads were good, by wagon. Having reached Cumberland, Md., in safety, he dispatched the following letter to his parents : —

CUMBERLAND, MD., April 30, 1828.

DEAR FATHER AND MOTHER, — In haste I inform you that we arrived in Cumberland on Wednesday, 30th, all well. Rachel was very sick the first and second day, but the limestone water has done her much good. Rachel and myself

walked over Sideling Hill from its foot on one side to its base
on the other, with the babe in our arms [this was his daughter
Hannah, then an infant but ten months old], with a great deal
of comfort. The babe is doing well, and the other children are
getting fat. What I have written is in great haste. I will
write you more particularly from Wheeling. It has cost us
but five dollars to Cumberland, exclusive of our provision;
this is cheap travelling. Love to all.

Yours, &c.   J. II. W. HAWKINS.

———

WHEELING, May 9, 1828.

DEAR FATHER AND MOTHER, — We arrived safely in this
place yesterday afternoon, without the least accident happening
to us. The wagoner treated us with all the kindness and attention possible. We are at present boarding with Mrs. Simmons,
until a house is finished which Mr. Thompson engaged for us.
As respects my prospects, I cannot say anything at present,
but will let you know as soon as we get a little settled. I expect next Monday to go up to Steubenville on a little visit with
all the family, a distance of twenty-two miles. The passage
for all about two dollars. We remained all night in Washington on our way out, and breakfasted with Uncle Charles Hawkins, who treated us kindly and desired to be remembered to you
all. Mr. Thompson and Charlotte desire to be remembered to you
all. Rachel and the children are in good health, and desires to
be remembered particularly to her father and to Mr. Tuttle's
family. I have nothing more to write at present, but remain,

Yours, &c.   J. II. W. HAWKINS.

Of the great conflagration that took place in Wheeling in 1828 he thus writes: —

(TO MR. JOHN BAXLEY.)

WHEELING, Dec. 7, 1828.

DEAR SIR, — It is with much pain I communicate to you
the intelligence of a great fire in this place. On Wednesday

evening last, about six o'clock, while Mr. Young, the bearer of your letter, was sitting with us, we heard the cry of " Fire ! " It proceeded from the stable of Messrs. Graham and Fisher, or in the stable of Charles Knox, adjoining, it is not known certainly which. There was a strong south-west wind blowing at the time, and every thing was dry. The flames spread with appalling rapidity, and it appeared for a time as if a large part of the town would inevitably be destroyed. [After recapitulating the losses, which embraced a large part of the town, he proceeds]. Much is due to the ladies of the place; one hundred and fifty to two hundred placed themselves in the ranks, handing buckets of water, others standing in the river handing water, while others were busily engaged in saving goods, and among them the most respectable and wealthy in the place. One of Mr. Thompson's [his brother-in-law] stores was several times on fire, and burned off nearly half of the roof. Mr. T. was down the river at the time. I would write you more about the fire, but you will no doubt hear more particularly through the papers.

Rachel has been sick, but is getting better. Poor little William has been very ill of an attack of bilious fever; I thought at one time I should lose him, but he is getting better. He has not eaten a pound for two weeks. The rest of the family are well. As respects my business I am still doing beyond my expectations. I have done well both at wholesale and retail, and have several hundred dollars' worth of hats and material on hand. I have in my employ two journeymen and two boys, at making hats, and I am busily employed in finishing them. I have some notion of visiting you in the spring or fall. I will however let you know very soon. Tell Cousin Dennis to send my paper regularly.

I wish you to send me by private conveyance Alexander McCaine's Reply and the proceedings of the Convention.*

---

* Some little disaffection, it seems, had occurred about this time amongst the Methodists of Baltimore. It was thought that arbitrary

As respects reform in this place every thing is quiet. I know not what course to pursue; I would have written to the Convention on the subject of my case, but took it for granted some one would think of me.   I now wish you to mention it to the association, or some member thereof, to give me some instructions which way to steer my course, as there is no Union Society here and no probability of forming one.   Let me hear from you soon.   No more at present.

I remain, yours, respectfully, .

J. II. W. HAWKINS.

In several letters that follow he speaks of the general depression in business in Wheeling, and in one of them, to his mother, communicates the intelligence of the birth of twin daughters, one of whom he named Frances, for his sister, and the other Susan, for his wife's sister; both of them died in infancy.   In a letter written in May, 1829, after making mention of the fact that his wife had connected herself with the M. E. Church, he adds: —

I am like a sheep, wandering, wandering, I scarcely know where; however, I trust Providence will provide a way for me ere long. * * *

I must hasten through; John Brown * is about starting.   I have written for all the small conch shells you can raise amongst you, as well as for some *oysters*.   I must now close, by requesting you to give our love to all friends without discrimination. You write that you heard Pompey [a faithful watch-dog] did not arrive.   Mr. Crawford brought him safe to me, and he

measures had been pursued in reference to some.   Most of the difficulties were soon after reconciled.

* This was the faithful teamster, who with his *six-horse* wagon had brought Mr. Hawkins and family safely over the Alleghanies.

is with me yet. I have been offered fifteen dollars for him, but am too much attached to him to part with him.

I remain, as ever,

J. H. W. HAWKINS.

Failing in his business operations in Wheeling, he began to entertain the project of re-crossing the Alleghanies, and seeking a home and employment in his native city. His failure was attributable, in part at least, to the general depression in trade, and losses sustained in business; but there were other causes contributing to the same result. There is no doubt that he at this time indulged daily, although perhaps moderately, in the use of intoxicating beverages; he was exceedingly social in his habits, and his expenses were thereby increased; he was liberal, almost to a fault, and generous, and never refused to aid a friend.

But the days of darkness were now beginning to draw nigh. His wife, whom he tenderly loved, and whose only source of grief was his waywardness, began to decline in health. Influenced by the consideration that the change to Baltimore would be beneficial to her health, he decided to remove. The writer of this, then a child seven years old, well remembers that journey under the careful guidance of John Brown, the faithful Western teamster; often did the kind man place him upon the saddle-horse, where, with reins in hand, he imagined in his childish heart that the noble team was moving under his direction; frequently his father would procure a private carriage and drive onward to an advanced station, and thus enable his mother to rest until the team came up. Railroads were not then in existence, at least in the West, and the only

5

modes of travel were by the rough stages or by private conveyances.

It was in the summer time when the returning emigrants passed along amid the wild scenery of Western Pennsylvania, and into the territory of Maryland. It was the fourth journey which the father had made through the Western wilderness, and every portion of the way had become associated in his memory with some interesting incidents, which, as they travelled along, he narrated to his wife and children. Here he once met the chiefs of Indian tribes, returning from Washington, laden with presents from their " Great Father ; " there the stage-coach in which he was riding came near being dashed over the precipice by a careless or drunken driver. Now he would call their attention to a deer bounding across the highway into the depths of the dense forest; and then, when approaching the confines of agricultural industry, where the waving grain glittered in the noonday sun, he would go off into the fields and orchards and purchase of the obliging farmers milk and fruits to gratify their simple tastes. Thus the journey, for the children at least, was relieved of its tediousness. But the mother's health was far from improving; she was falling into a gradual decline; she was siezed with a consumptive cough, which no remedy seemed able to reach. The best medical advice was sought for, and every remedy employed which was supposed to possess any virtue; but in vain.

A kinder husband and parent than Mr. Hawkins did not exist, and no comfort that his means enabled him to provide was denied to his family. The chief object of his solicitude at this time was his wife; could any thing be done to preserve her life? The conviction

was fast forcing itself upon his mind, that she must
ere long take her departure from earth, and leave him
in darkness to finish his course alone.

. Reaching Baltimore, he was soon comfortably established at housekeeping, and being an industrious and
expert workman, he immediately obtained employment
at the hat manufactory of Jacob Rogers and Son.

CHAPTER VII.

" Can this be death ? there's bloom upon her cheek :
    But now I see it is no living hue,
    But a strange hectic — like the unnatural red
    Which Autumn paints upon the perished leaf.
    It is the same !   O God ! that I should dread
    To look upon the same ! "

THE numerous relatives who gathered around the death-bed of that wife and mother, on the 23rd of February, 1832, testify that a more triumphant vindication of the power of the blessed religion of Jesus to soothe the dying hour, they had seldom, if ever, witnessed. Her countenance was illumined with a brightness which seemed not of earth ; her parting words touched every heart, as she spoke to her stricken partner of her loved offspring, then standing by her bedside.   Her womanly faith felt that she could leave them in the hands of God, with a confident assurance that he would preserve and defend them on earth, and at length conduct them to that home above, where parting and tears are unknown.

Having spoken her final words in feeble accents, the sweet song of Zion was sung, —

" Jesus can make a dying bed
    Feel soft as downy pillows are ;
    While on his breast I lean my head,
    And breathe my life out sweetly there."

It was a dark and gloomy day on which they bore

(52)

her to her final resting place in the cemetery. She was but thirty-three years of age when she parted from us: —

> " Early, bright, transient, chaste as morning dew,
>   She sparkled, was exhaled, and went to heaven."

That dark day, to her bereft partner, was but the precursor of a darker night. It did not come suddenly, but gradually and surely. Left with four children, the youngest an infant, the others, five, seven, and nine years of age, for a few years he entirely reformed his drinking habits, was devout in the performance of his religious duties, and sought the consolations of religion. His pious mother was unremitting in her attentions, and in administering consolations, and to her he constantly looked for sympathy. The infant, Frances Ann Hawkins, died in the month of August succeeding the death of her mother.

The letters at this period from the bereaved husband to his mother, are brief; his heart is sad, but he struggles to maintain his usual cheerfulness. The cholera had made its appearance in Philadelphia, and was increasing with fearful rapidity. " The cholera has increased in that city," he writes, " from one hundred and twenty-three cases, to one hundred and seventy-one, in the last twenty-four hours." It soon made its appearance in the city of Baltimore, and so great was the panic, that many employers discharged their men, fearing to keep such large numbers together. " Jacob Rogers," he writes, " discharged *every man* in his establishment this morning, myself among the rest." He expresses his thankfulness that his mother is in the country, away from the danger. She was residing at

5*

this time a number of miles from the city, near Meredith Ford, on the Gunpowder Falls. Her sons often visited her, and kept her advised in respect to the health of her numerous offspring, and their families in Baltimore.

Early in the summer after their mother's death, the two daughters, Elizabeth and Hannah, were placed at a private boarding-school in Baltimore, where they remained for more than a year. During this period, and until his second marriage, on May 4th, 1834, their father was steadily engaged at his trade, and doing all in his power to educate his children. His daughters remember his constant visits at their boarding-school on Sabbath afternoons, the labors of the week over, and his Sabbath duties, sometimes as superintendent and at other times as teacher, performed. Being an ardent lover of nature, he often, with his children at his side, strolled away into the green fields, and by appropriate conversation strove to lead their youthful minds to contemplate the Maker's ways, in the sky and earth and air. Frequently, when in a contemplative mood, would he visit the humble grave where Rachel, the affectionate wife, the pious and tender mother, reposed. This visit always brought tears to his eyes, as he remembered the past; as the harrowing thoughts of his former waywardness rose to his view. How was his heart wrung with anguish! Had he ever brought a pang of sorrow to that dear one's heart? "My children," he would say, "your precious, sainted mother, lies here; let us strive to meet her in the mansions above." Year after year, in the summer time, often early in the spring, did he visit that grave.

In process of time came the second marriage. He

was married to Mrs. Ann Gibson Ruth, in Baltimore,
by the Rev. W. W. Wallace, on May 4th, 1834.   His
son had been placed under the instruction of his grandfather, the Rev. John Baxley ; the daughters were cared
for by a thoughtful mother.

Mr. Hawkins, soon after, was again without employment.   Then came days and months of suffering.   The
years 1836–8 were years of great financial distress.
The general failures of the mercantile interests which
took place in 1837, affected, through them, the business
of the mechanic and the farmer, nor did the evil stop
until it had effected the reduction of the wages of even
the day-laborer.

Notwithstanding his many trials and misfortunes,
and his occasional departures from virtue's ways, Mr.
Hawkins, constantly gave evidence of the possession
of a tender conscience, and of desires to do right.   Nor
was he left without the influences of heavenly grace ;
struggling in the enthrallment of appetite and passion,
he did not utterly forswear or abandon his allegiance
to his Maker ; — while he would do good, the evil was
present with him.   He had often, by the exercise of his
own strong will, broken away from the tempter's horrid
enchantments, and fled with hurried steps from the
haunts of inebriation.   Then would the noble qualities
of his heart shine forth ; and every Sabbath during a
year at a time, perhaps, would he walk to the house
of God in company with his son, a youth of tender
age.   His solicitude that that son might lead a virtuous and a Christian life was never intermitted, until at
length, in 1837, he saw his youthful footsteps approach
the altar of consecration to the Master's service, and
heard the venerable minister pronounce his blessing,

praying that he might lead the rest of his life according to this beginning. The parent never ceased to feel the deepest interest in the instruction of his son in all useful knowledge ; and often after the weary hours of severe labor were over, would he sit patiently down to the task of educating and training his opening mind.

The year 1836 witnessed one of those terrible relapses, which was not only distressing to the family and friends of Mr. Hawkins, but which left him in a deeply depressed state of mind. He began to think that there was no hope for him ; that he must be lost, morally and physically, for time and eternity. But he resolved to make one more struggle. After days of entire abstinence and attention to business, an incident occurred which produced a decided change in his feelings, and led to the formation of new and important resolutions. Returning home one evening, passing by a Roman Catholic Church at the hour for prayer, he observed a miserable foreign beggar kneeling, and engaged in earnest prayer, on the steps of the church. " Well," thought he, " if this poor wretch is thankful to Heaven for his crust of bread, how ungrateful a being must I be to pervert the greater blessing bestowed upon me." The reflection was followed by the resolution to reform his life, and to reënter upon the performance of his religious duties. He sought religious guidance in the prayer meeting of the Methodist chapel near his dwelling, and God listened to his earnest entreaties.

The following letter written to his son, who was still in the country, pursuing his studies under the tuition of his grandfather, Rev. Mr. Baxley, exhibits the state of his mind at this time.

BALTIMORE, May 15, 1836.

MY DEAR SON, — It gives me pleasure to inform you what has happened in our family since your grandmother left here. On Friday night last, while we were sitting in the room, *the power of God came down and converted the souls of myself and your mother.* Oh, what an ungrateful sinner I have been against so good and merciful a God ; how kind he has been to me, while I willingly and wickedly, with my eyes open and his spirit knocking every day at my heart, warning me of my sins, was yet resisting, until at length he has spoken in more powerful terms, " REPENT OR YOU WILL BE DAMNED FOREVER ! " Glory to God ! I have obeyed, and can now say of a truth, he has power on earth to forgive the worst of sinners. Your *two sisters* have consented to go with us to heaven. And now I ask you, my son, my dear son, will you agree to go with us ? Yes, I seem to hear your young heart say, *Father, I will go with you,* and by the help of God possess the land.

Last Sunday I was at class meeting, and there I saw little boys, no older than you, declare that God has power, on earth, to forgive sin ; and why can you not realize that power ? You can, if you will but pray. My dear son, do not rest until you feel the pardoning love of God. I could write more, but want to see you all, to tell you all I feel.

Give our love to grandfather and grandmother, and tell them their prayers are answered. Yes, their *midnight groanings* they have so often poured out for the salvation of my soul.

Keep this letter, and read it often, and pray that the contents of it may be fulfilled to your salvation. No more ; I subscribe myself your father, most affectionately. Your sister and your mother join me in love to you all.

J. H. W. HAWKINS.

To WM. G. HAWKINS,
    Ellicott's Mills, Md.

How those glad tidings affected his parents, he appears impatient to learn ; for he adds in a postscript, —

I want you to come in [to Baltimore], on Friday, without fail, and bring a letter of consolation from your grandfather and grandmother.   J. H. W. H.

The years 1837–8, as has been remarked, were seasons of great distress throughout the country. Mercantile and mechanical operations were extensively suspended, and artisans of almost every kind were thrown out of employment. The manufacture of fur hats was rapidly declining — other textures taking their place.

During these years, and the succeeding, Mr. Hawkins found but little to do at his trade, and was forced to seek other means of supporting his family. Sometimes he became discouraged, and sought, too often, alas! to drown his sorrows in the inebriating cup ; a fatal appetite for which had wrought in him a dangerous proclivity to excess.

His wife, and his daughters, Elizabeth and Hannah, sought in every way in their power to comfort him in his distresses, and by affectionate entreaty to win him from the fatal indulgence. He had always a tender conscience, and the pleading of his youngest child seemed deeply to affect him, while it sent many a pang of remorse to his sorrow-stricken heart. But the fatal appetite too often made him deaf to entreaty, and hushed the whisperings of conscience.

The following letters, one from his mother, and the other his reply, will throw some light upon his condition and feelings at this period.

HAVRE DE GRACE, MD., Feb. 7, 1838.

DEAR SON, — I send by Mrs. S—— the articles I promised for your wife and daughter, which I hope will make them comfortable this cold weather. We are all well, and hope to hear that yourself and family are well, and that you are engaged in some employment which enables you to provide for your immediate wants. It is likely your son William George will come to town in a few weeks, perhaps the last of this month, if he finishes his course of book-keeping in which he is now engaged.

I have only to add, that our earnest prayers for your salvation, and that of your wife and children, are daily offered at the throne of God's grace. Oh, let them not be offered in vain! *Remember what you once were*, and, my dear son, return to the Lord with all your heart; *you will never be happy* till you get religion; be prevailed upon *to give up every thing that hinders you*, and pray in secret, and in your family. It will be my great comfort in my dying hour, to know that all my children are following their father and myself to heaven and glory.

Wishing you and yours the choicest blessings of the gospel, and the earthly blessings promised to those who seek the kingdom of God and his righteousness, I remain, my dear John,

Your very affectionate mother,
ELIZABETH BAXLEY.

BALTIMORE, Feb. 12, 1838.

DEAR MOTHER AND FATHER,— Your letter of the 7th came safe to hand by Mrs. S——, and we are thankful to you for the articles sent; they have come in good season.

You cannot imagine the trouble of mind I have and am still passing through for the want of employment at my own business; and there is but little prospect yet. I have had about three weeks' work, in a bake-house, for one dollar per day, working from one, two, and three o'clock in the morning until seven and eight at night, with scarcely any rest, and that at my meals only, which I have sent to me.

I am willing to work, but I could not stand it and was compelled to quit it for awhile. I feel, however, relieved; my rent is all paid and I have a good supply of wood on hand.   I shall move from where I am, should I ever get at making hats again, to a street more convenient to my old place of business.

You write me that your prayers are daily offered up to God for the salvation of my wife, children, and myself. *Mother*, you seem to think we do not pray. Yes, we do; and in my present situation it requires me to double my diligence to *keep my head above water*.   I have, and always have had, *confidence* in my Heavenly Father, that he would *keep me and protect me, and in the end save me*, notwithstanding my many, many forfeits of his favor.   I beg you still to pray for me and my children; *I have not a doubt your prayers will be answered.*   I must now close, and pray that God may keep you and father, and in the end gather us all into his bosom, where we shall have no more trouble.

Your son, affectionately,

J. H. W. HAWKINS.

   *   *   *   *

The year 1839 was one of much misery to Mr. Hawkins and his family. The compunctions of conscience which he experienced during this period, no language of his could describe. Conscious of having fallen from the position he was entitled to occupy in the scale of moral being, the change from his former to a new life, when it did come, came with power, and was decided and entire.

CHAPTER VIII.

" The ransomed drunkard, once a hopeless slave,
Snatched from a vicious life, an early grave,
Once more to friends, wife, children, home, restored,
And taught the way that leadeth to the Lord,—
Shall keep thy memory treasured in his heart
Amid its holiest things, till life depart;
And bless thy name, while lip, and eye, and breast,
The strong emotions of his soul attest ! "

IT is not the intention of the compiler of this memoir to give a history of the temperance reformation
which began in Baltimore in 1840, except so far as
that history is connected with, and illustrated by, the
life and labors of Mr. Hawkins ; such a history would
require a volume of itself. Besides, it would be going
over ground with which the public, through numerous
publications, are already familiar.

The organization of the Washington Temperance
Society took place in the city of Baltimore, early in the
month of April, 1840.*

* See Eleventh Annual Report of the Maryland State Temperance
Society. By Christian Keener. Baltimore : 1842.

Six individuals, who were in the habit of associating together, were
seated, as usual, on Friday evening the second of April, 1840, in Chase's
tavern, in Liberty Street, Baltimore, where they were accustomed to meet
almost every evening, for the purpose of enjoying mutually all the benefits which the conveniences of the establishment and the society of each
other could possibly afford. These were William. K. Mitchell, tailor; John
F. Hoss, carpenter ; David Anderson, blacksmith ; George Steers, blacksmith ; James McCurley, coachmaker ; and Archibald Campbell, silver-
plater. A clergyman who was preaching in the city at that time had

Mr. Hawkins connected himself with the society

given public notice that on that evening he would deliver a discourse upon the subject of temperance. Upon this lecture the conversation of our six heroes presently turned ; whereupon it was determined that four of them should go and hear it and report accordingly. After the sermon they returned and discoursed on its merits for some time; when one of the company remarked, that "After all, temperance is a good thing."—"Oh," said the host, "they're all a parcel of hypocrites."—"Oh, yes," replied McCurley, "I'll be bound for you ; it's your interest to cry them down, anyhow."—"I tell you what, boys," says Steers, "let's form a society, and make Bill Mitchell president."—"Agreed," cried they. The idea seemed to take wonderfully, and the more they laughed and talked over it, the more they were pleased with it.

After parting that night they did not all meet again until Sunday ; when they took a stroll, and between walking and treating they managed to arrange the whole matter to their entire satisfaction. It was agreed that one of them should draw up a pledge, and that the whole party should sign it the next day. Accordingly, on Monday morning, William K. Mitchell wrote the following

PLEDGE.

" We whose names are annexed, desirous of forming a society for our mutual benefit, and to guard against a pernicious practice, which is injurious to our health,
standing, and families, do pledge ourselves as gentlemen, that we will not drink any
spirituous or malt liquors, wine, or cider."

He went with it, about nine o'clock, to Anderson's house, and found him still in bed, sick from the effects of his Sunday adventure, He arose, however, dressed himself, and after hearing the pledge read, went down to his shop with his friend for pen and ink; and there did himself the honor of being the first man who signed the Washington Pledge. After obtaining the names of the remaining four, the worthy President finished this noble achievement by adding his own. On the evening of that day, they met at the residence of one of their number and duly formed themselves into a society, by assigning to each the following offices : President W. K. Mitchell ; Vice President, Archibald Campbell ; Secretary, John F. Hoss ; Treasurer, James McCurley ; Standing Committee, George Steers and David Anderson.

Having thus summarily provided themselves with offices, they next turned their attention to obtaining members and to devising means to defray the expenses of their meetings ; it was therefore agreed that each

about the 14th of June, in the same year.   He imme-

man should bring a man, and every one should pay twenty-five cents upon becoming a member, and twelve and a half cents, monthly, thereafter.

The next debate was as to the name they should give to their society. A number were proposed, among them that of Jefferson; when it was finally agreed that the President and Secretary should be a committee to draft a Constitution, and select a name; which they did, and gave to the association the name of the WASHINGTON TEMPERANCE SOCIETY.

At their second meeting they had two new members; after this they met for some time, every week, at their old rendezvous in Liberty Street; but the landlord's wife complaining that their company was no particular advantage to the house, the lady of the President kindly offered them the use of one of her own rooms, where they continued to meet until their numbers had increased so much as to make it necessary for them to seek more extensive accommodations. Their next move was to a carpenter's shop in Little Sharp Street, where they remained until some weeks afterwards, when they removed to their present quarters.

At this time the society had enlarged so considerably that it became a question how they could employ their time so as to make their meetings interesting. Their worthy President, ever ready with expedients, suggested that each member should rise in his place and give his experience; and, by way of commencement, he arose and told what he had passed through in the last fifteen years, and the advantages which he had derived from signing the total-abstinence pledge. This was the origin of that most excellent plan, which the Washington Society and all its auxiliaries have adopted, for giving interest and effect to all their meetings. From this time the society increased very rapidly. It was proposed that they should hold a public experience meeting; and arrangements were made for one to be held on the 19th of November, in the Masonic Hall in St. Paul Street. At this meeting Mr. Mitchell and others related their experience with great effect; a number of signers were obtained, and the attention of the public was attracted to the movements of the society.

Too much praise cannot be awarded to these men; they spared neither their money nor their time in carrying out the principles which they had espoused. Many a poor fellow who from the effects of liquor had become a burthen to his family and himself, was fed and clothed by them, and won by kindness to reform his life; even more than this; they have supported the families of those whom they had induced to join with them, until the husband and father had procured work, and was enabled to support them with his own hands.

The peculiar characteristics of this great reform are first, a total-ab-

diately commenced the work of a temperance mission-

stinence pledge. The idea of a partial pledge seems never to have entered the minds of these honest fellows. Secondly, the telling to others what they know from experience, of the evils of intemperance, and of the good which they feel to result from entire abstinence. They knew of but one way to rid the world of the evil, and that was, to strike directly at its root. They knew, too, if others could know as they did of the suffering which resulted from the custom of drinking, that they would renounce forever this social yet destructive habit.

> "Vice is a monster of so frightful mien,
> As to be hated, needs but to be seen."

By this reformation, commencing as all great reforms, whether religious or political, ever have, among the people, a class has been reached which otherwise might never have been affected by the labors of those good men who had for so many years been engaged in diffusing the principles of temperance; resulting as it has, from a singular combination of providences, it is fully adapted to all the necessities of the people.

By the Christmas of 1840, the reform had become so popular, that thousands had flocked to its standard, and enrolled themselves as the friends of temperance. But a new feature was about to be added to the character of these movements, which was to complete this already wonderful system.

A merchant of Baltimore, who was a friend to the cause, was in the city of New York, and happened to be present at one of the simultaneous meetings which were held in that city; being requested, he gave a short account of the history of the Washington Society, and temperance at home. After the meeting, while in conversation with Dr. Reese of that city, the idea was suggested of procuring some of the "Washington" men to come on to New York, and tell their experience. After his return to Baltimore, this gentleman learned that such a delegation could be had, and wrote immediately, through Dr. Reese, to the New-York City Society, a proposal to send five men, who should engage to hold experience meetings twice every day for one week, in such places as the friends there might select, if privilege were given to draw on them for a sum sufficient to defray their expenses. This letter was promptly responded to, and in one week, on Monday the 22nd of March, Messrs. Hawkins, Pollard, Shaw, and Casey, took passage in the cars for New York, and on the next morning were followed by Mr. Mitchell.

Their first meeting in New York was held on Tuesday evening, in the M. E. Church, Green Street; being the first Washington missionary

ary among his old companions, who were addicted to intemperate habits. He was punctual in his attendance at the weekly meetings of the society, and did all in his power to add interest to them by detailing his own past, sad experience, and in encouraging others.

He spoke at several public meetings, and in the winter succeeding his reformation, on the 25th of February, he attended the anniversary of the Maryland State Temperance Society, at Annapolis, and related his experience there, before the members of the State Legislature, with great power and effect. The singleness of his aim and his simplicity of manner seemed to carry every heart with him.

The following communication from Christian Keener, whose name cannot be mentioned in connection with temperance without love and veneration, conveys a very vivid idea of Mr. Hawkins' visit to Annapolis. " The House, it is said, was dissolved in tears."

BALTIMORE, March 14, 1841.

REV. J. MARSH, — * * * We held our annual State meet-

meeting ever held in the United States. This meeting was a type of that success which was ever to accompany this new system of temperance. The New-York *Commercial Advertiser,* speaking of it next morning, says : " During the first speech, a young man rose in the gallery, and though intoxicated, begged to know if there was hope for him, declaring his readiness to bind himself, from that hour, to drink no more. He was invited to come down and sign the pledge, which he did forthwith, in the presence of the audience, under deep emotion, which seemed to be contagious, for others followed ; and during each of the speeches, they continued to come forward and sign, until more than a hundred pledges were obtained, a large proportion of which were from intemperate persons, some of whom were old and grayheaded. Such a scene as was beheld at the Secretary's table while they were signing, and the unaffected tears that were flowing, and the cordial greeting of the recruits by the Baltimore delegates, was never before witnessed in New York."

6*

ing at Annapolis, on Thursday, the 25th ult., and had a Mr.
Hawkins, a member of the Washington Temperance Society
with us. He commenced his speech by letting them know that
he stood before them a reformed drunkard, less than twelve
months ago taken almost out of the gutter; and now in the
Senate chamber of his native State, addressing hundreds of
the best informed and most intelligent of men and women, and
they listening with almost breathless, I was going to say, but
certainly tearful, attention. The circumstances had an almost
overpowering effect on his own feelings and those of his audience. He is a man of plain, good common sense, with a sincerity about him, an easy way of expressing himself, that every
word told like a point-blank shot. His was the eloquence of
the heart; no effort at display; indeed, none is needed where
all is honesty and sincerity.

The great advantage of the Washington Temperance Society has been this; they have reached hundreds of men that
would not come out to our churches, nor even temperance meetings; they go to their old companions and drag them, not by
force, but by friendly considerations of duty, and a sense of
self-respect, into their ranks, and watch over them with the
solicitude of friends and brothers. This work can, must, and
will go on.

Believe me to be,

Your friend and fellow-laborer,

CHRISTIAN KEENER.

These personal efforts of the members were eminently
blessed, and the reformation spread through the city
with amazing rapidity. In less than one year over one
thousand drunkards were reformed.* The Rev. Dr.
John Marsh, Editor of the *American Temperance
Union*, New York, was early advised of these move-

---

* See John Zug's "Account of the Foundation, Progress, and Principles of the Washington Temperance Society."

ments by John Zug, Esq., in a letter dated Baltimore, December 12th, 1840, which we give in a note.*

BALTIMORE, Dec. 12, 1840.

* To the Editor of the Journal of the A. T. U.

DEAR SIR, — In a communication which I addressed you some months since, from Carlisle, Pa. (my former residence), I had the pleasure of giving you an account of the recent temperance movement in that place.

Since my coming to Baltimore, I have interested myself in ascertaining the state of things here on that subject, in order that I might coöperate with the friends of the cause in whatever way my services might be of advantage. There is in this city a society of recent origin, the beginning, progress, operations, and prosperity of which will, I think, be interesting to the numerous readers of your journal. I therefore give you the following sketch.

The association to which I refer is called the " Washington Temperance Society," and is based on the principle of *total abstinence* from all that can intoxicate. Some time in April last, about half a dozen drinking characters (most if not all of whom were noted drunkards, and had been so for years), while sitting in a tavern in this city, conceived the idea, and formed the resolution, that they would cease to use intoxicating liquor from that time forth. Satisfied that its use was ruining their health, character, fortunes, and comfort, and the peace and happiness of their families, — in short, " evil, only evil, and that continually," — and that they could in no way consult their own interests better than by resolving in their own minds, and pledging themselves to each other, to abstain forever after from touching, tasting, or handling the unclean thing.

Their resolution was no sooner formed than carried into execution. In a few days a constitution was adopted with a total-abstinence pledge, and they all signed it. These half a dozen men immediately interested themselves to persuade their old bottle-companions to unite with them, and they in a short time numbered nearly one hundred members, a majority of whom were reformed drunkards. By their unprecedented exertions from the beginning, they have been growing in numbers, extending their influence, and increasing in interest, until now they number *about three hundred members, upwards of two hundred of whom are reformed drunkards —reformed, too, within the last eight months.* Many of these had been drunkards of many years' standing, — notorious for their dissipation. Indeed, the society has done wonders in the reformation of scores whose friends and the community had despaired of long since.

The interest connected with this society is maintained by the continued

Early in March, 1841, it was determined to send for

active exertions of its members, the peculiar character of their operations, and the frequency of their meetings. The whole society is considered a " grand committee of the whole," each member exerting himself, from week to week, and from day to day, as far as possible, to persuade his friends to adopt the only safe course, total abstinence ; or at least to accompany him to the next meeting of the " Washington Temperance Society." It is a motto of their energetic and worthy President (a drinking man of fifteen years' standing, and who was one of the founders of the society), in urging the attendance of the members at the stated meetings, " Let every man be present, and every man bring with him a man."

They have rented a public hall in which they meet every Monday night. At these stated weekly meetings, after their regular business is transacted, the several members rise promiscuously and state their temperance experience for each other's warning, instruction, and encouragement. After this, any persons present wishing to unite with them are invited forward to sign the Constitution and Pledge. Those who have never attended any meetings of the kind can hardly conceive how thrillingly interesting they are. To hear the tales of degradation, woe, and crime, which some describe as the condition to which they had reduced themselves by strong drink, is enough to melt the heart of stone. And, again, to hear these regenerated men contrasting the health, comfort, prosperity, and happiness which now are shed around them, with their former lives, characters, and wants, and the wretchedness they had brought upon their families, would make the most insensible heart leap for joy.

In addition to these stated weekly meetings, they have also been holding, of late, one or more public meetings every month, to which the friends of temperance of both sexes are invited. These meetings have been uncommonly well attended, and full of interest. After the general exercises of an address or two, the meetings have been continued by the members (who have experienced the ills of intemperance, and who now reap the benefit of abstinence), stating frankly to the public their former habits, and their present condition and prospects. Most of those who have thus spoken, are men who had never, on any occasion, spoken in public before. But the strains of eloquence which flowed from their hearts as well as from their mouths, equally astonished the minds, and moved the hearts of the congregations. Some of the most affecting speeches to which I have ever listened, have been these simple, unaffected narratives of men who spoke from their own experience. If I had time and space, I might repeat to you some of these experiences of these Washington temperance men. Indeed, I can not deny myself the pleasure of men-a delegation of these Baltimore reformers, to come to New York, and add the enthusiasm of their addresses to the interest which was then but slightly awakened. Mr. Hawkins accordingly proceeded to New York, with four or five companions, and commenced a series of public meetings. The first meeting was held in the Methodist Church in Green Street, on Tuesday evening, the 23d of March, 1841, Anson G. Phelps, Esq., presiding. Thousands flocked to their meetings, and in the space of several weeks hundreds of the most debased drunkards were reformed, and an impulse given to the cause there which was not likely to die soon.

The Rev. Dr. John Marsh has preserved a circumstantial account of these extraordinary meetings. This account is published in the April number of the *Journal* for 1841.

"For the past few days," he says, "our city has been the seat of an exceedingly interesting temperance movement. Feeling deeply for a sister city, suffering under the ravages of intemperance, the Washington Temperance Society of Baltimore,

---

tioning one or two cases, at least. One of these men assured me that he had wasted, within the last fifteen years, the round sum of fifteen thousand dollars; not in gambling, — not in general extravagance and dissipation, but purely for drink, — declaring that he had laid that amount upon the counters of the taverns and grog-shops of this city, for poison with which to destroy himself and his friends.

In conclusion, allow me to say, this society is composed of men of all classes and professions. It is one in which men of all political parties, and religious opinions, unite and act in harmony. Their numbers are growing weekly, and I should not be surprised if they numbered a thousand before another twelvemonth rolls around.

Very respectfully, yours &c.,

JOHN ZUG.

consisting now of more than *one thousand reformed drunkards*, made an offer to the New-York City Temperance Society of a delegation, to state to its citizens what had been effected in Baltimore.   The offer was gladly accepted, and on Tuesday they came to our city and held their first meeting in the Methodist church in Green Street.   Although the weather was unfavorable through the day, yet the house was well filled with an audience drawn together by great curiosity *to see this new thing.* The meetings have been continued afternoons and evenings, until the churches have not been able to hold the people who have pressed to them.   So great was the desire to hear the delegates that it was thought best on Saturday afternoon to hold a meeting in the Park.   More than three thousand people gathered around the platform and on the steps of the City Hall, all listening with deep interest to hear their statements and appeals, and cheering them onward in their glorious career.   On Friday afternoon a Washington Temperance Society was formed in New York.   A large number of intemperate men have been brought out to sign the total-abstinence pledge, besides nearly two thousand of our fellow citizens who had never before given their names.   The meetings still continue as our *Journal* goes to press.   For the gratification of our readers we have taken some notes at a few of these meetings, and give them the substance of what has been said.   At the first meeting Mr. Hawkins first took the stand.   Mr. Hawkins said he stood there a reformed drunkard.   At the age of fourteen he was apprenticed to a hatter for eight years.   It was then customary to teach the rising generation to drink, and he contracted a habit of daily drinking.   * * *   He afterwards went to the West, where he gave way to dissipation; a course commenced on wine and beer and cider.   Though he had been educated by a minister of the gospel, he never once thought he could be a drunkard, yet the use of ardent spirit crept upon him and slew him.   No tongue could tell the degradation and misery to which he had been reduced.   Last April he woke up for the first time to a sense of his dreadful condition; he discovered that his health was gone, his property gone, his peace gone; the peace of his family and of an aged and beloved mother was gone. 'Never,' said he, 'shall I forget the 12th of June last. The first two weeks in June I averaged — it is a cross to acknowledge it — as much as a quart and a pint a day. That morning I was miserable beyond conception, and was hesitating whether to live or die. My little daughter came to my bed and said, "I hope you won't send me for any whisky to-day." I told her to go out of the room. She went, weeping. I wounded her sorely, though I had made up my mind I would drink no more. *I suffered all the horrors of the pit that day.* But my wife supported me. She said, "Hold on — hold on." Next day I felt better. Monday I wanted to go down and see my old associates who had joined the Washington Society. I went and signed. I felt like a freeman. What was I now to do to regain my character? My friends took me by the hand. They encouraged me; they did right. If there is a man on earth who deserves the sympathy of the world it is the poor drunkard; he is poisoned, degraded, cast out, knows not what to do, and must be helped or he is lost. We have saved more than a thousand drunkards in Baltimore.' Mr. H. said if time permitted he could give a history of his whole course. He became a drunkard on an article which the law makes right. 'What,' said he, 'should we do with a man who sold bad meat in the market; or a baker, dishonest in his bread? Put him in the penitentiary. The law allows a man to rectify (his liquor). What does he do? Reduces his liquor so that a drunkard would not touch it. If a liquor will not intoxicate, it is bad liquor; and when he gets it so low that it is just good for nothing, then he puts in his poisonous drugs that destroy men. This is rectifying by law. I can see the distiller in his distillery, sitting in his comfortable chair, watching his distilled damnation as it oozes out of his pipe. As it goes into the world will it fill my pockets? will it make my family comfortable? Is there a being on earth whom it will bless? No, he knows there is not one. I have suffered from it ten thousand deaths. They have trusted me for whisky when they would not trust me for bread. Oh, if hell could be opened and the distiller and vender could see the miserable lost wretches there, they would see there was no blessing in their cup. I feel for drunkards; I want them to come and sign the pledge and be saved.' "

At this point in the address of Mr. Hawkins, a scene occurred which possessed many of the elements of true moral sublimity. It communicated a thrill of excessive joy to the hundreds there assembled, which has never been forgotten. An impulse was then given to the reform, which was soon to sweep over the world with increasing and resistless power.

Out of the depths of that dense crowd of human beings came a faltering voice from the gallery, exclaiming, " Can I be saved? I am a poor drunkard. I would give the world if I was as you. Is there any hope for me?"—" Yes, there is, my friend," answered Mr. Hawkins; " come down and sign the pledge, and you will be a man. Come down, and I will meet you, and we will take you by the hand." " Every eye," says one who witnessed the scene, " was fixed upon the two speakers, and silence prevailed. Many a silent prayer ascended for the poor man, and many a heart beat with breathless anxiety. Summoning up resolution, the man started for the stairs. Your father," continues the writer, " sprang from the stand, and, followed by others, met the poor man literally half way, escorted him to the desk, and guided his hand as he signed his name; and then such a shout broke forth from the friends of temperance as must have reached the angels above.

Others followed and signed the pledge, and then commenced the good work in the city of New York. As for myself, my feelings were much excited, and the scene has fastened itself indelibly upon my memory. I looked around for the scoffers, but they were few, and more solemnity have I seldom seen in any gathering, except it may be at a funeral." [*]

." The victory," says the Rev. Dr. John Marsh, " was now gained. The work of redemption among poor drunkards commenced. Another uttered forth his feelings from the gallery, and was led to come down and sign the pledge. Five or six others of this miserable class followed, and some thirty or forty others, well-known as hard drinkers and drunkards. The animation and zeal imparted to the speakers became great." [†]

Mr. Hawkins continued: "Is there a man," as the poor fellow signed the pledge, " who does not rejoice in this ? What does not all this promise to him and his family, if he has one? [‡] In Baltimore, we obtained ninety-six in one night. The axe is laid at the root of the tree. Numerous families among us are rejoicing. One man, who, last February, had not for himself and family the least comfort, scarce a rag to clothe him, owned in November a small house, and had plenty of comforts. Little children are rejoicing. A little boy, in going down one of our streets, was hailed by another, ' Ho, you've

---

[*] Rev. O. W. Morris' letter to Rev. Wm. G. Hawkins, dated Institution of the Deaf and Dumb, New York, Oct. 25th, 1858.

[†] See *Journal*, p. 50, 1841.

[‡] This man was completely reformed, and restored to his family and society, and became the first President of the New-York Washington Temperance Society.

got a new pair of shoes.'—' Yes,' said the boy, ' Father
has joined the Washington Temperance Society.' On
the 5th of April we are going to finish up the work in
our city, and put an end to the traffic. We shall have
fifteen thousand men in procession. God is on our
side, and he who puts his trust in God cannot fail."

The modesty and earnestness of Mr. Hawkins in his
address, was a subject of special remark in the public
journals of the day.

Mr. Hawkins and his missionary brethren continued
their labors in New York for three weeks, addressing
crowded audiences almost every night. He did not,
however, intermit his labors during the day, but sought
out those unfortunate men who had been induced to
visit their meetings, and commence their reformation.
He administered what consolation he could, and encouraged them to press onward in the work of amendment. In some instances, husbands were found separated from their wives and children. So great was the
confidence inspired by Mr. Hawkins in these once
wretched men, that he was solicited to act as mediator
between the wife and husband, to effect their reunion,
and aid in restoring them to their former social happiness. Mr. Hawkins took so deep an interest in such
cases, that he visited different cities to search out the
wife who had been compelled to desert her once happy
home.

We select one among the many instances that came
to his knowledge. Among the miserable inebriates
snatched, as thousands were, from the depths of degradation and wretchedness, was James McC——; once
in the enjoyment of the society of a loved partner. The
Fiend of inebriation had entered their once happy

home, and drove from his bosom his companion, the sharer of his joys and sorrows. To escape the miseries of her situation and to save her scattered offspring, she had gone to a distant city in search of employment, to procure the means for her support. This was in 1840. Mr. Hawkins learned these unhappy circumstances from the now rescued man, and advising him to industrious habits, set himself immediately about the restoration of the scattered family to the enjoyments of home. The wife had left her husband in utter hopelessness of ever witnessing his reformation; dark despair seemed to have thrown its pall over her heart.

It was in this state of feeling that Mr. Hawkins found her in the city of B——, toiling at some menial service for the loved ones at her side. The history of her husband's reformation was joyous news, told to her by a heart that yearned over her with compassionate sorrow. She believed his words, and consented to return to the deserted home, and to her renovated husband. Oh, who can tell the joy of such a meeting, and the emotions of pleasure which must have thrilled the bosom of their benefactor! He left them, but not to forget them; this he never did. He lived to witness their restoration to social happiness, to society, and to the church; the father walking in company with his family, Sabbath after Sabbath, to the sacred portals of God's house. As years rolled on, he continued to prosper in business, and there were added to his circle of loved ones, two babes, one of whom was called Hannah Hawkins, and the son, John Hawkins. Could they have given him more gratifying tokens of their love and gratitude? Mr. Hawkins enjoyed the fruit of his

labor before he passed to his reward on high. On his
return from Vermont in July last (1858), he stopped
for a night and a day in the city of New York. On
the morning after his arrival, he proceeded with his
wife and daughter Hannah to the residence of Mr.
James McC——, and had the pleasure of dining with
them. Little did they think that they should see his
face no more.

During the stay of Mr. Hawkins and his companions
in New York, the interest in the meetings was unabated; over two thousand five hundred were induced
to sign the pledge, many of whom were confirmed
drunkards. An impulse was given to the cause which
soon spread to all parts of the country, and invitations
for the services of these novel reformers came from the
North, South, East, and West. These labors over,
Mr. Hawkins returned to Baltimore, to be present at
the Anniversary of the founding of the Washington
Temperance Society, to take place on the 5th of April.
On this occasion, six thousand individuals walked in
procession with banners and music. This was indeed
a great triumph for the cause of temperance in Baltimore. It was said that during six months of 1841,
the whisky inspections for the city of Baltimore alone
had fallen short of those of the preceding six months
in 1840, by four hundred and five thousand, five hundred and eighty-two gallons, being a decrease of
twenty-five per cent. The number of licenses granted
in 1841 for the same place, was less than that of the
former year by one hundred and sixty-six.

CHAPTER IX

*"And on, and on, a swelling host
  Of temperance men, we come,
Contemning and defying all
  The powers and priests of rum ;
A host redeemed, who've drawn the sword,
  And sharpened up its edge,
And hewn our way, through hostile ranks,
  To the teetotal pledge."*

Mr. Hawkins remained but a few days in Baltimore, and then, in company with Mr. Wright, proceeded to Boston, where they had been invited to spend some time, while in the city of New York.* His journal of his visits to various parts of the United States commences with this visit to Boston. We shall have occasion to make frequent and copious extracts from it.

These extraordinary temperance movements which were in progress in Baltimore, Philadelphia, and New York speedily reached the city of Boston. Extracts from the daily journals of New York appeared in the Boston papers, particularly the Boston *Mercantile Journal*, a paper of great respectability and influence. The accounts published in this journal were always well written, and commanded the serious attention of the public. As early as March 22d, 1841, attention was called to the wonderful reformatory movements in the cities already alluded to, the agencies employed, and

---

* See Eleventh Annual Report, by Christian Keener, 1842.

the rapid progress already made.*   The Rev. John

* (FROM THE BOSTON MERCANTILE JOURNAL.)

It is stated that four hundred persons have joined the temperance societies in the city and county of Philadelphia within the last three months.
The whole number belonging to the societies is about seventeen thousand.
In the city of Baltimore the cause of Temperance has progressed wonderfully. Within a few months more than thirteen hundred reformed
inebriates have subscribed the total-abstinence pledge, among whom were
great numbers of those whose condition was most debased and hopeless.
In order to interest a similar class of our population in the great work of
reform, and also venders of strong liquors, and drinkers of every description, the New-York City Temperance Society have made arrangements
to receive a deputation of five reformed drunkards, from the city of Baltimore, who have volunteered to visit this city for the purpose of addressing public meetings. — *March, 22, 1841.*

The following interesting article from the N.-Y. *Commercial* of yesterday
will be read with great pleasure by all who wish well to the Temperance
Reform. "Last evening an overwhelming meeting was held at the Methodist Episcopal Church in Green Street. Addresses were made by Messrs.
Hawkins, Casey, Shaw, and Pollard, delegates from the Washington
Temperance Society of Baltimore, and by Captain Wisdom of this city.
These gentlemen have all been reclaimed from intemperance within a
short time, and the delegation from Baltimore declare themselves to be
'reformed drunkards.' The speakers are all men of strong sense, and
some of them truly eloquent, though at this meeting they simply stated
their experience, and urged upon others to share the benefits they have
received from abandoning the use of intoxicating drinks; still it was done
in a style at once forcible and pathetic, the effect of which upon the large
audience was astonishing. During the first speech a young man rose in
the gallery, and though intoxicated, begged God to know whether there
was hope for him, declaring his readiness to bind himself from that hour
to drink no more. He was invited to come down and sign the pledge,
which he did forthwith in the presence of the audience, under deep emotion, which seemed to be contagious, for others followed, and during each
of the speeches they continued to come forward and sign, until more than
a hundred pledges were obtained, a large proportion of which were from
intemperate persons, some of whom were old and gray headed. Such a
scene as was beheld at the Secretary's table while they were signing — the
unaffected tears that were flowing, and the cordial greeting of the recruits
by the Baltimore delegates — was never before witnessed in New York.
This afternoon at the Methodist church in Duane Street, and this evening

Marsh, D.D., considered the subject of such surpassing

at the Presbyterian church in Rivingston Street, similar meetings are to
be held; and Mr. Mitchell, the President of the Washington Temperance
Society of Baltimore, will address both meetings, he having joined the
delegation last night, and will attend the subsequent meetings during the
week, in company with his colleagues. A class of our population who
have been heretofore inaccessible by temperance efforts it is believed will
now be reached by this new and attractive measure of employing reformed
drunkards in this agency." — *March* 25, 1841.

New York, March 26, 1841.

John S. Sleeper: *Dear Sir,* — We have the greatest movement
here on the subject of temperance that we have ever witnessed. The delegation of the Baltimore Washington Temperance Society, now embracing
more than one thousand reformed drunkards, have been addressing our
citizens in several successive meetings, with a power and eloquence seldom
known on any occasion. The houses will not hold the people that flock
to hear them.

The subject of the addresses is their own experience in the path of the
drunkard, and the wishes of the rumseller, for fifteen or twenty years,
and their happiness, health, and prosperity under the sway of total abstinence. It astonishes our community to see men once so degraded now
like other men, appearing indeed as if they had always been temperate
kind husbands and fathers, and useful citizens. We ask, as we mingle
with them, can it be you were ever the fiends and brutes you say you
were? and can men in a Christian land ever be permittted to manufacture and sell a poison that should produce the effect which alcohol does? This afternoon we are to form a Washington Benevolent
Society, and to-morrow we are to have a public meeting in the Park.
Several intemperate men have signed the pledge. If you want to put an
end to the grog-shops in Boston, get the Baltimore delegation to address
your citizens; they will not merely arouse public indignation against them,
but will convert that class of your population who support them.

Yours truly,   John Marsh,
— *March*, 29, 1841.   Sec'y Am. Temperance Union

There is to be a great temperance procession in Baltimore on the 5th
instant under the direction of a committee of the Washington Temperance
Society. All the clergy of all denominations, Judges of the courts, members of the bar, the medical faculty, Mayor and city council, members of
Congress, members of the State Legislature, officers of the army and

magnitude as to address a letter to John S. Sleeper,

navy, and all persons friendly to the temperance cause, are invited to par
ticipate in the celebration. — *April* 2, 1841.

The temperance meeting held on Saturday evening in the hall at the
corner of Tremont and Bromfield Streets, agreeably to the call in the
papers, was very fully attended. William B. Spooner called the meeting
to order. William T. Eustis was chosen chairman, and Isaac F. Shepard
and George W. Bazin, Secretaries. — *April* 6, 1841.

The temperance meeting at the Odeon last evening was well attended
and very interesting. A letter was read from the Secretary of the "American Union at New York," giving an account of the temperance celebration in Baltimore, in which *six thousand* persons marched in procession
around the city, while forty thousand were looking on the amazing spectacle. He further stated that the Baltimore Washington Temperance
Society delegates will be here *to-morrow*, and that they made a most powerful impression in New York, having spoken twenty times to houses, and
in the Park to an immense audience. Over *two thousand* signed the
pledge. Extracts were read from the remarks of these reformed inebriates
of a most touching character, after which the meeting was addressed by
Rev. William Howe and Rev. A. Phelps, city missionaries to the poor,
occasioned by grog-shops and bar-rooms, and urging the signing of the
total-abstinence pledge. Captain Holbrook, who had been much at sea
and about the world, made some feeling remarks on the use of intoxicating drinks among sailors, and the great destruction of property it occasions, remarking that enough had been lost by drunken sea-captains to
"purchase the whole United States." John Tappan gave a brief notice
of the state of temperance as he had witnessed it during a recent tour to
many parts of the Old World, all of which encourage the hope that this
cause of humanity, at home and abroad, is rapidly progressing. Between
two and three hundred persons then gave their names to the total-abstinence pledge, and the interesting meeting dissolved. — *April* 12, 1841.

The exercises at the temperance meeting at the Odeon last evening possessed a deep and thrilling interest. The hall was crowded, and the
meeting was addressed by Messrs. Hawkins and Wright, delegates from
Baltimore, with a force and eloquence and a pathos which has seldom
been surpassed, and which brought tears into the eyes of many present.
Another meeting will be held at the Odeon this evening. — *April* 16, 1841.

The meeting last evening was one of unparalleled interest. The "Reformed" spoke with great eloquence and power for more than two hours,
and when, at ten o'clock, they proposed abridging somewhat they had to
say, shouts of "Go on! go on!" were heard from all parts of the house.

Esq., of Boston, giving in detail the doings of the reformers in New York, and urging upon the temperance men of Boston to secure a delegation for their city; this letter was read at a public meeting, and afterwards published in the *Mercantile Journal.* Several preliminary meetings were held, and Mr. Hawkins and Mr. Wright were invited to visit Boston as soon after the 5th of April as possible, to commence their labors in that city.

The following are extracts from Mr. Hawkins' journal, commencing April 14th, 1841.

William E. Wright and myself left Baltimore Saturday, April 10th, 1841, for Boston, by especial invitation of the Boston City Temperance Society, to spend a few weeks in lecturing on the subject of temperance. We arrived in New York at two o'clock on Sunday morning, in a heavy snow storm, which prevented us from proceeding on our journey; the captain of the steamboat considering it dangerous to go through the sound in the day or night in such a storm. We thought to improve our short stay in New York. We therefore got up a meeting in the Rev. W. W. Wallace's church (Methodist Protestant). The house was crowded and much interest manifested in the subject of temperance. One hundred and fifty-three signed the pledge.

We believe more tears were never shed by an audience in one evening than flowed last night at the thrilling recitals that enchained the mighty host. Old gray haired men sobbed like children, and the noble and honorable bowed their heads and wept. *Three hundred and seventy-seven* came forward and made "the second declaration of independence," by pledging themselves to touch no intoxicating drink; among them were noticed many bloated countenances, familiar as common drunkards; and we promise them health, prosperity, honor, and happiness, in the pursuance of their new principles. We extend to them the right hand of fellowship. Brothers, welcome! thrice welcome to paths of peace! — *April* 16, 1841.

We left New York for Boston in the steamboat Mohegan, on Tuesday morning, April 13, at six o'clock. Arrived in Boston twelve o'clock same night. We were here welcomed and received cordially by many warm-hearted friends of the temperance cause; amongst them may be found the names of Moses Grant, Dr. Walter Channing, William B. Spooner, John Ball, Henry Plympton, J. C. Converse, John Tappan, Henry Edwards, and many others. Much has been done in the (old) cause of temperance here, but little comparatively for the reformation of the unfortunate drunkard. At our first meeting, gotten up at Tremont Chapel, under the Museum, the people appeared to look with astonishment and doubt at the two strangers, especially when we introduced ourselves at our first public lecture as reformed drunkards; but before the meeting closed, doubts and fears appeared to be dispelled, and resolutions were offered by William B. Spooner, Esq., and passed, to sustain and stand by us while our visit lasted. During our stay we lectured in the following places: — First, Tremont Chapel, Wednesday evening, April 14th; second, Thursday evening, Odeon, April 15th, eighty-two signed; third, Friday evening, Marlboro' Chapel, two hundred and seventy-nine signed; fourth, Saturday, Bennet-Street Methodist Church, one hundred and forty signed.

Sunday Morning. — Went with Deacon Moses Grant to the Houses of Correction and Reformation. Addressed sixty-two boys in the House of Reformation. We then visited the House of Correction. Addressed one hundred and seventy-two men and one hundred and fifteen women; they appeared to feel much on the subject. At night addressed a crowded assembly at the Bethel, Rev. Mr. Taylor's; four hundred and twenty-nine signed. Same night addressed a crowded house at the Odeon; two hundred signed the pledge. The work was now fairly begun; many that signed were notorious drunkards.

Monday, April 19th. — Held a meeting in Rev. Dr. Sharp's Church (Baptist); ninety-four signed.

Tuesday, 20th. — Held a meeting in Roxbury ; full house ; adjourned till Saturday afternoon.

Wednesday evening, 21st. — Held the first meeting in Faneuil Hall ; the house crowded to overflowing, notwithstanding the rain.

The *Mercantile Journal* of the 22d thus speaks of this meeting : —

The great meeting, last evening, at Faneuil Hall, to receive the delegates from the Washington Baltimore Society of reformed inebriates, was numerously attended, notwithstanding the severe storm. Theodore Lyman presided, and on taking the chair addressed the meeting in language glowing with sympathy for the poor inebriate, and his afflicted family. He described in an impressive manner the evils inflicted on society by the use of intoxicating drinks. He inquired who were accountable for all this misery and suffering? Certainly, said he, some persons are, and we are bound to do what we can to remove it. He alluded to the benevolent and successful efforts now making for the unfortunate drunkard (referring to the Baltimore Washington Society), and then introduced one of the delegates from that society, John Hawkins, who riveted the attention of the vast assembly for over one hour.

The following is the language used by Mr. Hawkins on that ever-memorable occasion, as reported :

When I compare the past with the present, my days of intemperance with my present peace and sobriety, my past degradation with my present position in this hall, the Cradle of Liberty — I am overwhelmed. It seems to me holy ground. I never expected to see this hall. I had heard of it in boyhood. 'Twas here that Otis and the elder Adams argued the principles of independence, and we now meet here to declare ourselves free and independent; to make a second declaration of independence — not quite so lengthy as the old one — but it promises life, liberty, and the pursuit of happiness. Our forefathers plegded their lives and fortunes and sacred honors; we, too, will pledge our honor, our life, but our fortunes have gone for rum! Poor though we drunkards are, and miserable, even in the gutter, we will pledge our lives to maintain sobriety.

The cause of temperance! what is it but the cause of humanity? I need not talk long to show its connection with humanity. I have suffered from every description of drunkenness — have borne the heat and burden of the day in *rum-mills* (grog-shops), and know all about it — and I rejoice to say, in this Cradle of Liberty, that whereas I was once a drunkard I am now a sober man, and always mean to be.

[After the accounts given of himself in our last, Mr. Hawkins proceeded.] Drunkard! come up here; you can reform; — take the pledge in this Cradle of Liberty, and be ever free! Delay not. I met a gentleman this morning who reformed four weeks ago, rejoicing in his reformation. He brought a man with him who took the pledge, and this man has already brought two others. This is the way we do the business up in Baltimore; we reformed drunkards are a *Committee of the Whole on the state of the Union!* are all missionaries — don't slight the drunkard, but love him. No; we *nurse* him as the mother does her infant learning to walk. We go right up to him and say, How do you do? and he remembers our kindness. I tell you, be kind to him and he'll never forget you. He has peculiar feelings when the boys run after him and hoot at him; — take his part and he'll never forget it. He has better feelings than the moderate drinker; — don't lay a stumbling block in his way. One man — poor, miserable, wretched, ragged — *a real wharf-rat* — (I expect you have such here, we had plenty of them in Baltimore, but much lessened now) — he was a buster about a year ago, his clothes not fit for paper rags, his family had nothing to eat, no fuel, not even clothes, —

I'd give you his name, but won't trouble you, as he and his were not worth a *"fip'ny-bit;"* — well, he told his brother that he was going to quit, and wanted him to go his security for a horse and cart, but he would not. Our members then went to his brother, and he was persuaded. He has paid for his horse and cart, his family and himself are well clothed, cellar full of wood, a barrel of flour, and he has become a gentleman and a Christian. And all this in one short year.

Just let me tell you about one of our reformed men. We all of us changed a great deal in our appearance; some grew thin, some pale; but a dark-complexioned man grew yellow; and the grogseller, noticing the change in others, and seeing his old customer not becoming *white*, said he did not believe he had quit it altogether. The man heard of it, and prepared himself for an interview — so happened in his way.

These taverners are apt to complain; say we do them an injury because we save our money for the support of our families — quite villainous to be sure! And so they charge us with drinking a little; but I tell you that we keep close watch of each other; we are very loving, and we take care to get along-side the mouth and know what has been going on there.

As I was going to tell you, the taverner said to the member " It appears to me you don't alter quite so much as the rest." —" Don't I," said he, "well, why don't I?"—" Why you don't look pale; you grow *yallar*." — " I grow yallar, you think?" — " Yes."—" Well," said the man, drawing out a handful of gold pieces from his pantaloons pocket, " these look yallar too; but you don't get any more of them; they belong here," returning them to his pocket, " and my wife will have them. You'll get no more of them — that is the trouble with you."

These grogsellers know how to fix the drunkards, — they understand their business. They keep a big platter of salt fish, cheese, herring, and crackers, to fix the appetite — all free; don't ask any thing, of course, for them; but when they see a

8

man take hold and eat a little, they think they have him; he'll
want to wash it down,—he'll get started and "he'll do well
enough yet." Well the stuff is very apt to stick in the throat,
so it is washed down, and then the breath must be changed,
and a little more fish or cheese is taken, and that must be
washed out of the throat; and so it goes. But if a man eats
and dont drink, he is pretty sure to be told that that will not do.

This drinking has killed more men, women, and children,
than war, pestilence, and all other evils together. You cannot
bring upon man so awful a curse as alcohol; it cannot be done ;
no machinery, or invention of death can work like it. Is there
a moderate drinker who says he can use "a little," or "much,"
and "quit when he pleases?" I tell him from experience he
can't do it. Well, he can *if he will*, but HE WON'T WILL! that
is the difficulty, and there is the fatal mistake. Does he want
to know whether he can? I ask him to go without his accustomed morning bitters or his eleven-o'clock, to-morrow, and he
will find how he loves it! We have come up out of the gutter,
to tell him how he loves it, and how he may escape. It is the
moderate use—the little, the pretty drink, the genteel and
fashionable, that does the mischief. The moderate drinker is
training to take the place of the drunkard.

Go to Baltimore and see now our happy wives and families.
Only look at our procession on the 5th of April, when we celebrated our anniversary. Six thousand men, nearly half of
them reformed within a year, followed by two thousand boys,
of all ages, to give assurance to the world that the next generation shall all be sober. But where were our wives on that occasion? at home, shut up with hungry children in rags, as a year
ago? No, no! but in carriages, riding round the streets to
see their sober husbands!

My family were in a hack, and I carried apples, cakes, &c.
to them, and wife said "How happy all look; why, husband,
there is —— all dressed up; — and only think, I saw old ——
in the procession, as happy and smart as any of them;" and so

she went on telling me whom she had seen. And where do you think the grog-sellers' wives were? were they out? Not they! Some of them peeped out from behind their *curtains!* We cut down the rum-tree that day in Baltimore, under ground; not on the top of the ground, leaving a stump, but under ground, roots and all!

We have not seen six drunkards staggering in the streets since we have been in Boston; and we have been all around, even in Ann Street. They must hide themselves. If they are put into the House of Correction, I don't wonder they hide. I said when I talked to them on the Sabbath, over there, that I wished I had a distiller at my right hand and a rum-seller at my left, and let them answer the question, what brought all these here? and we would have had the answer, RUM. This making the drunkard by a thousand temptations and induce-ments, and then shutting him up in prison, is a cruel and hor-rible business. You make the drunkard, and then let him come into your house, and you turn him out; let him come to the church, and you turn him out; friends cast him off; the grog-seller turns him out when his money is gone, or midnight comes. When he serves his time out in the prison, he is turned out with the threat of a flogging if he is ever caught again; and yet you keep open the place where he is entangled and destroyed. You are bound to turn the whole tide of public opinion against the traffic. The seller will pour down your son's throat a tide of liquor, and you do so to *his* son, and he would cut your throat. Ask him if he is willing you should make his daughter a drunkard? and why should he make your son one?

At the close of Mr. Hawkins' address, he introduced Mr. Johnson, of Boston, a shoemaker, recently reformed, who now for the first time spoke in public; he spoke with great effect, bringing tears to many eyes.

The scene, altogether, was a solemn and imposing

one. The hall was draped in mourning, in token of the deep grief of the nation at the death of the lamented Harrison. The resolutions* presented and

* The following preamble and series of resolutions were read, and unanimously adopted, and the meeting adjourned to Friday evening, at the same place, — the " Cradle of Liberty," — to continue the subject of a "second declaration of independence," by signing the total-abstinence pledge from all intoxicating drinks. The delegates and others will continue the great subject : —

We are assembled amidst the emblems of a nation's sorrow. In this venerated hall, sacred to all the associations of freemen, the voice of eloquence has hardly ceased to dwell on a calamity which has awakened the sympathies of an afflicted people. Subdued by a common misfortune, *here* they have united in the expression of their grief, and have forgotten the divisions of party strife, in the nobler desire to pay appropriate honors to the memory of their chief. At such a time, and in such a place, chastened by all the influences which circumstances so imposing are calculated to throw around us, we have come to deliberate upon an evil which is spreading misery and desolation throughout the land ; carrying want and disease into the abodes of domestic peace, and filling up the broad limits of the community with pauperism and crime ; therefore,

Resolved, That when the passions of men are soothed by a common misfortune, it is a proper time to present to their calm deliberation an evil of such magnitude, and that the character of the people to whom it is presented, who are capable of such generous sacrifices in political controversies, is a sufficient guaranty that our views will be received with candor, and examined with impartiality.

Resolved, That we receive with gladness, in this Temple of Liberty, the delegates from the Washington Baltimore Temperance Society of reformed inebriates, and hail the noble stand they have taken in the cause of humanity, as marking a new era in the temperance reformation ; that their example is a living argument which nothing can refute, and that it is expedient to form a similar society in this city.

Resolved, That the approbation of distinguished patriots and statesmen encourages us to persevere in the cause in which we are engaged, and that we will not relax our efforts until the land is redeemed from the pestilence which invades it ; that we will invoke the dealer, until he shall say from his heart, in the language of the lamented Harrison, "Whereas, I have sinned, — I will sin no more ; " and those who are in bondage to the tyrant Alcohol, we will urge to break their fetters, and bo " as of right they ought to be, free and independent " citizens ; and to the young and rising generation, who have not yet put on the chains of this moral despot, we will echo around these consecrated walls, glowing with the almost speaking resemblances of the sires of our country's freedom, the impressive injunction of one of the earliest martyrs to her liberty, " My sons, scorn to be slaves ! "

This was a noble meeting ; I remember nothing like it. The evening was stormy with rain, but men and women showed they had no fear of *cold water*. The lower part of the hall was, with the exception of several women, filled with men. From top to end it was full ; the galleries, with

passed at the close of the exercises, were most beautifully and eloquently worded, alluding in the most touching manner to the nation's grief on the one hand, and
on the other to the joy which the inauguration of the
new reformatory movement was calculated to inspire.
Two hundred and ten persons signed the pledge, and
the meeting adjourned to Friday evening.

On Thursday Mr. Hawkins addressed a meeting in
the Baptist Church, Chelsea; one hundred and sixteen
signed.

women. Rev. Mr. Gray offered prayer. General Theodore Lyman, an
ex-mayor of the city, presided. He opened the meeting in a strain of true
eloquence; showed what was the evil of intemperance, and how much it was
the duty of all good and true men to do all in their power to remove it.
Everybody was happy to see our respected fellow-citizen presiding over
such a meeting, and manifested their deep pleasure to hear from him such
sentiments. The President introduced to the meeting, John Hawkins, a
delegate from the Baltimore Washington Temperance Society of reformed
drunkards. I have often heard Mr. Hawkins, but to my mind he was
never so happy as on this occasion. He came to us with a story of misery
unparalleled in interest, and told with a simplicity, a natural eloquence,
that cannot be surpassed. You saw all round, your own eyes filled with
tears, weeping men, women, and children. Never was sympathy so perfect; never more contagious. Would that the hall could have held
thousands more. Mr. H. has great power of voice, and could have been
heard by the whole. Mr. Hawkins introduced to the meeting, Mr. Johnson, a reformed inebriate of Boston, who occupied a few minutes in telling his personal experience of the miseries and horrors of intemperance.
Mr. Johnson spoke with true eloquence, for his words came from his heart.
Everybody manifested joy at his perfect emancipation from the slavery of
intemperance, and wished him "God speed." Before Mr. Hawkins spoke,
resolutions were offered by Mr. Converse, embodying most important
truths. Moses Grant followed Mr. Johnson, in a few remarks, in his best
manner, showing how important is the good work, and how nobly it is
advancing. Dr. Walter Channing then moved the acceptance of the resolutions, and everybody gave them his and her hearty vote. Then followed three cheers, which made the old hall ring with its encouraging
sound. The meeting was adjourned to Friday (to-morrow) evening.
Pledges were then taken in great numbers.—*Mercantile Journal.*

8*

We extract the following from Mr. Hawkins' journal: —

Faneuil Hall, *Friday Evening, April 28.* — Meeting according to adjournment — General Theodore Lyman in the chair; interest increasing; a vast number signed the pledge."

From the public journals we extract the following account of the meeting: —

An immense concourse of people assembled at the Cradle of Liberty last evening. General Theodore Lyman presided, and opened the meeting by a neat and happy speech. He spoke of the reformation of the drunkards in Baltimore in a manner alike honorable to himself and them, and in reference to the degrading vice of intemperance related a most interesting case of the fall of one of the brightest ornaments of the bar, that had come under his own observation. The dense throng united in singing, to the grand tune of " Old Hundred," the hymn beginning, —

> "Here Freedom's life-cry taught the brave,
> Our belted fathers, to be free."

and the old hall rang again with the sublime and majestic sound. Mr. Lyman then introduced Mr. Hawkins, who enchained the audience until ten o'clock, in his most happy manner. Alternate smiles, shouts, and tears, bore witness to the effect he was producing by the simple recital of what he himself had suffered and experienced of intemperance and misery. Nor was he deficient in his pictures of the happiness attendant on his reformation. He laid down the position that the drunkard can be saved, and he labored effectually to convince him of it. Numbers, even then under the influence of the cup, came forward and signed the total-abstinence pledge.

The following is the address of Mr. Hawkins, in

which he gives a more minute account of his past life
and his then recent reformation. We give the whole
of this address as there are several things alluded to
which have been intentionally omitted, preferring to
have Mr. Hawkins speak as much as possible for himself: —

I was born of respectable parents, and was educated by a
minister, and then bound out to the hatting business, in as perfect a grog-shop as ever existed. [Passing over what has
already been quoted, he proceeds.] For fifteen years past,
time after time, I rose and fell, was up and down. I would
quit all, and then take a little glass. I would earn fifteen dollars a week, and be happy and well, and with my money in
hand start for home, and in some unaccountable way, imperceptibly and irresistibly, fall into a tavern, and think one glass
would do me good. But I found that a single glass of ale
would conquer all my resolutions. I appeal to all my fellow-
drunkards if it is not exactly so; if the one glass of any intoxicating drink does not annihilate, by revival of the appetite, all
resolutions to resist drinking on. June 13th, 1840, I drank
and suffered awfully; I cannot tell how much I suffered in
mind; in body every thing, but in mind more. I drank dread-
fully the two first weeks of June, — bought by the gallon,
and drank, and drank, and was about taking life, — drunk all
the time.

On the 14th I was a wonder to myself; astonished I had
any mind left; and yet it seemed in the goodness of God uncommonly clear. I laid in bed long after my wife and daughter
were up, and my *conscience* drove me to madness. I hated
the darkness of the night, and when light came I hated the
light. I hated myself, my existence. I asked myself, " Can I
restrain? is it possible? Not a being to take me by the hand
and lead or help me along, and say, '*you can.*' " I was friend-
less, without help or light; an outcast. My wife came up-

stairs, and knew I was suffering, and asked me to go down to breakfast. I had a pint of whisky, and thought I would drink; and yet I knew it was life or death with me, as I decided. Moderate drinkers, beware! take care you dont get into this condition. Well, I told my wife I would come down presently. Then my daughter came up and asked me down. I always loved her more because she was a drunkard's friend — my only friend. And then she said, "Father, don't send me after whisky to-day." I was tormented before, but this was unexpected torture. I told her to leave the chamber, and she went down crying, and said to her mother, "Father is angry with me." Wife came up again, and asked me to take some coffee. I told her I did not want any thing of her, and covered myself in the bed. I soon heard some one enter the room, and I peeped out and saw it was my daughter. I then thought of my past life, my degradation, misery of my friends, and felt bad enough. So I called her, and said, "Hannah, I am not angry with you, and I shall not drink any more." She cried, and so did I. I got up and went to the cupboard and looked at the enemy, my whisky bottle, and thought, "Is it possible I can be restored?" and then turned my back upon it. Several times while dressing I looked at the bottle, but thought I should be lost if I yielded. Poor drunkard! there is hope for you! You cannot be worse off than I was; not more degraded, or more of a slave to appetite. You can return if you will. *Try it, try it!*

Well, Monday night I went to the society of drunkards, and there I found all my old bottle companions. I did not tell anybody I was going, not even my wife. I had got out of difficulty, but did not know how long I would keep out. The "six-pounders" of the society were there. We had fished together — got drunk together. We stuck like brothers, and so we do now that we are sober. One said, "There is Hawkins, the 'regulator,' the old *bruiser*," and they clapped and laughed, as you do now. But there was no laugh or clap in me. I was too sober and solemn for that. The pledge was read for my accommodation; they did not say so, and yet I knew it. They all looked over my shoulder to see me write my name. I never had such feelings before. It was a great battle.

At eleven I went home. Because when I staid out late I always went home drunk, wife had given me up again, and she began to think about breaking up and going home to mother's. My yard is covered with brick, and as I went over the brick, wife listened, as she told me, to determine whether the gate opened drunk or sober, for she could tell; and it opened sober and shut sober; and when I entered, my wife was standing in the middle of the room, to see me as I came in. She was astonished; but I smiled, and she smiled, as I caught her keen black eye. I told her quick, — I could not keep it back, — "*I have put my name to the temperance pledge never to drink as long as I live!*" It was a happy time. I cried, and she cried; we could not hush it, and our crying waked up our daughter, and she cried too. I tell you this, that you may know how happy the reformation of a drunkard makes his family. I slept none that night; my thoughts were better than sleep. Next morning I went to see my mother; old as she was, I must go and see her, and tell her of our joy. She had been praying twenty years for her drunken son. Now she said, "It is enough; I am ready to die." It made all my connections happy.

The next thing was to determine what was to be done. My mind was blunted, my character gone; I was bloated, and I was getting old; but men who had slighted me came to my help again, and took me by the hand, held me up, encouraged and comforted me.

I'll never slight a drunkard as long as I live; he needs sympathy, and is worthy of it, poor and miserable as he is; he did not design to become a drunkard, and people have too long told him he cannot reform; it is no use; he must die a drunkard. But now we assure him he can reform, and need not live or die so; and we show ourselves, two hundred in one year, as evidence of the fact. The poor wretch here is crammed into the poor-house or prison, and when he comes out he meets temptation at every step; he begs you to succor him; but he is led by appetite and neglect straight to the grog-shop. Drunkard! come up here. You can reform! Take the pledge in this Cradle of Liberty, and be forever free! Delay not.

After Mr. Hawkins sat down, Mr. Grant offered the following resolutions, which were received with three cheers:—

Whereas, This is the last opportunity we shall have to hear the delegates from the Washington Baltimore Temperance Society plead for the poor, unfortunate drunkard and his family, within these consecrated walls; therefore,

Resolved, That this meeting tender their warmest acknowledgments and sincerest gratitude, for the eloquent manner in which Mr. John Hawkins has advocated the claim to sympathy for the forlorn, and too often forsaken, inebriate, and for the deep interest he has awakened in the public mind, on the great subject of temperance.

Resolved, That we regret he cannot longer remain with us than on Thursday next, and that we wish him a safe return to his beloved wife, and daughter Hannah, hoping that he will conclude to make us another early visit, and be sure to bring them with him, that so he may be willing to remain and continue his work of philanthropy.

Here a scene occurred similar to the one in New York. A man influenced by the remarks of Mr. Hawkins arose in the gallery, under feelings of deep emotion, and thanked him for being the instrument in inducing him to reform his mode of life. He bade him God speed! and promised his hearty support. He came down, says the account, went up to the rostrum, and enrolled his name upon the pledge as Dennis William O'Brien. A host of pledges were taken at the meeting.

On Saturday, according to appointment, Mr Hawkins met the people of Roxbury; many signed the pledge, and a Washington Temperance Society was formed. At night, he lectured in the North-Russell Street Methodist Church: one hundred and fifteen signed the pledge.

On Sunday evening, 25th, he addressed the prisoners in the State Prison at Charlestown, three hundred and twenty-seven in number. " They seemed," he says in his journal, " to feel much their situation, knowing the primary cause of their misery was the use of intoxicating drink; they wept like children." The thrilling interest of this meeting seemed to impress itself on many minds. The following account appeared in the Boston *Mercantile Journal* on Monday morning, April 26, 1841 :—

We were present yesterday forenoon at the services at the State Prison in Charlestown. The convicts were collected in the chapel. The services consisted of prayer, and reading of the Scriptures, by Rev. Mr. Curtis, the excellent chaplain of the prison, and sacred music, and an address to the convicts by John Hawkins of Baltimore, who is now, with his friend and co-laborer, Mr. Wright, effecting so much good in this city. Mr. Hawkins delivered a most touching and eloquent address, one which came home to the bosoms and feelings of every one present. It was an address calculated to produce a most beneficial effect, especially when we consider that intemperance is the rock on which many, nearly all, of those convicts have been wrecked. He was listened to with closest attention while he described what he *knew* of the evils of intemperance, of the terrible effects it had produced upon himself and his family; and he showed that the drunkard, although by many regarded as incorrigible, and treated as an outcast from society, *can be reformed*, and become a respectable and useful member of society. He spoke *feelingly;* the words seemed to come from the bottom of his heart; and they were not unheeded. Those convicts seemed to feel the force of this language; this appeal to their feelings, to their better nature, was not in vain. All of them seemed to regard him as a friend, as a monitor, who came among them to fortify their souls against crime; and many of them wept, yes, those rough-looking, despised men, wept like children, and those were precious tears.

Mr. Hawkins' journal contains this entry:—

Sunday night 25th April.—Lectured at the Odeon; the house was filled to overflowing; exceeding great interest was manifested in the cause of temperance; great numbers signed the pledge.

The *Mercantile Journal* of Monday thus speaks:—

The temperance meeting at the Odeon last evening was a glorious affair. At an early hour every seat, and indeed every standing-place, was occupied. Hundreds were obliged to go away, unable to obtain admittance. Mr. Hawkins addressed this numerous audience about two hours, and was listened to throughout with intense interest. Such a temperance meeting has seldom been held in this country. His remarks were exceedingly eloquent and seemed to produce a wonderful effect on the vast congregation who listened to him. No other speaker addressed the audience. Upwards of *two hundred pledges* were given at the close of the meeting. In the course of his remarks Mr. Hawkins referred in a beautiful and impressive manner to the scene which he had witnessed at the State Prison in the morning. To-morrow evening he will lecture in South Boston, and on Wednesday evening at the Marlboro' Chapel. Every one should go and hear him.

The activity of Mr. Hawkins in this reform was truly amazing; his whole being seemed to be engrossed in the work of saving the drunkard. " I will never slight a drunkard as long as I live," was a principle to which he adhered to the last day of his labors on earth.

Mr. Hawkins' style in these addresses, and his personal appearance, may be gathered from the record of eye-witnesses. " Mr. Hawkins," says one writer. " is a man about forty-four years of age, of fine. manly form; he spoke with much fluency, force. and effect, in a vein of free-and-easy, off-hand, direct, manly, bang-up style; at times in a simple. conversational manner, then earnest and vehement, then pathetic, then humorous; but always manly and reasonable." — " Mr. Hawkins always succeeded in ' working up' his audience finely. Now, the house was as quiet and still as a deserted church, and anon, the high dome rung with violent bursts of laughter and applause. Now, he assumed the melting mood, and pictured the scenes of a drunkard's home, — and that home his own, — and the fountains of generous feeling, in many hearts, gushed forth in tears; and again, in a moment. as he related some ludicrous story, those tearful eyes glistened with delight, sighs changed to hearty shouts, and long faces were convulsed with broad grins and glorious smiles."

A letter from Deacon Moses Grant, of April 15th, 1841, to the editor of the *American Temperance Union*, N. Y., thus speaks: —

I have delayed writing from a press of duties connected with the visit of our friends, Messrs. Hawkins and Wright; and as you wrote, they exceeded *all* expectation, particularly

9

Mr. Hawkins, who is a powerful man. You will see by the *Mercantile Journal* how the meetings go on ; they are crowded, and intensely interesting. We go into Faneuil Hall on Wednesday afternoon and evening. It is dressed in mourning for the eulogy to-morrow, when we avail ourselves of the entire seats and fixtures for the funeral obsequies, I hope, of old King Alcohol. We never had any thing like the interest now felt on this great subject. Last evening we filled the Odeon and Mr. Taylor's church also.

" The meeting on Wednesday evening in Faneuil Hall," says the *Mercantile Journal*, " was one of thrilling interest. Mr. Hawkins arose amidst great applause, and spoke an hour with much fluency and appropriateness of diction. His soul overflowed with intense feeling for the poor drunkard, and often he was obliged to stop to brush the tears from his manly cheek. His address abounded with anecdote, and was frequently characterized by deep and impassioned eloquence."

To return to his journal.

Monday, 26*th:* — Afternoon, held a meeting in Tremont Chapel ; formed a " Martha Washington Temperance Society." Evening, held a meeting in Marlboro' Chapel ; formed a " Boston Washington Temperance Society," of reformed inebriates ; *one hundred and thirty gave in their names.*

The friends of temperance now thought the work was fairly and effectually begun. " This is doing well," said one of the public journals, in giving an account of this meeting ; " we believe that by this act a blow is given to intemperance in this city from which it will not recover. Several of these true reformers came forward and in a forcible and feeling manner sketched the miseries which attended the drunkard and his wretched family. This new and interesting association was then addressed by Mr. Hawkins, at considerable length, in which he exhorted them to be steadfast in the resolution which they had nobly formed, and to look to their God for aid in carrying out the great principles which they had adopted."*

Tuesday, 27th. — Held a meeting in South Boston; one hundred and sixty signed the pledge.

Wednesday, 28th. — Boston W. T. Society met in the Marlboro' Chapel according to adjournment; one hundred and fifty signed the pledge.

Thursday, 29th. — Held a meeting in Danvers; crowded house; large numbers signed the pledge; adjourned to meet again for the purpose of forming a society.

Mr. Hawkins, feeling that he had now been absent from his family as long as he could be conveniently, began his journey southward. It will be seen from his journal that he was industriously and usefully employed by the way.

Friday morning, April 30th. — Left Boston for Baltimore, by way of Worcester; remained in Worcester till Monday morning, May 3d; three hundred and eighteen persons signed the pledge.

Monday. — Arrived in Norwich, Conn.; lectured in the Town Hall; left same evening for New York;. *five hundred and twenty signed the pledge.* Reached New York Tuesday morning, May 5th, 7½ A.M. At 12¾ P.M. took the cars for Patterson, New Jersey.

Tuesday evening. — Held a meeting in the Methodist church · house crowded; no pledges circulated.

* See *Boston Journal*, April 27th, 1841.

Wednesday evening, 6th.— Meeting in the same house ; large congregation ; one hundred signed the pledge.

Continuing still in Patterson, he met the females in the Free Church, and formed a " Martha Washington Temperance Society."

Friday evening, May 8th. — Held a meeting in the Methodist Church ; formed a Washington Temperance Society , *three hundred and fifteen signed the pledge.*

Saturday afternoon, May 9th. — Held a meeting in Brooklyn at three o'clock ; not well attended ; at night held a meeting in the " Log Cabin," Brooklyn.

This was the remains of the "log cabin" and " hard cider " enthusiasm which had so lately swept over the country.

Sunday morning, 10th. — At 8 o'clock held a meeting in the Methodist Church, Brooklyn. At ten held a meeting on board the steamship Fulton ; eighteen seamen signed the pledge. In the afternoon met the children in the Sunday school of Mr. Spencer's church. Sunday night addressed a large congregation in Rev. Mr. Spencer's church.

Monday. — Addressed, at 3 P.M., a large congregation in the Free Church ; at night addressed a very large congregation in the " Log Cabin."

Tuesday, 12th. — Held a meeting in Allen Street.

Wednesday, 13th. — Addressed the hatters in Columbian Hall ; same evening addressed a meeting in Pearl Street, near Broadway.

Thursday, 14th. — Addressed the Young Men's National Temperance Convention, which had been holding meetings in the city. Held a meeting in Carmine-Street Church ; eighty signed the pledge.

Friday, 6 A.M. — Left New York for Baltimore; arrived in Philadelphia at 1 P.M. I was arrested on the wharf by a constable for an old grog-bill, which I paid, but was detained by it until next day.* Left Philadelphia Saturday morning, at 7½ A.M. ; reached Baltimore in the afternoon ; found my family well.

* The New-York *Organ* for June, 1841, thus referred to the incident : " After Mr. Hawkins left this city on his way to Baltimore, some weeks ago, as he was standing on the wharf at Philadelphia with a number of friends, waiting for the boat to start, he saw a person who seemed to watch him very closely. It seemed that he had seen him somewhere before, but couldn't for his life bring to mind where, but thought he had been an old bottle companion. They stood watching each other until the boat was nearly ready to start, and as Mr. Hawkins was about to go on board, he was in the gentlest manner possible tapped on the shoulder by his unrecognized friend, who very politely informed him that he was his prisoner. 'What!' exclaimed the astonished Hawkins: 'what do you mean ? ' — 'Mean ? ' says the stranger, 'I mean what I say ; you're my prisoner.' — 'Where is your authority ? ' demanded Hawkins. — 'Here,' returned the other; sure enough, pulling out a warrant, which proved to be for an old grog-bill, incurred years ago, and which since his reformation he had frequently sought to find the man for the purpose of settling, but had been informed that he had given up business, and was unable to get a clue to his whereabouts. Hawkins offered the money but was refused; 'twas too good a joke to arrest this apostle of temperance for a grog-bill. Hawkins remonstrated; stated how anxious he was to get to his family ; but it was no use ; — before a magistrate he must go. This was an awkward fix. One spell he had a notion to get angry, but he thought it would be too good a text to preach temperance from, so like a good citizen he 'yielded to the majesty of the law,' and accompanied the man to the police office; where he planked down the ready and was discharged. Now we would advise every man who has any old grog scores standing against him to go right off and square them up."

9*

CHAPTER X.

"And when the triumph comes — as come it will,
When baffled flies the *Demon of the still*,
And heaven-born *Temperance* pours o'er every land,
Her richest blessings with a liberal hand;
Thy prayers and tears and toils to haste the day,
When all may joy in her benignant sway,
Remembered still, shall oft recounted be,
And glad thanksgivings shall be poured for *thee!*"

THE rapidity with which the temperance reform was progressing through the land, was arresting the attention of all classes. Thousands of degraded men were leaving the haunts of vice; thousands of families were revisited with the blessings of peace and sobriety. In many instances liquor dealers were induced to give up their business, and the contents of their barrels were burned amidst the shouts of the multitudes, now disenthralled. City governments were beginning to rejoice at their diminishing expenditures, and the hearts of all true philanthropists were filled with joy. The hearts of old temperance-men were rejoicing at the powerful instrumentalities now placed in their hands. The old temperance pledge, which admitted the use of "wine and cider," was numbered among the "things that were." Doubting physiologists were convinced that all intoxicating beverages might be abandoned, and the human system suffer no evil. The army of total-abstinence men, putting on all the freshness and vigor of youth, constituted an argument that could not be

(102)

resisted. Instead of being still the despised and neglected of all, these reformed inebriates became the
champions and missionaries to their brethren in bonds.

The fifth anniversary of the American Temperance
Union was held on the 11th of May, 1841, under the
most encouraging circumstances. Its friends were
found among the most distinguished of the land.
" Never before," said its honored secretary, Rev. John
Marsh, " have the committee come up to the anniversary of the Temperance Union with such cause for
gratitude and praise. The Almighty Ruler of the
universe, who will overturn and overturn and overturn, until every knee shall bow, seems to have taken
the enterprise in which we are engaged into his own
hands, and to have given it an impulse in the past year,
wholly unlooked for by its warmest advocates. We
are nothing. Human thought stretched not to what
has been accomplished. Human action would have
stamped it as folly, had it labored to do it. God de-
vised, and God executed. We look and we adore."

After glancing at the results accomplished by Father
Matthew in Ireland, at the successful tour of Rev.
Robert Baird in the north of Europe, the report thus
speaks of the American movement.

In the city of Baltimore, without any special agency ex-
cepting their action one upon another, more than a thousand
reformed drunkards stand upon their feet, and walk forth erect
in the conscious dignity of freemen. Several of these individuals, long deceived, robbed, beaten, tossed by friends, suffering
the horrors of the pit, now plucked from the burning, joyful in
their deliverance, affected to tears at what they have been and
where they have been, yet willing to acknowledge all and confess all, and desirous of raising every inebriate from degrada-

tion and ruin, have visited sister cities, and by telling to crowded houses their simple tale, have waked up this great community to the practicability and possibility of the drunkard's reform, and arrested many a miserable man, who was abandoned by his friends to hopeless ruin. Already, in New York more than four hundred, and in Boston more than five hundred and fifty have signed the pledge of total abstinence.

It is not, perhaps, too much to say that in the United States, in the last six months, fifteen thousand drunkards have ceased using intoxicating drinks. The physiologist has been confounded, the caviller silenced, the fearful shamed, the distiller and vender struck dumb, and à tide of unlooked-for blessings has been poured into the bosoms of many miserable families.

Addresses were made at this meeting by Dr. Charles Jewett, of Mass., Prof. Goodrich, of Yale Theological Seminary, Rev. Mr. Scott, of Stockholm, in Sweden, Rev. Robert Baird, who had visited several of the courts of Europe and received the favorable expressions of their monarchs on this subject, Rev. Mr. Bingham, of the Sandwich Islands, and John Hawkins, of Baltimore.*

The new principle of love to the fallen, which Mr. Hawkins had promulgated in Boston, took a deep hold upon the people; the more it was revolved in their minds, the deeper became the conviction that hitherto a great mistake had been made; that instead of imprisonment and correction, the mild persuasions of love should be employed to win him from ruinous indulgences. This power melted and subdued his heart; correction soured, and blunted his sensibilities.

The new society in Boston rapidly increased, and before Mr. Hawkins' return from Baltimore it num-

* See *Boston Journal*, May 13, 1841.

bered upwards of eleven hundred. While they were counselled to be unremitting in their attentions to one another, they were reminded of their duty to remember those who were yet in bonds. The long-tried friends of temperance were advised to improve every opportunity of encouraging those who were entering on a new course of life, and to evince their kindness and regard in every suitable manner. Should the work go on as prosperously as there was reason to believe it would, it was hoped that although there might be a decline of business in the court-house, and many vacant cells in the House of Correction and State Prison, the fireside of many a domestic circle which had been lonely and desolate would again present a cheerful aspect.*

These principles are distinctly and forcibly enunciated in the following letter to the writer of these pages from Dr. Walter Channing; the brief *resumé* which it gives of the state of the cause at the time Mr. Hawkins came to Boston on his first visit, makes it a valuable addition to this memoir : —

BOSTON, September 25, 1858.

REV. W. G. HAWKINS : *Dear Sir,* — The Massachusetts Temperance Society, one of the earliest organizations for promoting temperance, had faithfully labored for this object. Its constitution declared that this was to be accomplished by checking the too free use of intoxicating liquors, which threatened to make us a nation of drunkards.

The first President of the society was Samuel Dexter, one of the most distinguished jurists in the land, and holding some of the most important offices in the republic. Its next President was Nathan Dane, the author of the Ordinance which declared the great Western Territory forever free. The so-

---

* See *Boston Journal*, May 21, 1841.

ciety had no pledge, and obtained no aid from public laws. It had a large number of members from among our ranks, and a faithful agent; its Recording Secretary was the late Dr. J. G. Stephenson, whom I never name without remembrance and record of the public and private respect and affection in which he was held. Dr. Stephenson was obliged by declining health to resign his office, and I was appointed in his stead. The society continued its labors. Other societies were formed. The public, especially the churches, began to feel and express an interest in the work. New societies adopted the pledge. There was doubtless good done. Progress was slow. With the increase in numbers and in wealth, the manufacture and sale of intoxicating drinks were increased. The traffic was protected by license laws, which, although designed to check an immoral and destructive custom, gave it *direct* patronage. The right to sell could be procured with a very small sum. How small was the gain to the public treasury by this purchase money, when compared with its expenditure to support the intemperance which the license system produced! The general government paid a bounty for the export of New-England rum, and thus was the patron of its distillation.

It was in this state of things the "Washingtonian Movement," so called, was made. It began in Baltimore, and by the direct agency of drunkards. I need not give an account of the circumstances under which this movement began, for you have in your possession its whole history. Sufficient for me is it to say, that your father was one of its authors, and that we both know with what heroic fidelity he continued in its service till his death.

It was wholly new, both in its principles and its agents. It laid aside law punishment, and made love, the new commandment, its own. It dared to look upon moral power as sufficient for the work of human regeneration — the living moral power in the drunkard, however degraded he might be. It had faith in man; and with this principle in action, it regarded success as certain. The drunkard became a moral teacher. Yes; he who had lived in daily violation of the paramount principle in the constitution of human nature, felt that he was yet a MAN; and in virtue of his divine investiture as a moral being, he rose from the lowest depths of degradation, and became an apostle of the highest sentiment in his nature; viz., the love of man, the acknowledgment of the inborn dignity of man.

You know how this announcement of individual conversion to truth, and from a source never looked to before, was received. It attracted universal and deep attention. Those Baltimore meetings were published throughout the land, and soon were heard of abroad. Drunkards were now the teachers of temperance! They came before the people with the story of their wrongs; how they had wronged their own souls, and their "living temples," their bodies; how they had made their homes desolate, — their wives widows *with living husbands*, their children orphans with *living fathers*. These men (for such again they were), told of their sins, their crimes, making the nation — the world, their confessional!

Your father came to Boston. I remember — I can never forget — the welcome he received at the meeting in Faneuil Hall, by the multitude who met him there. He told his story with the eloquence of personal experience, and with the simplicity of truth. You felt that you was in the presence of a brother — of a man. Your heart sunk within you as you listened to the story of a terrible delinquency. How did it swell with joy at his power, and his victory, when he told you of his moral resurrection. Whose eyes were dry in that great assembly, when he told us of the long night-watchings of that little child — his daughter, — for him, her wretched father, and that she was his deliverer!

A result of your father's visit to Boston, was the formation of a Washingtonian Temperance Society, upon the same platform as that of Baltimore. Samuel F. Holbrook was chosen

President, and I was appointed Treasurer. Its success was
great; money was needed, and was asked for; the appeal was
answered, and several thousand dollars were contributed. It
came in various sums, from two hundred dollars to six and a
quarter cents; the old and the young, the poor and the rich,
— all classes gave. It was of the widow's mite, and of the
rich man's wealth. I could relate touching incidents of giving,
for it often involved sacrifices where it seemed that self-denial
could no farther go. They came to give, and claimed the privilege to help such a work.

But why money? Intemperance, while it produces the se-
verest want, deprives it for a time of much of its suffering. To
cease to be drunk is to feel the whole misery of a drunkard's lot,
— he has no friends, no work, it may be, no home. Let such a
man resolve on a better life, you must stand by him lest he fall;
you must feed and shelter him till he has fully come to himself,
— you must give, or get him work. Money here was raised
to help such men. To provide for them shelter, food, clothing.
Much money was collected, and in the distribution of it those
men were employed who had known the claims, the wants of
the reformed.

You know that questions have been asked as to the expediency of the intemperate appealing to the public, in the way of
relating experiences, revealing their delinquencies, sins, crimes,
in public assemblies. It is bad taste we are told; it comes of
some form of vanity; it is very apt to be exaggerated, on the
ground that the greater the crime the more merit in the reformation; it **may** be done to make money, and the imagination
may be taxed to make the confession more telling. We hear
all sorts of objections made to this feature of the Washingtonian
movement, as you doubtless know. I do not mean to argue
these points, but I will say to you, that I have known no genu-
ine, true member of this body, who has ever for a moment led
me to question his sincerity. There may have been, and there
may be, men who have entered into the public service for

lucre; but I have known no such hypocritical disciples in this great work, and trust I never may. Many may have fallen from their pledge, and denied the faith; they have been tempted beyond their strength and have fallen.

I turn from the proper object of my note, to speak again of your father, to whom every lover of man owes the deepest obligations, and, for one, to offer my sincere thanks for his important services. I can never forget the earnestness, the simplicity, the humbleness, with which he declared his obligations to that cause which had saved him from terrible self-murder, and had enabled him to resist a temptation to which habit had given strength, leaving only moral weakness which is of all things most fatal to successful resistance of temptation. I felt sure that he would stand. I felt sure that with his honest eloquence he would win hosts of men to his doctrine and to his practice. And having done all, he did stand. He worked for his brothers to the last day of his life, and in peace passed away.

I thank you for calling on me, and only regret that in complying with your request, to write you concerning my impressions of your father, and of his visit to Boston, I have so imperfectly done what I promised to do. I rejoice to hear from you that you are preparing a memoir of him. If this note will serve you, I place it entirely at your service. If you have any questions which I can answer let me have them, and I will do what I can to answer them.

I remain, very truly yours,

WALTER CHANNING.

Mr. Hawkins remained but a short time in Baltimore, seven days only, making brief visits to his mother and to his numerous relatives, detailing to them incidents in the astonishing reformation at the North. We continue our extracts from his journal.

The Boston Temperance Society having engaged my services on a mission of Temperance, I accordingly gathered my family together, [consisting of his wife, his daughter Hannah, and two orphan children, a nephew and niece of his wife, his daughter Elizabeth being then with her grandmother, and his son learning the business of a grocer in his uncle's store] and left Baltimore at 3 P.M., for Boston, on Friday, May 21st; reached Philadelphia at eleven o'clock at night. Left next morning, 7 A.M., reached New York at 2½ P.M.; was kindly invited to make our stay with Mr. Asa Bigelow.

Sunday afternoon, 23d. — Lectured in Sullivan-Street Church. Sunday night lectured in Methodist Protestant Church, Attorney Street.

Monday, 24th. — Met the Washington Temperance Society; an interesting meeting.

Tuesday, 25th. — Left New York for Middletown, Ct., in company with Rev. John Marsh; lectured at night.

It is to this journey, without doubt, that Dr. Marsh refers in the little volume entitled "Hannah Hawkins, the Reformed Drunkard's Daughter." This little work, though defective in some of its statements, is nevertheless admirably written, and calculated to do much good; we learn that sixteen thousand copies have already been distributed through the country.

Wednesday, 26th May. — Left Middletown for Hartford, Ct.; lectured same evening in Rev. Dr. Hawes' church.

Thursday, 27th. — Afternoon, lectured in the session-room of same church, and at night in the Town Hall. Friday, lectured again in the Town Hall.

We learn from the Hartford papers of that day, that the Washington Temperance Society of that city was founded by John Hawkins the last of May, that it speedily increased to one hundred in number, embracing

many who, a month before, were miserable inebriates.
The young men were also stimulated during that month
to the organization of a large and efficient society on
total-abstinence principles; it soon numbered over
eight hundred members; such an onward movement in
the cause of temperance was never before known in
that city.

Saturday, May 29th. — Reached Springfield at 7 P.M., and
lectured same evening in the Presbyterian church. On Sunday
afternoon, 30th, addressed an interesting congregation of children, with their parents; much interest felt; and at night
addressed a large congregation in the same church.

Monday, May 31. — Arrived in Boston with my family, and
took boarding at the National Temperance Hotel, kept by Mr.
Louis Boutelle.

During the late extraordinary movements in Boston,
Mr. Boutelle, the keeper of this hotel, became so impressed
with the evils of keeping intoxicating liquor in a public house, as to come to the conclusion to banish it at
once and forever from his premises. Mr. Hawkins took
much interest in sustaining so laudable an enterprise
and wherever he lectured commended the example to
others. Mr. Boutelle addressed a most sensible letter to
S. F. Holbrook, President of the Washington Temperance Society, in which he gave it as his opinion, as a
vender of intoxicating drinks, " *that this was the first
time intemperance had ever been attacked in the right
way.*" Mr. Boutelle was not neglected in his under-
taking, but was for years nobly sustained by the friends
of the cause.

The rapidity of the new reform, and the dignity and
importance which it was now assuming, gathering

everywhere to its standard men of talent and influence, was a subject of daily remark in the journals of that period. *

The moral grandeur of the work made a deep impression on the public mind. Thousands of hearts beat in sympathy with the new reformers, and many earnest prayers ascended for their ultimate triumph. It was God who guided the impulses of the people, and led them onward to the amazing conquests that have been won in eighteen years over this department of the " Kingdom of Darkness."   A very just allusion to the moral character of the work we append in a note ; it is a communication to the *Mercantile Journal* of May 28, 1841. †

* (FROM THE MERCANTILE JOURNAL.)

The formation of this society in this city established a new and important era in the history of the temperance reform.   The inebriates themselves are awakened to their errors, and have embraced the great work of reform.   They understand the whole nature of intemperance in all its different phases; they are acquainted with the monster in every shape which he assumes ; they know the avenues to the drunkard's heart ; they can sympathize with him ; they can reason with him ; they can convince him that it is not yet too late to reform ; that by signing the pledge of total abstinence from *all* that intoxicates, he may yet become a respectable member of society, and peace and prosperity may again visit his dwelling, and happiness take up her abode in his heart.   This society numbers now nearly twelve hundred persons, and the numbers are daily increasing.   Among them are men of talent and energy of character, who are deeply interested in extending the great principles of the temperance reform. — *May* 27, 1841.

† Mr. SLEEPER, — I wonder with rejoicing at the developments which are now making in the temperance reform among the drunkards of our city and in various parts of our country.   There is a new principle in this movement, which should inspire hope for the friends of man, of man degraded by intemperance and vice ; new tongues in this resurrection. " Hear we not," says the drunkard, " every one speak in our own lan-

The arrival of Mr. Hawkins in Boston with a portion of his family on the 31st of May was immediately announced in the newspapers. "We are requested," says the *Mercantile Journal*, "to state that there will be a public meeting of the Washington Total-Abstinence Society, at the Marlboro' Chapel, this evening. Mr. Hawkins has reached this city to-day, last from Springfield, with his family, and will be present at the meeting and address the audience."

Of this meeting Mr. Hawkins makes this brief record in his journal: "Met the Washington Temperance Society in Marlboro' Chapel; it was an interesting meeting." Its modesty is worthy of note. The *Mercantile Journal* of June 1, 1841, says: —

guage?" The voice of the drunkard comes home to those of his own class. Their inmost experience makes them one soul. The good can only speak to the degraded in any form of vice by uniting with the good yet left in them. The most degraded man living is our brother. Our souls should vibrate in unison with the sublime sentiment of Hawkins, one of the reformed drunkards; "I'll never slight a drunkard as long as I live." No! nor slight any man, however degraded by any form of vice.

It is not the least advantage growing out of the new aspect of the temperance reform, that it creates a noble and God-like sympathy for that class of men whom Hawkins represented when he said, "Not a being to take me by the hand, and lead or help me along, and say, 'You can free yourself from intemperance and vice.'" We must seek a fellowship with the intemperate in our lanes and cellars, even in the very gutters of our streets, if we would save them from the ruin that must otherwise come upon them. Brother-like we must take them by the hand, and lead them forth from the cellars of their degradation into the clear air and bright light of heaven. "Is this not the carpenter's son?" What eloquence from illiterate men! Lips parched by intemperance, quivering, steeped in very death, now moving in utterance of heroic sentiments, full to overflowing with divine thoughts and great resolves. In the reformed drunkard beautiful and sublime sentiments spring up spontaneously, and his lips move to the utterance.

The Marlboro' Chapel was crowded to overflowing last evening to welcome the return of Mr. Hawkins, with his family. His entrance into the hall was the signal for acclamations which were long and reiterated. For upwards of an hour he enchained the attention of the numerous audience, while he sketched the scenes through which he had lately passed, and recounted his labors in other States, and gave cheering evidence of the progress of the temperance reform. His arguments in favor of temperance were forcible, and his appeals to the drunkard to abandon his cups were strong and affecting. On the one hand he placed misery and ruin to himself and those whom he loved — on the other, health, competence, cheerfulness, and happiness. He portrayed in strong and burning characters, the cupidity, the heartlessness, the rapacity of the dram-seller, and described the various lures to which he was wont to resort to entrap the unwary or weak-minded toper, when he had once resolved to reform. His eloquent and impassioned language must have raised the blush of shame even on the face of the dramseller, if he had been present. He adduced some strong arguments to show that the cause of justice would be better subserved, if the dram-seller should be sent to the House of Correction, instead of the miserable victim, the *drunkard ;* and a large portion of the audience seemed to be of his opinion. Mr. Hawkins is a very effective speaker ; few men possess the power in a greater degree of deeply interesting an audience ; and the reason is plain — he speaks from the fullness of the heart. He describes what he knows, what he has seen, what he has felt, and his audience are convinced that he is sincere in what he says, and his language sinks into the hearts of his hearers. After Mr. Hawkins concluded his remarks, Mr. Holbrook, the President of the Washington Total-Abstinence Society, addressed the meeting in his straight-forward, animated style, and clinched the nail which Mr. Hawkins had driven. He told us that a cab would be sent to the House of Correction this morning, to receive some offenders

whose term of imprisonment had expired, and who were desirous of enrolling themselves among the members of the society.
In this way he hoped to put an effectual check to intemperance
and crime. Another public meeting, called by the Boston
Temperance Society, will be held at the chapel on Wednesday
evening next, when Mr. Hawkins will again address the audience, and a collection will be taken in aid of the funds of the
society. " The work goes bravely on."

We return to Mr. Hawkins' journal.

Thursday, June 3d. — Met the County Convention at Concord, Mass.; it was well attended; about two hundred and
fifty delegates were present, besides others, especially ladies,
who attended the meeting of the convention. The proceedings were of the most gratifying character, and gave evidence
that a good feeling is awakened in old Middlesex, which augurs
well for temperance. Samuel Hoar presided, and addresses
were made by several gentlemen from the county; and also
by Rev. John Pierpont, Mr. Crosby, of Boston, Mr. Parsons,
of Salem, and by myself.

Friday and *Saturday.* — Rest.

Sunday, June 6th. — Lectured in Charlestown to a large
concourse of people; great interest was manifested.

Monday, 7th. — Lectured in Marlboro' Chapel; house
crowded.

Tuesday, 8th. — Lectured again in Charlestown; increasing
interest.

Wednesday, 9th. — Lectured in Chelsea; the people are here
wide awake to the subject of reform.

Thursday, 10th. — Lectured in Cambridgeport; the people
are aroused to the subject of temperance; the pledge was circulated, and three hundred and ten names obtained.

Hitherto we have sketched the public life of Mr.

Hawkins as the champion of the fallen; we have seen the estimation in which he was held, and the modesty with which he received all exhibitions of public favor. His interior life has hitherto been unwritten; — this can best be learned from his private correspondence, which he never designed to meet the public eye. We are much mistaken if the admiration for his character is not much increased by a perusal of these letters. The Christian will certainly be encouraged and animated by the consideration that the power upon which he relied for success was drawn from the blessed religion of Jesus of Nazareth. In all his sympathy, in all his labors and self-denials, he did but follow in the footsteps of Him who was a man of sorrows and acquainted with grief. Jesus was sympathetic; he met objects of compassion at the corner of every street. What would he not do to relieve human suffering, — what sacrifice would he not make to wipe away the tear of grief, to bind up the broken heart! How promptly did he hasten to perform a good deed! " My son dieth," said a certain nobleman." " Go thy way," said Jesus unto him, " thy son liveth." How kindly he bends over the leper, the crippled, the blind and impotent! Such, the Gospels inform us, was the spirit and mind of Jesus. " Now, if any man have not the spirit of Christ, he is none of his."

However nearly Mr. Hawkins may have approached the character of a *practical* Christian, it never made him proud or vain-glorious. Whatever he possessed, he ascribed to the grace and goodness of God.

BOSTON, June 10, 1841.

MY DEAR MOTHER, SISTERS, BROTHERS, SON, DAUGHTERS, AND FRIENDS, — I thus head my letter from the deep feelings of affection I have for you all. For you, my mother, when I remember, by you I was nourished and cherished at the breast, when unable to help myself, and have been the subject of your prayers from my birth; *which you well remember.* But, mother, although you have been praying for a drunken son for many years, your prayers have been answered, and I am now restored to sobriety, to my friends and family, and to the favor and fellowship of Him who died that I "might not perish, but have everlasting life." For years past *I did not expect, when I died, ever to meet you or any of my friends in heaven;* but now my fears and doubts are all gone, and I have a well grounded hope that when I die I shall see you at God's right hand, "where parting shall be no more."

My sisters and brothers, I love them much, for they do love me. Yes, they love me more because I have reformed my life and am trying to save my soul, and doing all in my power, by the help of God, to save others. My children, I love them, and rejoice that my bad example did not injure them; *but the time has come, by the providence of a good God, that my life and death will not bring disgrace upon my children and friends, especially upon you, my dear mother.* I know I have given you much trouble, trouble beyond all calculation; and I pray to God, from the bottom of my heart, that there shall never be another "black sheep" in the flock, who will bring disgrace on you, or any of their friends.

Mother, we are all doing well, and comfortably situated; boarding at the National Hotel, a strictly temperance house, kept by Mr. Louis Boutelle; he is a gentleman, and his wife is a lady. We are surrounded by good friends. I have sent you some papers showing the work the committee has laid out for me this month. My family go with me to most of the places; they are from five to fifty miles from Boston; all expenses paid, independent of my salary, which is one thousand dollars per year, besides the many gifts put into our hands.

A miniature painter called on me, and I am now sitting for

my likeness; I shall send you all a copy. A portrait painter has also called, and I am sitting for my portrait, which is to be presented to the Washington Temperance Society, of Boston. They call me the Father of the Society. The portrait is to be hung up in the hall of the society. All this is done without one cent of cost to me. * * * It is impossible for me to tell you how high I stand in the affections of the people of this State; and not only in this, but in Maine, New Hampshire, Vermont, Connecticut, and Rhode Island. I stand high, I know, *but my trust is in God, and not in the arm of flesh.* I pray much to God to sustain me. I have established family prayers. Pray for me that God may keep me. I shall soon get Hannah into one of the best schools in the city. My friends say they will make a woman of her; I know they will. Give my love to my son William George. Mr. John Tappan and two or three others are beginning to ask me a great many questions about William, and are much disposed to do something for him for my sake. Mother, I thank God that there is a good day coming to us all yet. I want to see Elizabeth very much, and when I send for her don't refuse her, for I am now about to do well, and wish to see my children with me. There will be some gentlemen in Baltimore shortly, from Boston, who will tell you how I am doing, better than I can write. I wrote from Hartford, Connecticut, but received no answer. Answer this to Boston without fail.

Your son, affectionately,
J. H. W. HAWKINS.

The following letter from Mr. Tappan to Mrs. Schaeffer requires no comment:—

BOSTON, June 29, 1841.

MRS. F. McC. SCHAEFFER — will without doubt be gratified to hear that her brother John is doing much to promote temperance in this State, and that his success does not appear to have any injurious effect upon him. If he can be kept humble, so as to feel his constant dependence upon God, he may be the instrument of effecting great good among those who were recently in the path to the drunkard's grave; and for this his friends should pray, as such applause is dangerous to any man, and especially to one so situated as he has been. At his request I direct some tracts to be sent to you for your distribution, and it will gratify me to be informed if they, or the former parcel which I gave him, have done good in your city. I send you some others, and if you wish more of *any* of them, it will give me pleasure to supply them on addressing me through the post-office. Respectfully yours,

JOHN TAPPAN,
President of the American Tract Society, Boston.

CHAPTER XI

" Hail! thou glad, primeval glory,
    Beacon of the drunkard's soul,
Watch-light on the lurid ocean
    Where the waves of ruin roll.
Hail! thou Star of Temperance, gleaming
    Through the clouded spirit's haze,
And the feet of Error guiding
    Into Wisdom's pleasant ways."

MR. HAWKINS' journal continues to furnish evidence of untiring industry, from the 11th of June to the 13th of July, in lecturing in and about Boston, as often as twice every day. On the 16th of June he attended the Essex County Convention, held at Lynn. The *Mercantile Journal* of the 17th of June, says :—

A meeting of the Essex County Temperance Society was held at Lynn yesterday, which was well attended by delegates from all parts of the county of Essex, and from the neighboring counties. Rev. Mr. Perry, of Bradford, presided, and the doings throughout were of the most interesting and cheering character. In the afternoon, the children belonging to the town, forming a Cold Water Army, numbering twelve hundred oys and girls, who had resolved never to touch the intoxicating cup, were introduced into the gallery of the church. It was a glorious sight, and which will not be soon forgotten by those who witnessed it. This army was addressed by Samuel Hoar, of Concord, by Moses Grant, of Boston, and by John Hawkins, of Baltimore. The address of Mr. Hawkins was one of the most truly eloquent and moving addresses to which we ever listened, and appeared to make a deep impression on the

(120)

minds of the children; indeed, on the minds of the whole audience. The citizens of Lynn, with a hospitality deserving of commendation, had kindly made arrangements for a collation at · the Town Hall, of which all were invited to partake, when the meeting adjourned at noon, and at five o'clock in the afternoon. In the mean time a platform was erected on the Common, and at six o'clock, a large number of people being collected, amounting to some thousands, the assembly was addressed by several gentlemen, and by Mr. Hawkins in one of his most powerful and effective speeches. Indeed, the proceedings throughout were of a nature deeply calculated to spread new light on this important subject through the community; to show the partaker of intoxicating drinks the dangerous abyss on which he is standing, to convince the rum-seller of the iniquity of his business, and to infuse new energy and spirit into the hearts of the active friends of temperance.

The same paper of June 29th, says: —

There was a noble gathering of the friends of temperance at Medford, yesterday. At eleven o'clock the delegates assembled in the church; prayer was offered, and the society was re-organized for the year. Delegates attended from Middlesex and Suffolk, and took an active part in the debate. At three o'clock, the church pews, aisle, pulpit, all were crowded to listen to a short but very able address from Dr. Wyman, the President of the society; excellent music from the choir followed, and then John Hawkins' unvarnished tale of a drunkard's sufferings; at which not only the tender female wept, but the rugged farmer, the hardy mechanic, the able lawyer, the learned divine, all sympathized and wept too.

Throughout the country extensive preparations were now being made for the celebration of the nation's anniversary, on total-abstinence principles. In these movements Mr. Hawkins was particularly active.

11

Speaking of the excessive labors of Mr. Hawkins, the Rev. John Marsh thus remarks in the *Journal* of the American Temperance Union : —

We are happy to state that this individual, who has for some time filled a large space in the public eye, has been received as an agent for the Massachusetts Temperance Society, and that his family have been removed to Boston, where their latter end will be better than their beginning. On his way with them from Baltimore on the first of June, Mr. H. addressed large assemblies at New York, Middletown, Hartford (where most of the Legislature were present), Springfield, and Worcester. When he arrived at Boston an immense assembly convened at the Marlboro' Chapel to receive him, and, when he rose to speak, we are told the enthusiasm of the people beggared all description. On the next day we find him at a large county meeting in Middlesex, holding an immense audience at his will, in perfect silence, in tears, or in laughter at his sallies of wit and humor; and soon after at Concord, N. H., addressing the Legislature and polished citizens of that place with great power. On the 12th of June, we find him at Framingham, where the anniversary of his reform was celebrated by a large number of his friends, and the 15th, the anniversary of his signing the pledge was celebrated at Marlboro' Chapel, Boston, in a most enthusiastic meeting. Scarce a day passes in which he is not engaged in some large meeting in city or country, giving his own history and the history of every drunkard, picturing the work and blessedness of reform, the traffic in ardent spirit in all its horrors, and the certain and glorious triumphs of temperance.

The fourth and fifth days of July, 1841, should be ever memorable in the nation's annals; they constituted an epoch in the history of moral reform, such as neither this nor any other country had ever before witnessed.

Over two hundred thousand ransomed inebriates greeted with exulting hearts its coming. Divines, philanthropists, statesmen, jurists, physicians, hailed its advent. Millions of children — a cold water army — marched to pleasant groves, with banners flying and music playing, to assure their sires that the next generation should be a generation of sober men and women. A nation but recently presenting the mournful spectacle of three hundred thousand of its people in the various stages of drunkenness, suddenly arrested in its downward progress, beholds the resurrection of almost countless myriads, who, casting off the habiliments of mental and moral degradation, stand forth, the emancipated signers of a "second Declaration of Independence."

"When and where," says that noble veteran in the temperance reform, Dr. Marsh, "was it ever known, from the rising to the setting sun, that on a nation's proudest anniversary, her conquest over herself was thus her greatest glory. We went forth in city and town, young men and old men, matrons and virgins, by thousands and thousands, in songs and dances, to say that our self-invoked chains were broken and the nation is free."

In New York the joy of the people was unbounded. An immense crowd filled the Broadway Tabernacle, to listen to a patriotic oration from the late Benjamin F. Butler, Esq., in which he alluded most appropriately to the source of the nation's increased joy.

In Boston, thousands upon thousands of "cold-water" men and children marched through the streets, from old Faneuil Hall to the Common, where, on platforms erected for the purpose, addresses were made by Mr. Hawkins and others. At a later hour in the day,

Temperance Celebration on Boston Common.

the members of the Washington Temperance Society having accepted an invitation from Charlestown, visited that place, and in the shadow of Bunker Hill Monument were addressed by Mr. Hawkins. The procession as it moved through the streets presented a most imposing spectacle; the " Cold Water Army " was a host of itself. " The windows," says the correspondent of the *A. T. Union*, " and balconies were crowded with women ·and children, whose happy faces gave evidence of the joy which filled their bosoms, in seeing husbands and fathers, sons and brothers, enrolled, a mighty army, marching with firm step and firmer resolution to exterminate from our beloved country the great cause of misery and crime."

Among the speakers on the Common was Mr. Dennis W. O'Brien, the individual who at the second address of Mr Hawkins in Faneuil Hall proclaimed from the gallery his conversion to total-abstinence principles. " He spoke," says the *Star*, " with great energy and effect; his fine, manly voice, with just enough of Irish accent to make it rich and pleasing, rang out clearly, and fell with melodious sounds on the listening ear."

When Mr. O'Brien had concluded, Mr. Hawkins was introduced, and was received by the multitude with acclamations. In the course of his remarks he said, that this was the second sober Fourth of July he had passed in twenty years; and so full was his heart with joy that he had celebrated it three times this year; at Worcester and Brookfield on Saturday, at the Odeon on Sunday, and here, this day, on the Common.

A number of songs, composed for the occasion, were set to charming music; among them the following: —

11*

SONG OF JOHN HAWKINS AND HIS COMRADES.

BY WM. B. TAPPAN.

Hurrah! hurrah! we've burst the chain
  O God! how long it bound us!
We run! we leap! O God again
  Thy light, thy air, surround us.
From midnight's dungeon-depths brought out,
  We hail Hope's rising star;
Ho, comrades, give the stirring shout,
  Hurrah! hurrah! hurrah!

The world has kissed the tyrant's throne,
  The Beast! the Man of Sin!
"Legion!" "Apollyon!" better known
  As Brandy, Beer, or Gin!
Roused up at Reason's clarion cry,
  We go to holy war,
To slay the dragon *or to die,*
  Hurrah! hurrah! hurrah!

Hurrah! hurrah! there's joy within,
  Where all before was woe,
And sunk is passion's dreadful din,
  And crushed for aye's the foe.
Yet *one charge more* in glorious strife,
  Stout hearts! to end the war:
'Tis done — our spoils! the babes! the wife!
  Hurrah! hurrah! hurrah!

Debased by drink, we'd lost the sign
  Of manhood God impressed —
The open face, the look divine —
  To show what he had blessed.
Behold! erect, with honest brow,
  Restored to Nature's law,
We're men, we're men! heaven knows us now,
  Hurrah! hurrah! hurrah! ·

Of ten men cleansed did one return
  To bless the healing hour?
All of our rescued thousands burn
  To praise redeeming power.

Come! bless God now! and what for us
  He's done — so reads the law —
WE'LL DO FOR OTHERS! and the curse
  Root out — hurrah! hurrah!

Tom Moore may drug the golden cup
  With costly pearls that shine
Bright as his face, and drink them up,
  Dissolved in rosy wine;
In undiluted streams *we* dip
  Our crystal glasses; nor
Refuse the pledge will Woman's lip,
  Hurrah! hurrah! hurrah!

Hurrah! hurrah! we've burst the chain;
  O God! how long it bound us!
We run! we leap! O God, again
  Thy light, thy air surround us.
From midnight's dungeon-depths brought out
  We hail hope's rising star;
Ho, comrades! give the stirring shout,
  Hurrah! hurrah! hurrah!

On the 13th of July Mr. Hawkins left Boston on a
lecturing tour "Down East," in Maine, from which
State pressing invitations had been received. How he
was received, will appear in the following selections
from the many accounts published of his efforts there,
and his encounters by the way. The following was
communicated to the *Mercantile Journal:* —

BANGOR, July 17, 1841.

MR. SLEEPER, — Mr. Hawkins arrived here on Wednesday
evening, and has been at work ever since. He has lectured
four times in this city, and to-day has gone to Orono, where he
will lecture this evening. To-morrow he will lecture at Old
Town, on Monday at Frankfort and Hampden, and here again
on Tuesday and Wednesday. Applications for him are received every day from all quarters, and it is to be regretted that

such arrangements could not have been made as to allow of his remaining longer with us. He must come into Maine again ; I do not know of a State in which he could do more good. His meetings have been held in the churches, except the last, which was on Friday evening at the City Hall. The galleries of this building were crowded with females, and the body of the house with all kinds of the other sex. All grades, from the lowest drunkard upward, were there, and such a temperance meeting I never attended. Mr. Hawkins' speech was cheered from beginning to end. It was one of those happy efforts by which he has obtained so much celebrity. He was occasionally interrupted by a quick-witted inebriate who sat in a corner of the room, and he would turn his sallies to so good an account, that the applause would come down upon him like a thunder-clap.

While he was speaking, a man came up and signed the pledge under circumstances related in the *Bangor Whig and Courier* of to-day. It is reported, with how much truth I am not able to say, that after the meeting had closed, and before the poor fellow had got entirely free from the effects of the liquor he had drank, a miserable sot-pimp sought him out, got him into his "hell," or confectionery as he calls it, poured liquor enough down his throat to get him thoroughly drunk again, and then kicked him out of doors. If this shall prove to be true, and I fear it will, the name of the soulless scoundrel will be given to the world, that he may be treated with the contempt he deserves. After Mr. Hawkins had concluded, an old man whose head 'had been visited by the frosts of about seventy winters, arose and wished to make some remarks. Mr. Hawkins gave him leave. He then commenced in a strain of abuse of Mr. Hawkins. The audience were so disgusted with this course, that they immediately commenced hissing him. This was promptly rebuked by Mr. Hawkins. — " Fair play, fair play, gentlemen ; that's the jewel ! " The old man went on. It was difficult to keep the audience quiet. The old man saw it, and hastened to a conclusion. " I have been invited," said he, " by the best men in this town to sign the temperance pledge, and I never would do it. I consider myself a temperance man, and I wouldn't sign that pledge," pointing to the Washington pledge which laid near Mr. H., "for if I did, I should acknowledge myself a drunkard! a drunkard!"—"Sign it, sign it," shouted several persons. "No, I'll not acknowledge myself to be a drunkard; every man that signs that pledge, acknowledges himself to be a drunkard. *Yes, a drunkard.*" Mr. Hawkins could not keep the people silent any longer, and the confusion became so great that the old man was glad to make his escape, cursing this "temperance business" all the while, however. This man was no less a personage than one of the electors of President from this State in 1826.

Mr. Hawkins is busily engaged in Maine in awakening a feeling on the subject of intemperance. The last number of the *Bangor Courier* says that he visited Stillwater and Old Town on Saturday and Sunday, at which places he addressed crowded assemblies. The people are awake there on the subject of temperance, and great good is anticipated to result from the labors of Mr. Hawkins. At Stillwater eighty-two individuals came forward, and fifty-four at Orono, and signed the pledge.

Referring to the above incident of his venerable opponent, Dr. Marsh observes : " In Maine, John Hawkins has performed a triumphant tour, obtaining three hundred and four hundred pledges in almost every place visited. The archers have shot at him, but he laughs at the shaking of their spear. He knows too well what he is about to be killed by friend or foe, or to be tied up to the will of any individuals."

On the 28th of July, 1841, the State Temperance Convention assembled at Portland, Maine. A deep feeling had been awakened on the subject, and large numbers were in attendance. During its session Mr.

Hawkins addressed the assembled multitude in the following simple and effective style : —

Mr. Chairman, — It affords me pleasure and satisfaction to have an opportunity of stating the progress of the temperance reform in the now happy city of Baltimore. It is truly astonishing. When I contrast one year ago with the present condition of that city, I sometimes wish I could stay among them, and look upon their happy faces. When I think of this I scarcely know how to begin or go on talking. Four thousand, nearly, have been saved. On the 8th of April, one year ago, six companions, greatly under the influence of liquor, not influenced by any temperance men, talked over among themselves their misery, and by agreement one of them made a pledge to drink no more intoxicating drink, and they all signed it. That pledge stands now, with no alteration, to rule and govern sober men. They met at the chairman's house, and brought five more with them, and five more ; and soon after that I cast my lot among them. I had refused before because the society were not for total abstinence. I knew from experience that nothing but total abstinence could prevent me from being a drunkard. It was the weaker drinks that made and kept me a drunkard. I didn't make it known, because I didn't like the truth. We saw the gain in our persons and in our families. We could sit under our own vine and fig-tree. We helped our old bottle companions to get up out of the gutter. They came timidly, and asked, "Is it possible that I can quit drink without being killed ? I shall have fits, and delirium tremens." But they came ; and if they fell we picked them up again, until they were strong enough to go alone. In a very short time our little band was exposed to public scrutiny, and people said, "They can't stand long ; they will soon go back again." Good men said this, and temperance men said, "You can't stand." But we did stand. Our Heavenly Father's hand was upon us ; he had us under his care ; we didn't know it, but when our hearts swelled with gratitude then we knew it. I could name cases, and I will name one, the worst we had. The man scarce looked like a human being; he was truly an object of pity. His wife and children were emaciated and crying for bread. The children were shrivelled and drawn up like old men. He had a thing that was once a bed, but no clothing on it; no fuel but a few shavings. He came and took the pledge, and with a faltering tongue. He used to drive a dray on shares. He went to his brother and was supplied with food and clothing, but he didn't let them have all they wanted. In February he went security for a horse, and in November it was all paid for, his cellar was filled with wood, he had a barrel of flour, and a barrel of meat, his wife and children were well supplied with clothing, and he had a double suit, besides paying ninety dollars of an old grog bill; and he is a Christian too. He was the last man that I shook hands with when I left. He is happy, and his wife and children are happy too. We have many more in the city of Baltimore like this; but it is not confined there. Several thousand have taken the pledge within a few weeks in Boston. But there are human beings in society that take every means to get them drunk again. It seems cruel that when the poor drunkard once gets up they should attempt to ruin his character. It would be better to rob and cut throats at once than to keep on robbing by degrees. Sometime since there appeared to be a resting-spell; but they have waked up again with renewed strength and vigor. They have rubbed their eyes and crossed the Alleghanies and gone further South. At Pittsburgh twelve hundred have reformed.

Mr. Chairman, I have heard it said since I came here that the old temperance men don't strive to save the drunkard. I have said ever since my reform that they do. I know it. I watched the old temperance men; I persecuted them, and tried to injure them in their property, and took every opportunity to do them hurt. I delighted in it. But I had a guilty conscience, and I look back over fifteen years and see how I fought against it. They strove to save the drunkard, but he would kick, and they were compelled to let him alone. I saw in my own heart that they were friends, and I was ashamed, and would go to them for two or three months at a time.* I remember when they said, "Let the poor drunkard alone," and I felt it, if other drunkards didn't; I felt sorry; and I feel it my duty to make these acknowledgments. I am sorry to hear it said that old temperance men didn't do this, that, and the other; they did all they could. It is true the poor drunkard knew nowhere to look for help. The rum-sellers knew this, and if they can get but one little drop down his throat he is gone. Are they sensible of the guilt of this? I cannot conceive what can induce them to sell spirits; it is worse than robbing. I know not the feeling of this community on this subject, but I know mine is the strongest indignation. But I must close. God is forever on our side. He has blessings yet in store for us, and this country, called the land of freedom, will yet be free.

While Mr. Hawkins was unrelaxing in his efforts and sympathy to save the drunkard, he began to discover that the efforts of the friends of temperance would prove in a great degree unavailing, while the manufacture and sale of intoxicating drinks continued. He began, therefore, to fortify himself with facts, and soon directed the whole power of his indignation and sarcasm against the making and vending of them. His humble instrumentality in stirring up public opinion on this subject has perhaps never been fully realized. It will be observed that he began, cautiously, to express his sentiments in his speech at Portland.

Mr. Hawkins remained twenty days in the State of Maine, and delivered in that time thirty-six lectures,

---

* Mr. Hawkins frequently took the old pledge, and made ineffectual attempts to reform.

and raised up, it is said, a mighty army of teetotalers. " His march was indeed gloriously triumphant; crowds of attentive auditors hung on his lips wherever he went." In many towns votes of thanks were paid him for his invaluable services. *

On his return to Boston, in the first part of August, he met with a warm reception.

" The church in Green Street," says the *Mercantile Journal,* " was filled at an early hour on Sunday evening, and many went away, unable to enter, every part of the house being crowded. Mr. Hawkins fixed the attention of the numerous audience for an hour and a half, in depicting the miseries of the drunkard, his wife, and children. He was truly eloquent in his appeals to save the drunkard, and by a variety of facts proved that it can be done ; and that throughout the land thousands who were once drunkards are now sober men. He stated that in all his tour through Maine, New Hampshire, and many parts of this State, he found the deepest interest to prevail on the subject of temperance, and related some astonishing cases of reformed drunkards. His appeal to the manufacturers and dealers in intoxicating drinks, was strong, unanswerable, kind, and to the point, and must have produced a strong effect. Public opinion, that mighty lever which can not be resisted, will soon overthrow, and render the whole traffic too odious to be pursued by those who set any value on the favor of their fellow-men, or an approving conscience.

The most of the month of August he spent in visiting the camp-meeting at Eastham, the camp-meeting on Martha's Vineyard, the island of Nantucket, New

---

* The *Portsmouth Journal* says that a little girl, eleven years of age, from a neighboring town, who heard Mr. Hawkins lecture, when he invited those present to circulate temperance pledges, went home, and in a week obtained one hundred and fifty names. Who is there that can do nothing ?

12

Bedford, Fairhaven, Mattapoisett, Fall River, Taunton, lecturing in them and other places. Three large meetings were held in New Bedford, and a cold water army formed of four hundred children. Mr. Hawkins had at this time many able coadjutors, but our limits forbid any extended remarks upon their services, such as they deserve. At the camp-meeting at Martha's Vineyard he occupied the attention of the assembly of about three thousand persons nearly the whole of the afternoon. Between four and five hundred signed the pledge on the spot. *

He arrived at Boston on the first of September. Feeling confident of maintaining the position he had assumed, and encouraged by the liberal support of the friends of temperance, he began to turn his attention to the education of his children and the two orphans, children of his wife's sister, with whom it was a pleasure to share the bounties bestowed on him.

* See *Journal* of American Union, 1841, p. 156.

CHAPTER XII.

"Ah, who can tell what wonders it hath wrought!
Home to the soul what long-lost comfort brought!
What virtues started from a hopeless grave,
When, wandlike, o'er it Temperance came to wave
Her own pure banner! Oh, what torn hearts healed!
What deep, deep founts of love have been unsealed!
What rosy light, what living streams now flow
Where all was black and sterile with long woe!"

(FROM JOHN H. W. HAWKINS TO MRS. SCHAEFFER.)

BOSTON, Sunday morning, Sept. 5, 1841.

MY DEAR SISTER, — Your kind letter dated August 24th came safe to hand, and would have been answered before this, but I was out of the city. You write me that Elizabeth will be ready by the 16th inst. I wish to be in the city when she arrives, and to meet her at the cars; and in order to accomplish this, it is necessary for me to know when she will leave Baltimore, and whether she will arrive here by way of Providence or Worcester R. R., and let me know who is her protector. Tell my dear daughter she must be watchful and very guarded in her words and deportment while travelling, and when she arrives here I will tell her what kind of people they are here; all about their intelligence, and how scrutinizing they are towards us; but as kind people as live on the earth; very much so towards me and my family.

You did not mention in your letter whether James received the draft for one hundred dollars ($100). I requested him in it to answer me; it may at some time be in my power to render him assistance for his kindness to me.

After writing the above I went to church to hear Mr. Maffit;

he preached a gospel sermon; he has more religion than he formerly had; at any rate he preaches and talks as if he had. My poor heart was warmed up, and my soul is in full stretch for happiness and heaven. My sister, you say you pray for me, and that while you was writing your sight was almost blind with the tears in your eyes; just so it is with me at this very moment. Glory to God for the prospect of meeting as an unbroken family in heaven. I am made to think who of our flesh and bone are now resting in Abraham's bosom, looking out for us: — a kind father, two brothers, a husband and wife, and, praise God, our dear little children; can you not see them by the eye of faith, (I can,) around the throne of God?

Bless the Lord, O my soul, and all that is within me, bless his holy name." While I write my soul is happy, and I have to stop to wipe the tears away; it is not the tear of sorrow and regret; no, my dear sister, it is the tear of joy and gladness, that God has answered the many prayers that have been offered up for me. Oh, my mother, my dear mother, how often she has prayed for me; nearly forty-four years; and how much she loves me. You say mother is complaining. My dear sister, soothe her in her *downward — upward* course. Tell her Jesus has said, "I will be with you;" tell her God will bless her more abundantly, the nearer she approaches life and glory. She may look down through the dark valley of the shadow of death, but beyond the vale Jesus stands, holding out a crown of glory. Amen, amen, so let it be, my heavenly Father.

When I came to that part of your letter which says, " Archy has paid us a visit and tells us he visited the Washington Temperance Society last night, and went forward publicly and signed the pledge," you say to your great joy, it was good news to me. I love my dear brother Archy. Tell him he has talents, and that there is a work for him to do, and that God expects him to work; tell him to remember his poor brother John's past condition, and what I am now by the grace of God.

Tell him also to remember his own, and praise God we are out of hell and within the reach of mercy; tell him to hold out faithful and I should be glad to see him in Boston. I was glad to hear that N—— W—— signed the pledge.

My dear sister Frances, it gave me much pleasure to hear that William George went to church with you every Sunday night; why not in the morning too? Tell him, "Remember now thy Creator in the days of thy youth," and "to pray in secret and God will reward him openly." I want him to write and let me know how it is with him; tell him it will give me pleasure to hear from him by letter. Enclosed is five dollars ($5) for him; God bless him. Lizzie, does she feel the need of a Saviour? tell her to pray much in secret, and God will pardon her sins. Isabella and David, tell them I love them and the Saviour loves little children, for he said, "Suffer little children to come unto me, and forbid them not." Tell them, "Honor thy father and mother," &c. Tell them the poor drunkard is still reforming. O sister Frances, it surely is God's work, for how could man do such things? Sometimes I am on the mountain-top, sometimes in the valley. God is there, I try to live near him; his grace supports me, for without it I could not be sustained under so much applause. Continue to pray for me, dear sister, that God may supply me with sustaining grace.

I want Elizabeth Schaeffer to write me a long letter. I sometimes look at myself with wonder and astonishment, and ask myself, "Am I the same person who was a poor, unhappy drunkard a short time ago." Let us praise God, my dear sister, for his long forbearance towards me, and let the language of our hearts be, "not unto us, not unto us, but unto God be all the praise of our salvation." Nothing, my dear sister, but the grace of God can sustain me in this great work. It is true I have been called into this great field of labor without much fore-thought on my part, but what of that? My heavenly Father

12*

has promised: "My grace is sufficient for you;" "I will never leave thee nor forsake thee;" "Though he slay me yet will I trust in him."

Ann [his wife] is in better health than formerly. Hannah is in excellent health and will soon write a letter to her grandmother; she was much pleased with that part of your letter relating to mother's coming to Boston. I will pay her passage to and from Boston, and something more, if she will come here in the spring.

After my return from Maine I took a tour through Cape Cod; was at Eastham camp-meeting; a great time you will see by the papers. After my return from the Cape, only one day with my family; off again to Nantucket, New Bedford, &c., &c. On my return from Nantucket stopped a few days on Martha's Vineyard Island, at a camp meeting; how kind the people were to me. I lectured at this meeting from 1 P.M. till $4\frac{1}{2}$ P.M. I never saw the like before in all my life.

I lecture to-night in Dr. Jenks' Church. I returned from Nantucket to this place on Friday, September 3d, and commence another tour to-morrow. The following are the towns I shall visit: Lexington, Salem, Medway, Kingston, Plymouth, Duxbury, Scituate, which will bring me home on the 16th inst. I shall then expect to hear from you, and will remain in the city until Elizabeth's arrival; if she can leave on the 13th or 14th, it will bring her here about Friday or Saturday, the 17th or 18th, if you can so arrange it; if not, do the best you can. I pray God that no accident may happen. I shall be anxious until her arrival. We are all in high expectations. I have sent you some papers; if you have not received them they are in the post office.

I fear I tax you and James too much, but do not fear of taxing me, for it does me good to hear from you. My wife sends her love to you all. Hannah, Arthur, and Sallie are well. I want William George to find Mr. Holmes, and tell him his children are well, in good hands, and all their wants are supplied. Give my love to mother, and to all my nephews and nieces.

I remain your brother,

JOHN H. W. HAWKINS.

Between the 6th and 15th of September, 1841, he visited and lectured in Lexington, Salem, Medway, Kingston, Plymouth, Duxbury, and Scituate. " The meetings in all these places were well attended ; much real interest felt and carried out in the cause of temperance ; a vast number signed the pledge."

On reaching Boston he addressed the following letter to Rev. John Marsh ; it was published in the *Journal*.

BOSTON, Sept. 16, 1841.

MY DEAR SIR, — The cause of temperance is going on here, gloriously. We shall commence a series of protracted temperance meetings to-morrow (Sabbath) evening, and it is our intention to carry the *war* into the ENEMY's camp, as did Putnam with the *wolf*. I shall use my influence in getting up a Merchants' Temperance Society here. One is *needed*. My health is *good, very good ;* you will be surprised when you see me. The first of June I weighed one hundred and sixty pounds ; I now weigh one hundred and eighty-two pounds. I thank God for the good health of my body and the peace of mind I enjoy. God is with me ; he sustains and comforts me in my labor. I pray that God will keep me humble at his feet. My dear brother, I do feel thankful and humble for what he has done for me ; and I do feel that nothing short of the grace of God can sustain me.

Yes, my dear brother, he has raised me out of a deep pit of wretchedness ; he has plucked me as a brand from the burning, and made me an humble instrument in his hand in doing much good. I cannot write what I feel. My poor heart is full. I am almost blind with the tears in my eyes. I brush them away to say, Glory to God in the highest. Salvation has come to my poor soul. Pray for me, that God may keep and sustain me.

I trust that I shall pay you a visit in October.

J. H. W. HAWKINS.

We continue our extracts from his journal : —

Left Boston, Sept. 27th, on a long tour through Massachusetts, New Hampshire, and Vermont. Commencing my lectures at Lancaster, Mass., I delivered one lecture to a crowded house ; much interest is felt, and the cause beginning to prosper ; one hundred and twenty signed the pledge. At Fitchburg lectured to a crowded house. Here a military company was out on parade, and by special invitation from me attended my lecture. Many of them came forward, with others of the congregation, and took the pledge. This place bids fair to triumph in the temperance cause. One hundred and fifteen signed.

Templeton, 29*th.* — Pledges, one hundred and eight. Lectured in the Unitarian Church ; but little interest felt here by the community generally. Many of the professed friends of temperance not setting the example they should by signing the pledge.

Chester, Vermont. — Lectured in this place morning, afternoon, and night ; deep interest is felt in the cause. Mr. Baxter, a reformed drunkard, is very active in the good work. In this place they have formed a Washington Temperance Society, and are doing well ; three hundred and four signed the pledge during my stay.

Windsor, Vt., Oct. 8*th.* — Lectured once in this place ; one hundred and thirty-two signed. Left in the morning for Dartmouth College, with Rev. Mr. Richards. Stayed Oct. 9th and 10th with Deacon Long ; a good work has been done here at the college among the students ;* with most of the Professors at

* TEMPERANCE AT DARTMOUTH COLLEGE. — A letter from Hanover

their head, they have formed themselves into a temperance society.

The number of pledges obtained in Barry was fifty; Greenfield, fifty. In Brattleboro' he delivered in two days six lectures, and took two hundred and sixty pledges. At Keene, three lectures. Here the whole population were wide awake, and four hundred signed the pledge; at Bellows Falls, one hundred; Hanover,

states that of ninety-one members of the Senior Class, seventy-one have signed the pledge; sixty-nine out of eighty-five of the Junior; forty-one out of seventy-nine of the Sophomore; twenty-two out of seventy-six of the Freshmen; two hundred and three out of three hundred and thirty-one. And some of the students who have not signed have signed elsewhere. Surely this is an encouragement to parents to send their sons to Dartmouth.

The sound principle of total abstinence is gaining ground in the community. The *N. Y. Observer* contains an extract of a letter from Princeton, N. J., showing that the Faculty of Princeton College have adopted the total-abstinence pledge; and in the explanations they have given while taking this ground, they have only expressed sentiments which are entertained by multitudes who are willing to lend the weight of their names and examples to the cause of temperance. "Our temperance meeting on Tuesday evening was the commencement, I hope, of good in Princeton. Professor Henry opened with an address on the force of habit, and concluded by saying, that as far as his example went, total abstinence should have it; and he stepped forward and signed the pledge. Professor James Alexander, after stating his protest against three things; viz., 1. That it should be thought that the friends of temperance considered it a sin to drink. 2. That the society should at all interfere with the communion. 3. That any one should be constrained to say, that Scripture wines were not intoxicating; said, he had come to do what he had never done before, to sign a total-abstinence pledge: and he accordingly signed it. Professor M'Lean said, he had been wrongly considered an enemy of the total-abstinence society; he was an enemy of ultra measures, and had never signed a total-abstinence pledge, but would now do it, and he did it. Many of the students also signed. Professor M'Lean then stated, that the President and Professor Dodd were prevented by sickness from attending and signing." — *Mercantile Journal, Sept.* 28, 1841.

eighty-nine; Woodstock, two hundred and sixteen. At Rutland he attended a mass meeting. The county poured in its vigorous population. From Pittsford came fifty wagons, bringing from two to three hundred people, including twenty-five drunkards, with a good band of music. Six hundred in Pittsford signed the pledge. In Montpelier eight reformed drunkards pledged themselves to the cause, and commenced vigorously the work of reform. At Burlington he delivered two lectures; some interest was felt in the cause. Journal continued: —

Left Burlington 19th October, in the steamboat, for Whitehall; there took passage by stage and canal packet for Saratoga; thence by railroad to Troy, remaining all night in Troy.

Left, 21st, in steamboat Troy for New York; arrived at night in time for my lecture in Clinton Hall before the Merchant's Temperance Society.

After reaching New York he received a letter from Brattleboro' with the following pleasing information: —

We have already in our Washington Society one hundred and fifty members, six or seven hard cases. We have raised by subscription one hundred and eight dollars, for the relief of the suffering families of those who have joined us. The ladies have three hundred and fifty on their list, and have agreed to send a petition to the rumsellers in the village, requesting them to discontinue their business; to be presented by three interesting young ladies. The young men are moving on well. We have now eight hundred names of a population of fifteen hundred. Your visit did us great good. It set the ball in motion. You will long be remembered by us.

His friend, Rev. John Marsh, thus speaks of the merchants' meeting above referred to: —

In expectation of hearing an address from Mr. Hawkins, a meeting of the Merchants' Society was called at Clinton Hall on the evening of the 21st. As he did not arrive in the city until a few minutes before the hour appointed, the meeting was at first thin; but a large meeting of the Washingtonians at their hall, hearing that he had arrived, at once adjourned, and poured in a dense crowd, well occupying all the vacant seats. Mr. Hawkins was affected and animated at the sight of his redeemed comrades, many of whom he had himself been instrumental in saving, and for more than an hour and a half he entertained and moved the audience sometimes to laughter and sometimes to tears, by a relation of his travels. The meeting was closed by an address from Mr. T. N. Woodruff.

One result of the inauguration of this great reform, was the assembling of large masses of the people in County and State conventions, in a number of which, it will be seen, Mr. Hawkins took a very prominent part, and gave advice as to the proper measures to be adopted to make the reformation efficient and permanent. Similar assemblies, it is true, had formerly been held; but they were not so frequent, nor did they exhibit the enthusiasm which characterized these meetings.

The result of these movements was the calling of a great national temperance convention, which assembled at Saratoga Springs on the 27th of July, in the year 1841. Five hundred and forty individuals attended as delegates, gathered from nearly every State in the Union, judges, divines, lawyers, statesmen, mechanics, farmers, and merchants, of all sects in religion and of every school in politics. They came to consult upon subjects pertaining to the best interests of humanity; their discussions were harmonious and highly encouraging to every lover of his race.

In the course of his remarks upon the second resolution offered to the convention, referring to the movement begun in Baltimore, Rev. Dr. Beaman of Troy
expressed the following sentiments : —

This is the first time that the temperance movement could
be justly called a *reformation*. Hitherto it has been no reformation. It has been the great object and endeavor to hold
one another up ; good business, indeed, as far as it goes ; but
it has scarcely accomplished any thing, until recently, towards
the reclaim of those who had fallen under the power of alcohol. But these reformed drunkards — and I rejoice that they
choose to call themselves by this name — it indicates a humil-
ity which is the best proof of the genuineness of their repentance, and gives a cheering pledge of its permanence — show
us that the work has been begun in earnest, and in the right
quarter. This impulse has been felt all through the land. We
have many more here present than would have been but for
their efforts.

William B. Spooner, of Boston, electrified the convention by a narration of the wonderful work that
had been accomplished there; pledges to the number
of four thousand two hundred had been taken there
and in South Boston. "What a prodigious result
has been brought round; *four-fifths* of the drunkards
of a city numbering one hundred thousand entirely
reformed within a few months! When or where has
the world ever looked upon the like? But not only at
Boston, in every place where this electric fire of reform
has reached, it is producing the same astonishing effects."

The heart of the worthy and indefatigable Corresponding Secretary of the A. T. Union was filled with

joy at the marvellous results of the new movement, and at the harmony of the proceedings. On returning to his post he thus wrote: —

Life, it has been well remarked, is made up of the exciting anticipation of a series of important events, and of short spaces of relief when they are past; spaces either of bitter mortification or of complacent triumph — enduring until summoned to the next in course, and so continuing until our frail bark is lost in the ocean of eternity. We have returned to our post from one of those exciting and important movements, and returned with rich causes of gratitude that it has been in every respect such as was most desirable for the great work in which we are engaged.

We refer to the note for a fuller account of the proceedings at this Convention.*

*(FROM THE MERCANTILE JOURNAL.)

SARATOGA SPRINGS, July 28, 1841.

MR. SLEEPER, — We have had a noble Temperance Convention, probably never surpassed for talent, wisdom, harmony, and efficient action. Five hundred and sixty delegates and members have attended; from the State of New York, 386; Massachusetts, 50; Rhode Island, 2; Vermont, 46; Connecticut, 23; New Hampshire, 4; Maine, 3; New Jersey, 7; Pennsylvania, 9; Maryland, 4; Michigan, 4; Louisiana, 3; Alabama, 2; Wisconsin, 3; Ohio, 3; Indiana, 2; Georgia, 2; Iowa, 1; Montreal, 1; Sweden, 1; Sandwich Islands, 1; from places not known, 3. Among the bright lights of temperance present, were Chancellor Walworth, Mr. Delavan, Dr. Edwards, Dr. Humphrey, John Tappan, Rev. J. Pierpont, Gerrit Smith, Dr. C. Jewett, Dea. Moses Grant, Dr. Charles A. Lee, J. C. Lovejoy, Rev. Mr. Scott, of Sweden, &c.; while a number of reformed drunkards graced the scene, and gave life to the day, as so many captives from the terrible foe. Never, perhaps, has there been a business meeting in the world, so full of joy, love, and praise. The bursts of feeling on the first afternoon, as the delegates from Boston, New York, Baltimore, &c., — I may say especially your Mr. Spooner, — told what God had wrought, and described the incidents in the delivery from

13

During the deliberations of the Convention, Mr.
Hawkins was performing a most successful tour of duty
in the State of Maine.   As he gathered from the daily
papers an account of its proceedings, his heart was encouraged and animated with redoubled zeal to carry out
the good work.

But to return to our narrative.   After his address before the Merchants' Society, he remained a few days,
lecturing in the city and neighboring towns, until the
29th, when he thus writes: —

I left this day for Baltimore; remained there until the 8th

King Alcohol of more than ten thousand drunkards, were indescribable.
And when the Convention turned back to look at even the work which
seemed in some measure hid, the Irish reformation, the enthusiasm was
rather increased than diminished.   The discussion of the great principles
of temperance, and the best method of carrying on the work of reform,
were calm and dignified, all receiving a new interest from the existing
state of things in the country.   During the sittings of the Convention,
six public meetings were held; three in the large grove east of Congress
Spring, and three in the churches.   The evening meeting in the grove on
Tuesday, was peculiarly beautiful and solemn; some thousands surrounded the platforms hung with lamps, all deeply interested, first in the
statements of Mr. Scott, from Sweden, then in the cutting satire of your
Mr. Pierpont, then in the wit, and thrusts, and affecting narrations of Pollard, the reformed Baltimore drunkard, and, last of all, in the solemn appeal of Gerrit Smith.   At the close of the Convention, Dr. Humphrey
expressed it as his opinion, that so large a body of men had never assembled from such an extent of country, transacting so much business with
perfect harmony.   In three days' discussion of near thirty resolutions, he
had not heard an unkind word.   I should have mentioned that the chair
was first taken by His Honor Chief Justice Savage, who, after the prayer
by Dr. Beaman, opened the meeting by reading an address from General
Cooke, President of the American Temperance Union.   Chancellor Walworth was made President of the Convention; Rev. John Marsh, Dr.
Edwards, E. C. Delavan, J. B. Segur, John J. Norton, Rev. Mr. Slicer,
Francis Parsons, and Elisha Taylor, Business Committee.   Their resolutions, reported and adopted, will soon be before the public.

Yours, &c.,   E.

of November. Lectured in the Rev. Dr. Breckenridge's
church, Rev. Dr. J. Morris', Rev. Mr. Hill's, at Milk St., before the Howard Society twice, and once to the Washington.

Nov. 8th. — Left Baltimore with my daughter Elizabeth.
Arrived in Philadelphia, sojourned with Dr. Burgin, and at
night lectured to the Jefferson T. A. Society. The meeting at
their hall was well attended; here met with Mr. Pollard on his
way to Baltimore.

9th. — Took the cars for New York, at 5 P.M.; reached Newark at midnight; remained there to lecture next evening, 10th;
· lectured to a crowded house. Much interest is felt here on
the subject. The Washington T. S. formed, and in a prosperous condition.

November 11. — Arrived in New York, and remained until
Monday, November 15th. While there, on Sunday morning,
lectured at the Catherine Market; in the evening at Allen-Street
Methodist Church.

Monday, Nov. 15. — Left for Boston by way of New Haven
and Hartford. In the former place delivered a lecture to a
crowded house, in the Methodist Church. On Tuesday to the
children, and at night to a large audience in the Rev. Mr. Dut-
ton's church (Orthodox). This place seems to be wide awake
in the cause of temperance.

The *Journal* of the American Temperance Union,
thus refers to the return of Mr. Hawkins to Boston :—

This bright advocate of the poor unfortunate drunkard
stopped a few days in our city, on his return from Baltimore
to Boston, and addressed a very large meeting in the Methodist
Chapel in Allen Street; also an immense meeting at Newark.
We had the happiness to see him throw himself into the arms
of his reformed brethren at the Washington Hall. He alluded
very happily to his first address in Green Street, where the first
of the reformed drunkards of New York cried out from the gal-

lery, "Is there any hope for me?" Speaking of his happiness in his family, he suddenly asked, "But am I the only happy man?" Twenty voices answered from all parts of the hall, "No, No." From this place he went to New Haven. A letter from that place says, "We gave him a full house Monday night. About one thousand children were out yesterday afternoon, and last evening it was a perfect jam. The aisles were full, quite up to the pulpit. He was very happy in his remarks. All were pleased. One hundred and fifty names were added to the pledge." Mr. H. is now in Providence speaking to immense audiences.

On his arrival in Boston he wrote to his son as follows: —

BOSTON, Nov. 20, 1841.

MY DEAR SON, — We arrived in Boston after a very pleasant journey of more than ten days. We stopped at Philadelphia, Newark, New Jersey, New York city, New Haven, Ct., Hartford, Ct., Springfield, Mass. In all these places I lectured to crowded houses. I found your mother in excellent health; also your sister Hannah, Arthur, and Sallie. Your mother and myself leave here to-day for Providence, and return on Wednesday next, the 24th of November, the day before Thanksgiving. I wish you could be here on that day. It is always a great day here, when parents gather their children together, and return thanks for the goodness of God to them. My dear son, "Remember thy Creator in the days of thy youth;" remember what our good Heavenly Father has done for your poor father, and is still doing. Serve him with an undivided heart, a perfect heart, and with a willing mind. I shall be lecturing in and about Boston until your arrival here. My trip to the South is postponed for the present. I want you to write me positively on what day you leave Baltimore. I wish you to leave as soon as possible, as I am desirous, as soon as may be, to go to my distant appointments, which I cannot do till you arrive and I have you fixed at school.

Instructions. — Leave Baltimore at 9 A.M., arriving in Philadelphia at 4 P.M. Take the cars immediately; you will arrive in New York that night about eleven o'clock. Get a porter to carry your trunk to Mrs. Ballard's boarding-house, which will cost you twenty-five cents. Mrs. Ballard's is at the corner of Broadway and the street you land at. Next day you leave New York for Boston, I think at five o'clock in the afternoon. The porter at Mrs. Ballard's will give you all attention, and the information you desire. You must introduce yourself to Mrs. B. as my son; they anticipate your coming, and will be glad to see you. You must go and see Mr. Cutter; he will point you to Mr. Bigelow across the street; see him. You will have all the morning and afternoon to look about New York. *Watch your baggage.* When you arrive in Boston, which I think will be midnight, take a cab, telling the driver to bring you to the National Temperance Hotel, Louis Boutelle, corner of Blackstone and Cross Streets. I believe I have written all that is required. You must by all means call on Rev. John Marsh, Clinton Hall, at the American Temperance Union. Say to those friends, plainly, without any seeming embarrassment, "My name is William George Hawkins, son of John Hawkins;" that you are on your way to join your father in Boston, *and you will see their eyes beam with delight.* Enclosed I send you ten dollars. I am very scarce of money at present. If it is not sufficient to bring you on, get your Uncle James to advance you a little more and charge me. The money I send you, convert into specie; don't bring any railroad money, and watch the money you receive on the road; the best way is for you to have the even change in paying your passage. Your cousin Lizzie was to negotiate for your free passage to Philadelphia or New York; see to it. We are all well. Give our love to all, especially to your Aunt Frances. I want to hear from them, particularly from her.

Your father, affectionately,
J. H. W. HAWKINS.

November 20th. — Left Boston for Providence with my wife; lectured in the Methodist Church in the afternoon, to a crowded house; at night, in Richmond-Street Church; crowded to excess.

Monday, 22d. — Lectured in Pawtucket; rain, and meeting slim.

Tuesday, 23d. — In Dr. Tucker's church, Providence; large audience.

Wednesday, 27th. — Left Boston for Thompson, Ct. Stopped at Worcester; lectured to the Cold Water Army in the afternoon; lectured the same day, at night, in Thompson, to a crowded house.

Sunday, 28th. — Lectured in the Rev. Mr. Dow's church to a crowded house; much interest manifested in the cause here; one hundred and thirty signed the pledge.

Monday. — Heavy snow storm; rode in a sleigh to Chestnut Hill to lecture; very few in attendance on account of the storm. Thirty-six signed the pledge. The society formed in this place now numbers over two hundred in two months. After lecture returned with Mr. Mowrey Aimsbury to Killington Centre.

Wednesday, Dec. 1st. — Lectured at Westfield, in the Rev. Mr. Whitmore's church; two hundred and fifty signed the pledge.

Thursday, Dec. 2. — Lectured at Moosop Depot; a good work has been begun in this hard place, through the instrumentality of twelve reformed drunkards.

Friday 3. — Returned to Boston and rested.

The following letter, dated the day following, was written to his sister : —

BOSTON, December 4, 1841.

MY DEAR SISTER, — I returned yesterday from Connecticut, where I have been laboring for a week past with great success, and leave again at 2 P.M. this day. Truly the Lord is good to me in blessing my efforts.   On my return I was indeed glad to read your letter, and to hear that you were. *crawling* about the room, somewhat better.*

My dear sister, I have given your case some study and prayer.   I often ask myself, " Why is the hand of the Lord thus upon you?"   Why are you, my dear sister, called to pass thus under the rod of our heavenly Father?   I hope you are not impatient under a chastisement administered by one whose wisdom and whose goodness you cannot call in question.   Though the stripes of our heavenly Father are often laid most frequently and heavily upon those whom we should think need them least, yet we do not know what important purposes are to be effected by such a course of divine procedure.   If it is a proof that our heavenly Father loves us to be thus chastened, may it not prove a special favor to be *greatly chastened?*   I do believe, judging from the observation I have been able to make, that those persons who have become what we call eminent for piety, have generally been made so, under God, by suffering.   This seems reasonable ; for how can poor depraved human nature ever rise heavenward when it can be satisfied with earthly objects?   " Every branch in me that beareth not fruit he taketh away, and every branch that beareth fruit he purgeth it, that it may bring forth more fruit."   My dear sister, what has Jesus wrought for us " before our ravished eyes."   Yes, he laid down his *life* that we might not perish but have *eternal life.*   " Whilst we were yet sinners, Christ died for us. "

> " Oh, what a blessed hope is ours,
>   While here on earth we stay :

* His sister, the year before, in passing out of her house on Sunday morning on her way to church, trod upon a needle, which broke off, half of it remaining in her foot; supposing it had all been removed she walked to church, but was unable to put her foot to the ground to walk for more than a year afterwards.

We more than taste the heavenly powers,
And antedate the day."

My dear sister, with all your afflictions you have enjoyed much of the presence of God. A sentiment in one of your letters, written August 24th, rings continually in my ears. It is that we may be kept and saved an unbroken family around the throne of God. God has done much for me; he has raised me up to become an instrument in his hands in doing much good. I feel humble and thankful, from the bottom of my heart, that I am not in a drunkard's grave, and in a drunkard's hell.

How comfortable and happy my family are; we have a family altar raised, *that when I am out preaching temperance, — they promised me, and they keep their promise, — my family may assemble every morning and evening, read the Scriptures and offer up prayer and thanksgiving to God for his goodness and mercy to us.* We have just this moment, by my asking each one, viz., wife, Elizabeth, and Hannah, agreed to redouble our diligence in the service of God. Hannah attends the prayer meetings and has asked to be prayed for; Elizabeth begins to feel much on the subject.

Tell my dear son to search the Scriptures and pray much in secret, reading the Word of God on his knees. Shall I ask how it is with Eleanora and Elizabeth? Tell them to pray in secret, " and the Lord will reward them openly." I must close, for it is past twelve o'clock, and I have to travel in a carriage twenty miles this afternoon to lecture at night. You see that I am but little with my family; but God is with them, and that is the best of all. My son William George may remain with his uncle, say until early in the spring; I wish him then to enter a good school in Massachusetts. Give my love to dear mother; God bless her.

I had like to forgot B—— M——. I felt happy by the interview with her while in Baltimore. God has indeed afflicted her with one hand and blessed her with the other. He will no doubt give her the kingdom he has prepared for her from the foundation of the world.   May the Lord bless you and keep you unto eternal life, is the prayer of your

Affectionate brother,

JOHN.

P. S. — I want a " spiritual " letter from my son *soon*, that is, next week.   Please inform Mr. James McFaile, at Eli Howard's, that I received a letter from him.   He writes me that there was a report in Baltimore that I had broken up a temperance meeting in Bangor, Maine ; the report is false.   I have written to the President of the society there, and he will hear from him on the subject.   No man could be received with more respect than I was, for it was there the society gave me a public dinner.   I wish this to be read to Mr. McFaile by James Baxley.

J. H. W. HAWKINS.

Sunday, December 5th. — In Dedham village, lectured in the Town Hall to an overflowing assembly.   In this place, some few do not seem to feel that interest in the cause they should ; it is thought they may *" take a little,"* therefore are not friendly to *total abstinence.*

December, 8th. — South Dedham.   Thursday, rest.   Friday, in West Dedham ; returned to Boston in the morning, and left at 3 P.M. for Ipswich, Mass.   On Sunday evening lectured in the Rev. Mr. Fitch's church (Presbyterian) to a crowded congregation.

Monday, 13th. — Lectured in Rev. Daniel Wise's church (Methodist), to a large audience ; much good done here ; over three hundred signed the pledge.

Tuesday, 14th. — In Newburyport.

Wednesday, 15th. — Attended a convention in Exeter, N. H. with the Rev. John Pierpont.   Not much had been done here in the cause of temperance, but do hope the present meetings of the friends of temperance in convention will give the cause a fresh impulse.   The meetings were very interesting, and the people seem willing to lay hold of the cause.

December, 17th. — Returned to Newbury, with the intention of delivering another address ; but a very heavy storm of wind, rain, and snow came on, and it was thought there would be no people out.   I therefore returned to Boston to fill up other appointments.

Saturday. — Rest.

Sunday, 19th. — Lectured in Waltham.

Monday, 20th. — Lectured in Upton to a crowded house. Much has been done here in the cause ; a heavy snow-storm.

Tuesday, Dec. 21st. — Attended a county convention ; it was well attended and much interest manifested.   At night lectured to an overflowing house.

Wednesday, Dec. 22d. — Lectured in New England Village to a crowded house ; great interest felt here.

Thursday, Dec. 23d. — In Shrewsbury to a crowded congregation, in the basement of the Orthodox Church.

Friday, 24th. — Lectured to a crowded and interested audience in Millbury.

Saturday, 25th. — Christmas-day.   In Boston with the Cold Water Army in Faneuil Hall ; Marlboro' Chapel at night.

Monday, Dec. 27th, 1841. — Lectured in Thompson ; also in Plainfield ; much has been done here and the work has been *thorough.*

In speaking of the celebration in Faneuil Hall on Christmas-day, and the review which that day called forth of the year's progress, the *Mercantile Journal* of December 27th thus speaks : —

The temperance celebration at Faneuil Hall on Christmas-day was of an exceedingly interesting character, and was calculated to encourage the friends of this great and glorious cause, and excite them to renewed and still more strenuous exertions in behalf of the great moral reformation which is now going on throughout the whole length and breadth of the land; a reformation which, when perfected as it promises to be, by elevating hundreds of thousands from degradation and want to respectability and competence, will increase to a wonderful degree both the moral and physical powers of this republic. Since the first of January last much has been done to extend the blessings of the temperance reform. Those who acted as pioneers in the cause do not pause in their efforts, and have welcomed, within the year, an accession to their ranks which promises the most successful results. New societies have been formed, composed of men most of whom have heretofore been worshippers of the bottle, but who have awakened to a sense of their moral duties, and who now go forth proclaiming, with native eloquence and arguments supported by an array of facts which cannot be resisted, the mighty evils of intemperance, and the blessings of abstinence from intoxicating drinks. This noble band have already produced an influence on public opinion. The drunkard is every day quitting his cups forever; and the dram-seller, ashamed and conscience-stricken, is forsaking the odious traffic in which he has been engaged and seeking a reputable employment. Even the man of wealth, who is accustomed to luxuries of an enervating tendency, is roused from his moral apathy, and is heard to declare that the traffic in rum is not only unnecessary and demoralizing in its nature, but infamous also; and by banishing wine from his table he has set an example as well as uttered a precept.

The Cold Water Army, on the forenoon of Christmas-day, assembled in large numbers at Faneuil Hall, where the exercises were of an exceedingly interesting character, and appropriate to the occasion which called them forth. The hall was decorated with evergreens and temperance banners, and with the vast array of smiling countenances, animated with the elastic spirits which are the attendants of youth and hope, presented an attractive scene. After an appropriate prayer from Rev.

Mr. Lothrop, the children were addressed by Moses Grant, a well-known working man in the temperance cause, who presided on the occasion, by H. W. Dwight, Mr. Hawkins, and Mr. O'Brien.

In the afternoon there was another meeting at Faneuil Hall, at which Samuel F. Holbrook, the zealous and indefatigable President of the Washington Total-Abstinence Society, presided. John Hawkins, in his quaint but effective manner, then addressed the meeting. This was one of his happiest efforts. After which Mr. Dwight and the Rev. John Pierpont made a few short and pithy remarks, quite to the purpose. The meeting then adjourned until half-past six o'clock, to meet again in the old " Cradle of Liberty," and a large collection of our citizens were present, and listened to the burning eloquence of those who sought to free their country from the thraldom of the monster Intemperance.

This was the grand meeting of the day. Long before the appointed hour the hall was literally crammed from floor to ceiling. A greater array of beauty, or a more respectable assemblage, *perhaps* never before graced the walls of the " Cradle of Liberty ; " and certainly *never* in a more noble cause. Dr. J. C. Warren presided, and a prayer was offered by the Rev. Dr. Sharp. Messrs. Hawkins and Davis then addressed the meeting; hymns were sung, in which the whole audience joined.

CHAPTER XIII

"The wife, whose husband thou didst toil to save,
Not vainly, from the drunkard's yawning grave,
Shall teach her little ones, in coming days,
To tell thy story and to lisp thy praise;
The child, redeemed from all the shames that fill
A rum-cursed house, from woes that blight and kill,
Lisping thy name, shall link it morn and even
With the sweet prayers that tremble up to Heaven."

A YEAR'S experience in addressing popular assemblies, together with the possession of good judgment, a clear mind, and a remarkable memory, enabled Mr. Hawkins to speak upon the drinking usages of society, and against the traffic in intoxicating drinks, in such a manner as no sophists could withstand. His industry and enthusiasm increased as he comprehended more clearly the amazing work which remained to be accomplished.

On the 3d of January, 1842, he has this brief entry in his journal: —

Lectured in Newport until Saturday, January 8th; during my stay in that city over eight hundred persons affixed their signatures to the temperance pledge. In no place that I have visited has so much been done for the cause.

"We have," says the *Mercantile Journal*, "been favored by Mr. Hawkins with the following summary but interesting sketch of his trip to Newport, R. I., and the proceedings while there."

14

Monday morning. — Left Boston for Newport; in the evening lectured in Zion (Episcopal) Church; crowded house; much interest felt on the subject.

Tuesday. — Lectured in same church; interest increasing; a great many drinkers signed the pledge.

Wednesday evening. — Lectured in Methodist Church; people felt more at home; the interest increasing to an astonishing degree; drinkers and drunkards giving up their cups, and the rum-sellers, like Felix, tremble and quake for fear. No wonder there is a cry made, " By this craft we have our wealth."

Thursday afternoon. — Met the children; the house literally jammed. It was the most imposing sight I ever beheld; a large church crowded to overflowing with children and parents. Many a tear trickled down the cheek of parent and child at the redemption of the husband, father, and son. More than a hundred of these dear little ones,·with pledge in hand, are acting as home missionaries, in getting signers to the " Second Declaration of Independence." In the evening, lectured in the same church. It is impossible to pen a description of the interest felt in Newport. Suffice it to say, I have never, in all my travels, seen any thing like it. " Truly, it is the work of the Lord, and marvellous in our eyes."

Friday evening. — The house full; the people have truly taken hold in the proper style. This evening three hundred signed the pledge. Over eight hundred signed the pledge during my stay. Three thousand have signed the pledge since Thanksgiving-day, when the work commenced! I shall ever remember the people of Newport with gratitude, notwithstanding the false reports that have been published in the papers. It-would seem hard to condemn a whole town for the want of interest in a subject they have not felt. If they never before felt the importance of the subject, they feel it now, and are doing more than any place I ever visited. I cannot close without saying, *much* credit is due to the females. They, like Mary of old, " last at the cross and earliest at the grave," are foremost in administering to the wants of the poor and needy; they have a Martha Washington Society, and meet every Tuesday to receive clothing, and prepare them for the reformed drunkard, his wife, and children, who no doubt will rise up and call them blessed.

The President of the Washington Temperance Society, Edward W. Lawton, Esq., is a first-rate man and thorough-going in the work of reform. Many of the most respectable men in the place have come forward, and do not feel it derogatory to their characters to publicly place their names to a pledge of total abstinence, for the sake of the reformed drunkard; and to use their influence in saving their fellow-men from a drunkard's grave, and dry up the tear of the almost broken-hearted wife and children. Indeed, it gives me pleasure, and I hope I am not doing wrong, in mentioning the name of the Hon. Dutee J. Pearce, among many that I do not remember who have taken this bold stand, and will be workers in the cause. Several rum-sellers have already abandoned the sale. May the work go on until not a drop may be found on the island.

The following letter from a dear friend of Mr. Hawkins, giving the circumstances which preceded and accompanied his visit to Newport, will be read with interest : —

(EDWARD W. LAWTON, ESQ., TO THE COR. SEC. A. T. U.)

NEWPORT, Jan. 8, 1842.

DEAR SIR, — On the subject of temperance in Newport, previous to the last five or six weeks, there was little to gratify the feelings of the philanthropist. The blighted remains of some thirty or forty distilleries, where liquid poison was made to barter in Africa for the souls and bodies of men and women, seemed to have set their seals upon us with a strength of impression that nothing could efface. All the efforts to get up a

reform in this matter were almost entirely abortive. Temperate men in small numbers formed societies, one after another,
which had a short-lived existence, and were heard of no more.
They were honest and well-meaning men, true to their principles *as far as they had light*, and perhaps sowed some of the
seed that has lately sprung up so abundantly; the pledge of
total abstinence was adopted among them early, but like their
contemporaries elsewhere, almost all their *labors* began at the
wrong end. This may be considered as a true sketch of the
subject up to Thursday, the 25th of November, 1841 (Thanksgiving-day). On that day two gentlemen arrived in town, as
lecturers, from some part of Massachusetts, and held their first
meeting in the evening. It excited so little attention at first,
that I did not hear of it until the afternoon of the next day,
although I was in the practice of attending such meetings.
These men seemed to possess but moderate talents as lecturers,
but were animated by a very proper spirit for the work, and as
the result leads us to suppose, began at the right end; at any
rate, they, and those by whom they were met, succeeded, under
Providence, in raising up a feeling in favor of the cause, hitherto unparalleled. They staid about three weeks, held meetings almost continually, and which continually increased in
numbers, until upwards of a thousand names were put upon
the pledge, being about one-eighth of our population. Among
the signers were many of our most noted drunkards. One
circumstance occurred during the time above mentioned which
made a strong impression on the public mind, and which was
improved by the lecturers. A soldier of the garrison, during
the violent snow storm which occurred the last of November,
came into town and got very drunk at one of our shops; he
was found in the street and taken in by a humane individual,
and kept till he was measurably sober, who advised him to go
to the Fort without drinking, so as to get there in time to
escape punishment. He set off, apparently with that intention,
but the next morning he was found frozen to death, about half

way between the town and Fort, with a bottle of gin buttoned under his frock. It is supposed that he drank from the bottle on his way.

At this stage of the enterprise I wrote to Mr. John Tappan, of Boston, from whom I had an immediate answer; his kindness and assistance have been very great. Through his instrumentality we had one very powerful lecture from Col. Dwight, of Stockbridge. This lecture produced a great sensation, and caused the subject to be much examined by those who had before been indifferent, and constituted one great step in our progress onward. From this time up to the 3d of January, much was done in various ways, by lectures from clergymen and others (four of the former having heartily espoused the cause), by conferences, and by individual visiting and exhortation. On the 3d, Mr. Hawkins arrived here in the evening and commenced lecturing in little more than an hour after, and from that time until this morning it has been a perfect jubilee. The whole public mind has been engrossed and absorbed by this one question. Immense meetings every evening, and continual visits through the day; constant applications to sign the pledge left the friends of the cause but little time to spare for other avocations. Mr. Hawkins several times expressed the opinion that it exceeded any movement he had yet seen, even that of the celebrated reformation in Springfield, Mass. Our pledge roll now numbers upwards of two thousand five hundred, many of whom were drunkards, or hard drinkers, *not one of whom has yet broken his pledge.* Rum-sellers in all directions are giving up their business. Several bars have been taken down this day, since Mr. Hawkins went away. Townsend's coffeehouse (so miscalled), that has been a great drinking-house for nearly a century, this evening closed its bar; several have thrown their liquors into the street; some into the back yards. I called on one man to-day who had signed the pledge, and told him there was a feeling of uneasiness among the friends from a report that he had some liquors left. He thanked me most

14*

cordially, and said if he had been always thus kindly treated, he should have been a temperance man two years sooner, and added, "What shall I do? I have but one cask, and that I have determined not to sell." I replied that if he would throw it away he would get rid of the poison and the imputation both together. He said immediately if I would help him to get it out, it should go. It was accordingly set to running in the back yard; his family lived in the same house, and his children, discovering what was doing, came out and danced round it for joy. Believe me, sir, I do not state this circumstance to celebrate my own part in it, but only to add my testimony to many others as to the efficacy of *kindness* in conducting this enterprise. It has been a general feeling among us, and has evidently been productive of the best results; under its influence the utmost unanimity has prevailed among us, "the eye has been single (to the object), and the whole body (seemingly) full of light." I would not be understood as taking any credit to ourselves in this matter; the hand of God is evidently in it, and if his servants are but faithful, it will prosper to their everlasting benefit. Mr. Hawkins, during the few days he staid among us, got a strong and most affectionate hold upon our feelings, and I trust we have imparted something of the same to him.

January 9. — This evening I have attended a lecture by the Catholic priest before our society, at his own church. He is an Irishman; evidently a man of learning. His discourse was peculiar, convincing and forcible, and formed an interesting variation from the many we have heard lately. The house was crowded to an extreme, and I should think as many went away as got in. In mentioning the number of signers I do not include the Catholic pledge, which would bring the number nearly up to three thousand. A very numerous juvenile society was formed yesterday, and a numerous and active Martha Washington Society has carried on its active labors for three r four weeks. Mr. Rogers, the lecturer on India, is here, and we are making arrangements to have the drunkard's stomach exhibited with the aid of the magic lantern, which we hope may convince some. Notwithstanding this detail of good (which you may think is rather long), we have still evil among us. One great distillery; many grog-shops; two or three ministers who do not come up to the total pledge, and of course their congregations are lukewarm; and the self-sufficient moderate drinkers, they are here; still, if we " go on " as we have done, it will soon be their turn to come in. God grant that it may be so till not one is left. Excuse the length of this letter, and believe me truly yours,

EDWARD W. LAWTON.

There can be no doubt that Mr. Hawkins early perceived, that no matter how great the effort to rescue the intemperate from the misery of their condition, while the enticements of the rumshops continued his labors must prove, in very many instances, fruitless; and if permitted always to exist, the complete reformation of many would prove but an idle dream. While he manifested, therefore, a boundless sympathy for the drunkard, and kindness towards the rumseller, personally, he began to turn the whole force of his accumulated facts and arguments against the *manufacture and traffic.*

He did not abandon moral suasion; but while he applied it to the victims of the traffic in inducing them to forsake their cups, he did all in his power to persuade the rum-seller to abandon his calling. He early sought to arouse a healthy public sentiment against the granting of licenses to sell, hoping that, ultimately, law-makers would be elected who would place upon the statute-book enactments prohibitory of a trade so

pernicious in its tendencies.   In September, 1841, a
Boston temperance journal used this language : —

There is a strange feeling manifested by a multitude of our
temperance men respecting the dealers in intoxicating drinks.
Some say, "Oh, let them alone ; they will soon give it up."
Others say, "Moral suasion is the way ; don't drive ; you can't
drive."   Others still object to have us use sharp or pointed
language.   "Now don't be severe ; our taverner is a good sort
of a man, and if you say any thing to touch him, it will only
make him worse," &c. &c.   It is time to use plain English
with the rum-seller of every grade ; and as we have tried "tufts
of grass" long enough, without bringing him down from his
rum casks, it is time to try the "virtue of stones."   John
Hawkins is doing more than any other man to give right
impressions upon this subject, and to bring down upon this
enemy of man just indignation and rebuke.   A man who
sells rum in the midst of us, where there is so much light
upon the subject, so great a struggling among drunkards to escape, such a multitude of men giving their time, influence, and
substance to counteract his influence, might, under other circumstances, become a robber or a pirate ; and the sooner we
pounce upon him, hoot at him, and let him know in long and
unmeasured withdrawal of all respect for him or endurance of
him, that we give him no rest, the better.   Let us turn our backs
upon him, as we would upon the murderer of our children and
the destroyer of our race.   Let our indignation come upon him
like a tempest, and our rebuke like a fire.   IT IS TIME, AND
THERE IS OCCASION.

In his first address in Faneuil Hall, Mr. Hawkins
alluded in strong terms to the enormous inconsistency
of shutting up the drunkard in the House of Correction, and of inflicting punishment upon him, while the
enticements to indulgence were still allowed to be held
out by the rum-seller.   "*You are bound*," he said in

conclusion, "*to turn the whole tide of public opinion against the traffic;*" and he never faltered for a moment, in his whole subsequent career, in acting up to these settled convictions of his mind.

The principle of " Prohibition " was here most distinctly announced. Mr. Hawkins did not, at first, advocate legal enactments against the rum-seller, but sought rather to win him by kind entreaty to abandon his business. He would go to him and kindly invite him to attend his meetings, and then, instead of denouncing the man, would appeal to his reason and conscience, by detailing in the most touching manner the effects of intemperance in destroying social happiness, as a direct result of the sale of his liquors, until he became heartily ashamed of his occupation, and was constrained to abhor the nefarious traffic. In many instances the business was abandoned. It was not until this policy failed, that temperance men were compelled to resort to the agency of legislation.

However strong then his convictions of the evil of the traffic, Mr. Hawkins never allowed himself to be diverted a moment from his daily work of saving the inebriate from the results of his unfortunate delinquencies. With the new year his zeal was renewed, and his labors became more abundant.

About the first of January, 1842, a tract appeared in Boston, bearing the following title: " The New Impulse ; or, Hawkins and the Reform. A Brief History of the Origin, Progress, and Effects of the present astonishing Temperance Movements, and of the Life and Reformation of John H. W. Hawkins, the Distinguished Leader. Embellished with a correct likeness of said Hawkins. By a Teetotaler.".

This pamphlet was, without doubt, the means of doing much good. In summing up the results, the author says: " The whole number who have signed the pledge and joined the Washington Total Abstinence Societies in the principal cities, and in various parts of the country, is surprisingly great; the exact number cannot be ascertained, but is estimated in round numbers, by those best acquainted with the facts, to be : In Baltimore, about 12,000 ; New York, 10,000 ; Boston, 5,000 ; all other places in New England, 73,000 ; other Northern States, 100,000 ; total, 200,000. A majority of these are supposed to have been hard drinkers, and a large proportion hardened drunkards; all reformed from the example and exertions of one man. How wonderful! How sublime!" However great Mr. Hawkins' instrumentality in producing such results, his humble estimate of himself, and his sense of justice to the multitude of his co-laborers in this reform, would hardly have permitted him to be satisfied with this wholesale laudation.

The *Journal* of the A. T. Union, at the time the tract appeared, made the following very just remarks : —

This is a well-timed and popular tract, issued with numerous and high recommendations. We are surprised, however at the prefixing of a face in which we can see nothing of our friend Hawkins, especially as the Bostonians have a fine likeness of him. A few statements are made which need correction. It was not in a steamboat, but in the counting-room of Mr John Tappan, of Boston, that Mr. Hawkins was induced to throw away his tobacco. The work is somewhat too local for one which would give a general history of this wonderful movement. The legislation of Massachusetts was all absorbing there, but it little affected the rest of the country ; and though to a Bostonian, the names of Sargent, Crosby, Perry, Pierpont, and Jewett, stand prominent as pioneers in the cause, yet one who would trace the origin of the Baltimore movement, should understand and let the world know, that in that matter all the foundation walls were laid by that old veteran, Christian Keener. We perceive also in this little work a disposition, which we have noticed elsewhere, to make this wonderful reform, not merely the work of God, this we fully believe, but a religious reform in itself, and something superior to the piety found in ministers and churches. Such language we notice as this: " The new system is practical Christianity, Christianity carried out." " The practical Christianity of these humble reformers may well put many of the pastors and churches of the land to the blush for their cold, formal religion and dead faith." pp. 20 and 21. Every thing in its place; temperance in its place; philanthropy in its place; and religion in its place. Many of the reformed, we rejoice to say it, have become hopefully pious men. We hope all will be truly so. But reformation from drunkenness is not, of course, religion, nor is the most intense interest or arduous labor in reforming others. It may all be found without even a belief in Christianity, and in those who discard all religion. It therefore is not to be elevated above piety in pastors and churches, though even like warm political zeal or zeal for the security of any philanthropic or worldly object, it may well put some to the blush. We mention these things, because correct language in these popular tracts is all-important. With a few corrections, and a better likeness of the " Major-General," we could wish to see this tract scattered throughout the nation.

Temperance publications now began to pour from the press, thus affording the best evidence of onward progress towards the nation's ultimate recovery from the thraldom of its besetting sin.

Says Dr. John Marsh: —

We have at no period been flooded with so much interesting intelligence from every quarter. The public mind, well prepared by the long, untiring labors of the friends of temperance, is now almost universally yielding to the summons of surrender from the bold and persevering Washington reformers. Two glorious meetings have been held recently in Boston. One on Thanksgiving-day, in Brattle-Street Church, for praise, and another on Christmas-day, in Faneuil Hall. The great work loses none of its interest; eight thousand have here, during the year, signed the city pledge, eight thousand the Washington pledge, four thousand the Catholic, twenty thousand in all. Over twenty lecturers are now out, lecturing in the country, and John Hawkins is cannonading every strong fortification.

On the 8th of January, Mr. Hawkins returned to Boston, and, as appears from the *Mercantile Journal*, addressed the Washington Temperance Society: —

At the first anniversary of the Boston Temperance Society, held last evening, the Marlboro' Chapel was crowded in every part ; many persons left the doors, being unable to enter. The sight was impressive to witness ; such a mass assembled for so good a cause. Thomas A. Davis, President of the society, in a brief and appropriate address, described the operations and success of the society during the past year, which have been truly cheering and encouraging. After which the drunkard's friend, John H. W. Hawkins, riveted the attention of the immense assembly for over one hour. The interest in this able champion for total abstinence is unabated ; he was listened to with the same attention which he always commands.

His journal continues: —

Wednesday, January 12th. — Took the cars for Norwich, Ct. Thursday, 13th, lectured in Central Baptist Church, Rev. Mr. Clark's ; in the afternoon of Friday, to the Cold

Water Army; at night to a crowded house in the Methodist Church.

Returned to Boston, and on Sunday, 16th, addressed a large audience in the Odeon.

Monday, 17th. — Took the cars for Albany and Troy, N. Y. On Tuesday evening, lectured in Rev. Dr. Sprague's church; the house was not crowded. Wednesday, 19th, in the Baptist Church (Dr. Welch's), church crowded.

Thursday, January 20, 1842. — Took stage to Troy. Lectured same evening to a crowded house of men only. The Rensselaer County Convention met in Dr. Snodgrass' church.

Friday. At 2 P.M., met the children and lectured to them in Rev. Dr. Beaman's church; a great deal of interest is felt; the children were much affected. At night lectured to a very crowded house in the Methodist Church in Fifth Street.

January 22. — Lectured to a house full of children in the Second Presbyterian Church; at night in the Methodist Church, State Street.

Sunday, 23. — Addressed the Sabbath School attached to the Rev. Dr. Snodgrass' church. Same day, at 3 P.M., lectured to an overflowing congregation in Lansingburgh, immediately after the lecture of Mr. H. W. Dwight. The congregation was deeply affected. Same night (Sunday), lectured to a large congregation in the Methodist Church, State Street; immediately after the lecture repaired to the meeting of the Washington Temperance Society, in session at their hall. Much interest is felt in the cause by the Trojans; they are wide awake.*

*(FROM JOURNAL OF AMERICAN TEMPERANCE UNION.)

TOUR OF JOHN HAWKINS. — Our friend Hawkins, during the month of January, made an excursion from Boston to Troy, Albany, and some other places in New York. On the 18th, he spoke in the Rev. Dr. Sprague's Church, Albany, and on the 19th, in Dr. Welch's. On the 20th, he attended the Rensselaer County Convention at Troy, with Hon. H. W. Dwight. On his return to Boston, he furnished the following interesting items respecting the work at Troy: —

A physician and surgeon, for the last ten years intemperate, and for

15

The state of his feelings at this time may be learned

the last two or three years grossly so, signed the pledge just before Christmas, and carried his pledge certificate *as a Christmas present* to his mother. He was a lost son, restored after hope had expired.

Mr. K. was picked up in the street, in the night, drunk — head lying on the curb-stone. A four-horse stage passed over the ground immediately after he was removed. He belonged to a highly respectable family —ruined by fashionable tippling—visited by Washingtonians and induced to sign the pledge — now looks well.

A wholesale hardware merchant, connected with the highest circles, went from fashionable drinking to the most abandoned drunkenness, rapidly—family broken up — he had delirium tremens repeatedly, and was considered a hopeless case till a Washingtonian got him to sign the pledge. He is now very active in the temperance cause, and doing good — restored to his family and now happy.

A young man, son of an elder in a church, became intemperate soon after leaving college — was mortified by a public exposure — signed the pledge, and was asked to drink wine at his father's table afterwards,— thus far stands firm, though his father opposes the temperance movement. If this man falls, will not his father one day see blood on his raiment ?

In one instance a reformed drunkard (who had been generally known as an abandoned case, lost to friends, honor, and happiness), went to an elder in the church, and claimed his influence and support in maintaining his pledge, adding, " How can I be expected to hold on when such men as you offer wine freely at public entertainments ? " The elder confessed afterwards that he was conscience-smitten, gave up his wine, and signed the pledge.

There is now an old gentleman there who is a professing Christian — has four sons ; the father opposed the temperance movement from the first — his breath smells of wine — his sons have all been hard fashionable drinkers — the hostility of the father operates to prevent his sons from signing the pledge. The old man thinks he has done well enough without the pledge, and is blind to the danger of his children. He has been seen the worse for liquor, while, from his position, he should be an example of piety.

The whole history of the work here has been interesting ; the most unlikely instrumentalities have been most powerful. Since the visit of Pollard and Wright, the fire has been kindling " at the bottom of the grate," and slowly burning up through, so that it may truly be said that the most abject cases have been more easily reached than the drunkards in high

from the following letter to his sister, written in the midst of these labors : —

TROY, N. Y., Jan. 21, 1842.

MY DEAR SISTER, — Your very kind and affectionate letter, bearing date Dec. 30th, came to hand after my return from a tour of duty.   It afforded me much heartfelt pleasure to hear from you.   Indeed, I found comfort in taking your old letters

life.   I think it may be affirmed, without doubt, that the very general reformation of the working classes has shamed some of the fashionable families into approbation of the cause.   The drunkenness of the genteel classes is more conspicuous now than formerly, and the idea that they should be sinking while the poverty-stricken portion are rising to comfort under the influence of the pledge, is mortifying to their pride.   A large number of heads of families, who have been accustomed to high life and fashionable use of wine, &c., &c., have within a few days signed the pledge.   A new society has been formed, of which the Mayor of the city is President.   It is open to all, and promises to sweep away the fashionable indulgence at parties and public festivals.

A circumstance occurred in Troy, some time since, which proves the truth of the old adage, " When rogues fall out," &c.   One deacon had a ball at his house.   A committee of the church waited upon him to discipline him for it, one of whom, another deacon, was engaged in the brewery business.   While urging upon his brother the impropriety of his conduct, in allowing balls at his house, he was asked the following question, which, it strikes me, was rather a leading one, as the lawyers say : " Which do you think has done the most injury, my ball, or your brewing ale and making drunkards ? "   But the brewing deacon was not to be put down ; so he asked in reply : " If it is wrong for me to brew, is it right for you to furnish me damaged grain for my brewery ? "   And so we go.

In Saratoga, the population is two thousand five hundred.   Two thousand have already signed the pledge, and the work is progressing.

Washington County, N. Y., is under the labors of Mr. Hyde, a reformed drunkard.   Five thousand five hundred have signed the pledge in two months.   He was urged by his brother to come to Troy, in the hope that he would be induced to sign the pledge for his own safety.   He came, signed, and went back and commenced lecturing, and has been constantly employed ever since, and now has engagements for every day till the 4th of March.

with me in my valise, and occasionally reading them. The Lord has done great things for me ; blessed be his holy name. The language of my heart is

> " Daily in his grace to grow,
>   And ever in his faith abide ;
> Only Jesus will I know,
>   And Jesus crucified."

You know, my dear sister, in a great measure, the heavy *weight of responsibility that rests upon me.* Oh, how I feel sometimes, when I look back upon my ill-spent life, and the narrow escape of falling into a drunkard's grave, and into a drunkard's hell !

My poor heart says, Praise the Lord, and I know yours does also. A brother, father, husband, and son, saved by grace. I bless God for the special blessings that attend my labors wherever I go. I am now in Troy, and shall remain here, and in Albany, until Wednesday next, when I return to Boston. On Thursday I have been asked to preach a dedication sermon in a new Protestant Methodist Church at Malden, a few miles from Boston. The text I shall take, from which I am preparing a discourse, is in Leviticus, 10 : 8, 9, 10, 11 : " And the Lord spake unto Aaron, saying, Do not drink wine nor strong drink, thou, nor thy sons with thee, when ye go into the tabernacle of the congregation, lest ye die ; it shall be a statute forever throughout your generations : And that ye may put difference between holy and unholy, and between unclean and clean ; And that ye may teach the children of Israel all the statutes which the Lord hath spoken unto them by the hand of Moses." My dear sister, pray for me, that God may sustain me in this stupendous work. Nothing but the grace of God can sustain me. I am very little with my family ; I am now two hundred miles from them, and may be in another week two hundred miles from them another way. They are well and comfortable ; indeed, Elizabeth has entered a private school, one of the best in Boston, kept by Mrs. Dwight, an accomplished teacher. For my sake, she says she will take especial pains with her; Elizabeth likes her very much; her teacher will instruct her also in the languages. I never saw a child improve so much as Hannah does; she loves her Bible, and walks so circumspectly. I love slyly to watch her movements when at home, there is so much of the lady in them; Elizabeth can't help seeing it, and takes the hint. Little Sallie is one of the sweetest children I ever knew; the most affectionate. We cannot help loving her; everybody loves her. She has become an excellent singer. On Christmas-day we held a meeting of the children in Faneuil Hall. The hall was a perfect jam; and little Sallie rose up amidst the acclamations of the multitude, on the platform, Dr. Pierce and myself standing by her side. She sang most splendidly, "Away, away, the bowl!" without the least apparent embarrassment. Arthur improves also. I want William George to see Mr. Holmes, and say to him that we are all well.

I should have answered your letter before this, but was waiting to know whether the committee would send me South; they have not determined yet. I shall write you, if they make up their minds to send me to Washington with Mr. Dwight. I am glad to learn that William George is in earnest about the salvation of his soul. It pleases me to hear also that you are getting well, and that Eleanora and Elizabeth are doing well. I thought it best to let William George remain until spring; in the mean time I want James to be ready, by a week or two's notice, if possible. Give my love to mother, and tell her Hannah is preparing a letter for her.

I arrived in Albany last Monday, 17th, direct from Boston On the day of my arrival, Governor William H. Seward, of New York, with many other distinguished gentlemen, signed the total-abstinence pledge. I lectured two evenings in Albany, then went to Troy, which is only six miles. Here the work of reform has gone on to an amazing extent. The mayor of the city of Troy, with more than one hundred of the most respectable wine-drinkers have not thought it *disgraceful* to sign a pledge of total abstinence. Many thousands have signed the pledge here and in Albany. Saratoga Springs has a population of two thousand five hundred souls, all told; two thousand have signed the pledge, and they are working rapidly into the five hundred. If we keep on, the whole world will be sober.

The most difficult to reform is the moderate drinker, because he thinks he is possessed of all the fortitude in the world. But we must remember, " Let him who thinketh he standeth take heed lest he fall." Fifteen thousand have signed the pledge in Boston during the past year! I have occasionally sent you papers with information relative to the cause of temperance. I shall continue to send them every opportunity. I must now close by asking you and all my friends to continue praying for me, that God may keep me humble. I want William George, my son, to write me immediately; a letter also from you; now don't neglect this. I should like to pay postage on a letter from my brother Archibald. I remain, dear sister,   .

Your affectionate brother,

J. H. W. HAWKINS.

On the 26th of February Mr. Hawkins returned to Boston, and on the next day was present and preached his discourse at the dedication services in Malden, and on the next lectured to a crowded house in Roxbury.

The sudden death of Mr. Holmes, the father of the two children he had taken under his protection, calls forth the following letter: —

BOSTON, January 29, 1842.

REV. JOHN BAXLEY: *Dear Sir,* — Your letter, dated January 21, has just been received, and would have been received and answered before this, but I was absent from the city. I have just returned from Albany and Troy, N. Y. I was somewhat astonished to hear of the sudden death of Mr. Holmes, but did not expect in the course of nature he could survive long, knowing his bad health. I presume, however, there is no necessity for my coming on immediately. I shall, God willing, be in Baltimore the last of February with the Hon. H. W. Dwight, on a temperance tour to the city of Washington. I hope the property of Mr. Holmes will not be sold, as there will be no absolute necessity for it, until I come on. I wrote to Sister Frances, from Troy. I mentioned a dedication I had to attend on the 27th, at Malden. It was indeed a sublime affair. I have not time to write the particulars, nor a long letter. I acknowledge the receipt of a letter from William George; was glad to hear from him. I hope he will be in readiness to come on with me when I return. Remember me to *mother*, and all inquiring friends. We are all well, and doing well. As regards myself, I now weigh one hundred and ninety pounds.

I remain, yours, &c.

J. H. W. HAWKINS.

The Hon. H. W. Dwight, above referred to, was at one time a distinguished lawyer, of high rank in the profession, and whose well-known talents would· have elevated him, it is said, to the highest posts of honor in our country, but for the "mocker" wine. He was a native of Stockbridge, Mass., and was induced during Mr. Hawkins' lectures in that State to abandon forever the use of intoxicating drinks. Like the reformers, he was unwilling to remain inactive, and very soon became an efficient temperance lecturer. How Mr. Dwight became associated with Mr. Hawkins, the following letter, which we extract from the *Journal* of the American Temperance Union, will explain :—

(REV. LOUIS DWIGHT TO JOHN TAPPAN, ESQ., OF BOSTON.)

STOCKBRIDGE, Oct. 4, 1841.

MY DEAR SIR, — My brother Henry signed the pledge of

total abstinence at Pittsfield, Sabbath before last, and made a short speech on the occasion, before a crowded meeting of the Washington Temperance Society. Since that time there have been the most favorable indications that the reformation might become permanent. On Saturday last I carried him to Pittsfield, where he was expected to address the meeting again last evening. He was received in the first instance with three times three most hearty cheers, and great expectation and delight was expressed on Saturday that he had come again. On Friday morning last, before I engaged to carry him to Pittsfield, he came to me and proposed of his own accord to engage in the service of the Washington Temperance Society as a means of usefulness and confirming habits of temperance. He requested me to write to Boston in his behalf, and offer his services to the society on such terms as they might propose. He said it was not so much for compensation as for usefulness that he was willing to engage in this service. If the society will employ and encourage him, it may be greatly useful both to him and others. He spoke of Mr. Hawkins as a person with whom he should like to be associated, and my opinion is that they would work well together. If Mr. Hawkins can come this way and go over the county of Berkshire with him, they might then move off together in some other direction. Your friendly aid in bringing about an arrangement of this kind would be most gratefully acknowledged by him and his friends. Please to write me as soon as convenient to yourself whether an arrangement of this kind can be made.

Most respectfully and affectionately,

Your friend,
LOUIS DWIGHT.

This arrangement was, without doubt, happily effected, as we find frequent mention in the journal of Mr. Hawkins of his friend Col. H. W. Dwight, and of their having addressed the same audience upon several occasions. We have every reason for saying that their acquaintance was of a mutually gratifying character.

Mr. Hawkins possessed the singular power of adapting his addresses to the constantly varying character of his audiences. He seems to have been equally successful whether he is addressing the inmates of a prison or of a poorhouse ; — a popular assembly or the members of a State legislature. He was exceedingly happy in his efforts to influence children. Many a little child has gone forth from his lectures a voluntary missionary to the neighborhood where they resided, and obtained hundreds of signers to the pledge. His influence upon the sailor was also great. During his days of *rest* in Boston, he frequently visited the ships of our navy, and induced many of their crews to abandon the use of intoxicating liquor. One result of his efforts was the formation of a Temperance Society among the sailors on board the frigate Columbus, at that time stationed at the Charlestown navy yard. On Sunday, 30th December, there was a meeting in the morning on board the schooner Grampus, and addresses made in a very forcible manner, it is said, by delegates from the Columbus Society. " In the afternoon," says the *Mercantile Journal*, " Messrs. Hawkins and Holbrook addressed, by invitation, the sailors, in a most affecting manner and with good success. The commander and officers generally have signed the pledge, together with most of the crew. They have now an excellent and efficient society on board each ship. Several sailors gave very interesting experiences. This day all liquor is to be sent on shore, being no longer considered worthy to be a ' messmate.' "

These services for the sailors were performed by Mr.

Hawkins upon days which he terms in his Journal
" days of rest. " Another result of these labors in
behalf of temperance was the voluntary relinquishment
of the " spirit rations" on board many of our national
ships. " We understand," said one of the morning
papers after the above meeting, " that $2,500 were yes-
terday paid to the seamen on board the receiving ship
Columbus, in lieu of spirit rations, which they had
voluntarily relinquished. We also learn that the crew
of the U. S. schooner Grampus, commanded by Lieut.
Van Brunt, which vessel is now ready to sail on a
cruise, all, with the exception of ten or eleven, receive
money instead of grog. It is time that the custom of
allowing spirit rations on board our ships was abolished."

The temperance movement was now extending over
the whole length and breadth of the land. The simple
but powerful words of the temperance advocates oper-
ated like a potent enchantment wherever heard, trans-
forming the miserable inebriate into a sober and useful
citizen, dilapidated and wretched tenements into abodes
of peace and plenteousness, where honest Industry
smiled at her accumulating joys.

In the far-off West the cause was making rapid
progress. Intelligence of the movements in those cities
visited by the subject of this memoir in his youth,
while they revived sad memories of early delinquencies,
filled his heart with inexpressible gladness. In Cincinnati, by the first of January, 1842, the number of
teetotalers was about eight thousand! of whom nine
hundred had been confirmed drunkards. In Dayton,
Columbus, and Chilicothe there was an average of
over one thousand ; in St. Louis, over two thousand-

at Louisville a large Washington Society was formed. The whole number in Ohio alone who had embraced the total-abstinence principle of the new movement was about thirty thousand.

This movement, commencing among the humble and the unknown, now began to command the respect of every class ; and for the reason that observation had begun to disclose the fact that drunkenness was not confined to the class of day-laborers, but was making its terrible inroads into every rank and profession. Legis- lative temperance societies were organized, and great respect was paid to the reformatory movement. On Wednesday, February 2d, agreeable to a public notice, a meeting of the members of the Massachusetts Legis- lature was held at the Hall of the Representatives, for the purpose of forming a Legislative Temperance Society. The meeting was of a highly interesting character. It was resolved that it is expedient to revive the Legislative Temperance Society, founded in 1833, on total-abstinence principles. The meeting was addressed by Messrs. Hawkins and Holbrook, and subsequently by Messrs. Walter Channing, M. D., Emory Washburn, and Foster Hooper.

On the first of January the Pennsylvania Temper- ance Convention began its session in Harrisburgh. By invitation, it is said, the Legislature adjourned, and proceeded in a body, with the Governor at their head, to the place of meeting, and for half a day, listened to the deliberations.

Nor did the movement rest here. The occasional reformation of individuals who had formerly been members of both branches of the National legislature, as well as of State legislatures, led the people to ask whether there might not be a greater degree of intemperance prevailing at Washington than had yet been disclosed.

The reformation of the Hon. H. W. Dwight, and of others who had held posts of influence in the country, members of Congress, lawyers, and physicians, had already been made public. The affecting circumstances attending the restoration of the Hon. T. F. Marshall, of Ky., to habits of sobriety, is thus related by Dr. Marsh in his *Journal* of February 1st, 1842 : —

At the meeting of Congress, some of the reformed inebriates of Baltimore were producing an excited feeling among the citizens of every class, especially drunkards and hard drinkers, and many were renouncing their cups and signing the pledge. But Dr. Sewall had prepared himself to reach and electrify the intelligent and reflecting mind, by illustrating his views of the pain, the sufferings, and destruction to which the poor drunkard is doomed, by means of transparent drawings of his stomach in the various stages from moderate drinking to delirium tremens. Some thousands attended his lectures ; many members of Congress said his exhibitions should be made all over the country ; and grog-sellers were heard to declare, that if their business made such stomachs, they would abandon it forever.

Amid this excited state of public feeling, while all were hoping for some blow which would drive the demon Intemperance from our capital, yet none knowing whence it would come, one of the most talented men on the floor of the House, the Hon. Thomas F. Marshall, of Kentucky, found himself in the very jaws of destruction. This gentleman had indulged to ʻreat excess, and on entering the House on the evening of the 7th of January, he found himself nervously affected to a degree th   alarmed him. The sensation was accompanied by a raging th   for strong drink. Terrified at the extent of his

passion, he resolutely determined to break at once from his destructive habits.   He inquired for a temperance member, and
was directed to the Hon. Mr. Briggs, who drew a pledge,
which was signed by Mr. Marshall.   But resolved on placing
himself beyond the power of temptation, he said he must make
a public confession, and join one of the temperance societies
of the city.   This he did on the same evening at a temperance
meeting which was then gathered at the Medical College.

" I was present," says Dr. Sewall in a letter before us, " and
saw him sign the pledge of total abstinence, after which he
made a most touching speech.   Several other members followed
his example.   Mr. Marshall's step has astonished Congress.
There is no man who compares with him in debate."

Our limits will not permit an extended account of
the meeting above referred to.   The Hon. George N.
Briggs, of Mass., made some eloquent and touching remarks.   The *National Intelligencer* spoke of the event
as one of the most thrilling which had occurred at
any of the meetings at the national capital.   A new
era in the cause of temperance then began, commanding as it did, the services of the highest talent in the
land.   Mr. Marshall in concluding his remarks, said : —

For ten years past I have been a politician in a section of
the country where candidates for office are expected to treat
the people, and drink with them ; to this custom, and the fes-
tive board, I attribute the power which the habit of intemperance gained over me.   Often after leaving those scenes have I
resolved never to repeat them, but temptation returning the
vow has again and again been broken.   Yet I never thought
myself lost, or in great danger, till this morning, when I found
upon me a quenchless, hellish thirst for drink.   I was alarmed ;
it followed me ; a crisis had come, and I knew it.   The thought
of joining a temperance society occurred to me.   I resolved

16·

upon it, and went to an honorable gentleman and asked if he was a member of that society; he answered "Yes." I asked him to draw me up a pledge, and to do it *quick*, that I might execute it. I did so.

Mr. President, the age of miracles is past, and I presume what at that moment occurred to me is explicable on familiar principles; but the fact I know, that when my hand was lifted from the paper, that appetite, which before drove me almost to madness, was *gone*.

But I did not conceive the step fully taken till I should meet and unite with you here; for there is peculiar strength in the tie of honor that now publicly binds us. I am not ashamed of what I have done. I wish Congress — the nation to know it. No doubt many will laugh when the intelligence shall reach them, but Sir, if I *redeem* my *pledge*, which I believe I shall do, *I will laugh too.*

It was resolved, thereupon, to send Messrs. Hawkins and Dwight to Washington the latter part of February, to add the influence of their examples and experience to the reformations there taking place.

In the mean time Mr. Hawkins was not idle, as may be seen from his journal. On the 6th of February he again addressed the sailors, in the sail-loft of the Navy Yard in Charlestown. The meeting was "attended by several officers, and the greater portion of the crew of the Columbus, and a number of ladies and gentlemen from Charlestown and Boston. The meeting was addressed with great power by Mr. Hawkins, who was listened to with great attention by his audience. At the close of his address, some fifty or sixty of the seamen pressed forward and signed the pledge."

February 7. — Took the cars for Lowell; lectured two evenings to the Washington Temperance Society, in the Town Hall.

Wednesday, 9. — Lectured again in the Representatives' Hall in the State House, to the Legislative Temperance Society.

Thursday, 10*th.* — Andover. In the evening lectured in the North Parish, to adults ; on Friday afternoon to a house crowded with children ; and at night to an overflowing congregation of men, women, and children ; much interest is here felt in the subject. Saturday evening again at the Marlboro' Chapel.

Sunday, February 13. — Lectured to an overflowing congregation in Wayland, in the Unitarian Church ; some few of the members opposed to the cause.

The following communication from Wayland, published in the *Mercantile Journal,* will be read with interest : —

Mr. Editor, — I had the pleasure of hearing Mr. Hawkins address the good citizens of Wayland on Sunday evening ; there was a full house, though the travelling was as bad as I ever knew it ; but this only goes to prove the intense feeling and Christian spirit which exist there on the great subject of temperance. He took up a variety of topics which the progress of the cause has developed and is daily developing, and as evidence that he touched some sensitive chords of the many which vibrate in the human bosom, a number came to the altar after the address and signed the pledge ; among whom I observed an old gentleman, nearly threescore years and ten, who for a great part of his life had been addicted to the use of intoxicating drinks, and he remarked that the lecturer had stated the cause and effects of intemperance truly and fairly. Another most touching scene occurred. It was the advance to the sacred altar of two men who were twin brothers, of about forty

years of age, both in a state of intoxication, and who in that
condition signed the pledge of total abstinence from all intoxicating drinks. They then pledged themselves to each other,
alternately, using the term *brother* in the most affecting manner,
— they had at times been estranged from each other, — promising most faithfully that one brother should not lead the other
into temptation, but should aid him to the utmost of his power
to keep that sacred pledge to which they had just affixed their
names, in the presence of God and the meeting then assembled.

During the heart-stirring address of Mr. Hawkins, the case
of these twin brothers had by entire accident been so minutely
sketched, one of them told me, that they became quite angry;
but, on reflection, they acknowledged the truth of Mr. Hawkins' remarks, and it was his peculiar power which finally
brought them to do this great act, which, probably, is to be the
means of the ultimate salvation of their souls. I was told they
came from a neighboring town to hear Mr. Hawkins for the
first time. Only think for a moment; if these two solitary
beings are only saved from degradation, what immense and
incalculable good was done in this single evening! The fruits
are heavenly; restoring to society two unfortunate beings, who
had been lost to themselves and the community for twenty years,
and making them good husbands, and kind, affectionate fathers!
Thanks be to God, that heavenly light is breaking in upon us
and around us in all sections of our favored country. In a
few short years more, a drunkard, I trust, will not be found in
our land, and the use of intoxicating beverages, will not be
known or recognized by a single human being.

It is proper here to refer to the peculiar faculty which
Mr. Hawkins possessed of rendering his lectures practical and effective upon his audiences. His custom on
entering a city, or village, which he generally did early
in the day, was to ascertain, by conversing with various

individuals, the moral and social condition of the place.
Oftentimes parents would reveal to him the intemperance of a son or of a brother; children would solicit
his interposition to save a father from his ruinous
habits.   He would seek information as to the general
progress of temperance in the place; who were its
friends, and who its enemies.   Any peculiar instances
of inebriation, where the circumstances were of an affecting and touching kind, he made his own ; possessing a retentive memory, he never forgot them.   His
judgment indicated which of these instances it would be
proper to refer to in his lecture in the evening.   He was
exceedingly cautious about injuring the feelings of individuals; never relating the facts in such a manner as
to lead members of the congregation to feel uncomfortable by unnecessary exposures of their errors or misfortunes.   But wherever there had been notorious injustice, where the humble and unoffending had been
wronged, or the easily tempted drawn into sin, he was
unsparing in the utterance of his condemnation, often-
times resorting to the most scathing sarcasm.

It was his custom also to make himself familiar with
all the " gossip " of the village; not for the purpose of
repeating what he heard to the injury of any one, but
to turn it over in his mind and decide what part of it,
if any, it would be proper to use, and how far to use
it, so that the *conscience* of the hearer might feel, as he
pictured the evils of intemperance, " thou art the man."
Hundreds of families in the land have detailed to him
with the utmost freedom their domestic griefs, brought
about by the evil of intemperance ; he never was known
to betray the confidence thus reposed in him.   Many a
tale of human suffering has he heard, with tearful eyes,
16*

which his lips never repeated even to the most intimate of his friends and relatives.

After lecturing in East Cambridge, Brookline, and Gloucester, to large congregations, and with his usual good success, he began his journey southward, to Washington, on Saturday, February 19th.

Took steamboat at Providence, at dusk, wind blowing so hard that we put into Newport for the night. On Sunday morning raised steam and left at four o'clock for New York, which place we reached at 6 P.M. Remained here to unite in the celebration of the birthday of the immortal Washington, in a truly temperance style.

The 22d of February, 1842, was noted throughout the country for great and splendid temperance meetings. In Boston, the cradle of American liberty was filled three times in the day, while the greatest enthusiasm everywhere prevailed. Thousands of happy hearts were there who had cast off the chains of the most galling tyranny that ever oppressed the human family. There was a feast of reason and a flow of soul, unalloyed by the presence of that "which at the last biteth like a serpent and stingeth like an adder.* Great was the rejoicing in Portland, Me; the

---

* (FROM THE MERCANTILE JOURNAL OF FEB. 23.)

Yesterday was a day memorable in the annals of temperance. The proceedings in various places which we have heard from, were conducted with a zeal and a spirit and an unanimity in the highest degree gratifying to all who take an interest in this holy cause, and calculated to excite the most sanguine hopes that the reign of intemperance is rapidly approaching its end.

FANEUIL HALL, Feb. 22d, 1842.

Resolved, That on this occasion we would reverently offer thanksgiving to Al-

Washingtonians were out in large numbers.   At Providence, R. I., four thousand, including a little army
of fifteen hundred " cold water " children, with ᴠenty
banners, ᴬ ᴄomᴘanied by ᴊeveral bands of music,
marched to the several churches to hear addresses by
different persons.   At New London there was a procession of three thousand.   At Cooperstown, N. Y.
there was a splendid celebration.   At Buffalo, Geneva,
Rome, and many other places, the people were out in
large numbers, with music and with banners, declaring
by their actions that the nation should no longer be
ruled by ᴛum.

But the festival in New York surpassed all others in
its extent, beauty, and appropriateness ; it is thus
described by Dr. Marsh : —

The Grand Festival at Centre Market Hall, on the birthday of our immortal Washington, was got up and carried
through in a style worthy of the movement with which it was
connected.   The magnitude of the halls, their appropriate
decorations, the immense crowd of people, the eloquence of
the orators, the beauty and rich supply of the table, the hearty
but innocent congratulations of the guests, the pith of the
sentiments, and the power of the temperance odes, sung by

mighty God for the signal mercies he has shown to the cause of temperance, in that
he has moved the souls of the intemperate to undertake the great work of their own
reformation, and with results equally worthy astonishment and gratitude.

Resolved, That to secure to the reformed the great blessings which have become
theirs, the friends of temperance everywhere are called upon for active sympathy in
their behalf, for that love for them which never faileth, for that steady aid and assistance which their destitution or their spiritual weakness may demand.

Resolved, That for this end, the comfort and support of the reformed, we now in
this vast assembly, and before the ever-seeing God, call upon him who manufactures
and upon him who traffics in intoxicating drinks, and in all kinds of them, that he
would, in the view of a fearful accountability, and the spirit of a true self-sacrifice, at
once and forever abandon a business which is full of misery, of sin, and of death.

thousands of voices ; these, gratifying as they were, did not fill our vision so much as the object of the festival, and the character and circumstances of the many there, once poor unfortunate drunkards, now disenthralled, reformed men, gathered together with their "happy families," as John Hawkins calls them, to rejoice in their wonderful deliverance ; — the whole forming an entirely new era in the moral history of our great city.

The four halls over the Centre Market give a floor of two hundred and seventy-five feet by forty feet on Centre, and eighty feet by fifty feet on Grand Street. They were all thrown into one, and splendidly decorated with flags, transparencies, portraits, temperance banners, and appropriate devices, and brilliantly lighted with gas. Tables of more than three hundred and thirty feet were placed in various parts of the halls, but leaving the whole centre as a promenade, and were, through the liberality of our citizens, especially the efficiency of the female temperance societies, loaded and even beautifully adorned, with every variety of cakes, sandwiches, smoked beef, tongues, crackers, cheese, apples, raisins, &c., &c., with two thousand tumblers of clear cold water. At six o'clock the doors were thrown open, and for an hour and a half the access was crowded with the thronging guests, who could not have been little less than three thousand in number, one thousand of whom were females. During their entrance, music was given by a fine brass band provided for the occasion.

Precisely at seven the vast assemblage was called to order by the Grand Marshals, Dr. E. Kirby, and Mr. E. L. Snow, at the two stands provided for speakers, when letters of apology for absence were read by Rev. J. Marsh, and Mr. E. Burns, Committee on Invitation, from Deacon Moses Grant, Rev. John Pierpont, Lewis C. Levin, Dr. Walter Channing, Christian Keener, William K. Mitchell, and other gentlemen, expressing the warmest interest in the occasion, and the most devout thankfulness for the progress of the cause, each also giving an appropriate sentiment. One of the stands was now to be occupied by the Hon. Theodore Frelinghuysen, but unfortunately he had been prevented from an entrance by the great concourse at the door. The Rev. E. N. Kirk was called to fill his place, who, though without the advantage of premeditation, closely riveted the attention of all within the sound of his voice for half an hour, while on the other stand, far distant, John Hawkins, the ever interesting and powerful advocate of the cause, poured forth his full and grateful soul in strains of thrilling eloquence. At eight o'clock thanks were rendered for the great temperance reformation, and the divine blessing was implored on the festival by the Rev. Drs. Patton and Bangs, when the collation was regularly but most rapidly dispatched, and with a hilarity and good humor that showed that temperance is no austere and lugubrious service. By the hour of nine order was again restored, the immense company having returned to their seats, when the regular sentiments were given by the Grand Marshal, and repeated by the assistant marshals through the length of the halls. Each sentiment was responded to by music from the band; three of them by Temperance songs appropriate to the sentiments, which were sung by the whole assembly, whose voices were as the sound of many waters. Volunteer sentiments succeeded, with short addresses and songs, and oft repeated airs from the bands, which continued until the hour of eleven. At the fourth regular sentiment two reformed men related their experiences on the stands, and at the sixth, expressive of commendation of female charity, the stands were occupied by Rev. Drs. Patton and Parker, who dwelt on the appropriateness and power of female action in this great cause. The Washingtonians, Latham, Madden, Snow, and others, spoke with great interest to the audience, while the temperance glee club and the firemen, who have united with the cold water army, drew forth by their appropriate and animated songs the loudest applause.

Never have we mingled in an assembly where were more

joyful countenances. A number of our respectable citizens with their wives and daughters came to see the happy scene. We only wish that every rum-seller in the land could have witnessed the spectacle, to learn that his destructive business here is fast on the wane.

CHAPTER XIV.

"In the strength of your might, from each mountain and valley,
   Friends of Temperance, arise! the time is at hand:
Around its broad standard we'll rally, we'll rally,
   While the star-spangled banner floats over our land.
Then let the proud eagle spread his wings wide asunder,
   And break from the trammels which strive to enchain;
If we rise in our strength, if we speak but in thunder,
   The Genius of Temperance will flourish again."

OF his journey to and arrival at Washington, Mr. Hawkins thus writes in his journal:—

On the 23d of February left New York; stopped in Burlington to lecture in the evening; left for Philadelphia same night. Remained in Philadelphia one night; reached Baltimore the next morning. I found all my relatives and friends well, and glad to see me. Took the cars next day, 25th, for Washington. At night attended a large and enthusiastic meeting in the Hall of the House of Representatives.

This meeting was largely attended by members of Congress and many individuals who had taken a prominent part in the late extraordinary movements. The cordiality with which Mr. Hawkins and those who labored with him were received, was exceedingly gratifying. The meeting was addressed by the Hon. George N. Briggs, of Massachusetts; also by the Hon. Mr. Williams, of Connecticut, who offered a resolution of thanks for the late signal interposition of Divine Providence, in so far delivering the nation from the scourge of intemperance.

He was followed by Dr. Thomas Sewall, who by his mammoth engravings of the interior of the stomach exhibited the terrible evils inflicted by alcohol upon its inner coatings. The Hon. Mr. Fillmore spoke of the importance of these illustrations of the physical effects of intemperance. The Hon. Mr. Gillmore, of Virginia, commended the whole subject to the serious attention of the young men of the nation, especially those occupying posts of trust, or who had devoted themselves to the service of their country. The Hon. Mr. Burnell, from Massachusetts, dwelt at considerable length upon the evils inflicted by intemperance upon the material resources of the people, and upon their morals, paralyzing the efforts of religion, and gradually undermining her institutions. The Hon. J. R. Giddings, of Ohio, denounced intemperance in the resolution which he offered, on the ground of its being at variance with the laws of our physical and moral being. Hon. T. F. Marshall thought that the custom of pledging each other in the social glass at fashionable entertainments, has no foundation in the natural principles of good taste, true hospitality, or refined manners. Hon. Mr. Morgan, of New York, dwelt upon the subject of female influence. Hon. Mr. Irving, of Pennsylvania, called attention by resolution to the extraordinary work of reform which is now blessing the country. Mr. Hawkins responded to the resolution, but the lateness of the hour (eleven o'clock), did not admit of any thing more than a brief account of what he had been permitted to witness in various parts of the country through which he had travelled. *

* For a more extended account, see *Journal* of American Temperance Union, New York, March, 1842.

So great was the interest at this meeting, that even at this late hour none of the audience had retired. In conclusion, Mr. John Tappan, of Boston, moved that the whole proceedings and speeches be printed in pamphlet form and circulated through the country. During the proceedings of the meeting the Corresponding Secretary of the American Temperance Union gave a highly entertaining summary of the astonishing results so far accomplished in the country.

Nothing is here attempted beyond the briefest outline; these deliberations exerted an extensive influence in the country, and many individuals of great ability and standing were led to give the subject their especial attention.

There was, without doubt, some intemperance among the members of Congress at this period, but far less than the statements in the papers led the country to believe. The distinguished reformations which had taken place exerted a good influence both there and abroad. There was one thing, however, in connection with intemperance at Washington, which occasioned great dissatisfaction among the people; viz., the existence of drinking saloons, styled *refectories*, in the basement of the Capitol. Mr. Hawkins exerted his influence with the members and proper authorities to procure the removal of these nuisances, and as a consequence they were for several years in a good degree *abated*. It was not, however, until the winter session of 1847–8 that drinking saloons in the Capitol were abolished by order of the officers of both branches of Congress. The Hon. George M. Dallas was at that time President of the Senate, and the Hon. Robert C Winthrop, Speaker of the House. Mr. Dallas had

17

ordered their removal from his department of the Capitol, thus throwing the responsibility of their continuance, under the *other wing*, upon Mr. Winthrop. Many
members of the House feeling annoyed at this state
of things, Mr. Winthrop gave orders to the Sergeant-
at-Arms to notify the occupant of the premises to va
cate them immediately. At first he was a little disposed
to resist the authorities, but finally complied with their
desires. To the Hon. Robert C. Winthrop, therefore,
belongs the credit of entirely banishing, for the *first time*,
inebriating beverages from the basement of the nation's Capitol.

Mr. Hawkins visited Washington subsequently, and
after due inquiries learned that notwithstanding the
efforts previously made, the keeper of a refectory down
in those gloomy recesses still sold the forbidden article.
Although suspected, he had thus far escaped detection;
no one had been actually seen to drink in his saloon.
Mr. Hawkins being satisfied as to his guilt, called upon
the Sergeant-at-Arms and stated his convictions; that
officer informed him that as soon as he could bring
certain proofs of the guilt of the party named, he should
be ordered from the premises, such being the instructions of the Speaker. Mr. Hawkins went immediately
to the saloon and ordered some oysters; then calling
the waiter, he inquired in a low tone if he had any
other refreshments. Being answered in the affirmative,
he called for a glass of brandy. This was brought to
him, and as soon as opportunity allowed he conveyed
the contents of the glass into a vial, which he carefully
placed in his pocket. He then called upon the officer
above named and stated to him these facts. The offender was speedily summoned into their presence.

" Do you not keep intoxicating drinks," was asked, " in your establishment ? " He began to equivocate, when he was immediately checked by the exhibition of the vial of brandy which Mr. Hawkins had but a few moments before procured from his waiter. It is needless to add that the offender was immediately ordered to remove the offensive articles. This was, probably, the end of tippling-shops in those localities.

Mr. Hawkins made many valuable friends among the members of Congress, who in after years, wherever they met him, gave him their hearty encouragement and sympathy. He was regarded by them as an honest lover of his race ; they loved him for his frankness, and confided in him.

While in Washington Mr. Hawkins lectured four times to large audiences, and with uncommon success ; in Apollo Hall on Saturday, February 26, 1842, on Sunday in the Methodist Church, in the Assembly Rooms on Monday, and in the Rev. Dr. Brown's church on Tuesday. Remaining a few days in Baltimore, he proceeded to Philadelphia ; here he found the cause of temperance making rapid strides ; the interest so great that meetings were kept up nightly. He reached New Brunswick on the 16th of March, where he delivered four lectures. " Much has been done," he remarks in his journal, " to reclaim the drunkard ; great interest prevails."

In all these addresses, while Mr. Hawkins exhibited unabated interest in the inebriate, he did not fail to call the public attention to the iniquity of the liquor traffic, and the great laxity of the license laws. He contended that unless these streams of death could be abated, the efforts of temperance men would in a good degree prove fruitless.

The reformation of so many thousands, both of habitual and moderate drinkers, had largely diminished the retail trade. It was estimated that on the 1st of April, 1842, the demand for whisky was not more than half what it was in the same month of the year previous. Its sale at that period (April, 1841) had been greatly reduced. The distilleries were now running not more than half the time, and there was a large stock on hand for which there was no demand. The consumption of grain in the manufacture of the article in previous years, in the city of New York alone, was four or five thousand bushels daily: now it was less than two thousand. " The distillers," says the *Journal of Commerce*, in March, 1842, " seem pleased with the change, and are reducing their works as speedily as possible." It was confidently believed that the demand for the next crop of grain would not exceed one-fourth what it was at the highest point, — that the falling off could not be less than a million of bushels for the year. The largest merchants in the city began to refuse any advances on whisky; a cargo of rum, failing of a purchaser, was put up at auction, and after paying all expenses there was not fifty dollars remaining for the shipper. Whisky was selling at eleven cents per gallon in Cincinnati, which was not half the price of the year previous. In Maine and Massachusetts sellers were daily abandoning the business. A young lady in Portland, who was engaged to be married to a merchant who kept liquors for sale, refused her consent to their union until he had emptied his casks; which, of

course, he did.   Many of the most notorious rum-sellers
in the land gave up the business from sincere convictions of duty.   In Brooklyn, N. Y., four shops were
closed in one week.   In Chillicothe all the poison from
the rum-shops was thrown into the streets.   At Jones-
boro', Tenn., an old dealer gave up his stock, for which
the citizens paid him, and a bonfire was made of it in
the public square.   At Conway, N. H., all the dealers
save one renounced the traffic.   Five distillers in Dan-
ville and two in Boston, it was said by the papers of
the day, put out their fires.   In Wilmington, Del., in
the interior towns of Virginia, and as far south as
Mobile, a considerable number of dealers closed their
shops.

We subjoin a note containing extracts from various
papers in the Union, compiled by Rev. Dr. Marsh for
his *Journal*, which will exhibit the rapid prevalence of
temperance principles at this exceedingly interesting
period in the reformation.*

---

* In one block, on Wednesday last, we counted " To Let " on eight
rum-shops, some of them large ones, hardly a stone's-throw from the Five
Points too ! — *N. Y. Organ.*

Strolling along up Division Street the other day, we saw a sign in
the window of a grocery which struck us as being somewhat peculiar ;
—it read after this fashion : " A bar, kegs, decanters, and stock of
liquors for sale, *below cost !* "   They would have been dear at that. — *Organ.*

At Worcester, Mass., the cause of temperance advances triumphantly ;
great numbers have signed the pledge ; most of the tavern keepers are
among the number.   One who sometime ago sold large quantities of the
fiery liquid by the glass, and therefore would not sign the pledge, has
had his business so reduced that he has rented his house and moved
away.

In Brighton, Mass., temperance has made such astonishing progress,
that Porter's Hotel is soon to be vacated by him who has dealt out the

Mr. Hawkins regarded this encouraging state of

poison to thousands, and gloried in his shame, in that once besotted, but now regenerated town. — *Letter.*

A quantity of brandy and gin of the best quality was offered at auction some weeks ago in Wilmington, Del. Great pains had been taken to advertise the sale by handbills, and the bell-man was sent round for customers. At the heat of the sale the people gathered in such numbers that we did not count them. The way the rum-sellers bid for the liquor was a caution. The greatest animation prevailed, and the thing went off finely. Competition was at its extreme point, and there was not a man in the crowd that did not appear anxious to — see the result. The first bid was twenty cents a gallon, by some strange gentleman, and so it went on — on — on. But the world was not made in a day, nor was the brandy and gin to be sold in a minute. The auctioneer cried with spirit; the spirits of the company rose as the sale went on, and the spirits in the casks were at length knocked down to the highest bidder. We have already said that the first bid was twenty cents a gallon. The reader will please bear this in mind. Well, the last and highest bidder of course got the liquor — and that was the very same stranger that made the first bid. Never before did brandy and gin bring the same price in Wilmington. But it was the *best* brandy and gin, and that may account for it. Have patience, reader, and you shall hear the end of it. How much do you suppose it sold for? *The first, and last, and only bid was twenty cents a gallon! — Standard.*

We believe that the consumption of intoxicating liquors has been reduced one fourth in 1841, and that it will be reduced in still greater proportion in 1842. — *Boston paper.*

Some weeks ago a cargo of St. Croix rum was brought to this city, but returned to that island on account of the low price of the article in this market. The cargo has since come back again, of course paying freight on three voyages. — *New York paper.*

In Belchertown, Mass., the last rum-tavern has abandoned the trade.

Mr. Samuel Palmer has turned alcohol out of his bar at Oriskany Falls, N. Y., and joyfully unfurled the banner of temperance.

Says the *Utica News*, — " Within one week we have seen accounts of sixty-three rum-selling taverns and hotels turned into temperance houses, and in many instances the wines and liquors were burned in the streets."

The *Pittsburg Gazette* says " it is a remarkable fact that while there were

things, with evident satisfaction.   He was encouraged in

in Washington and Alleghany counties, in Pennsylvania, in the year 1815, some fifteen hundred stills at work, there are at this time not more than fifteen or twenty still-houses at work in both counties."

Several merchants in Annapolis have turned their liquor into the street, and one of the keepers of the City Hotel has signed the Washington pledge.

Mr. S. Norton, of New Marlboro', has abandoned the sale of liquor. This is the first instance in Berkshire county, and was celebrated by a magnificent supper.

In Lynn, Mass., there were, six months ago, eighteen spirit shops sending forth a pestilential influence throughout the length and breadth of the town.   There are only three remaining.

At Elyria, O., Gen. Griffith has converted his mansion-house into a temperance-house, and on the 22d of February, at a teetotal dinner, was present the most extensive distiller and vender in the county, he and his family having signed the pledge.

At Norwalk, O., Col. James, of the Mansion, has removed every thing in the shape of alcohol from his bar.

At Medina, Mr. S. H. Bradley, of the Eastern Hotel, and Mr. Chidester and Mr. Miner, have all broken up their bars.

Mr. Marshall, the keeper of a tavern at Marcus Hook, Pa., in which liquor has been sold for the last seventy-five years, has sawed down his old sign, and removed ardent spirits from his premises.

The Franklin House at Owego, and the Hotel at Ovid, have recently ousted alcohol, and raised the cold-water colors.

One of the principal grocers in Wilmington lately remarked that he thought if a paper were taken round among the grocers, all but one of them would sign to give up the sale of liquor.

The two hotels in North Bridgewater, Mass., have raised the teetotal sign.

In Portland, Me., there were a year ago one hundred and thirty rumsellers.   Of these, twenty-four have discontinued the business.

A clerk of one of the largest rum-selling establishments in Portland, recently said that their sales were not sufficient to make it an object to keep liquors ;—and a large dealer said recently, that this reform was only a *little flurry*, which would soon be over, otherwise he would abandon the business, as no longer worth pursuing — and that his profits on liquors were diminished this year to the amount of $3,000.

A gentleman in Maine says, those who formerly transported hogsheads of rum by his house into the country, are now reduced to barrels,

his own efforts, and he spread abroad, wherever he lectured, the news of these daily conquests over the demon of the still.

On reaching New York, he found that his friend Mr. Asa Bigelow had made appointments for him in the following places: Rye, Southport, Fairfield, and Danbury, Ct. There were a multitude of towns which he had not yet visited in Massachusetts and Connecticut, where the people were clamorous for his presence and aid. The Massachusetts Temperance Union had printed and circulated seventy-five thousand copies of a tract containing his first speech in Faneuil Hall, and another edition was demanded. All these things tended to keep alive public interest, and added greatly to his means of usefulness wherever he went. We subjoin the following correspondence as evidence of the feelings entertained towards Mr. Hawkins by the people of Danbury, Ct.: —

NEW YORK, March 14, 1842.

MR. JOHN H. W. HAWKINS: *Dear Sir*, — I have come to this city — hearing that you were to be here on Saturday last — for the express purpose of urging you to come to the town of

and those who formerly transported rum by the barrel now do it by the keg.

Mr. Sergent, of the Mansion House, Portsmouth, N. H., has hoisted the temperance flag.

In the western district of the State of Maine, fourteen grog-shops have been opened during the year, and more than fifty-one have been closed, or their bars taken down. All the returns agree in saying that the sales of liquor have greatly diminished during the year. In some towns the diminution is set down at one-half — in others at three-quarters, and in others at nine-tenths, for in some of the towns in the district, all the traders and tavern keepers have ceased to sell intoxicating drinks. — *Rep. of Com.*

In Brunswick, Me., both of the public houses have closed their bars.

Danbury, Ct., to labor in the temperance cause. And did I not know that the reformation of the poor, drunken, and despised hatter lay nearest your heart, I should at once despair of prevailing upon you to leave unanswered the numerous calls from large places and cities, and come to us. We have a society now formed on the right principles. A reformed hatter for President, a reformed laborer for Vice President, a reformed baker for Secretary, and a reformed shoemaker for Corresponding Secretary. Many of our hatters, too, have reformed, but there are a great many that hold out yet. And now is the time, sir. Many of them *know you*, and the cry is, " Give us John Hawkins." Could you have heard the "ayes" when the question was asked to an overflowing audience, " Shall we send for him?" methinks you would not hesitate long.

Sir, I would not be too bold, but if I should speak the minds of my townsmen, I should say, " We must have you!" and my commission was, " not to come back without you." But as you are not here, I cannot take you with me. So confident were the people that you were in the city and could be prevailed on to come, that they have appointed this, Monday evening, for a meeting, and procured the largest church in the town, with the expectation that you will be among them to-night. Could I see you, I could give you some interesting facts which time will not allow to do on paper. And now, sir, what further shall I say to you? Do you not believe that we want you? Do you not believe that there is a field in which you can labor for a great amount of good? There are over twenty hat shops in the town, and among all these but a very few of the journeymen are temperate men. Will you come?

The most direct route is by the steamboat Nimrod, or Fairfield, to Bridgeport, thence by railroad to Land's End, thence by stage to Danbury; or, you can stop at Norwalk and take the stage direct to Danbury. Through the kindness of Mr. Bigelow, I have been put on this track for reaching you, otherwise, I believe I must have gone home as empty as I came.

Now I feel as if I could go with a much better grace. And now, sir, in conclusion, let me say, should you conclude to come among us, only write me a line through the post office, stating the day on which you will be there. You can start in the morning and reach there about 4 P.M. the same day. I give you my word you shall be "shopped" to as full an audience as any heart could desire.

                    With much respect I am, sir,
                         Your friend and obedient servant,
                              E. ARTHUR NICHOLS.

On reaching Southport, March the 22d, he was met by a gentleman from Danbury, who handed him the following letter : —

                              DANBURY, March 22, 1842.

JOHN H. W. HAWKINS: *Dear Sir,* — Permit me to introduce to your acquaintance, the bearer, Mr. James P. Saunders, who comes for the purpose of bringing you to this place, direct. Mr. Saunders is the person with whom you had some correspondence last fall. I should have come myself, but my business and public duties prevented me. The people here are all awake for ten miles round, and anxious to see and hear you. You will want to start pretty early in the morning in order to reach here by noon. Our arrangements are to have you address the children in the afternoon of to-morrow, when none *but* children will be admitted; in the evening, the men will occupy the house and children excluded. On Thursday there is a great desire to have a mass meeting; but in all these arrangements your opinion and comfort will be consulted. Mr. Saunders will give a detail of our late proceedings, etc., etc.

          Very respectfully, your friend and obedient servant,
                              ED. ARTHUR NICHOLS.

This communication was preceded by a petition signed by thirty hatters, urging his coming.

Mr. Hawkins says in his journal: —

March 23. — Was conveyed by private carriage to Danbury, Ct. Delivered three lectures in this place ; much interest felt on the subject, especially among the hatters. I delivered one lecture in an adjoining town, Bethel ; much has been done here for the cause.

What his success was in this place (Danbury), may be learned from the following letter, written some weeks after his visit to that place.

DANBURY, April, 29, 1842.

MY DEAR SIR, — On the other side you will find a list of Washingtonian hatters, residents of this town. I think you will come to the conclusion that the "Old Hat Shop" is nearly redeemed.

We are continually adding to our numbers : some "old bruisers" come up every Monday evening, and there is hardly time to give all a chance to speak. If things continue in this manner, we shall be obliged to hold two meetings in a week. We are now about procuring a banner, the expense of which will be in the neighborhood of $50. The cause is going forward all around us ; — new societies are forming, and we send out lecturers to them from among our own men.

The times are very much against us, as most of our men are out of employment, and can get nothing to do. But they hold on finely to the Car of Temperance. It would give us a great deal of pleasure to see and hear you once more, and we are indulging the hope, that before the summer is gone yo will be among us. We are making great preparations to have a great celebration on the fourth of July. The whole number of Washingtonians in the town is over thirteen hundred.

Don't forget us when you go to Albany this summer ; just

let me know when you are coming and we will have some *stock* for you to work upon.

Very respectfully yours,

ED. ARTHUR NICHOLS.

Then follow the names of one hundred and fifty-seven hatters, most of them reformed within one year.

DANBURY, 12 May, 1842.

MR. JOHN H. W. HAWKINS : *Dear Sir,* — The Washington Temperance Benevolent Society of this town have determined to celebrate the approaching anniversary of our nation's independence in an appropriate manner. Invitations have already been extended to every town in our county, to unite with us upon that occasion ; and we shall doubtless have an assemblage of from four to six thousand persons upon that day. Should the weather prove unfavorable, we shall defer the celebration until the 5th, as our ceremonies must necessarily be in the open air. We know of no man who would be so warmly welcomed to address us as yourself; as we consider that you may be emphatically called the pioneer in our glorious cause. Will you not, therefore, favor us with an address upon that joyful occasion? Fairfield County has taken the lead in temperance in this State. You have already assisted us in turning our lead to the other side, and we must yet cry " give, give." Don't refuse us. You will find thousands of warm and glad hearts to hear you.

Yours very respectfully,

NELSON L. WHITE,
ED. ARTHUR NICHOLS,
AMOS BISHOP,   } *Committee of*
JAMES P. SAUNDERS,   *Arrangements.*
WM. A. CROCKER.

At the close of Mr. Hawkins' first visit to Danbury,

on the 25th of March, he returned to New York, and
on the next day left in steamboat Worcester for Boston, by way of Norwich and Worcester. How he occupied himself on board will be seen from the following communication which we take from the *Mercantile
Journal*. The writer, after speaking of the greater quiet
and comfort on " temperance steamboats," says : —

I have been led to this remark after another passage in the
steamer Worcester of the Norwich line, under the command
of Capt. Coit. It is also to be remembered that in order to
secure that quiet and sense of safety so much desired on board
a steamer, a sacrifice has been made by the proprietors of this
boat. Rum, wine, and all other intoxicating drinks have been
banished from the bar and the boat. We had a fine run on
Saturday last, pleasant weather, a good table and attention,
and a company of passengers who, if not all teetotalers, were
at least disposed to hear reasons for becoming so.

Mr. Hawkins, the great apostle of Washingtonianism, being
on board, it was unanimously voted at the table to hold a temperance meeting in the forward cabin after supper, and request
an address from him. The meeting was called to order at seven
o'clock, when John Owen, of Cambridge, was appointed Chairman, and H. B. Claflin, of Worcester, Secretary. The company was then addressed by several gentlemen. Mr. Hawkins
made an eloquent appeal to the moderate drinkers, showing
the deceptive influence of all fermented liquors upon the minds
and feelings of those who use them in any quantity. The moderate drinker might not acknowledge this influence, and would
not be likely to, till reformation should open his eyes. Then
he would see and confess it all, with the two hundred thousand
inebriates in this country, reformed within the past year, who,
with united voice, have borne testimony to the insidious nature
of all intoxicating liquors. Mr. Hawkins introduced the anecdote of Judge M.'s definition of drunkenness, in his usual happy

manner of telling a story. A clergyman had been accused of intemperance by an individual whom he wished to have arraigned for a libel on his reputation. He applied for this purpose to Judge M., then an eminent lawyer in Baltimore. Having heard the clergyman's complaint, and after a severe scrutiny of the person of the complainant, Mr. M., not inexperienced himself in the effects of drink, questioned his client in the following manner: " Sir, in order to do my duty to you more faithfully, I wish to inquire, first of all, are you guilty of the charge? Do you ever get drunk?" Astonished at the question, the clergyman was about to say "never," but having a good degree of conscientiousness, he hesitated, and then he replied, "What do you mean by drunkenness?" " Why, sir, I mean by drunkenness that condition of the human faculties in which, by the use of fermented liquors, a man is enabled or induced to do certain acts which he could not do, or would not do, without such use. For instance, sir, and I beg you not to deem me personal or irreverent, a man may sometimes preach a more eloquent discourse, and utter a more fervent prayer, excited by drink, than he could do in the previous languid state of his feelings. He may not think so, but I call him drunk. This is my definition of drunkenness." The clergyman replied, " Mr. M., I withdraw my complaint!"

A few days previous to Mr. Hawkins' return to New York, a very important meeting of reformed drunkards was held in Concert Hall, Broadway. Dr. Kirby took the chair, and after making a few remarks introduced several reformed drunkards, each of whom, by arrangement, was to speak not over five minutes. The first one who came upon the stand was Mr. Latham, the individual who at the first meeting addressed by Mr. Hawkins, in Green Street, New York, cried out from the gallery to know "if there was any hope for him."

Mr. Latham said he was young to address an audience like that, being but one year old that day. One year ago he was a miserable drunkard. He did not tell of that to glory in it. No. He was ashamed of it, and sorry for it. But as he had been one, he was willing to confess it, and felt it his duty to do so. I went to the church in Green Street the day John Hawkins came here. I had been drunk twice that day. I drank to strengthen my resolution to go into the church. I heard what he said of himself, and I asked myself if he could be saved why might not I be ; and I felt so much that I spoke my feelings aloud ; — they brought me down and I signed the pledge, one year ago to-day. And oh, what a different man I have been ever since ! I have the same body, bones, and sinews, but oh, how changed in every respect ! I look upon myself as a wonder. The doctors said that we could not be reformed ; we should all die if we left off drinking. But the Almighty, in his goodness, was determined to break this illusion.· The doctors knew nothing about it, and to prove they did not, I will mention that it was six months from its commencement before a single member of our society died, though it got to be very numerous. If any man will sign our pledge honestly, and stick to it a little while, he will meet with no difficulty. He will meet with the greatest trials and temptations, but he must be firm. I lay on my bed three days, my wife sitting by and doing a little something, but no money and no food in the house. At length I took a basket and went out. I worked at beer-pumps. I met all my acquaintance, and all said, drink a little or you will die. But the words of John Hawkins were right before me — "LIVE OR DIE, NEVER TOUCH ANOTHER DROP ;" and that saved me, and has saved thousands of others, and has saved a great many temperate men, moderate drinkers, from becoming drunkards.

The experience of five others was given, all going to show the influence of the reform in snatching degraded men from the very edge of the yawning gulf, and restoring them to sobriety and happiness.

On reaching Boston Mr. Hawkins found the cause of temperance in a most hopeful condition. A host of temperance delegates, selected from the Washington Temperance Society, had been sent out into all parts of the New England States, and through their efforts societies had been formed and hundreds of unfortunate men snatched from the misery of a debasing appetite, restored to their families and homes. Says the *Mercantile Journal:* —

By letters received from various parts of Massachusetts, New Hampshire, and Vermont, the most cheering accounts are given from places that our delegates have visited. The Washingtonian reform is spreading rapidly in all sections. The amount of good done by our delegates abroad is beyond calculation. One short year more and the Northern States will be as free from intemperance as any spot on the whole earth.

Nor was this abatement in the use of intoxicating beverages confined to any one class in the community; it reached every grade of society; all seemed willing to admit the fact of the baneful influence of intemperance, and manifested a disposition to moderate, if not abandon, the use of intoxicating drinks. They began to be much less frequently provided at fashionable entertainments; moderate drinkers were becoming alarmed; the young were eagerly embracing the principles of total abstinence. In a letter from Washington, dated 5th February, 1843, to Edward C. Delavan, Esq., which we extract from the *Mercantile Journal*, the statement was made, that "at the great and splendid levee given on the occasion of his daughter's marriage, the President of

the United States of America had not a drop of wine
or other alcoholic drinks furnished.   Nothing but cold
water was to be had, and on a wedding occasion too.
What a noble step! one which will draw to him
thousands of hearts, warm and fresh, and will tell on
the future destinies of the nation."

" Fashionable drinking" was becoming unfashion-
able, and the traffic in ardent spirits was on the decline.
The most influential papers in the country were contributing their powerful aid in the advocacy of total
abstinence.   We have already spoken of the noble
stand taken by the Boston *Mercantile Journal;* now the
National Intelligencer, the *North American,* the *Journal
of Commerce,* the *New-York Express,* the *New-York
Tribune,* the *New-York Times and Star,* and a host of
other papers, were sending forth columns filled with
noble sentiments in praise of the reformation.   We
subjoin a few extracts.*

* (FROM THE NEW-YORK TIMES AND STAR.)

This practice, or rather habit of hard drinking and draining the wine
cup, and keeping up bacchanalian revels, has run through the many
ages of English kings, down to the Reformation, and then it presented a
more elegant and rational adoption of the same habits, with more refinement, but with less consumption of strong liquors.   There was not that
rude and boisterous hospitality, which, chaining a man to the table, and
compelling him to drain goblet after goblet, kept him there until brutal
intoxication followed, and himself and all the lords and knights and no-
bility of the land, sprawled on the floor in utter insensibility.   Brandy
yielded to light wine, and distilled waters to punch, a favorite beverage
from the time of Elizabeth to George the Third, when heavy Port and
Old Maderia chased away the immense china bowl and silver dipper,
which were the delight of all the clubs and fashionable houses.   We, of
course, in this country, followed the fashion of our ancestors ; we spoke
the same language and adopted the same habits as our forefathers ; and
up to 1815, it is doubtful whether men of easy fortune were not as fond
of the delights of the table, as they were at any period of our history.

18*

Much indeed had been done, but vastly more was

At that time champagne sparingly appeared, and was considered so choice and *recherche*, that a bottle or two passed around the centre table at an evening party of ladies, was deemed a rich and rare treat. But every thing is doomed to its changes, and all other kinds of wines were almost banished by the importations of whole cargoes of champagne, until a French cultivator wished to know of his correspondent here, "whether we bathed in champagne," such was the immense quantity of that article exported to this country. If we ask the importers, we shall find that the quantity of all kinds of wines introduced into this country, has greatly diminished. It is not true, therefore, as has been said, that there is more hard drinking, intoxication, lewdness, and profanity among the opulent than are found in the grog-shops; there never was at any time ground to institute the comparison. At all events, sitting long at table after dinner, drinking bottle after bottle of wine, is almost entirely exploded among respectable people. In former times the sideboard was thrown open, and the casual visitor invited to drink; that practice is almost entirely exploded. Down East, the great school of morality, the distilleries are a dead loss on the hands of their owners, and grog-shops are everywhere closing; and it is considered vulgar among genteel people to indulge in drinking liquors, almost of every kind. Our tavern and hotel keepers, and family grocers, sell less liquor than they formerly did; the Irish are gradually selling out their grog-shops to the Germans, who will soon discover that they are following a losing business. In our foreign *cafés*, so much frequented, there are few if any hard drinkers. A cup of coffee or chocolate, a glass of hot milk and sugar, a lemonade, or some such beverages, are the prevailing drinks. In short, it should be proudly conceded, that everywhere throughout our country, and in all classes, there are evident signs of great improvement in the temperance cause. There are some benighted regions of the republic where the cause has not as yet made much progress; but "Rome was not built in a day;" and if the press of our country will unite to advocate this great moral reform, we shall be in time a sober people, and, consequently, with all our great resources, a decidedly happy people.

(FROM THE MERCANTILE JOURNAL.)

The temperance reformation is making a great stir in the Bermudas, and the movement is strongly countenanced and aided by the Governor, Reid.

Among the stupendous reforms of the present day, nothing excites more grateful astonishment than the temperance reformation. It is as yet to be accomplished. Mr. Hawkins remained a few days in Boston with his family, to make arrangements for another temperance tour. In the mean time he visited all parts of the city to ascertain what had been the influence of the reformations on the traffic, and the appearance of those sections where the intemperate " most do congregate." He was, without doubt, often gratified at the evident improvement, but enough was still visible to spur him on to redoubled zeal. Says the *Mercantile Journal* of Dec. 6, 1841 : —

John Hawkins says it would be a first-rate business for some temperance man to stand at a certain corner near the Hay-scales, of a Sunday morning, and distribute a certain tract called the " Fool's Pence." He furthermore says, that any

vast as it is deep, and thorough as it is extensive. It does not merely pervade certain local sections, or the visible surface of society. It embraces the entire Union, and its healing influence extends from the refined classes down to the most besotted bodies of men. Persons from the East and the West, from the North and the South, from populous cities and obscure villages, alike concur in speaking of it as exceeding any thing in the annals of moral reformation. We find persons of every grade, who have been habitual drinkers, almost voluntarily abandoning their cups, and renouncing their accustomed haunts of dissipation. Crowds of men, acted upon by common sympathy, or by some other inexplicable cause, are abandoning habits of intoxication, and joining in reforming those whose appetites hitherto they have helped to feed and inflame. Men who have been conspicuous for their habits of intemperance and lawless disregard of the healthful laws of morality, suddenly are changed and become exemplary and sober men. Nothing could induce a return to their former habits ; it would be difficult to tempt these men again to pollute their lips with the " poison." Those who once needed the aid of friends to stop excess, now in turn are exhorting others to reform. The reformed everywhere have become successful and judicious reformers. God be praised, that this vast fountain from whence vice springs in such innumerable shapes, has already met with so blessed an amount of purification. May it continue to be cleansed, and happy will that day be when it no longer shall send forth turbid and bitter waters. — *Oct.* 4, 1841.

man who spends his money in such places for rum, while his
family is suffering at home for food and fuel, may well exclaim
in the language of John Randolph, " Remorse! *remorse!* RE-
MORSE!"

On the 1st of April, 1842, so rapidly had the cause
advanced among all classes of men, from the humblest
day laborer to the statesman in the halls of Congress,
as to be made a subject of especial comment by most
of the journals favorable to temperance in the land.
The *Journal* of the American Temperance Union, in
adverting to this encouraging state of things, used the
following language :—

We believe no month has exhibited more engagedness and
zeal, or has been attended with more signal triumphs in our city
than the one just brought to a close. Our happy celebration
of the birthday of Washington seemed to inspire every true
friend of the cause with a new determination to carry forward
the work; while the intelligence pouring in from every part
of the United States through the public press, and imparted by
the many who are at this season visiting our city, has satisfied
us that we are moving on amid a national enthusiasm, which
is to exterminate our country's worst enemy. It is impossible
for us to give the names of all the societies now in the field;
their places of meeting; names of speakers; the cheering, the
glorious results.

Speaking of the operations in the city of New York
alone, it says :—

We suppose there are not less than fifty meetings held
weekly, and most of them are perfect jams. Our accessions
are numerous, and often of the most hopeless characters. The
Washington societies have opened their battery in Broadway,
and already some of the higher classes, as they are called, men

of wealth, but sunk in intemperance, have come forward and signed the pledge. We at one time feared that our better families were not to enjoy this blessing which the common people receive so gladly; but we now believe it is to roll over them, and that many a family, yet having all the means of comfort and luxury, but afflicted with an intemperate son or father, is to be made happy by this great reform.

Almost weekly we have some interesting presentation of a banner to a fire or hose company, which has adopted the pledge. This transformation of these companies in the city, and the interest they manifest in the cause, together with the union and harmony among the temperance societies now in the field, and their joy in the hope that our city, by these movements, is to be relieved from the most intolerable burden, its thousands of licensed and unlicensed grog-shops, is exceedingly animating.

Bishop Berkeley thought that matter was ideal, and some men have deemed that there was no reality in pain. It is not surprising, therefore, that some should think that the cause of temperance is in a state of "retrogression" here, and that much at which we now grasp is "imaginary and deceptive." A blessed deception to many a poor drunkard's wife and famished children.

But comparisons with the past are not always wise. The Bible says "There is joy in heaven over one sinner that repenteth, more than over ninety and nine just persons who need no repentance." And so we have felt about these reformed drunkards. Old laborers in the field, "elder brothers," who have borne the heat and burden of the day, must have their reward; but we do say, "Welcome home the returning prodigals," and we must believe that the reform of some thousands of inebriates in our city is an achievement, in the good providence of God, with which no former one can at all compare. It is saving lost men, lost families, and will do vastly more than all former movements to break up the rum trade so ruinous to our city.

And in view of it all — a wonderful work, there is no mistake about it — it is doing great things for our city — we ask, is it not time for some of our distinguished lawyers, our Griffins, our Hoffmans, our Maxwells, and our O'Connors, like Messrs. Briggs, Marshall, and others, to come forward and sign the pledge, and advocate this cause? Can they be afraid of injuring their business? If they are, surely the ministry need not be. But is it not true that a considerable portion of the ministry of this city, and some of the most able divines, have never yet signed a total-abstinence pledge, nor spoken in behalf of the total-abstinence cause? Would they not now effect an immense good in all their congregations, if they would as a body come forward and sign that pledge, and publicly commend the principle it presents? We respectfully lay this subject at their feet; for they are men who love to do good, and who are the guides and leaders of thousands in the way of salvation. We see not how they can stand aloof at this interesting moment. The eyes of the city, the eyes of the nation, are upon them. If they fear evil from this mighty movement of the people, let them come forward and be its guides. We believe it is God's work, and that, as God's ministers, they are bound to engage joyfully in it.

At least, we will ask them to remember, in all their supplications at the throne of grace, the many thousands of men reformed in the wonderful providence of God in this city and throughout the land, that they may become men of righteousness, and thus have the only permanent security against any return to their unhappy and most ruinous courses.

One of the surest indications of advance in the cause, was the increasing number of temperance newspapers in almost every State in the Union. Many of these were weeklies, and were conducted with an ability highly creditable to the editors, and to the important reform which they sought to promote. We subjoin a list with the comments of the *Journal* of the American Temperance Union. * Their number, however, was constantly increasing, and a few years furnished large additions to the list.

So wide spread was the movement, and so thoroughly was the nation aroused to a sense of the misery resulting from the use and traffic in intoxicating drinks, that newspapers of all classes, religious and political, were filled with the most interesting details of the wonders that had been achieved. The sale and manufacture was rapidly declining, and thousands of hearts began to hail the rapidly approaching day, when the great scourge of intemperance should no longer afflict the

---

* A large number of new temperance papers have recently been commenced in various parts of the country; a sure index of the great advance of the cause.

Among the new papers on our table are—

The *New-York Washingtonian*, edited by E. Burns, a handsome and well-furnished sheet, weekly.

The *Louisville Washingtonian*, weekly.

The *Washington Banner and Reserve Temperance Herald*, Medina, O. semi-monthly.

Boyle's Temperance Herald, Massillon, O.

The *Troy Temperance Mirror*, weekly, eight page, quarto.

Essex County Washingtonian, Salem and Lynn, Mass., weekly, folio.

The *Columbian Washingtonian*, Hudson, N. Y.

Western Reformer, Madison, Indiana, weekly.

The *Temperance Union*, Raleigh, N. C.

The *Cold-Water Cup*, Fitchburg, Mass., semi-monthly.

The *Reformed Drunkard*, Montpelier, Vt., semi-monthly.

Temperance Agent, Thompsontown, Juniata County, Pa.

Washingtonian, Marietta, Lancaster County, Pa.

Washingtonian, Lexington, Ky.

Hampden Washingtonian, Springfield, Mass.

Temperance Gem, Boonsboro', Md.

Waterfall, Worcester, Mass.

Temperance Advocate and Juvenile Miscellany, North Springfield, Vt.

Crystal Fountain, New York.

people.   The following lines, by the Rev. John Pierpont, exhibiting the onward rush of the new-born enthusiasm of the age, have very justly been much admired. Thousands of hearts were inspired with new zeal by their glowing sentences.

We come, we come, that have been held
　　In burning chains so long;
We're up! and on we come, a host
　　Full fifty thousand strong.
The chains we've snapped that held us round
　　The wine-vat and the still;
Snapp'd by a blow — nay, by a word,
　　That mighty word, I will!

We come from Belial's palaces,
　　The tippling-shop and bar;
And as we march, those gates of hell
　　Feel their foundations jar.
The very ground, that oft has held
　　All night our throbbing head,
Knows that we're up — no more to fall,
　　And trembles at our tread.

From dirty den, from gutter foul,
　　From watchhouse and from prison,
Where they, who gave a pois'nous glass,
　　Had thrown us, have we risen:
From garret high have hurried down,
　　From cellar stived and damp,
Come up; till alley, lane, and street
　　Echo our earthquake tramp.

And on — and on — a swelling host
　　Of temperance men we come;
Contemning and defying all
　　The powers and priests of rum.
A host redeemed, who've drawn the sword,
　　And sharpened up its edge,
And hewn our way, through hostile ranks,
　　To the teetotal pledge.

To God be thanks, who pours us out
  Cold water from his hills,
In crystal springs and bubbling brooks,
  In lakes and sparkling rills!
From these, to quench our thirst, we come,
  With freemen's shout and song,
A host already numbering more
  Than fifty thousand strong

19

CHAPTER XV.

"They're gath'ring! they're gath'ring on mountain and plain,
   They grace every vale and o'ershadow each river,
Each mansion and cot shall be vocal again, -
   With the soul-cheering shout of ' Temp'rance forever!'
The pledge of the free to the breeze is unfurled,
   By it is transmitted our freedom and fame,
By it we will hasten the time when our world
   Shall be strong in the strength of Messiah's loved name."

ON Mr. Hawkins' return to Boston, in March, he was licensed to preach the gospel by his Christian brethren of the Methodist Protestant Church. The motives that induced him to take this step were of the purest kind — opening to him as it did greater facilities for being useful to his fellow-men. It frequently happened that no minister was present at his meetings, which he always insisted should be opened with prayer. He preferred that his lectures on the Sabbath should assume as much as possible the religious aspect; and it was his custom to introduce them with some appropriate selections from the Scriptures. A rumor having gone abroad that he intended to devote himself thenceforth to the duties of the ministry, the following article, under his sanction, was inserted in the *Mercantile Journal:* —

It has lately been stated that this distinguished lecturer on temperance had been ordained at Malden as a Methodist preacher, and the inference from this fact seems to be that he has quietly settled down at Malden as a preacher of the Gospel.

We assure our readers that such is not the fact. Mr. Hawkins, although ordained as a preacher of the gospel, will continue unabated his labors in the cause of temperance, for the work is not yet finished, and he will not relax in his endeavors to reform the drunkard and destroy the demoralizing traffic in intoxicating drinks, until the monster Intemperance is banished from the shores of New England. No pecuniary consideration whatever will induce him to desert his post until the temperance reform is established on a basis which cannot be overthrown or shaken.

After enjoying a few days rest, he hastened to make preparations for fulfilling his engagements in various parts of New England. So urgent were the invitations extended to him, and so ardent was his enthusiasm in the cause, that he seldom spent more than three or four days in a month with his family. He was sufficiently recompensed for the self-sacrifice, by the consciousness that there were thousands of families to whose happiness his labors had largely contributed.

From the 2d to the 15th of April he visited eleven towns and delivered fourteen addresses. In Haverhill, South Reading, Woburn, Lowell, Nashua, N. H., and in Billerica, large audiences were gathered and many pledges taken. During the remainder of the month he visited and addressed full houses in fourteen towns, witnessing the reclamation of hundreds from their ruinous ways. " On Saturday, April 30th," he remarks in his journal, " there being no appointment, and finding myself in Worcester, I took the cars to spend the Sabbath in Thompson, Ct. ;" where but a few months before some astonishing reformations had taken place. " I witnessed," he continues, " in this place the bap-

tizing of Capt. B—— S—— by immersion; a reformed
drunkard and a reformed tavern-keeper."

On returning to Worcester he wrote the following
letter to J. W. Goodrich, Esq., editor of the *Worcester Waterfall:* —

WORCESTER, May 5, 1842.

MR. GOODRICH: *Dear Sir,* — I have just finished something of a tour in some of the towns of Worcester Co., of
which, according to my promise, I will now give you a very
short but imperfect account. I commenced at Hopkinton on
the 22d of April. A good and full meeting. A great deal
has been done here in the cause of temperance. Next at Clapp-
ville and Leicester. They are wide awake to the good cause.
I next went to Sutton. Much has been done in this town. A
Temperance House has been opened in Sutton Village by
Mr. Woodbury, and is conducted on true temperance principles, and should be patronized. You and I, Mr. Editor, had
the pleasure of attending a temperance supper there, provided
by Mr. Woodbury on the occasion, an account of which you
have already furnished your readers in the last number of the
Waterfall. * In West Sutton rum is still sold at a place called

* The editor of the *Waterfall* thus alludes to the reformation in Sutton,
and the opening of the first temperance hotel. The intemperance of
this town, it seems, had given great offence to its neighbors.

"TEETOTALLERS' JOLLIFICATION.
" ' Sound the loud trumpet o'er mountain and lea,
The monster has fallen and Sutton is free.'

"This joyous event was celebrated last Monday night by the good
people of that village, with a series of very appropriate and delightful
exercises. At seven o'clock the great apostle of temperance, Mr.
Hawkins, commenced an address to a large audience assembled in the
church, and continued it for one hour and a half, in a strain of surpassing eloquence, argument, feeling, and power. The next subject to be
discussed was a most excellent 'supper, prepared by Mr. J. C. Woodbury,
keeper of the new Temperance House, and which, for want of room on
his own premises, was spread in the vestry of the church. Plates were

a tavern, and at a store, for the *public* good and to the *private* injury of the *neighbors* of those who have the public and private good of the people at heart. At Northborough, Oxford, and Spencer, they are doing much in the cause, but still there is yet much to be done. At Webster and Southbridge were two of the best meetings I have ever attended. The people seem to understand and feel the subject as they should. At Boylston, on Wednesday, May 4th, I talked in the afternoon to the children in the Town House; meeting well attended. The children looked well and paid good attention. At night I lectured in Rev. Mr. Sandford's church. Meeting well attended. A great deal has been done in this town for the cause. On Thursday evening I lectured in the hall at New Worcester; a smart little village, a mile or two from the centre of the town. Meeting well attended by the residents of this and the adjoining town of Auburn. Cause doing well. I cannot close my remarks without saying something of the town of Charlton, where, at my suggestion, Mr. Editor, you announced an appointment for me, in the *Waterfall*, and where, at the suggestion of the letter from your friend in Charlton, I did *not* go to fulfil it. A great deal has been said about its being a hard place. I would respectfully ask the question, has not its

laid for a hundred and twenty; but, on account of the weather only about one hundred ladies and gentlemen took seats at the table. The presidential chair was presented to, and very ably and gracefully occupied by, Mr. John Gambler, of Wilkinsonville. The blessing was asked by the Rev. Mr. Tracy, and then, after the subjects were properly subdivided and distributed for discussion under their appropriate heads, there arose such a *jaw* all along the line of the three extended tables as may seem somewhat surprising to those so unfortunate as to be absent, and especially when we tell them, that each seemed to take and reciprocate the JAWING of his neighbor with the greatest good humor and delight; and that although it continued, with some modification, for about two hours and a half, the *women* did not give the *last words*. The speeches at the banquet, of Mr. Hawkins, J. W. Goodrich and others, were interspersed with appropriate sentiments, and cheering songs, from several gentlemen."

19*

backwardness in the cause of temperance grown much out of
the manner in which they have been approached on the subject? Has not denunciation been too much substituted for
moral suasion? I merely ask the question. I am persuaded,
if properly approached, they are as easily convinced as their
neighbors; at all events, I am determined to go there and
spend two or three days with them, and form some acquaintance with the people; and if they will but listen to me, I will
pledge myself to say nothing that will wound the feelings of
any man, but, on the contrary, will treat every man with the
utmost respect, feeling assured that the same treatment will
cordially be extended to me.

I shall give due notice of my coming.

Yours, &c.,   J. H. W. HAWKINS.

In his journal, under date of the 19th, we find the
following entry : —

Met my son, William George, at Grafton Station, and conveyed him to Wilbraham Academy.

It was not until after much consideration and consultation with friends that he decided to send his children
to that institution. Never did he have cause to regret
the step. Returning to Boston on the 20th, he proceeded, on the next day, to Dover, N. H., thence to
Henniker, by way of Nashua; in all these places
the enthusiasm of the people continued unabated; the
churches were all well filled. After referring to the
great interest exhibited at Nashua, he says, "I fear
the cause will suffer some here by the loss of one of
its best friends, in the death of Judge Darling."

The 26th of May, 1842, was a proud day for Massachusetts. It witnessed the gathering of a larger
number of temperance men in the city of Boston than

had ever met there before at any one time.   It was the
day appointed for the assembling of the State Washingtonian Convention.   The cars on the different railroads brought into the city on the previous day a host
of delegates; but early in the morning of the 26th,
throngs of people were pouring into the city by every
avenue, some on foot, and hundreds by private conveyances, all eager to participate in the exercises of the
day.   At 9 A.M. the Convention assembled in the hall
of the House of Representatives.   The papers of the
day speak of its having been filled to overflowing.
The meeting was called to order by Samuel F. Holbrook, the active and indefatigable President of the
Washington Temperance Society of Boston.   The
Hon. Seth Sprague, Jr., of Duxbury, was appointed
President, supported by six Vice Presidents.   The Convention being thoroughly organized, it adjourned to
meet again at 3 P.M.   A procession was then formed
on the Common, under the direction of Capt. W. S.
Baxter, the chief marshal.   Over three thousand persons marched in its ranks, with banners and badges,
and what was best of all, clear heads, and warm hearts
beating with high resolves.   We subjoin a note giving
the particulars of this procession, which will well repay
perusal.*   On the re-assembling of the Convention in the

---

*(FROM THE MERCANTILE JOURNAL, MAY 27, 1842.)

After the Convention was organized, at a quarter past ten o'clock,
it adjourned to meet again at the State House at three o'clock, and a procession was formed on the Common, under the direction of Capt. W. S.
Baxter, the chief marshal, whose arrangements were well conceived, and
promptly and faithfully executed.   The procession was formed by counties, and when it took up its line of march, to the sound of music, with
banners waving, and striking and ingenious emblems of the blessings of
temperance displayed, it presented a noble and imposing sight.   All so-

afternoon, according to adjournment, an immense con-

cieties, or persons who had joined the ranks of total abstinence from all
intoxicating drinks, were invited to march in the procession.

Here was a broad and elevated platform on which all could meet, and
here were seen men of all political parties, of various religious creeds, of
every occupation and calling, individuals of all ages, from the youthful
stripling to the patriarch of three score and ten, all engaged in one un-
dertaking, all united in promoting a single object, and that object one of
the noblest that ever excited human beings to action ; to raise the lowly,
to comfort the afflicted, to prevent crime and woe, to carry hope and joy
where sorrow and despair had long reigned, to scatter blessings through
the land, and bid the heart of the philanthropist rejoice, — in a word, to
banish from our midst, forever, the monster Intemperance !

The procession took up its line of march at twenty minutes after eleven
o'clock.   The Chief Marshal was followed by the societies and delegates
from the County of Middlesex, preceded by the Naval Washington Total-
Abstinence Society, apprentice boys, and men from the receiving-ship
Ohio, and the Navy Yard temperance seamen.   Then came the Counties
of Essex and Suffolk ; after which, officers of the convention, the reverend
clergy, strangers in the city, and others professing the Washingtonian
principles.   Then, in succession, the Counties of Worcester, Hampshire,
Hampden, Franklin, Berkshire, Norfolk, Bristol, Plymouth, Barnstable,
Nantucket, and Dukes.

There were many banners in the procession, some of which were very
neat and appropriate to the occasion, and attracted much attention.   We
are able to give but a few of the devices and inscriptions.

The banner of the Roxbury Total Abstinence Society represented
Hannah, the daughter of John Hawkins, destroying the hydra of Intemperance.   Another banner in the same delegation represented Christ at
the well with the Woman of Samaria ; motto, " Give me this *water*, that
I thirst not."   The banner of the Dorchester Total Abstinence Society
represented the figure of Hope, beautifully executed ; motto, " Hope for
the fallen."   The East Weymouth Total Abstinence Society had a banner
which displayed a cluster of grapes, and a sheaf of grain ; motto, " *Food,
if eaten ; poison, if drunk.*"   The Fall River Total Abstinence Society had
a banner giving a neat view of Justice with her scales ; motto, " Our
cause is good, and we will do it."   Pawtucket and Central Factory Total
Abstinence Society had a banner with a fine representation of a well ;
motto, —

> " Drink from the bubbling fountain — drink it free ;
> 'Twas good for Samson, and 'tis good for me."

course of people filled the Representatives Hall; every seat was occupied, the galleries were crowded, and many stood in the passage-ways.

On motion of Mr. Holbrook, the four following resolutions were adopted unanimously, and without discussion.

South Boston Total Abstinence Society had a banner representing a rum tavern, with its landlord thrusting out of his doors a poor inebriate; a well in perspective. The Rehoboth Total Abstinence Society had a banner with four views, representing Poverty, Death, Health, and Prosperity. The Boston Temperance Society had a banner with a fountain; motto, "That's the drink for me." The East Cambridge Temperance Union had a banner on which was inscribed, "Kindness the most efficient Law." The banner of the Washington Total Abstinence Society, of Lynn, represented a man drinking from the bucket at a well; motto, "The old Oaken Bucket." This society numbers two thousand four hundred members. The New York Washington Temperance Society bore a banner on which was painted a portrait of Washington; motto, "Total Abstinence from all that Intoxicates." This society also carried a beautiful banner presented to them by the ladies of New York, representing "a happy wife," with appropriate mottoes.

The head of the procession reached the Old State House at twelve o'clock, and a large crowd was collected in State Street to witness the scene. The time occupied in passing, at quick step, was fifteen minutes, and the number of persons in the procession is variously estimated at from three thousand to three thousand five hundred. The number of seamen and apprentices from the receiving-ship Ohio was about three hundred. They were accompanied by the Naval Band, and looked exceedingly well. A detachment of the "Boston Cold Water Army," numbering some hundreds, was also in the procession, with banners representing various emblematic devices.

It is hardly necessary for us to state, that as the procession moved through the principal streets, it attracted the attention of our citizens, who gathered in groups on the sidewalks and door-steps, at the casements and on the house-tops, and welcomed them with warmth, and cheered them as they passed along. Many a silent prayer for their continued success was offered to Heaven by the fair beings who gazed with a deep interest on the scene, and many a blessing was invoked on their heads by the wife, the mother, the sister, or the friend, whose happiness had been destroyed by Intemperance.

Resolved, That we rejoice at this mighty assemblage of free-men — freemen in the highest sense of the word — in this venerable hall, devoted to the great public interests of this ancient Commonwealth; and with our congratulations and thanksgivings we would now mingle fervent prayers to God, that he would bless always this enterprise of benevolence, of religion, of Christian charity; and in making those who act in and for it faithful to their pledges and to all their duties, — that he would cause this great work to be now and forever instrumental in accomplishing the greatest human good.

Resolved, That we see in this and similar conventions throughout the land, a principle in operation about which no question can be raised, as it applies equally to men in every situation in life, and knows no difference in sect or party, whether of politics or religion.

Resolved, That in union for the right there is true strength ; and that to promote such union has been the constant effort of the real friends of temperance. Let every friend of the cause now see to it that he labors for union, that he is ever ready to make a sacrifice of unimportant considerations, in the conviction that by so doing he studies his own progress in the truth, and by his example commends it to the love and obedience of his fellow-men.

Resolved, That reformation from intemperance is the conquest of principle over a most debasing and enslaving habit; and that to secure all the blessings of that reformation it must be followed at once by an untiring industry, which can alone produce true independence, and by an habitual reliance on the divine aid, which can alone deliver from the power of temptation.

Upon the reading of the fifth resolution, a discussion arose, which was commenced by Mr. Grant. This resolution was as follows : —

Resolved, That the unparalleled success of the Washingtonian movement in reforming the drunkard, and inducing the retailer to cease his unholy traffic, affords conclusive evidence that *moral suasion* is the *only* true and proper basis of action in the temperance cause ; and that we therefore earnestly recommend to its friends not to compromise the high and commanding position it now occupies.

Mr. Grant stated that he himself was opposed to the passage of the resolution; he thought it too strong, but that he was instructed by his colleagues to draw it as above. His objection was to the expression, " the only true and proper basis," etc. Mr. Hawkins followed. He said that the rum-seller had no principle. He avowed himself opposed to the resolution as it stood. He wanted the aid of the law. Moral suasion was an excellent thing, but it should go hand in hand with the law. Dr. Jewett next addressed the convention at some length, and advocated the same doctrine as Mr. Hawkins. He did not wish the Washingtonians to prosecute as a society, but he would have individuals do it if they wished. The Doctor thought we must have law as rum-sellers had no principle, or it was so steeped in rum it could not be got at, and they must be driven, as they could not be persuaded. Mr. Baxter moved that the word " only " be stricken out, and Dr. Carpenter withdrawing his amendment, Mr Baxter's passed unanimously; 'the resolution was accepted.

The above report presents but a very brief statement of the addresses made and the arguments adduced by the various speakers, in support of their opinions ; but .there is sufficient to indicate the change that was gradually taking place in the public mind. *Moral suasion,* the law of love, affectionate entreaty with the rum-

seller, had in a great measure failed.   These principles
addressed to *the victims* of the business had been wonderfully successful.   But those thousands of rescued
human beings were not all endowed with such powers
of resistance as to withstand temptation, and the wiles
and blandishments of the tempter.   Hundreds, alas!
were too often entrapped in the net of the destroyer;
such instances were known to have occurred in every
village and town in the United States, where these unholy trades, the making and vending of intoxicating
drinks, were unchecked.

To entreat the rum-seller was, too often, only to invoke insult and denunciation.   The conviction from
this state of facts was fairly and truthfully arrived at,
that no radical cure for the evil could be found, except
in withholding licenses, and, if necessary, a resort to
prohibitory enactments, as in cases of trades regarded
as *nuisances to society;* the object of this convention,
so far as this question was involved, was accomplished
in presenting the subject fairly to the public.   We return to Mr. Hawkins' journal: —

Wednesday, June 1st, 1842. — Rest.   June 2, lectured in
the Town Hall in Manchester, N. H., to a crowded house.
This is a flourishing manufacturing village, destined no doubt
to become a second Lowell; but intemperance prevails here
to some extent.   Lectured again, June 3, in the Town Hall;
the people are waking up to the cause.

After fulfilling a large number of engagements in
New Hampshire, he returned to Boston on the 8th of
June, when he makes this entry in his journal: —

Being much worn down by constant labors, I gave up many

of my appointments in New Hampshire, and shall remain in Boston some days to rest.

Becoming convinced that the climate of Boston was injurious to his wife's health, he determined to take up his residence in Worcester as soon as circumstances would permit. He regarded that town as nearer the centre of the field in which he proposed for several months to labor, and he would there be nearer to his children, who were all, in a short time, to be placed in the academy at Wilbraham.

The people of Worcester were much attached to Mr. Hawkins, on account, perhaps, of the wonderful changes which through his agency the year previous had been wrought among them. A vigorous Washington Temperance Society was formed soon after he delivered his first three lectures in that place. He found also in J. W. Goodrich, Esq., then residing in Worcester, a gentleman of most estimable character, a devoted friend; and during the many years in which he had the editorial care of the *Worcester Waterfall*, he never failed to speak in the most encouraging manner of Mr. Hawkins and his labors. Both have now gone to the enjoyment of the rest above. With these remarks we introduce the following letter from Mr. Hawkins to his son, at the date of which his other children had not been placed at the academy : —

BOSTON, June 15, 1842.

MY DEAR SON, — I fully intended to have removed with the family to Worcester, but your mother was taken very ill yesterday, but is much better to-day; it is thought best by Dr. Channing not to move for a few days.

On Saturday I return to New Hampshire to complete some

20

appointments which I left unfinished; shall return on or about the 30th of this month, and move to Worcester on the 1st of July; and on the 4th be in New York, and return the 7th or 8th. Should you wish, you can come down to Worcester on the morning of the 1st, [July]. If we have, or have not arrived, go to Mr. Congden's; you can spend the 4th there. Remember, this is as you please. I want you to write me immediately on the receipt of this; direct your letter to Boston, whether I am here or not, and let me know *every thing ;* how you get along, with whom you board, and how you like the institution.

I cannot now write what I wish to say to you in regard to your future welfare. I have now an opportunity of giving you a finished education, and wish to see you and talk with you on the subject. I therefore think you had better come down to Worcester, as I shall not have time to come to Wilbraham, and then we will have a talk about "matters and things."

Pray, my son, "and in every thing give thanks," and God will direct your steps aright. Pray for me, pray for the family, read your Bible, read it on your knees with prayer.

While writing, your mother is sitting up and is much better, and entirely out of danger. I am not now under the direction of the Committee.

I know nothing more to write at present.

I remain, my dear son,
Your father, in haste,
JOHN H. W. HAWKINS.

Mr. Hawkins had now successfully completed his engagement with the Boston Committee; their encouragement and patronage had been the means of placing him in a position of extensive usefulness. His earnestness and simplicity of character had everywhere inspired confidence, and applications for his services poured in from all parts of New England. Resuming his labors in New Hampshire on the 18th of June, he visited Franklin, Boscawen, Canterbury, Loudon Village, spending several days in each, and speaking with great effect to large audiences. His journal furnishes evidence of a vast amount of labor performed in each village by constant visiting through the day, in addition to his public lecturing.

His journal continues : —

Thursday, June 23d. — Lectured in Chichester ; something has been done here in the cause; but cider-drinking exerts considerable influence against the cause, as many of the most influential men drink largely, and are therefore a hindrance in the way of the drunkard's reformation. Their influence is now the greatest with which we have to contend in New England ; but we are fast gaining ground.

On the 26th he gave two lectures to the people of Meredith Village ; here a large meeting had assembled. At 2 P.M. he addressed them in a grove near the town, and at 5 P.M. in the " Old Saw Mill "; much feeling was exhibited. He alludes in his journal to a good Temperance House which had been opened in the place. So deep was the interest felt that he was induced to remain the next day, and spoke to an overflowing house ; a large number of pledges were taken. The same enthusiasm followed him to Lake Village, Francestown ; "a beautiful village," "an overflowing house," and "deep interest in the subject of temperance."

On the 1st of July Mr. Hawkins removed with his family to Worcester, and was cordially welcomed. His friend Goodrich thus heralds his coming in the *Waterfall* : —

J. H. W. Hawkins, the celebrated pioneer and efficient advocate of Washingtonian principles, we are authorized to say, has closed his year's engagement with the Boston Committee, has removed his family to Worcester, and will make this the place of his residence. He will then have his time and movements at his own disposal, and will attend to any application for his services, as a Washingtonian Missionary, that may be directed to him at Worcester, post-paid, or to the care of Jesse W. Goodrich.

On the same day of his arrival he "continued his journey to New York, to celebrate the 4th of July, which was done by a mass meeting of the Chelsea Temperance Society, at the foot of 49th Street, in a beautiful grove." " On the 7th of July returned to Worcester, and after some consultation with my family and friends, came to the conclusion to place my daughters Elizabeth and Hannah, with William George and Arthur Holmes, at Wilbraham Academy."

The commemoration of the national independence in 1842 was made the occasion for great rejoicing among the friends of temperance in the United States. Perhaps never before had that day witnessed the assembling together of such large masses of men, women, and children, in churches, in halls, and in groves, to rejoice with each other over the emancipation of thousands from the slavery of a debased appetite. Almost every town in New England, in the Middle, Western, and in most of the Southern States, celebrated the day with processions, speeches, music, and banners. But while there was cause for rejoicing, there was yet much cause for humiliation.

The judicious editor of the American Temperance Union seemed disposed to moderate, and very justly

too, the transports of the people; in the August number of his *Journal* he remarks : —

Many an army has sent up the shout of victory, but an hour
before its downfall. While there are forty million gallons of intoxicating drinks annually sold and drank in the country, it is
no time for a temperance jubilee; and while some ministers
and Christians, patriots and statesmen, and some of our most
enlightened and influential families, will at every social party
circulate and drink fiery liquors, seeming to take pleasure in
bidding defiance, with open windows, to all our efforts, and
even some of the best men in our national councils are dying
of drunkenness, there is cause for humiliation and deep anxiety.
But the 4th of July, 1842, has told great things for us. It was
a day of wonders. Could an angel from heaven have flown
over our land and witnessed, on that day, the hundreds and
thousands of beautiful processions, seen the lost reclaimed to
life, and witnessed the universal sobriety, order, and joy — the
blessedness of ten thousand hearts but recently miserable beyond what language could express in their connection with a
drunken husband and father, surely he would have sounded
long and loud the trump of praise to Him who has remembered
us in mercy. Every political paper agreed in saying that
our city presented an unusual spectacle of sobriety and order.
There were comparatively few booths around the Park and but
little drunkenness was anywhere visible.*

* While Mr. Hawkins was in New York, July 4th, his services in the
cause of temperance did not fail to receive honorable notice at the various
celebrations elsewhere on that day. At the town of Sutton there was a
large gathering, and several distinguished speakers were present; among
them the Rev. John Pierpont, of Boston. Mr. Hawkins' valuable efforts
for the spread of temperance in this town, have already been noticed;
once notorious for its intemperance, it now began to be noted for sobriety.
    After the conclusion of Rev. Mr. Pierpont's speech, which is spoken of
as an able effort, the company sat down to a well-loaded table, in the

Lecturing every day in various parts of Massachusetts, from the 10th to the 17th of July, he returned to
Boston. " On this day, Sunday," he says in his journal, "lectured to the inhabitants of Somerville (a
suburban town of Boston), from the top of Prospect
Hill; the attendance was very large." On the same
day he addressed the following letter to his sister, Mrs.
Schaeffer: —

BOSTON, July 17th, 1842.

MY DEAR SISTER, — I have suffered too much time to pass
without letting you hear from me, knowing how glad you are
at all times to hear from one you so much love. My dear sister, at times I can hardly realize the great contrast in my condition, comparing the past with the present. The longer I live,
and the farther I advance in this holy cause, the greater and
heavier I feel the responsibility resting upon me, and the more
confidence I have that my heavenly Father will sustain me.
Yes, my dear sister, he has sustained me in soul and body, and
I have faith to believe he will continue so to do while I put
my trust in him.

Since my last visit to Baltimore I have been constantly
travelling, and preaching or lecturing; lecturing most of the
time; and the cause has not lost any of its energy in New
England. I think I can say it is gaining confidence, and is
working powerfully on the minds of a class the most difficult
to reach; I mean the *moderate drinker of strong drinks*. He,
like every poor unfortunate drunkard, thinks himself secure in
his own resolutions; and how many ministers of the Gospel,
and professing Christians, of the best standing in church and
state, have tampered with the weakest even of intoxicating
drinks, yes, the purest wine and cider, until it has stung them
to the very soul. No man in first drinking ever intended to

largest hall of the Temperance House. Many sentiments of great beauty
and appropiateness were offered.

make himself a drunkard ; the strongest-minded men that ever lived have been slain by this *monster,* and yet the moderate drinker sings himself to sleep in the arms of self-security, but to wake up and find himself *a drunkard,* and then, the difficulty of reforming, and when reformed, to stay so! He no longer can be a moderate drinker ; his resolutions, his promises, and his prayers, are as empty as the wind ; he has only to see or even smell the poison, and he is borne away by an uncontrollable thirst. Thus he lives a miserable slave to one of the worst appetites formed in man.

My dear sister, I write from experience. None of you ever knew the half of my sufferings, not of body, but of mind. Yes, my dear sister, I was a drunkard ; "and no drunkard," it is said, in the sacred volume, "shall inherit the Kingdom of God." But why dwell so long on the dark side of the picture? Has not our heavenly Father promised life and salvation to the returning prodigal? Yes, my very soul has realized this promise and I am now happy, happy in my family ; and you, with mother, brothers, sisters, all rejoice, that I (by the mercy of God) have been plucked "as a brand from the burning," "and my feet placed on a rock," "with a new song in my mouth," even praise unto Him who "hath redeemed us with his most precious blood."

It will give you all great pleasure to hear that on Wednesday last I sent Elizabeth and Hannah to join William George at Wilbraham Academy, the girls to remain at least one year, if not more. And furthermore, I have made up my mind with William's consent, to fit him for college ; if he lives he will make a professional man ; this is all I can do for them. You will see they are all placed at the same school ; the girls are under the immediate protection of their brother, and, what is best of all, they are seeking the salvation of their souls. Elizabeth is awake, Hannah is awake, and William George is wide awake. What a satisfaction this is to me, and how much gratification it must be to mother, and to you all.

Now the fact is, you and mother must come on here and make us a visit. Let the boys "club together," and send or bring you on, and I will take care of you while you are here; and it will do my heart good to meet and introduce you to some of my friends; and when you want to go home I will furnish you with the means to take you there; so the boys shall not bear all the burden of your expenses. Come! Write me about this immediately, and make a long story short.

My wife, with Arthur and Sallie, have taken their summer residence in Worcester, Mass., one of the most beautiful and healthy villages in the Union. She has gained two pounds since the 4th; her health is fast improving; the children are well. I want you to write me immediately (as I said before), and let me know how you all are, especially whether Uncle Harry keeps his pledge. Send my respects to John Zug by Samuel Martin, and tell him I should like to have him send me one of the books he has published in reference to the Washington Temperance Society.

I spent the 4th in New-York city by special invitation, and had it not been for the many appointments and engagements which constantly occupied my time, I would have come to Baltimore, but shall now wait patiently an answer saying when you and mother will come, for now is the season for a visit to this part of the country. I shall cease my labors for a time to rest and enjoy your society; nothing will be spared to make your visit agreeable.

We all join in love to you all. Direct your answer to Boston; write so as I can get it by the 3d of August. I shall be in the city at that time. I want you to write a long letter to Elizabeth and Hannah, to Wilbraham.

Your brother, affectionately,   JOHN H. W. HAWKINS.

Returning to Worcester for a rest of two days, he wrote the following letter to his children, then at the Wilbraham Academy: —

WORCESTER, July 19, 1842.

MY DEAR SON AND DAUGHTERS, — I arrived here on Monday from a tour of duty in Plymouth County, and to-day and to-morrow (Wednesday and Thursday), I lecture in Groton ; Friday in Shirley. Saturday in Leominster, Sunday in Stirling, Monday in West Boylston, Tuesday in Charlton. Thursday I go again to Plymouth County, commencing at Middleborough Four Corners, where I shall labor till the third of August ; then I think I shall go to New Hampshire. Your mother and Sallie are going with me to Groton ; Arthur will board with Mrs. Congden while we are away. In the mean time she (your mother) will visit Boston ; had I time I should have come up to see you.

My object in writing to you is to let you know that I will return to Worcester from Stirling on Monday or Tuesday next, on my way to Charlton. I therefore wish you to write to me ; direct to Worcester, letting me know how your sisters are situated, and how they like the place ; also what books are wanted, etc., etc.

I intend your mother shall make you a visit shortly, and stay one week at least ; we will write when she will come in time for you to engage a place for her and Sallie.

My dear son, your sisters are under your immediate care ; watch over them affectionately ; love each other, and compare the past with the present. Remember what I once was, and let us join in prayer and praise to our heavenly Father for what he has done for your poor father, by which I have been able to do for you what I could not otherwise have done. My dear Elizabeth, remember you have a soul ; pray to God to convert you and fill your heart with pure and undefiled religion. My dear daughter Hannah, you have commenced early in life to seek the Lord, which gives me inexpressible joy ; never look back until you have found full redemption in the blood of your heavenly Redeemer.

My dear son, what shall I say to you ? Give your heart

entirely to God; watch and pray constantly, relying on God; it may be he will lead you to turn sinners to repentance.

You know that Hannah is not as far advanced as your sister, and that she has not as much confidence; it will require you and your sister's affectionate attention in affording her all the instruction you can without a jar. Give my compliments to your teacher, requesting his or her special attention to her. We are about to leave in the stage, so I must close with my love to you all.   Your father,

JOHN H. W. HAWKINS.

CHAPTER XVI

"Have ye heard of our triumph, that far o'er the nation
  Is sending its echoes so deeply and clear ?
Have ye seen our bright flag with its beams of salvation
  The rainbow of promise that lighted us here ?
Have ye heard that the bands of the tyrant are broken,
  That link after link hath been rent from his chain ?
That the conquest is gained, and the word hath been spoken
  That gives us the gladness of freedom again ? "

AFTER meeting and lecturing to large audiences in the towns referred to in the letter which closed the last chapter, Mr. Hawkins passed on to Halifax, in which town, he remarks, all the liquors have been burned, and the traffic suppressed. He found great interest in the cause and much enthusiasm prevailing in Bridgewater, East Bridgewater, North and South Bridgewater, Weymouth, and Quincy. "This town," he remarks in his journal, " is wide awake ; but there is still one rum-tavern ; but they are determined to drive rum from the town."

He was well received in Dover, Mass., and from thence passing into New Hampshire, he lectured in New Ipswich, Fitzwilliam, Hancock, Mason Village, and Amherst. In Manchester he spent four days, lecturing to very large audiences ; here he found the cause in a most flourishing condition. His former visit was remembered with pleasure. August 18th he closed his tour by a lecture in Hollis, to an attentive and delighted audience. On the 19th of August he returned to Boston ; we quote from his journal : —

Went this day to Eastham camp-meeting, and remained until its meetings broke up. The number of persons who went down from Boston by steamboat, and returned, were as follows:—

```
        Number that went down, adults,.............. 1031
         "     "     "     "   children,........... .   50
                                                      ——
        Total, .....................................  1081

        Number that returned, adults,.........  .... 1108
         "     "     "              children,.............   60
                                                      ——
        Total, .....................................  1168
```

Numbers also proceeded by land; to these were added the multitudes who poured in from the adjoining towns. Here the cause of temperance received large accessions. The addresses of Mr. Hawkins were frequently spoken of by the press as able and happy efforts.

The number who signed, during the continuance of the religious services, are noticed in Mr. Hawkins' journal. Number of pledges, 1200; also of ministers, 72; total, 1272.

It was at this camp-meeting that Mr. Hawkins was reminded of an incident which occurred in Maine while he was on a tour in that State several months previous. It is characteristic of his peculiar mode of approaching the most hopeless cases; it is thus related by the *New-York Organ:*—

At a recent temperance meeting Mr. John Hawkins related the following circumstances which occurred some months since in Brunswick, State of Maine, where he went by invitation to deliver an address. On arriving there an individual informed him that there was one of the most desperate cases at a tan-yard in the vicinity, and expressed a conviction that it would be useless to attempt to save him; however, they decided to make the attempt, and started for the tanyard. On their way they fell in with several gentlemen, who, on learning their errand, resolved to accompany them on their mission of love. Ex-Governor Dunlap, Dr. ——, and others, who rank high among their fellow-men, were of the party, "following," as Mr. Hawkins forcibly observed, "the reformed drunkard, to save the sunken and hopeless inebriate." The person they sought, whose name was Walker, was a man of gigantic stature, raw-boned and muscular, but fearfully had he fallen. As some one of the company made known their object in visiting him, Mr. Hawkins observed the neck of a bottle protruding from his pantaloons pocket. Walker saw the glance, and ere a word had been spoken by Mr. Hawkins, apologized to him with, " Indeed, sir, I cannot do without it."

The conversation now became general, and expostulation and argument for awhile seemed powerless. Turning to the doctor, Walker observed to him, " Sir, you know I cannot reform. Don't you remember the calculation we made some time ago, that I had averaged one quart of liquor per day since my birth, forty-two years ago; and do you now think I could stop drinking?"

After considerable parleying, he promised to attend the meeting that night; and then he took the bottle from his pocket, and digging a hole in a heap of tan, there buried it, saying, " Lay there; I'll not take any more till to-morrow, anyhow." Then turning to those who surrounded him, " Oh," said he, " when the horrors come upon me (as I know they will if I leave off), will you stand by me, will you help me? I will tell you what I want you to do; get a chain and a staple, drive the staple into the floor of the tanhouse, and secure the chain around my body, and then keep by me. Will you promise me this?" The sympathizing gentlemen assured him they would do all in their power, if he would come to the meeting that night and sign the pledge, and left him with a faint hope of effecting his salvation. Night came; Mr. Hawkins went to the

21

church, and almost the first one he saw was poor Walker, in a front seat, apparently all eye and ear.

To use Mr. Hawkins' own words, "When I began to talk *into* him, and at last the tears began to flow, then I felt sure of him! I gave the invitation for those who wished to sign to come forward. Walker rose, stepped out into the broad aisle, came up to the table, and grasping the pen, leaned forward to affix his name, when suddenly he dropped the pen, lifted both hands above his head, clasped them, and thus stood the image of despair, as he exclaimed, "I can't write my name! I can't write my name!" A thrill ran through the assembly, while the wretched man seemed losing the faint ray of hope, and yielding himself to dark, remediless despair. Mr. Hawkins seized the pen, and checking his despondency, reminded him that another could write his name and he affix his cross thereto, and it would be as binding as though entirely his own writing. Again Walker stooped, and made a broad black cross in the place pointed out by Mr. Hawkins, who had written his name, and then with a glad, triumphant glance at his handi-work, took his seat.

The next morning Mr. Hawkins took his departure, and for a few months heard nothing more about his *protegé ;* but a few weeks ago, at a camp-meeting, a Methodist minister informed him that there was to be a temperance meeting in Brunswick the next Sabbath, and Walker was to relate his experience.

In his journal, under date of August 24, we find the following : —

Attended a large picnic at Norton, Mass. The supposed number in attendance was over three thousand ; it was a glorious time ; speakers present were Rev. John Pierpont, Dr. Charles Jewett, Mr. Woodman, &c.

Mr. Hawkins spent a part of the week succeeding the above meeting in various parts of Rhode Island, lecturing several times in Bristol. He found the cause in a state of depression, " in consequence," as he remarks, " of the political difficulties from which the people were at this time suffering."

On returning, he addressed a meeting of children on " the Green " at Taunton, giving two evenings to the people. He addressed a crowded house next day, August 31, in Foxboro, Mass.

September 1st. — Attended a picnic in Brookline — a delightful time.

We append in a note an interesting account of this picnic, by one who was present, which we find in the *Mercantile Journal.* *

* THE PICNIC AT BROOKLINE. — The Ladies' Grand Picnic, and Washingtonian and Cold Water Army Celebration, at Brookline, yesterday, was one of the most delightful celebrations of the kind which has ever taken place. The day was beautiful, the place very happily chosen, and all the arrangements were made and carried out in the most perfect manner. About ten o'clock in the forenoon, the procession, headed by the Brigade Band, was formed at the Baptist meeting-house, under the direction of Samuel A. Walker, Chief Marshal, and took up its line of march to the Rev. Dr. Pierce's church, about half a mile distant, which was very tastefully decorated with temperance banners, bearing appropriate devices and mottoes. At the church, the exercises were opened by the song, " Come ye children, learn to sing," sung by the Cold Water Army, a numerous body of children of both sexes. This was followed by prayer, and then the song, " If for pleasure, health or treasure," was sung. Next followed addresses by the Rev. E. Thompson of Dedham, E. K. Whittaker, of Needham, Daniel Kimball, of Ipswich, John Hawkins, and the Rev. Mr. Shaler, of Brookline. The addresses were all short, and pertinent to the occasion, and some of them were eloquent and impressive. Mr. Hawkins spoke with even more than his usual effect, and brought tears to many eyes by the force and beauty of his descriptions. The procession was again formed, and marched to the place where the dinner was to take place — a beautiful grove about a

On the 2d day of September Mr. Hawkins returned again to New Hampshire, and visited a number of towns where he had not been, including a few where societies had already been formed.

The attendance on his lectures was large and the interest unabated. From Keene he wrote the following letter to his son: —

KEENE, N. H., Sept. 8th, 1842.

MY DEAR SON, — I have just time to write a few lines to you and your sisters, to inform you my health is very good. I hope you and your sisters are in good health, and in the enjoyment of much of the love of God. What pleasure it gives me to know you are all together, at so good a school, and trying to serve God and save your immortal souls. O my dear children, pray for your poor father; remember the pit from which God in his mercy has raised me. Rejoice in God, for he has become our salvation and our song. I want to see you all very much.

By a paper I send you, you will see my appointments, which will end on the 22d inst. I shall be in Boston on the 23d, in Worcester on the 24th, and, if I can, I will try and pay you a visit on the 25th.

Your mother is to spend a week with you before we go to Baltimore. I want to be there on the 28th September, which is my forty-fifth birthday. Your mother will return to Worcester on or about the 15th inst., to prepare herself for the intended visit. I wish you to write immediately; direct your letter to Milford, N. H. I shall be there Saturday and Sun-

mile from the church. Speeches, songs and sentiments followed, with such rapidity and in such profusion that we have not space to report them, and are compelled to give but two, as a specimen of the rest. John Hawkins gave, "The temperance cause; may nothing impede its ultimate triumph;" by another, "Cider; the *nest-egg* of intemperance."

day, 17th and 18th. I feel anxious to hear from you; don't fail to write. Love to mother and sisters.

Affectionately, your father,

JOHN H. W. HAWKINS.

His visit to Baltimore was a delightful one; meeting there many relatives who loved him, and that aged mother whose prayers had never been intermitted for her son's return to the paths of virtue and religion. The reunion on that forty-fifth birthday, September 28th, 1842, where parents, brothers, sisters, nephews, and nieces, interchanged their thoughts and feelings, filled his heart with gratitude and joy. Nor did he forget his brethren in the cause of temperance; he visited their meetings night after night, and encouraged them in their progress.

That veteran in the good cause, Christian Keener, of Baltimore, thus writes in the *Herald*, referring to Mr. Hawkins' visit: —

John Hawkins, the famous Apostle of Temperance, is among us again, receiving hearty welcome wherever he goes, and imparting power to every society he addresses.

Mr. Hawkins left Baltimore on the 11th of October, and reached New York in time for "The Croton Jubilee," which took place on the 14th. It was an occasion of great rejoicing. The day was ushered in by the firing of one hundred guns. At ten o'clock precisely, the procession began to move from the Battery; between twelve and fifteen thousand men marched in its ranks; the procession extended seven miles. The most striking fact in this celebration was its temperance character, the procession being in a large measure com-

21*

posed of teetotalers. Many temperance men marched
in the ranks of the military and fire companies. Between two and three hundred thousand people were
abroad on that day fraught with so many blessings to
the city. And yet, in this vast multitude, scarce a
drunken man was to be found; but few arrests were
made, and " during the ensuing night," says Dr. Marsh,
" none were committed for drunkenness." In the address
made by Samuel Stevens, Esq., in behalf of the Board
of Water Commissioners, a highly complimentary allusion was made to the beneficial effects of the temperance reformation upon the city, its internal quiet, and
greater domestic enjoyment.

The following lines composed by George P. Morris,
Esq., were sung at the Park fountain. Their appropriateness, their classic beauty and taste, and the exqui-
site fancy which flows along almost every line, render
them worthy of preservation. While more ancient as
well as more modern poets have thought it worth their
while to sing the praises of the sparkling wine, it is re-
freshing to recur to what was said of cold water in
October, 1842, when rushing up from the fountain's
depth, it flashed in sight of the good people of New
York, on that memorable day: —

> Gushing from this living fountain
>   Music pours a falling strain,
> As the goddess of the mountain
>   Comes with all her sparkling train.
> From her grotto-springs advancing,
>   Glittering in her feathery spray,
> Woodland fays beside her dancing,
>   She pursues her winding way.
>
> Gently o'er the rippling water,
>   In her coral-shallop bright,

Glides the rock-king's dove-eyed daughter
  Decked in robes of virgin white.
Nymphs and Naiads, sweetly smiling,
  Urge her bark with pearly hand,
Merrily the sylph beguiling,
  From the nooks of fairy land.

Swimming on the snow-curled billow,
  See the river-spirits fair,
Lay their cheeks, as on a pillow,
  With the foam-beads in their hair.
Thus attended, hither wending,
  Floats the lovely Oread now,
Eden's arch of promise bending
  Over her translucent brow.

Hail the wanderer from a far-land!
  Bind her flowing tresses up!
Crown her with a fadeless garland,
  And with crystal brim the cup.
From her haunts of deep seclusion,
  Let Intemperance greet her too,
And the heat of his delusion
  Sprinkle with this mountain-dew.

Water leaps as if delighted,
  While her conquered foes retire!
Pale Contagion flies affrighted
  With the baffled demon, Fire!
Safety dwells in her dominions,
  Health and Beauty with her move,
And entwine their circling pinions
  In a sisterhood of love.

Water shouts a glad hosanna!
  Bubbles up the earth to bless!
Cheers it like the precious manna,
  In the barren wilderness.
Here we wondering gaze, assembled
  Like the grateful Hebrew band,
When the hidden fountain trembled,
  And obeyed the prophet's wand.

Round the aqueducts of story,
  As the mists of Lethe throng,
Croton's waves, in all their glory,
  Troop in melody along.
Ever sparkling, bright and single,
  Will this rock-ribbed stream appear,
When posterity shall mingle,
  Like the gathered waters here.

Mr. Hawkins returned to Boston on the 19th of October, and passed the remainder of the month in New Hampshire, visiting and lecturing in fifteen towns with great success. November 4th, 5th, 6th, and 7th, he spent in Nantucket. This visit is spoken of in the papers of the day as a highly successful one; many reformations were effected, and temperance men were much encouraged.

After visiting several other towns he returned to Boston, from which place he wrote the following letter to his children : —

BOSTON, Nov. 17, 1842.

MY DEAR SON AND DAUGHTERS, — Since I saw you I have been lecturing most of the time in New Hampshire. I am now here attending a protracted temperance meeting now being held in Faneuil Hall; it commenced last night and will continue during the week. It is a union of all temperance men to take into consideration the alarming increase of grog-shops in this city, and to prosecute indiscriminately all who sell without license ; and there is not one licensed seller in the city. I will send you the papers containing the proceedings when published. I have not heard from Baltimore since I left. I received your letter dated 13th, and was glad to hear you were well. I feel a great anxiety about you and your sisters. Do you pray often and in secret? Do you read your Bible on your knees with prayer? Do you watch your thoughts and words? O my dear children, how thankful we all should be, especially that our situation in life has been so changed, and above all that I am no longer a drunkard, but able to educate and provide for my dear children, and striving to do all in my power to bring the poor drunkard into paths of sobriety, and point him to the " Lamb of God that taketh away the sin of the world." My dear children, pray for us that God may keep us by his power.

I expect soon to have some appointments in your part of the country, and shall call and spend a day or two with you. I send, enclosed in this, thirty dollars, to pay your expenses. I was much pleased to hear you had so pleasant a time in Middletown. But I must close for want of time. Write me a letter, a full one, how your sisters and yourself are progressing; be particular; I want to know especially about Hannah. Mail your letter on the 25th. I shall be in Boston the next day.

In your answer to this let me know what will be the entire amount of your bill, board, tuition, etc., etc., to the end of the term, and when this term will end.

I remain, my dear children,

Your father, very affectionately,

JOHN H. W. HAWKINS.

On the 16th, 17th, and 18th of November, Mr. Hawkins attended several extraordinary meetings of the citizens of Boston, held in Faneuil Hall, for the purpose of devising measures to check the alarming increase of dram-shops in the city. The debates were animating, and exerted an exceedingly beneficial influence upon the citizens. Temperance men of the old and the new schools united harmoniously; John Tappan, Moses Grant, Dr. Walter Channing, John Hawkins, Rev. J. Pierpont, and many others, moving shoulder to shoulder in the great enterprise.

The remainder of the year was spent by Mr. Hawkins in visiting a large number of towns in Massachusetts.   His visit to Hampshire is thus spoken of by the editor of the *Hampshire Washingtonian:* —

'This indefatigable lecturer has been visiting the towns in this county.   We have visited many of these towns since his lectures, and the universal approbation of the people is not only given, but they ask when can we have him again?   This is truly gratifying to the Washingtonians, and serves to induce them to renewed exertions and to hold them more firmly together.   Mr. Hawkins will do much in dispelling the fears of the timid in relation to the partisan purposes into which this great and good cause was thought to be merged, and enlist thousands in its favor who have as yet taken " no part or lot in the matter."

He speaks in his journal of addressing large meetings in Northampton, Montague, Sunderland, Hadley, Amherst, South Hadley, East Hampton, Williamsburg, Whately, and Greenfield.   From East Hampton he wrote to his children as follows: —

EAST HAMPTON, Dec. 27, 1842.

MY DEAR SON, — I have just a moment to spare to inform you that I have written to your mother to send Arthur up to Wilbraham.   He is to take the seven o'clock train of cars on the fourteenth day of January, which will be Saturday ; you will therefore be at the depot to receive him.   This will not interfere with your going to West Boylston on the eighteenth as contemplated.   He can be with your sisters, who I know will treat him kindly ; remember he is a poor little orphan, depending on me as a father and protector.   I have all confidence in placing him under the care of you and your sisters.

Yesterday I was at South Hadley, and lectured to a crowded audience ; this you know is the location of the far-famed Mt. Holyoke Seminary for young ladies, many of whom attended my lecture. In the afternoon I spent several hours at the institution, going through it and being introduced to the teachers and students. I was accompanied by the President, Rev. Mr. Hawks, and the Principal, Miss Lyon. I never saw an institution equal to it in all my travels; it is the most complete in all its arrangements of any in this country. It has, in a measure, been misrepresented in regard to the domestic labor imposed upon its students. I am decidedly in favor of it, as being wise and healthy. I intend that you and your sisters with me shall pay the institution a visit before I return to Boston.

Mr. Hawks, the President, intends, by my request, to write to you for the purpose of advising and giving you some good instruction in regard to your future prospects. I told him that your mind was directed to the study of the ministry; he was very much pleased. In conversation with him, he said he would advise me to put you, at the proper time, with some worthy, pious clergyman, to receive of him private instruction in his family; this will be a matter for conversation when we meet.

My dear son and daughters, you cannot imagine the anxiety I feel for you in regard to your education, as well as in other matters. Be diligent! Love each other! Tell Elizabeth and Hannah to love each other, and endeavor to make each other happy. I shall probably be in Wilbraham about the last of January.

My dear children, give your whole soul to God in prayer; he has done much for me, whereof we have cause to be glad. Pray for me; and that God may of his infinite goodness and mercy bless and keep you by his power, unto everlasting life, is the prayer of your dear father,

JOHN H. W. HAWKINS.

During the early part of January, 1843, we find Mr. Hawkins in Boston, delivering addresses several even-

ings during the week, and visiting the intemperate and
the recently reformed during the day.   Sunday, January 15th, he lectured in the Bethel in North Square;
the daily papers spoke of the audience as being "large
and highly respectable."   "The audience seemed gratified to welcome that long-tried friend of the drunkard,
and able lecturer on the cause of temperance, J. H. W.
Hawkins.   He enchained the attention while describing
the magic transformations which the pledge, under
God, had effected."   On the 15th he departed on a
tour of lecturing through a part of Worcester County
We make the following extract from his journal: —

I lectured in Gardner, Monday, January 16; crowded house;
the people seem to be awake to the subject, and have done
much to advance the cause.   There is a Temperance House in
this place; it was formerly a dram-shop, kept by a CLERGY-
MAN.   My next visit was to Hubbardston (17th).   The
cause has progressed here rapidly, notwithstanding the opposition; they are cursed with two rum-taverns and two rum-
stores; their time, however, is short.   They are, however,
blessed with a fine set of young men.   It is said that there is
not a young man in the town who has any pretension to respectability, that drinks a drop of intoxicating liquor; and, much
to their credit, they have formed themselves into a company,
not exactly a military company, called the Hubbardston
Washingtonian Guards.   No young gentleman can be admitted into the company without first signing the pledge.   In the
fall they visited Fitchburg, at a military parade, and did themselves much credit.   They are commanded by Charles O. Bar-
rows, Esq., a fine-looking young man, and as fair a specimen
of a *cold water man* as I ever looked upon.   Their uniform
consists of a plain blue coat, white pants, with a dark stripe
down the side, blue sash, cap with gold lace; their arms a
wooden spear; their number is forty-five, and increasing.   They

did me the honor of escorting me to the church, taking their seats in the body of the house. My next visit, Wednesday, was to Templeton; the meeting was not attended as well as I had expected, owing no doubt to a Miller meeting held in the Town Hall the same evening. There, also, much has been done, notwithstanding much opposition. The landlord had better sign the pledge and save himself. They are cursed here with rum in three taverns and one store. These are approbated by a selectman, a deacon of a church, whose character as a *man* and a *Christian* is *unblemished,* notwithstanding he was put into office last spring, since this great reform commenced, and therefore could not be blind to the "*sinning effects.*" Oh! how long will the people suffer these pitfalls to be left uncovered for their *children* and the poor drunkard to fall into? The reformation of the drunkard, the past and present condition of his family, imperatively demand that they be closed up, and that immediately. The inmates of our almshouses and houses of correction, and more beseechingly do the inmates of our States prisons, call upon the powers that be, to pity their condition, and to remove the temptation out of their way, that when they come again into the world they may be able to stand. "He that knoweth my will and doeth it not, shall be beaten with many stripes." Lectured in Phillipston, Thursday, January 19, to a crowded house. Much has been done here to suppress intemperance. The sale of rum is not licensed in the town, yet they have to contend against the influence of the surrounding towns. Lectured in Petersham, Friday, Jan. 20th. It has been up-stream work in this place, yet much has been done. Lectured in the Orthodox Church; it was crowded to overflowing; the people much interested, and many signed the pledge. Lectured at Athol, Saturday and Sunday. This place has done much in the good cause. Rum, however, is sold in a tavern in the village, approbated by a selectman, a member of the church, and a *member of the Washington Temperance Society.* O consistency! Monday, lectured in Royalston; this

22

is a teetotal town; no license is granted to make drunkards, paupers, and thieves, for the public good. Tuesday, lectured in Winchendon; they have done well in this town; the Cold Water Army is wide awake."

We make the following extract from the *Journal* of the Rev. Dr. Marsh, of New York :—

A letter from our friend Hawkins, dated, Boston, Feb. 20th, says, — "I am still travelling, and doing all I can, in my weakness, but in the *strength* of God, to save the poor drunkard. I have witnessed many, very many happy scenes of reformation. I long to see you, to talk to you, and relate some of them to you. I know they would warm up your heart. I see from the papers you are going ahead in your city. We are doing well here in this city; in fact, the cause is in a most prosperous condition throughout New England.

"I have travelled, since March, 1841, over seventeen thousand miles, and delivered over seven hundred addresses, and these not very short. You may judge from this that my labor has been very great. But what is it for? Thanks be to God for the thought, it is for the reformation of the poor drunkard, and the ultimate salvation of his soul. Now, some would say, there is too much religion in this. Oh! how can any one say so? especially the reformed drunkard, when he owes gratitude to God for every drop of water that he drinks."

We are sorry to see, by a public statement which has been drawn out from Mr. Hawkins, that he has been very poorly supported. Such things ought not so to be. If any men should be well sustained it should be the men who are doing the good in our country that John Hawkins is.

The following letter shows that the Bostonians, at least, were not indifferent to the temporal comfort of Mr. Hawkins and his family :—

BOSTON, March 31st, 1843.

MY DEAR CHILDREN, — My object in writing you at this time is to inform you that on next Fast-day eve the Boston Temperance Society propose to give a concert in Marlboro' Chapel, for my benefit. We are anxious that you should be here. I have, therefore, enclosed ten dollars to pay your fare on the railroad : this will more than pay for yourself and sisters. Arthur will remain at school, and when his aunt and sister come up he shall take a trip with them to Springfield. I want him to be a good boy and I will reward him for it.

You, with your sisters, will take the cars on the morning of Wednesday, the 5th day of April. I am to be in Holliston, five or six miles from Framingham, on Tuesday evening, and will meet you in Framingham on the morning train ; I need not say, Do not fail to meet me.

My respects to Mr. Goodnow and wife, the young ladies, and the keeper of the boarding-house.

Your father, affectionately,   J. H. W. HAWKINS.

We have omitted to mention a very important meeting, held in Faneuil Hall, Boston, on the 22d of February, Washington's birthday, and which was continued on four succeeding evenings. The object of these meetings was to arouse public sentiment to the iniquity of the traffic in intoxicating drinks, and to devise measures for its abatement or entire suppression. Men of distinction and influence united in the movement. Addresses were made by Dr. Warren, Mr. Brimmer, the Mayor, General Lyman, Mr. Rantoul, and Mr. Hawkins. The house on Friday evening was filled to its utmost capacity ; the galleries were crowded with ladies. At one of the meetings several fire companies were present, the members of which were all temperance men. We can find room for a part only of Mr.

Hawkins' remarks, as they were reported in one of the daily papers. They were spoken of as being peculiarly eloquent and effective.

He said he could not look back on his past life without emotion, and recall to memory his former intemperate habits, and reflect that it was not three years since he had signed the pledge. He spoke of the terrible evils which intemperance had caused to the hard-working mechanic and laborer. This was the class which had contributed most to the support of the still and the brewery, and this they had done at a terrible expense — at the expense of property, honor, their own happiness, and the happiness of their families. He said that if the ravages of intemperance were confined to the most worthless of society it would not be so bad; but its victims were frequently found among the best workmen, and those who possessed many estimable qualities. He traced the progress of the temperance reform from 1823 to the present time, and paid a beautiful passing tribute to those noble minds who, in the face of public opinion, dared then come forward and attempt to close the floodgates of intemperance. He spoke of the habit of drinking wine, and rejoiced that all distinctions in the character of the drink used no longer existed — that the brandy-drinker and the wine-bibber, the poor and the rich, all stood on the same platform and saw themselves through the same glass. He quoted a beautiful sentiment from an address of Father Matthew, that "Temperance was a green spot in the desert of life, where all men could meet in peace and harmony." He rejoiced to see men of influence and standing enter into the temperance ranks and give their aid to the cause.

The seventh anniversary of the American Temperance Union was held on the 11th of May, 1843, in the city of New York. Chancellor Walworth was chosen President, and the Hon. Theodore Frelinghuysen, Vice

President. It was an occasion of great interest, and resolutions were passed expressive of the liveliest gratitude to Almighty God for the progress that had been made in abating intemperance during the past year. The meeting in the evening, at the Broadway Tabernacle, called together an immense assemblage, to listen to the report of the Secretary, and the addresses expected from distinguished individuals known to be in the city. Effective speeches were made by Hon. George S. Catlin, of Connecticut, Dr. Patton, and Rev. John Chambers. Mr. Hawkins was present, but preferred being a listener to the older friends of the cause. He did, however, make a few remarks, under the circumstances thus referred to by Dr. Marsh. At the conclusion of Rev. Mr. Chambers' remarks, the Secretary stated that he had hoped to have the pleasure of introducing the Rev. Dr. Beecher to the meeting, one of the old pioneers who first caused his battle-axe to ring on the walls of King Alcohol, sending terror into the heart of the demon and his allies, but he was engaged in speaking in another part of the city; and as Mr. Hawkins, the apostle of Washingtonianism, who had been announced, wished to be excused from speaking, the meeting would be closed by another song from the vocalists of New Hampshire (the Hutchinsons). The name of " Hawkins," however, was loudly called from several parts of the house, and Mr. Hawkins came on to the platform made a short speech of unusual power and a heart-touching appeal. Before he closed Dr. Beecher entered, and came upon the platform amid the cheers of the immense audience. Mr. Hawkins expressed his most lively gratitude at being permitted for

22*

the first time to set his eyes upon Father Beecher, whose six sermons had often strengthened, cheered, and animated his heart. He said he would gladly give way to him that he might hear the same words from his own lips. He sat down amid deafening applause.

CHAPTER XVII.

"Hurrah! hurrah! we've burst the chain
O God! how long it bound us!
We run! we leap! O God again
Thy light, thy air surround us.
From midnight's dungeon-depths brought out,
We hail Hope's rising star;
Ho, comrades, give a stirring shout,
Hurrah! hurrah! hurrah!"

Mr. HAWKINS having completed his engagements in the following places, delivering effective and stirring addresses in each; viz., West Brookfield, Springfield, Cabotville, West Springfield, Hartford, Wethersfield, Middletown, New Haven, Bridgeport, and Danbury, made his arrangements for an extensive tour in middle and western New York.

On reaching Albany he commenced the following letter to his sister, Mrs. Schaeffer, which he did not conclude until he reached the Falls of Niagara: —

ALBANY, June 15, 1843.

My DEAR SISTER, — I promised that you should hear from me upon my arrival in New York. I have neglected to comply with my promise, for the want of sufficient matter to communicate; I need not ask your forgiveness.

My wife did not meet me here until Surday morning, June 4th, on account of her health, which has in a good measure improved. We are stopping with Mr. Jonas Wickes, who is the clerk of Albany County Court; I stopped with him a year ago last January, when on a visit to   city. He is is a very kind and good man. I shall be here for several days. My wife will go to Wilbraham when I leave here, and stay with the children to see to their clothes, &c., &c., and meet me at Saratoga Springs about the middle of July, spending a few days there.

What a pleasant jaunt; I wish you could be with us. She will leave S—— with the other children, so as not to be encumbered and her pleasure consequently lessened. After our tarry at the Springs, we shall return to Boston by the way of Wilbraham, stopping there a few days.

You see by the above that I do not at present settle in New-York city, owing to the difficulty in raising funds for my support. Since I left you I have been to New London * and Sag Harbor (on 'Long Island), by special invitation, to lecture; they were very kind to me.

We left New York on the morning of Wednesday, June 14th, for Albany, in the large steamboat Empire; the longest boat, it is said, in the United States, being three hundred and thirty-five feet in length. The fare was fifty cents, distance one hundred and fifty miles; sometimes the fare is as low as twenty-five cents, and even twelve and a half cents, the opposition is so great.

I have laid out for myself a large field of labor in western New York, ending at Buffalo, and thence to Niagara Falls, taking in my route the principal towns on the great Western Railroad and Erie canal, and returning the same route, take in some of the same towns in connection with others, and shall endeavor to be at Saratoga Springs by the middle of July, if possible, where I have a *special* invitation to speak to drunkards and drunkenness in *high places.*

---

* Of the results of this visit the *Journal* of the American Temperance Union remarks : —

"New London, Ct. — John Hawkins has lately visited this city and delivered three temperance speeches. At a recent election for city officers, the temperance men ran a ticket of their own, which was carried by an overwhelming majority."

NIAGARA FALLS, July 7, 1843.

MY DEAR SISTER,—You will see by the above, that I commenced writing you while in Albany, and not only finish that letter, but commence writing another on the same sheet, at this, as it were, the great "jumping-off place" of the United States. The grand cataract of Niagara! the most sublime sight I ever beheld! It would be useless for me to attempt to give you any thing like a correct description of the sight which my eyes are now resting upon from the window of my room, in the "Exchange Temperance Hotel." I stop, and solemnly lay down my pen, and adore the goodness and greatness of God in his wondrous works; his ways indeed "are past finding out." Only think! that over this stupendous cataract, passes nearly all the water of the great lakes; first, Lake Michigan into and through Lake Huron, thence through Lake Superior, all of these emptying their surplus waters into Lake Erie, and passing onward through Niagara River, over the Falls into Lake Ontario, thence into the river St. Lawrence, and thence into the mighty deep. What a feeding of the mighty ocean, upon whose waters so many human beings are constantly passing and repassing; where thousands of poor, suffering wretches, seeking an asylum in our happy land, too often find a watery grave, and thus suddenly appear before the Great Judge of heaven and earth, with all their sins upon their guilty heads! oh, what awful thoughts rush upon the mind when we contemplate the dying and the dead! Great God, upon what a slender thread hangs all that we have and are. My dear sister, he has been your friend, he has indeed been mine. Oh, what shall we render to him for all his forbearances and his mercies? to God be all the glory! to man the boundless bliss; and this far more than he deserves.

The following is a list of the towns where I have lectured on my way to this place: Schenectady, Utica, Syracuse, Auburn, Rochester, Buffalo, where I spent the 4th of July, and where we had indeed a glorious temperance time. I remain here at

the Falls and lecture two evenings. Saturday and Sunday
(8th and 9th), I spend in Lockport, then returning to Buffalo by way of the Falls, stop in Buffalo by previous engagement to lecture on Tuesday, July 11th.   On the next day I
leave on my return home to Boston, taking the following places
in my route ; it may take me till the last of the month before
I reach the Springs ; you shall then hear from me again : Batavia, Rochester, Geneva, Auburn, where I hope to be on Sunday, July 16th, to address the inmates of the State Prison,
seven hundred in number, by special engagement on the
part of the prisoners; thence to Syracuse, Rome, Little Falls,
Schenectady, and thence to Saratoga Springs, where I hope
to meet my wife in good health and spirits.   Remaining
there a few days, I take the cars and boat to Albany, then the
railroad over the Berkshire hills to Wilbraham, where the
children will hail us with joy and gladness.   As God has so
kindly protected me from harm and accident in all my travels,
I pray he will still continue to take care of me, and bless my
labors, ever keeping me humble before him, remembering that
" he that humbleth himself shall be exalted, and he that exalt-
eth himself shall be abased."   My dear sister, pray for me ;
and may all my friends pray for me.   My position in society
is a responsible one, but God is on my side ; I should, therefore,
have nothing to fear, but trust in him, and follow him as my
leader, and fear no danger.   The path of duty is the way of
safety.   At this moment, while I write, I am called to dinner.

The " Falls " is literally crammed with strangers coming
and going, from all parts of the United States and Canada.
After dinner I took the stage, which runs every hour for the
Rapids and Whirlpool, about three miles below the Falls ;
what a grand and awful sight, to see such a body of water
rushing through a narrow defile of about one hundred yards wide,
dashing and whirling with the appearance of wicked anger, as
if it was striving to tear up the very foundations of the earth.

I came near forgetting to give you a short description of

my journey to this place from Buffalo. I left Buffalo in the steamboat Waterloo; proceeding down the Niagara River, we stopped
and landed some passengers at Schlosser, about three miles above
the Falls; the wharf where we landed them was the one from
which the Canadians cut adrift the steamboat Caroline, set her
on fire, and then towed her into the stream, and sent her over
the Falls. From this place we passed over to Chippewa, on
the Canadian side. There we all landed and took the cars
through this portion of Canada, and arrived at the foot of the
Falls. There we crossed over to the American side just below
and almost under the great Cataract, amidst the boiling surges.
The only way of safely crossing here is in strong row-boats
built expressly for the purpose, having for their oarsmen strong
men, who understand how to tug against the raging waters that
lash the rocks and banks of the river in angry fury. After
landing we ascended a stairway, made with great difficulty up
the almost perpendicular side of the river's bank, more than
two hundred feet in height. Arriving at the top, we have the
Falls in full view, with the awful deep below. The traveller
is now well paid for the fatigues of his journey in getting here,
many of them not very slight. In crossing the river in the
steamboat already mentioned, three miles above the Falls, we
are exposed to great hazard. If the boat should become dis-
abled and unmanageable, she must inevitably — there is no
way of escape — go over the Falls and be dashed in pieces.
But, to guard against dangers of this kind, the anchors are
made ready, the men stand by, and in case of accident they
are thrown over, which is the only means of safety. I have
written you a long letter; I know, however, it is not too long,
as you are always glad to hear from me. Had I more space
I could have spread out my thoughts more, for I had much
more to say. My love to *all*.

Very affectionately, your brother,   JOHN.

While at Albany he addressed the following brief
note to his children : —

ALBANY, June 16th, 1843.

MY DEAR CHILDREN, — This will inform you where I am, and of my usual good health, for which I feel thankful to my heavenly Father, who has indeed dealt very kindly with me. He has, as you know, raised me out of the pit of wretchedness, "put a new song in my mouth," and made me the happy, humble instrument in his hands of saving my fellow-men. My dear children, you have, with me, great cause indeed to rejoice in the "God of your salvation," for what he has done for me.

If either of you have grown lukewarm, and have cause to reproach yourselves for your want of zeal, go straight to the throne of grace, go to your heavenly Father, who "heareth in secret, and he will reward you openly." O my dear children, you do not know how anxious I feel for your temporal, and more especially for your spiritual, welfare. My dear son, permit me to say to you in solemn seriousness, prepare yourself, for I feel that God has a work for you to do in calling sinners to repentance. I have a great deal to say, but must defer it till some other time.

Probably, I shall be with you some time in July; you shall hear. I send you in a small bundle two fine pineapples; you must take care they do not make you sick.

It is *important* to me, the moment you receive this and read it, that you answer it, that it may come by return mail (of Monday), and let me know the day of vacation.

Your father, affectionately,   JOHN H. W. HAWKINS.

The foregoing letters furnish no statement of what Mr. Hawkins accomplished in the various towns visited; this he gave in detail in his letters to the *New-England Washingtonian,* published in Boston; and even those letters do not contain full information of his labors through the day, in each place visited, which he usually spent in calling upon unfortunate men and women at their humble dwellings.

Nor were his services unappreciated in the mansions of the wealthy. On one occasion he received a note in the hand-writing of a female, desiring him to call at her residence at an hour appointed. He repaired there at the time specified, conjecturing that it was the case of a wife or mother, solicitous for the rescue of a husband or a son from intemperance. He found the residence on one of the most fashionable streets in the city, exhibiting every appearance of luxury and wealth. Having announced his name, he was asked to walk into the drawing-room. In a few moments the lady entered, magnificently attired. He was gratefully and modestly received ; but what was his astonishment on being informed that the person before him had sent for him to consult and advise with him in regard to *her own* habits of intemperance, which she feared were rapidly working out the ruin of her soul and body. She made a full confession of her sin, with tearful eyes, appealing to him as if he alone possessed the power of rescuing her. He gave her the best advice he could, and had the pleasure afterwards of hearing of her entire restoration to sobriety and peace of mind. Mr. Hawkins never divulged the name of the party, or the scene of this incident.

We make the following extracts from his letter to the *Washingtonian*, before referred to.

BUFFALO, July 6, 1843.

To the Editor of the Washingtonian:

RESPECTED FRIEND, — When I parted from you in New London, June 12th, I promised I would write you. I have neglected to do so until this time for want of accumulated interesting matter. I hope it will not be uninteresting to sketch briefly my sojournings, etc.

My passage to Albany by steamer Empire was delightful.
I at once reported myself to the friends of temperance,
who immediately went about getting up meetings for me, by
publishing notice of them in the papers, and by posting handbills all over the city, stating that I would lecture at the Washingtonian Hall on Thursday, Friday, and Saturday evenings. No
address, however, was given, for there were not enough people
at all the meetings put together to fill a common country school-
house. At this period the people of Albany are but little
aroused to the evils that afflict their city. The weather was
good. I give you the facts without comment; they, in this
case, are sufficiently indicative of the state of feeling there.
This is certainly the hardest place I have found in twenty
thousand miles travelling. I lectured in Troy on Monday and
Tuesday, the 19th and 20th inst.; they have done much here
in the cause. I had made appointments in Lansingburg and
Waterford, but was so ill with influenza that I could not fill
them. As soon as I got better I went down the river to
Hudson to fill appointments there. Lectured on Saturday and
Sunday to crowded audiences in the court house. They have
done a great deal here in the cause of temperance.

While Mr. Hawkins was at Hudson another effort
was made in Albany to rally the friends of the cause.
Notice was given on Sunday in many of the churches,
some of the ministers refusing to read the notice, that
there would be a lecture in the Rev. Dr. Welch's Church
on Monday evening. Monday evening came and the
vestry was about half filled. Mr. Hawkins remarks
that several of the clergy of Albany refused to sympathize with the new movement, and adds, " I make no
comments."

     * * * On Tuesday I took my departure in the cars, the
fastest mode of travel, for Schenectady, and lectured at night
to a crowded house. They are wide awake here; I shall stop

here again on my return. I don't know that I shall pass through Albany; if I do I think it will be in a hurry. There is a good Temperance House in Schenectady; I recommend it to the temperance public. Wednesday arrived in Utica. Found a good Temperance House; its proprietor, Mr. Ray, I found an obliging landlord; his house is convenient to the canal and railroad. Utica has done more than most places in the reformation of the drunkard. They have made thorough work of it. Thursday, June 29th, I lectured to a good audience at Syracuse. I shall stop again on my return. I was met here by a delegation of temperance men from Auburn, who gladly welcomed me to their city. On Friday, June 30th, I lectured to a large audience at Auburn; much has been done here; I shall stop here again on my return. Saturday and Sunday, July 1st and 2d, in Rochester. Here they came near taxing me beyond my powers of endurance, making four appointments for me to lecture on Sunday; I filled them to the best of my ability. At night I lectured in the theatre; it was a perfect jam, pit and gallery; I felt much freedom in my remarks to the assembled masses. I shall delay here a short time also on my return, by their special request. I am stopping at the United-States Temperance House, J. R. Parker, proprietor; this is a temperance house of the first class; the Croton House in New York, kept by Messrs. Ives and Moore, not excepted. His reading-room, table, attendance, and himself are all agreeable. July 3d I took my departure in the cars for Buffalo; great preparations are making for the celebration of the Glorious Fourth.

July 4th, Independence-day, was ushered in by the roar of cannon, not from the *Canada side,* but from our side, which I can assure you made the welkin ring. Many of the Canadians came over to celebrate the independence of America by getting beastly drunk; and very many of the Americans were not *free* from the effects of their *liberty.* The most drunkenness I ever saw in one day was among the Indians visiting the city, mingling with the citizens in the celebration of American freedom At 10 A.M. we mounted the rostrum. The "Second Declaration of" the reformed drunkard's "Independence" was read by Harlow S. Lowe, Esq.; after which the vast concourse of people were addressed by Mr. Du Boice, in a most eloquent manner. I followed him with a few remarks, after which the meeting broke up in fine spirits. At 6 P.M. we assembled again in the Methodist Church; the house was crowded. I gave my experience, which was listened to with profound attention, but interspersed with many a sob and flowing tear. Wednesday evening, July 5th, I lectured to a crowded audience in Park Church.

But I must conclude; you shall hear from me again shortly. I leave this day for Niagara Falls to fill a few appointments there, and shall then commence my return to Boston, which will be about the last of the month. You will please say to the friends of temperance in Massachusetts and New England who may want my services, that I shall be pleased to serve them on my return. I hope they will not forget me, as I have seemed to forget them from my long absence. I cannot, I hope I never shall, forget their many kindnesses to me.

No more at present, J. H. W. HAWKINS.

On again arriving at Auburn, he addressed another letter to the editor, the Rev. C. W. Denison.

AUBURN, N. Y., July 16th, 1843.

MY DEAR BROTHER DENISON, — I wrote you last from Buffalo. I then took my departure in the steamboat Waterloo for the Falls. On our passage down, a counterfeiter was recognized to be on board, whom we landed at Black Rock, in charge of two officers who were in pursuit of him. We next landed some passengers at Schlosser, who to all appearance were more honest. We then crossed the river immediately above the cataract, to Chippewa, on the Canada ide. Here we took the cars for the Falls. We then crossed to the American side, immediately below the Falls, in strong row boats, built expressly for that kind of ferry. I remained here two days and evenings, giving two addresses to crowded houses. They have done almost every thing that can be done to advance the cause of temperance among the inhabitants, all having signed the pledge that have come to the years of maturity.

Took the cars for Lockport. Held meetings Saturday and Sunday. Much has been done in this place to advance the cause of temperance. Monday, July 10th, returned to the Falls; remained a few hours and took the cars for Buffalo. There arrived here to-day from Toronto, Canada, a temperance party, in number five hundred. They could not all be accommodated on this side, and half of them had to take quarters on the other side of the Falls. I must here remark for the information of those who visit the Falls, that there is a *good* temperance house here, kept by Cyrus Smith, immediately opposite the Cataract House. I recommend it to the friends of temperance;—but it so happens with the *friends* of temperance, the moment they leave home on a journey they appear to have a propensity to run their heads into the first rum-hole they come to. Tuesday evening, July 11th, I addressed a crowded audience in the Buffalo M. E. Church. Between thirty and forty signed the pledge. The friends of temperance have done much to reform the drunkard in this place.

Notwithstanding the untiring efforts of the friends of temperance in endeavoring to give a character to the cause, and fixing it on a firm foundation, they have to contend against the influence of the mayor and aldermen, who are the true friends of rum and rum-sellers, and open and avowed enemies of the cause of temperance and good morals, by granting licenses to more than one hundred filthy, low grog-shops, to say nothing of the dirty ones in high places, especially the French one. Last week Mr. Charles T. Torrey, of Albany, editor of the *Weekly Patriot*, published a card in the paper of Buffalo, set-

23*

ting forth the fact that he counted on *Sunday*, fifty grog-shops in full operation, while those of a *higher order* were busily engaged in preparing more customers for the lower order of grog shops.

Wednesday, July 12th, I left Buffalo for Batavia. Same day, in the afternoon, addressed a crowd of people from the steps of the court house. In the evening held a meeting in the *old* court house; — all the churches closed against the cause for its want of holiness. However, the cause has many warm friends here, who have done much to advance it, notwithstanding the powerful influence they have to contend against; and some of this influence exerted by a distinguished divine, who sent forth a memorable sermon, I think in 1835, against total abstinence, in which he says that " the triumph of temperance will be the triumph of infidelity." Thank God for the triumph that many hundreds of the reformed have experienced in their happy conversion to God. It is not necessary for a man to be a *fool* in order to *err*, for many of our wisest and best men commit some of the grossest errors. For the credit of the M. E. Church, I must here record, that this is the first place, to my knowledge, in over twenty thousand miles travel, that I have not found that Church opened to the cause of temperance, which is acknowledged to be the cause of God. I was informed that the church here was closed by direction of the trustees; for the correctness of the information I cannot vouch, but I hope Dr. Bond of the *Christian Advocate and Journal*, and Br. Stevens of the *Zion's Herald*, will express themselves on this subject, ever keeping their minds on the fact that the Methodist Church has received the largest share of the returning, prodigal drunkards into its bosom, who make good *working* members, for above all other men they have the greatest cause to thank God for their miraculous and happy delivery.

Thursday evening, July 13th, I addressed an overflowing

audience in the Bethel, assisted by brother Van Wagner, who is on his way farther west. God speed him on his mission of mercy.

Friday evening, July 14th, I addressed quite a respectable audience in the beautiful village of Geneva, in the Presbyterian Church. They have done wonders here; their society consists of four hundred men, nearly three hundred of them reformed men.

Saturday, July 15th. I addressed a very large crowd in the streets of Auburn.

On Sunday evening addressed an overflowing audience in the First Presbyterian Church in this place. They have done nobly.

My present appointments will run out on Sunday next, 23d instant, at Lansingburg. I shall then pay my children a visit at Wilbraham Academy, and about Wednesday I hope to be at home in Boston. Farewell for the present. You shall hear from me again.

Yours, &c.,

JOHN H. W. HAWKINS.

On returning to Boston Mr. Hawkins furnished the following additional particulars of his late journey in a communication to the editor of the Washingtonian:—

BOSTON, August 6, 1843

REV. C. M. DENISON: *Dear Brother*, — The following extracts from my journal will finish the account of my late tour to and from Western New York. I wrote you last from Auburn, July 16th. I had fondly hoped that on my return to that place I should have had the pleasure of addressing the inmates of the State Prison. Application accordingly was made for that purpose to the inspectors, who were in session at the time in the prison; but they, in their *wisdom* and *judgment*, refused. * * *

Syracuse, July 17th. — In consequence of a tremendous gust of wind and rain, the meeting was poorly attended; however, they have done nobly in the cause of temperance.

Little Falls, July 18th. — This is one of the most picturesque villages I have ever been in; the Temperance Society here are independent of the churches, — *they* have closed their doors against the cause, — having a large and commodious hall for their meetings. They have done much to reform the drunkard, and have resolved, in order to keep him so, *not* to remove the reformed man out of the way of temptation, but *to remove the temptation out of his way;* that is to say, *moral suasion* for the unfortunate drunkard, and *legal suasion* for the drunkard MAKER. This is as it should be.

Schenectady, July 19th. — I wrote you, July 6th, that I should tarry here on my return by particular request, with a promise of a good house and good compensation. The first part only of their promise was complied with.

Saratoga Springs, July 20th and 21st. — Addressed two crowded audiences here, but it is up-hill work with the cause in this place: principally owing to the drinking, drunken, gambling, profligate, fluctuating population; partially resulting from the fathers of the town granting licenses to all who apply for the sale of the curse.

I ought not to omit stating that by *very urgent request* I went to Ballston Spa, on the afternoon of the 21st, to address the people, which I did. It cost me thirty-seven and a half cents to get there; they paid me, by way of compensation, two York shillings, leaving me minus only twelve and a half cents. Not so bad.

Waterford, Saturday, July 22d. — Lectured to a well-filled house; they have done a great deal to advance the cause in this place. Next day, Sabbath, addressed a crowded audience in the Presbyterian Church in Lansingburg; about one hour after I had returned to my lodgings from the lecture, a fire broke out in the bowling-alley of a grog-shop in the rear of a wholesale liquor store, owned and occupied by a Mr. F——; it communicated to the back building of his warehouse, in which was stored any quantity of rum, brandy, etc. The hogsheads, barrels, etc., began to burn, and the liquid fire to run out into the alley, thence through the *gutter* into the street, down the street for several hundred yards, into the Hudson, forming one entire sheet of flame. I heard many say, "Thank God," and I said "Amen," but felt sorry for the loss of their property. As soon as the burning liquid reached the edge of the water, it seemed to say, "Thus far shalt thou go and no farther." Oh, the power of cold water!

I forgot to mention another evil that abounds at the Springs, in the shape of ten-pin alleys, with which Boston is at this time doubly cursed. If I know any thing of these sinks of iniquity, by my own sad experience, I would here invoke the moral and religious attention of their honors the mayor and alder-men, and especially his honor the marshal, and his police, to these most complete schools for the education of the minor in drunkenness, and thereby preparing him for the house of cor-rection, and State Prison. Here in the city of Boston, a city held up as a moral light to the world, ten-pin alleys have in-creased to an alarming extent. The rum-seller has taken the matter into his own hands as it were, and in broad daylight, and on the Sabbath, has he strengthened his arm and set at defiance the mayor, aldermen, marshal, police, and the law, and bids them do their worst; and in this he is backed by owners of millions of dollars in property in and about the city, many of them, too, members of Christian churches! They do not wish the cause of temperance to triumph, for their property is at stake — it would depreciate in value, etc. For Heaven's sake let us deal justly! If the rum-seller ought not to be pros-ecuted for a violation of the license law, do not prosecute the poor unfortunate drunkard for a violation of the *drunken law.* "Deal justly, love mercy, and walk humbly;" we have a right to ask it, and, in the name of justice, we demand it, *as free Americans.* * * * It is my deliberate opinion that they

ought to be prosecuted forthwith; the cause of humanity demands it; the cries of the widow and the orphan demand it;
the blood of murdered thousands demands it; the cries pealing
forth from our almshouses, houses of correction, State prisons,
yea, even hell itself, peopled by millions of God's noblest work,
to fill the pockets of the importer, the distiller, and vender, demand it.   I am at this moment reminded that a distillery is in
operation here.   I dropped my pen; I repaired to the spot,
and, sure enough, the smoke of one was ascending.   I called a
friend to witness, that upon the Sabbath, August 6th, 1843,
God's day of holy rest is violated by the manufacture of rum.
There is a place, the torment of whose fires ascends forever
and ever; a place where there is weeping, wailing, and gnash-
ing of teeth.   From which may God in infinite mercy deliver
us.   JOHN H. W. HAWKINS.

It was during Mr. Hawkins' tour in Western New
York, if the compiler of this memoir is rightly informed,
that an incident occurred which is singularly illustrative
of his promptness in reading the character of his audi-
tory, and his tact in adapting his remarks to the
occasion as it arose.   The story was thus told in the
newspapers of the day :—

A gentleman of good standing in society gives the
following account of the manner in which he was cured
of wine drinking.   " I was," says he, " a cheerful, generous wine-drinker, and after drinking with some friends
at the T——, where we indulged ourselves as usual, we
strolled out in the edge of the evening, and on our
return passed the place where John Hawkins was
speaking.   Observing the thronged assembly I proposed
going in, but my companions laughed at my folly;
however I overruled them, and we sat awhile listening
to his experience.   At length my companions proposed

going, and rose for the purpose, when Hawkins observing us said, ' Ho, you gentlemanly wine drinkers : you
need not retire, for I shall say nothing to you this
evening.   My business lies wholly with the poor unfortunate drunkards.   I wish first to save them, and when
I have done with them I will turn to you ; and it will
be only a continuance of my work, for as sure as you
go on drinking your wine, by the time they are all
reclaimed you will assuredly be in their place and need
the same charity.'   The arrow thus shot sunk deep in
my soul.   The thought of taking the place of these
drunkards who over the country are reforming was too
much for me.   I instantly resolved on giving up wine
drinking, and became a thorough teetotaler."

CHAPTER XVIII.

" Ye who have marked the crimes and shames that throng
Like sateless fiends, the drunkard's way along —
Ye who can tell his everlasting doom,
When darkly over him shall close the tomb —
Up for the conflict ! — let your battle-peal
Ring in the air, as rings the clash of steel,
When, rank to rank, contending armies meet,
Trampling the dead beneath their bloody feet !
Up ! ye are bidden to a nobler strife —
Not to destroy, but rescue human life —
No added drop in misery's cup to press,
But minister relief to wretchedness."

Mr. HAWKINS did not remain long in Boston* after his return from New York. Spending less than three weeks with his family, he started for the State of Maine again, and the Province of New Brunswick. The invitations from these quarters were most pressing ; the manner in which he was received will appear from his letters, some of which were published in the Boston

---

* Mr. Hawkins was not idle while in Boston. He watched every movement which indicated the continuance of the destructive rum traffic ; he was bold, and oftentimes considered too severe in his rebukes. Passing along the wharves one day, his attention was attracted to a cargo which was being put on board a vessel bound to a foreign port, which led to the following communication, published in the *Washingtonian :* —

"NEW ENGLAND RUM *vs.* FOREIGN MISSIONS.

" Mr. EDITOR, — For the information of our Foreign Missions, and all others concerned, please give knowledge of the fact that the brig Lincoln, now lying at Lewis' Wharf, Boston, is loading with *molasses rum* for Smyrna. What a comment upon a civilized and Christian (?) nation !"

J. H. W. H.

papers, and others received by his family. The following was addressed to the editor of the *Washingtonian:*

SOUTH BERWICK, Aug. 19, 1843.

DEAR BROTHER DENISON, — According to the appointment, Sunday, the 13th, I addressed a crowded audience in Newburyport, in the Rev. Mr. Pierce's meeting-house (Methodist). There was present our old friend Rev. Dr. Pierce, of Brookline, who at the close of the meeting made some good and acceptable remarks, which, indeed, are always well received from so venerable a friend of the holy cause of temperance.

On my arrival at Portsmouth, Monday, August 14th, the first thing that attracted my attention at the depot was several freight cars loaded with the relics of the last distillery in this place; viz., several stills and the *worm* of the still, all bound to Boston, I suppose, as old copper. The ground on which the building stood is never more to be used for that purpose.

I lectured at night in the open air near Spring Market. I had not proceeded far before I received an egg in my back. Rather rough treatment all round! The next day the gentleman (?) was recognized as being a notoriously bad man by the name of *Rinaldo*, rather a famous name among robbers. I made application to a magistrate for a little "legal suasion" to mix with *my* "moral suasion." It was granted, and the egg cost him little short of ten dollars, and a lodgment in jail. I reckon he thought *eggs had riz*-en in price.

Many of the members of the society becoming indignant at the treatment I received, determined on having a house for Tuesday. They therefore obtained the South Baptist Church, the use of which was freely given for the purpose, and offered to me at any time I wished it. A crier was sent round, and at night the house was filled to overflowing, and we had a first-rate meeting.

At Dover, Wednesday, Aug. 16th, I lectured to a well-filled house.

At Great Falls, August 17th, I lectured to quite a crowd of men, women, and children, in a beautiful grove, in the afternoon, and at night to a full house in the Baptist Church. The temperance men of this place intend that the rum-sellers shall take a trip up " Salt river," in the same kind of boat as at Dover. May their voyage be an agreeable one, and may there be no falling out on the way. Those voyages, if I can understand men, matters, and things, are about to become very general and fashionable. I think a few trips from Boston would make a stir, especially among the ten-pin alleys, for every one of them has a *bar* attached to it.

Please don't forget to remind our friends, the mayor, marshal, and the police, that they are on the increase; and that for every accident that happens on the railroad by negligence or otherwise, the *company* is responsible. " Look out for the engine while the bell rings."

Rum has been driven entirely out of this town, and they who want it must go to North Berwick for it. What a stigma upon the character of those who grant licenses in that town !

While I was here, the only drunkard in town went over to North Berwick and bought a quart of rum. He had taken about two drinks out of it when some one told him that I was down at the Bank and wished to see him. He came there, — pretty well *corned.* After a great deal of talking and " moral suasion," we got him on the pledge. By our advice, he went home, brought his bottle containing the rum, and handed it to the President of the Bank, who handed it to the Cashier, with an order to seal it and place it in the vault for safe keeping — to the joy of the man, as well as of all present.

My intended route is up the Kennebec, across to and down the Penobscot; thence down east to Eastport; across to New Brunswick, and thence to Nova Scotia; thence by steamer home. How much of this contemplated journey I shall take I know not. You shall hear from me again.

Yours respectfully,   JOHN H. W. HAWKINS.

On reaching Eastport, Maine, he addressed the following letter to his children, who were still at school; his son had nearly completed his studies preparatory to entering college. Allusion has been made to instances where Mr. Hawkins was but poorly compensated for his services; it will be seen from the following letter that there were also instances in which those services were liberally appreciated.

EASTPORT, ME., Sept. 29, 1843.

MY DEAR SON, — The letter from your sister, dated September —, came safe to hand, and I was of course glad to hear from you, especially that you were all doing well, and enjoying good health, for which we have great cause to be thankful to Almighty God; let us not forget his goodness towards us.

You see that I have wandered "away Down East," well nigh as far as I can go without going into the Province of New Brunswick, which I intend to do, probably as far as St. Johns, and return to Boston towards the last of October. I have had quite a pleasant and profitable time. I have been paid better in this town for lecturing than at any other on my route. I left Boston on the 13th of August, and I have on hand, including the draft I send you, three hundred and twenty dollars, which will enable me to pay one year in advance when you enter college. I approve of your continuing another term before entering college; it is well not to be in haste; prepare yourself well, and, like David Crockett, "be sure you are right and then go ahead."

I propose that at the end of this term you come to Boston, and then take your contemplated trip to Baltimore. When you come to Boston we will talk more fully about matters which pertain to your and your sisters' future prospects in regard to education, etc.

Your sisters will of course enter another term, which I approve very much. As regards entering Mt. Holyoke Seminary

that must be a matter of future consideration; there is time
enough for that; do not be too hasty. I want you all, Arthur
also, to gather all the knowledge you can, and improve your
minds, and I will do what I can to help you along.

My dear children, live close to God in prayer; put your
trust in him, pray often in secret; read your Bible on your
knees in secret; pray for me.

I would write more, but have not time; the stage waits to
take me to Robbinston and Calais, and I must close. I have
not received any news from Baltimore since I left in the
spring.

Drop a line to your mother immediately upon the receipt of
this; *do not neglect.* My respects to all the friends in Wilbraham.

Receive the affections of your father,
JOHN H. W. HAWKINS.

Mr. Hawkins continued his journey into the Provinces of New Brunswick and Nova Scotia. Everywhere he lectured to crowded houses. His reputation
had preceded him, and there was no difficulty in bringing out large masses of people to hear him. As the
reform progressed, and the traffic in intoxicating drinks
was everywhere falling off, its supporters resorted to
every species of annoyance that malice and self-interest
could invent to render his position uncomfortable; they
exerted themselves to the utmost to throw ridicule upon
the new movement and its advocates. But the intre-
pidity which he always evinced, emboldened the friends
of temperance to make vigorous assaults in return upon
the enemy's entrenchments. It is not surprising that in
the fury of those assaults, and under the heavy blows
dealt by him upon his opponents, some were offended
whom he never designed to harm. But he felt that he

was fighting for the feeble and the oppressed, and he seldom paused to ask who the oppressor was, or what was the position he held in society. "That noble warrior, John Hawkins," says Dr. Marsh, "is doing great things in Maine."

During Mr. Hawkins' sojourn in New Brunswick, papers reached Boston, speaking in terms of high commendation of his labors there. The *St. Stephens Courant*, of October 10th, stated that "Mr. Hawkins addressed a large and most attentive audience at Middletown, on the all-important subject of temperance, and in the Methodist Chapel at Saltwater; and equally large and attentive assemblages at the Upper Mills, Oak Bay, and the Ledge. The earnest and touching manner of Mr. Hawkins, and his true description of the 'drunkard's progress,' have no doubt made a lasting impression upon the minds of his hearers. Mr. Hawkins was to hold meetings at St. George, St. Andrews, and St. Stephen."

The result of these efforts was the formation of vigorous and influential societies in all these places. "After lecturing three days in St. John," he says in his journal, "took steamboat, but concluded to put into Portland, Me., and deliver a lecture there by request of friends. October 28th took the cars for Boston; reached that city on the 31st, and rested until the 18th day of November."

On the third of November he thus writes to his son at Wilbraham: —

BOSTON, Nov. 3, 1843.

MY DEAR SON, — I have at last returned from my tour "Down East," and through the Province of New Brunswick, in good health. I send you, your sisters, and Arthur, each a

24*

handsomely bound volume of the last will and testament of our
blessed Lord and Saviour Jesus Christ, hoping that you will
take it as the rule and guide of your faith and practice ; for it
alone points out the way of life here, and will prepare you for
a full enjoyment of that which is to come.   I hope I need not
say to you all, pray much, and pray for me and the family.   I
have reason to hope we are not neglected.   My dear children, I feel much the want of the sustaining grace of God,
to strengthen and keep me through my arduous labors.   I am
now about to take a long and laborious journey through the
South ; first to Charleston, S. C., thence to Mobile, thence to
New Orleans, and return in the spring ; and then I may go to
London, to attend the World's Temperance Convention.   I
shall leave here for the South this month.   I have not made
up my mind as to the day, but wish you to hold yourself in
readiness to go to Baltimore in company with me, for I think
I shall leave here for Wilbraham on the morning of the 22d
inst., which is the day of vacation ; you will therefore be
ready to go with me on the 23d.   When I get to Wilbraham
we will talk over matters and things in general in regard to
your sisters' future movements, etc.   I saw the Rev. Mr.
Adams * the other day ; he looks badly, but says he feels that
he is getting stronger every day.   He said to me that there was
a boy at the institution whose influence over Arthur was not
good.   Have you looked into it ?   My dependence is on you to
see what influences are brought to bear on that boy ; don't
neglect it, but keep a close eye upon him.   You may expect
me on the 22d Nov.   I have nothing more to say at present.

 Your father, affectionately,   J. H. W. HAWKINS.

On the 19th of November Mr. Hawkins delivered a
parting address to his friends in Boston, in Warren

---

* The Rev. Charles Adams, at that time Principal of Wilbraham
Academy ; a gentleman much beloved and respected by his pupils.   He
was just recovering from a severe illness.

Street Chapel. On his way to New York he lectured in Monson and New Worcester. Remaining one day in New York * to lecture, he took the steamboat and cars for Baltimore. There he lectured once in the Light Street Methodist Church, and spending one day only with his aged mother and relatives, on the 28th of November he took the steamboat for Norfolk, thence by way of Wilmington, N. C., and arrived in Charleston on the 2d of December. He commenced his labors on the 4th of December in the Temperance Hall, under most favorable circumstances. The Charleston papers, in their notices of him and his labors, say that his power over the people was unbounded; that laying no claim to education, he touched the deepest chords of the heart; the manly and the delicate, the old and the young, were alike moved to tears. He continued to labor day and night in Charleston until the 13th of January; we refer to his letters for details. On the 11th he wrote thus to his son, then at Baltimore.

CHARLESTON, S. C., Jan. 11, 1844.

MY DEAR SON, — I embrace the present private opportunity of dropping you a line, which will inform you that I am in most excellent health.

You will be somewhat surprised when I tell you that such

---

* While in New York Mr. Hawkins called upon his friend Dr. Marsh, who thus makes mention of the call in his *Journal* for December, 1843 : —

"Our noble fellow-laborer, J. H. W. Hawkins, has just called upon us, on his way from the eastward to Charleston, Mobile, New Orleans, and St. Louis, etc., where he is to labor in the good cause. The archers have shot at him at the East, chiefly because of his determination to give God the glory of his reformation, and for his boldness in warning rum-sellers, rum-drinkers, and drunkards against the solemn retributions of eternity ; what they are pleased to call sectarianism. But he well knows what he is about."

is the mildness of this climate, that I have not seen a particle of snow or ice this winter, and have had no use for a cloak; and while I am sitting in my room writing, there is no more need of fire than in midsummer.

The quarters provided for me by the temperance society are at the Planters' Hotel, in the most retired part of the house. The family receive me as one of their own. It is kept by Mr. and Mrs. Myott; they treat me with great kindness; this makes it very pleasant. They attend all my lectures, and are as much pleased as the public at large; I seem to give general satisfaction, which to me is a great source of pleasure. I have had unbounded success in this city and at the capital of the State, Columbia.

The mayor of this city and the other officers of the city government have afforded me every facility for prosecuting my work, that could have been expected. I cannot go into a detail of my mode of operations; suffice it to say, that the first thing in the morning, after breakfast, I repair to the "Mayor's Court," where the drunkards taken by the guard the previous night are brought; some of them who are not so bad are then permitted to go; *i. e.*, after they have signed the pledge. The others, the worst, are sent to the poorhouse, a kind of workhouse and prison. I visit them every day, talk to them, encourage them, &c. They are kept there subject to my order; that is, until I think they are in a state to be discharged.

I have also visited a great many families who have sent for me, to talk to the father, husband, brother, or son, as the case may be, and, with a few exceptions, I have been successful, and have witnessed several very interesting cases.

I have given up the idea of going to New Orleans and returning home by the West, on account of my services being so much needed in this section of the country; and another reason is, that it would keep me too long from my family. I do not know precisely what time I shall be able to return; I think I shall remain no longer than the last of March. It would not be advisable for you to return now, as I wish you to enter college this spring, and hope you are so improving yourself that you will be fully qualified to enter. You should not let a moment escape; be diligent in your studies. I wish you could feel the great need of an education as your unworthy father feels it, situated as he is before the public; then I am sure you would be diligent. Do not think that I suppose you are not; oh, no; I would not discourage you.

I cannot close without thanking God for what he has done for me, for you, for all the family. He has done great things for us, for which we have great cause to rejoice. Oh, let us put our trust in him, "for his mercy endureth forever." Be often found in secret with your Bible, and remember that "He that seeth in secret will reward you openly."

Tell your Aunt Frances this must at present answer for the letter I promised to write her; she shall hear from me when I go to Savannah; I am engaged there for one month. To-morrow evening, Thursday, I take steamer for Georgetown, in this State, to spend a few days. I then return to Charleston, take the railroad for Augusta, Ga., and some other places. Feb. 6th return again to Charleston to attend the State Convention, then take the steamer for Savannah, to fill some engagements there. I then think of returning to Baltimore.

I forgot to mention, we have had one of the largest temperance "tea-parties" I ever attended. It was on the 1st of January. More than nine hundred tickets were sold, and the proceeds, after the expenses were paid, amounted to over two hundred dollars; pretty good for the first ever held in this city. It excited a great deal of curiosity, and they say we must have another.

When I return from Georgetown I shall expect to receive an answer to this.   JOHN H. W. HAWKINS.

Of his visit to Columbia, the capital of the State, and the impression produced there, his friend in the

good cause, Judge O'Neale, thus writes to the editor
of the *Charleston Courier*; this letter was copied into
a number of papers in the Northern and Southern
States : —

COLUMBIA, Dec. 17th, 1843.

MY DEAR SIR, — Mr. Hawkins' visit to this town has been
to me a source of inexpressible delight.   He speaks like one
who has felt and tasted in his reformation that God was (as
he is) good, and as merciful as he is just.   He blends, as I
think most properly, sublime views of Christian duty with the
practical results of the temperance reform.   In every point of
view he is calculated to do good ; and I wish that all our people
in South Carolina could hear him, and mingle their tears with
his as he recounts the story of shame and bitterness which he
has experienced.

His visit to Columbia, although at a time when the business
of the Legislature is rushing to a close, and when attention is
too much riveted upon it to be attracted elsewhere, has been
productive of much good.   The night he reached Columbia,
the notice was too short to permit information to be given so
as to call out the town.   A few, however, met on Thursday
night in the Methodist Church, which, with a characteristic
liberality, was thrown open to our use.   Mr. Hawkins was
barely introduced, and made a few plain but intelligent practical remarks.   The church was kindly offered for Friday
night, when a respectable audience assembled ; and I am sure
never were people more delighted with any address than they
were with the plain, simple, artless tale of suffering, shame, and
remorse which Mr. Hawkins has experienced.   His description
of his noble daughter's heroic effort to save him from a drunkard's grave, did not leave a dry eye in the house.

For Saturday night the Presbyterian Church was offered.
Here, again, another portion of the people of Columbia was
met, and before them he reasoned of righteousness, temperance,
and judgment to come.   He pointed the reform to its legitimate

result, the reformation of the drunkard for time, and his preparation for everlasting salvation. The Legislature (that is, the
House of Representatives), at his request, unanimously gave
the use of their hall for a lecture on Sunday night; the evening was rainy, and therefore a comparatively thin house attended. Notwithstanding these unfavorable circumstances, Mr.
Hawkins made one of his happiest efforts, and the representatives of the people who heard him will often speak of it as one
of the pleasantest and most instructive Sabbath evenings they
ever passed in Columbia. He successfully vindicated Sabbath
evening meetings for the discussion of temperance, and showed,
if they were properly conducted, how much good to religion
would be thereby accomplished. He painted with a master's
hand the wretched degradation of the drunkard, and wound
up with a thrilling chapter from his own life and sufferings and
reform. He leaves here in the morning for your noble city.
He will be with you before this reaches you. May God speed
and bless him on his errand of love and mercy.

The Temperance Convention will assemble in your city on
the first Tuesday in February. Before I leave here, I will,
through the *Advocate*, call the attention of the friends of temperance to it, and request the societies to appoint their delegates.   Most sincerely, your friend,

JOHN BELTON O'NEALE.

At the earnest desire of the friends of temperance
Mr. Hawkins spent over twenty days in visiting some
of the interior towns and cities of South Carolina and
a few places in Georgia. On the 15th, 16th, 17th, and
18th of January he lectured to good audiences in Georgetown; returning to Charleston on the 19th, he remained there until the 23d. The 24th and 25th he
spent in Augusta, the 27th in Hamburg, and the 28th
in Athens; thence he returned to Augusta, and re-

mained until February 2d. On the 3d he was again
at Hamburg, and on the 4th at Aiken.

He arrived at Charleston, from Aiken, on the 6th
of February, the day appointed for the meeting of the
State Temperance Convention. Never before was
there so large a gathering of temperance men and
women in that city. Almost every district sent up its
delegation. On the first day over seventy delegates
were present; the number was considerably increased
on the second day.

The Convention assembled at 10 A.M., in the Washington Temperance Hall. The President of the State
Temperance Society, Hon. John Belton O'Neale, being
absent, from indisposition, the Rev. Dr. John Backman,
one of the Vice Presidents was called to the chair;
Henry A. Meetze and J. D. Yates were appointed Secretaries. The aid of Divine Providence was invoked
by Rev. Dr. Leland. After the calling of the roll and
the appointment of several committees, the Convention
adjourned to half past three o'clock. The chairman of
the committee on preparing business reported the following subjects as worthy of special attention : —

1. That an address be made to the importers of spirituous liquors.

2. The subject of the " *Temperance Advocate.*"

3. The propriety of employing temperance lecturers
to labor in the cause throughout the State.

4. Seamen's Memorial to Congress for the abolition
of the spirit-ration in the navy.

5. Address to military men.

6. To take measures for a National Temperance
Convention.

On motion of W. Y. Leith, Mr. Hawkins was invited to take a seat in the Convention and to participate in its deliberations.

The memorial to Congress on the subject of the spirit-ration in the navy was earnest, reasonable, kind, and convincing. It asserted that the time had fully come when this relic of the age of folly and of mistaken kindness should be utterly removed. The address to importers and dealers was comprehensive and respectful. On motion of Mr. Hawkins it was resolved that the address be printed in letter form and addressed to the different importers and wholesale dealers in intoxicating liquors throughout the State.

On the second day the Hon. Mr. O'Neale appeared and took his seat as President of the Convention. On Thursday, the 8th, a large amount of business was transacted by the Convention, which the limits of this work will not permit us to notice. We find Mr. Hawkins' name frequently mentioned in the minutes of proceedings and as a member of several business committees. These particulars are drawn from the printed report of the Convention, and the temperance papers of the day.* Many incidents of stirring interest oc-

---

* See Proceedings of the State Temperance Convention held in Charleston, S. C., February 6, 1843. Issued from the press of the *Temperance Advocate*, Columbia, S. C. Letter from a Correspondent of the American Temperance Union : —

"CHARLESTON, Feb. 8, 1844.

"MR. MARSH : *Sir*, — I little thought when I promised you a letter, to have so much news of a temperance character to communicate. Having been favored with a quick and pleasant passage out, I arrived in time to *listen* to (I had almost said participate in) the deliberations of the South-Carolina Temperance Convention during the last two days of its session , and to attend, on the evening of the seventh, the second Anniversary of the Marine Washington Total Abstinence Society of the port of Charleston.

curred during the sittings of the Convention; we can-

"The Convention Assembled in Temperance Hall (which permit me to remark is the best arranged hall I have yet seen), with upwards of seventy delegates present at its first session. This number was considerably increased on the second day, and I rejoice at having been permitted to see so much of the moral worth of South Carolina assembled in behalf of temperance, as I there saw embodied. I will not pretend even to give you a synopsis of the business transacted by the Convention, but merely a wayfarer's impressions relative to the men there convened and the principles advocated. I will endeavor to send you copies of the *Courier* containing the resolutions and addresses passed at the meeting. I think you will be pleased at the action of the Convention in favor of the Seamens' Memorial; some of the members mystified themselves considerably as to the propriety of such action; but after a spirited debate, it was carried with but two dissenting voices, that I could hear.

"The address to importers and wholesale dealers in spirituous liquors, is a manly, respectful remonstrance, and I envy not the dealer whose conscience it fails to awaken. It seems rather invidious to particularize any addresses, when there were others, both excellent and appropriate.

"Mr. J. H. W. Hawkins was present, and took part in the meeting. He was listened to with attention, and from what I can hear, he has won many warm-hearted friends during his sojourn.

"Judge O'Neale's closing speech in the Convention was admirable, most admirable; — surely none of those *picked men* of the temperance army who listened to him, can fail of carrying to their homes a holy leaven that shall work out its own blessed reward.

"At the Anniversary of the Marine Washington Total Abstinence Society, a procession of the members and officers of the society then in port was formed at the Mariner's Church, bearing flags, banners, transparencies, glass lanterns, &c., accompanied by a band of music, and marched through part of the city, up to the theatre, which was ornamented for their reception. The night being dark, the procession presented a picturesque and imposing spectacle, and the interior of the theatre during the services of the evening was no less interesting. In the back-ground were seated the delegates to the Convention; in front of them, the offi cers of the society and the speakers; between these and the audience in the pit were placed a minature seventy-four, and a model of the revenue cutter, Van Buren, now in Charleston harbor (whose officers and crew are all members of the society, and, with the exception of the complement necessary to take care of the vessel, were all present). Beautiful

not refrain from alluding to one. There was considerable debate on the subject of the Seamen's Memorial, and for a time some doubt was expressed as to its passage; but it was finally adopted by a large majority, there being but two dissenting voices. A sailor's wife who was present, and listened to the proceedings, wrote the following sonnet; it was handed to the President, who read it to the Convention, and it was ordered to be printed.

"SONNET.

'DEDICATED TO THE GENTLEMEN WHO ADVOCATED THE ADOPTION OF THE RESOLUTION IN FAVOR OF THE SAILOR'S MEMORIAL TO CONGRESS.

" Thanks, deep and fervent thanks, my soul would breathe,
  To those who nobly seconded the prayer,
The sons of Ocean raise to be relieved
  From the last vestige of a legal snare.
Thanks, noble-hearted men ! a sailor's wife
  Listened with beating heart to each appeal,
Grew pale with doubt, lest in the wordy strife,
  Landsmen should cease for sailor's wrongs to feel ;
Lest Carolina's temperance host should be
  Neutral — while sailors battled to be free .

women and intelligent-looking men were seated indiscriminately on the flooring of the pit, and in the first tier of boxes were the sailors who had identified themselves with the society. The *coup d'œil* was really striking.

"Judge O'Neale, Rev. Mr. Culpepper, and Rev. Mr. Yates addressed the meeting. To say their remarks were eloquent is but reiterating what the names avow. Rev. Mr. Yates, as Secretary of the society, gave an interesting account of their present condition. He says that they have on their pledge-book two thousand and six members, one thousand five hundred of whom are seamen ! He also stated that since last June, ninety men on board the revenue cutter, Van Buren, have signed the pledge, and kept it. It rejoiced my very soul to see those officers present on the stage. They certainly have set a noble example ; God increase the number of such men in the service. A. C. L."

> Oh ! may this sanction of the " proud palm " speak,
>   In tones commanding the *whole nation's* will,
> Till sailors win the just reward they seek,
>   Ransomed, delivered, from each legal ill."

On the day succeeding the adjournment of the Convention Mr. Hawkins addressed a brief note to his son, saying, —

I have this day received a letter from Deacon Grant; he writes that they are all well in Boston. As regards my own health, it was never better. I leave to-morrow in the steamer for Savannah, Ga., where I expect to labor by special invitation for about one month, and then I propose commencing my journey homeward through North Carolina, Virginia, &c. I have nothing special to write you, only, that I meet with as much success as I could wish.

On reaching Savannah, Mr. Hawkins found time to prepare a fuller account of his operations than he had thus far been able to transmit to his northern friends. It is contained in a letter to Rev. Dr. Marsh. It was deemed by him to be of sufficient interest to lay before the public, and the letter was accordingly published in the March number of the American Temperance *Journal*. The circumstances attending his visit to the inebriates confined in the city prison, and their release, were published in the Charleston papers.

Says Rev. Dr. Marsh, —

The labors of our friend Mr. Hawkins are proving, we are happy to say, very efficient and acceptable at the South. We received a letter from him some time since, in which he expressed great gratitude for the manner in which he had been received in Charleston, especially by the mayor, who had taken him by the hand, welcomed him to the city, and made over to

him all the wretched inebriates who were then, for drunkenness, confined in the prison, with the promise of their deliverance, whenever Mr. Hawkins should report them reformed.
On entering the prison he found one interesting young man
who had been confined more than fifty days for drunkenness,
on bread and water, with a filthy bed, and almost fireless. Mr.
Hawkins told him that he had been a drunkard. "Then," said
the young man, "you know how to feel for me." They wept over
each other. On a set day he, with twenty others, listened to a

temperance address from Mr. Hawkins. All signed the pledge,
and the prison doors, at the order of the mayor, were thrown
open to them. Mr. Hawkins expressed a deep sense of gratitude to God for his own reformation, and his dependence upon
him for success in his great work. With these views and
feelings he cannot fail of being a blessing wherever he goes.

The following letter has just been received from him : —

25*

SAVANNAH, Geo. Feb. 19, 1844.

" RESPECTED FRIEND, — Your very kind letter dated Feb.
2d, has been duly received.   You rejoice that I came South ; indeed I have great cause to rejoice also, and that my feeble efforts, under the guidance of my heavenly Father, have been
so wonderfully and powerfully blessed.   The late State Temperance Convention in Charleston was one of the most important meetings I ever attended.   The measures adopted there, if
carried out, will tend so to revolutionize the State, that it ,will
place her alongside of good old Massachusetts.   The cause of
temperance, while it has for a leader such a man as B. J. How-
land, and the State such a noble philanthropist and advocate as
Judge J. B. O'Neale, has nothing to fear.

" The Marine Washington Total Abstinence Society, of
Charleston, has done wonders.   It was formed February 4,
1842, and now numbers considerably over two thousand, and
is still on the increase.   The past year over one thousand have
signed the pledge.   The Rev. Wm. B. Yates, pastor of the Seamen's Bethel and Secretary of the society, informed me that not
over six had been known to have broken their pledge.   There
are in this port about twenty-six pilots, twenty-two of whom
have signed the pledge.   He says it is impossible to arrive at
the amount of money saved by the seamen and pilots, by their
signing the pledge.

" The work has progressed on board the revenue cutter Van
Buren, wonderfully.   The captain, the first, and third lieuten-
ant are pledged men, with her entire crew, and only one has
been known to have broken his pledge.   One of her officers
told the Rev. Mr. Yates, that out of ninety men who had signed
the pledge since last June, only two have been known to vio-
late it.   In fact, such has been the work among the seamen
in this port, that several captains and officers with their entire
crew have come forward and signed the pledge.

" I have never visited a place in all my travels where the
people have taken hold of the subject of temperance as they

have here in Savannah. Before my arrival they had done but
little; and when I arrived, the friends of temperance told me
that I had a hard place to operate upon, and to the utter astonishment of every one, the house was filled to overflowing;
many had to go away; they could not get in. It was just such
a meeting as the first, you remember, we held in New York,
in March, 1841, when poor Latham cried out, ' Can I be saved ?
is there any hope for me ?' The next meeting was held in the
Methodist Church, a larger place; that was crowded to excess;
and oh! what a time it was! scarcely a dry eye in the house.
One hundred and thirty signed the pledge. The next meeting
was held in 'the Mariner's Church; the number that signed there
made over two hundred in three nights. Ought I to be discouraged at such results as these? No! I have never been
discouraged for a moment since, in the providence of God, I have
been called to this work. I now look back with astonishment,
and am compelled to say, 'Truly, this is the work of the Lord,
and marvellous in our eyes.' I shall remain in Savannah till
about the last of this month; and I think by that time, with
the aid of *such men* as *have* and *will* sign the pledge, we shall
route the enemy, horse, foot, and dragoons. I shall not at
present go to New Orleans as I contemplated, on account of the
health of Mrs. Hawkins. When I finish my engagement at Savannah, I contemplate visiting Macon and Milledgeville, then return to Charleston. Returning home, I contemplate spending
a few days at the following places, viz; Wilmington, Fayette-
ville, Raleigh, N. C., and Petersburg, Richmond, Fredericks-
burg, Va., Washington, and so on, home to Boston."

At the same date of the foregoing letter to Dr. Marsh,
he wrote to his son as follows: —

SAVANNAH, Ga., Feb. 19, 1844.

MY DEAR SON,—Your letter dated February 12th has
been duly received. I was glad to hear from you, and much

pleased with your sister's letter. I received a letter from Mr.
Spooner dated Boston, Feb. 8th. He states that your mother
has been very sick, but is getting better. I have nothing
special to write except that the cause of temperance is making
a tremendous excitement in this place ; they had done very
little previous to my coming. It would be impossible for me
to give you an adequate description of the interest which is felt
here. The people seem amazed ; such crowded houses I have
seldom witnessed anywhere ; the high, the low, the rich, and
poor, alike flock to the churches long before the hour of meeting. Over two hundred signed the pledge at two meetings,
many of them poor unfortunate drunkards, and the people take
notice of them and have given them employment ; this is as it
should be. I really suppose there will be a greater revolution
in this place than in any other that I have ever visited. The
talk is from morning until night, temperance, temperance ; and in
the taverns and grog-shops they talk it until long after midnight.
A tremendous blow has been struck at the sailor boarding-
houses, that have long been the ruin of the poor sailors of this
port. Several have been put into jail to await their trial for
stealing sailors from on board the ships, getting them drunk, and
then robbing them of every farthing. Remember me to *everybody.*

   * * * I thought you might call on Christian Keener and
give him a portion of the above relating to the work here, for
publication, if he thinks it worthy ; that is, you can copy it and
hand it to him. Write me before you leave Baltimore; don't
forget ; direct to Savannah.

     · Your father,   JOHN H. W. HAWKINS.

   The labors of Mr. Hawkins in Savannah and its
neighboring towns during the month he spent there
were productive of great good. He was engaged, as
appears from his journal, almost every day in some
work of philanthropy ; with the exception of two days'

rest, he lectured every day from the 12th of February to the 12th of March, 1844.

The rapacity of the agents of the sailor boarding-houses, as exhibited in their dealings with the sailor, excited his indignation, and he did not rest until he had aroused a healthy public sentiment against their unprincipled and outrageous practices. On returning to New York, while addressing a large meeting at the Sailors' Home, he thus adverts to this subject. Speaking of the "land pirates" on the Savannah River, he said, they actually steal the crews of vessels and lock them up in their rum boarding-houses, until they strip them of every thing. The captains and crews who came to hear him came armed. He boldly exposed the abomination, and while he was in Savannah one of these wretches was taken up by the city authorities for sailor stealing, and fined five hundred dollars.

On the 19th of February Mr. Hawkins addressed, in the evening, a large audience in the Methodist Church ; it was on the occasion of the regular weekly meeting of the Washington Temperance Society. The exercises were commenced, as we learn from a report of the proceedings, with an ode by the choir and a prayer by the Rev. Mr. Ross. It having been announced that Mr. Hawkins would address the meeting, the citizens turned out in great numbers to hear his " reasonings " upon temperance. " The church," says a Savannah paper, " was crowded, and to adopt a common mode of expression, ' much of the beauty and the fashion of our city was present.' " The writer expresses the wish that it might be more fashionable for the citizens generally to become the friends and advocates of the great temperance reform, and adds,

that from present indications it was thought there was
a strong probability that a large majority would be on
that side. The following is a brief outline of the
address referred to, as reported for the press : —

Mr. Hawkins commenced his address by observing that the
friends of temperance could not have selected a better time
than the present for bringing their principles to the notice of
the community. Fortunately the theatre is now closed, — there
is no place of public amusement open to divert the public
attention, and it can be fixed steadily and without interruption
upon this important subject. He was pleased to hear that the
operations of the society had become the subject of common
conversation ; especially was he rejoiced to know that temperance was being discussed in the bar-room and at the tavern.
This was carrying the subject to the right place. The truths
which may have been uttered are thus carried to many who
otherwise would never have heard them ; and let us hope they
may not be without some practical influence. The cause of
temperance has so far triumphed over all prejudice and opposition, that its enemies are now at a loss for arguments against
it. Driven to the wall they now attempt to decry the society,
and accuse the members of drinking behind the door. Mr.
Hawkins was willing to admit that to some extent the charge is
true. But this is no argument against temperance ; not any
more so than the defection of professors of religion would be
an argument against the truth and value of Christianity.
" They are not all Israel who are called Israel. "

But the importance of a subject can never be lessened, nor
its truth impaired, by the dereliction of those who profess to
advocate it. Our object should be to discuss this subject fairly,
to come to an impartial consideration of the *facts* connected
with the use of strong drink, and inquire whether a sense of
duty should not induce us to sign the pledge. If no other consideration can influence us, a regard to our own interest should

prompt us to inquire how far we are losers by the use of strong drinks, or what benefit we derive from them. Mr. Hawkins had within a few days conversed with a gentleman from the country, who had received a bill for groceries amounting to five hundred dollars ; of this sum three hundred dollars were expended for wines and other intoxicating drinks. What had this individual received for his money? A fair and honest equivalent? No! He had exchanged his money for that which destroys the intellect, and blasts the best hopes of man, both for time and eternity.

Mr. Hawkins was aware that in speaking upon this point he might be supposed to be hostile to the interests of that class of the community who make a living by the sale of strong drinks. His business was not so much with the vender as the consumer. The vender sees every day the practical effect of his traffic. Day by day he witnesses the misery and wretchedness which he entails upon his fellow-man, and we must leave it to his *conscience* to admonish him. Our main efforts should be directed to the rescue of the victim of intemperance. We wish to remove him from the scene of temptation, and to fortify him against the attacks of the enemy. If in these efforts we are successful, and a class of men suffer who are catering to the unhallowed appetites of their neighbors, upon themselves, their business, and not upon us, be the consequences.

The dealer in strong drinks boasts that his business is honorable and right, because it is legalized. He has his *license from the people.* Be it so. The poor drunkard has no license to get drunk, and he needs the kind interposition of friends to rescue him from ruin. And why is it that the law is so unequal in its enactments in regard to *drunkards* and those who make them? The *former* may be prosecuted and imprisoned, and fed on bread and water for fifty-two days, for indulging in strong drinks; the *latter* may make a *hundred drunkards* and the law *protects* them in their trade. Is this even-handed justice? He would, however, say to those who are engaged in this legalized work of death, "Friends, see well to it that you preserve your license; place it in an iron chest that it may be secure against all loss. When you are about to die, let your friends put it between your clammy fingers, and fail not to carry it with you to the judgment-bar of God, and there plead your *license* as a palliation for the evils you have wrought in the world."

Mr. Hawkins expatiated very happily upon the moral power of the pledge, and showed most conclusively, that when every other means had proved ineffectual, the simple act of signing the pledge had wrought a reformation in individuals whose recovery had been regarded as beyond all hope.

Mr. Hawkins presented a letter, which he had received during the evening. It was signed, "*A Sufferer*," and was doubtless written by some one who has suffered from a loss of *customers*. The author of the letter complained of the injury which he had experienced by intemperance and temperance, and requested Mr. Hawkins to remind some of his new converts that they had a duty to perform that ought not to be forgotten; viz., "*to pay off old scores.*" Mr. Hawkins made some very humorous and forcible comments upon this letter, and expressed the hope that there might be many more such " sufferers," here and elsewhere.

On concluding his address, he suggested to the friends of the cause the necessity of contributing something for the relief of the reformed inebriate. Donations of old clothes, hats, shoes, etc., would be thankfully received by the officers of the society, and distributed among those who were destitute.

The interest in this good work is certainly on the increase. Since Mr. Hawkins' visit to our city upwards of *four hundred* have signed the pledge, *and " still they come."* May God continue to speed the cause.

An incident occurred during his mission to Savannah which deserves particular notice. So great was the interest felt in his labors by the Roman Catholic population, that Father ——, of the Catholic Church, determined so far to dismiss his prejudices against a Protestant, as to invite him to address his people on a day which he should name. He accordingly called upon him, stated the extent to which intemperance prevailed among his flock, and solicited his aid in their behalf. Mr. Hawkins cheerfully consented, and at the time appointed repaired to the church, which was one of ample dimensions. He found to his astonishment, on entering, that every seat was filled. On advancing to the chancel, he observed that a table had been placed in front of it. Father —— inquired of the sexton why it was there. " And sure, sir, it is for the spaker to stand upon," was the reply. " Remove it immediately; Mr. Hawkins is good enough to stand within my chancel." He took his seat immediately in front of Mr. Hawkins, and as he proceeded in his remarks the tears began to course their way down the good father's face, and before he had concluded he wept, as hundreds of others in that congregation did, like a child. Mr. Hawkins had evidently produced a great effect upon his hearers. As soon as he had concluded, Father —— sprang upon his feet, under great emotion, and ordered the sexton to " Fasten every door of the church. Let not a man or a woman leave the house until you have all signed this pledge!" he exclaimed, pointing to it as it lay upon the table ; nor did he desist until his flock were all pledged to the principles of total abstinence.

On the 4th of March, Mr. Hawkins left Savannah for Milledgeville, where he lectured until the 7th, on which day he went to Macon, where he remained three

26

days and returned to Savannah on the 12th. On the
4th of this month he wrote a letter to a friend in Boston, Capt. W. R. Stacy, in which he says : —

It gives me great pleasure to inform you of the unexpected
and unbounded success I have met with in every place I have
visited in the South, and more especially in Savannah. In all
that I have travelled, which is more than forty thousand miles,
I have never seen the *people* take hold of the cause as they do
here. Every meeting is crowded to excess, and with all classes
of citizens. On my arrival the temperance society numbered
two hundred and twenty-five. I have been here twenty-one
days and it now numbers seven hundred and twenty-four, and
is rapidly on the increase. I have had several meetings of the
children, and I wish much you were here to see them, as I
know from the interest you have taken in the formation of the
" Cold Water Army," you would have been much pleased. You
will receive with this a request from Mr. John Ingersoll, President of the Savannah Temperance Society, to furnish him
with two full sets of " Cold Water Army " banners, three hundred badges, three hundred song books, for which he will forward the money as soon as received.

Mr. Hawkins remained at Savannah until the 18th
of March, and then left for Charleston, when he began
his journey homeward.

On arriving at Boston, April 6th, he received the following communication : —

CHARLESTON, March 30, 1844.

DEAR SIR, — At a meeting of the Board of Managers of
the Charleston Total Abstinence Society, held on the evening
of the 30th of March, the following resolutions were unanimously passed : —

Resolved, That this Board regards with feelings of deep satisfaction the labors of Mr. John H. W. Hawkins in the cause of temperance in this city. and in the neighboring towns of this State and in Georgia; and that his benevolent zeal in ameliorating the condition of the unfortunate inebriate, merits the approbation of the friends of humanity everywhere.

Resolved, That the President of the society communicate to Mr. Hawkins, the resolution just passed.

Extract from the minutes.

J. B. BETTS, *Recording Secretary.*

CHAPTER XIX.

"Pity dwelleth in thy bosom,
  Kindness reigneth o'er thy heart;
Gentle thoughts alone can sway thee —
  Judgment hath in thee no part.

"Hoping ever, failing never,
  Though deceived, believing still;
Long abiding, all confiding,
  To thy heavenly Father's will;

"Never weary of well-doing,
  Never fearful of the end;
Claiming all mankind as brothers,
  Thou dost all alike befriend."

ON reaching Boston Mr. Hawkins found his family in greatly improved health. He was thereby enabled to accept many of the invitations extended to him from various parts of New England. At an early date after his return he met his Washingtonian brethren in the Odeon, and addressed them at considerable length on the great progress of temperance at the South; the temperance papers spoke of his remarks as having been well received. He was greatly rejoiced at the new accessions to the already large number of able temperance advocates, and to every new co-laborer who gave evidence of moral worth he extended a hearty welcome.

Among the remarkable reformations in the city of Worcester, Massachusetts, was that of John B. Gough. This happy event occurred sometime in the month of

(304)

October, 1842. An extended account of his life and trials, and his final reclamation, may be found in an autobiography published some years after. Sincerely grateful for his escape from the path of ruin, possessng fine powers of imagination, a well-cultivated fancy, and a ready utterance, he soon became an able and a distinguished lecturer; he gave every evidence of being deeply and sincerely impressed with a conviction of the great evil of intemperance. He possessed the elements of popular oratory in a large degree, and few persons could remain unmoved while listening to him as he depicted, in chaste and eloquent language, the joys of temperance and the sorrows of the inebriate. On reaching Boston, Mr. Hawkins found Mr. Gough, with his friend Deacon Moses Grant making arrangements to visit a number of Southern cities in which Mr. Gough had been invited to lecture. Mr. Hawkins, with his accustomed generosity, rendered every facility in his power to make the visit a pleasant one. The following note will explain itself : —

BOSTON, May 8, 1844.

MY DEAR MOTHER, — This will be handed you by my much esteemed friend, Deacon Moses Grant, of Boston, of whom you have often heard me speak. He accompanies my friend and co-laborer, John B. Gough, who comes to Baltimore by the special invitation of Christian Keener, to lecture upon the subject of temperance; he is one of the best lecturers on this subject I have ever heard. I want you *all* to go and hear him.

Mr. Plympton is very thankful for the attention paid him by you all; he speaks of the visit with great satisfaction.

I remain ever yours, my dear mother,

J. H. W. HAWKINS.

26*

Among the many friends whom Mr. Hawkins made in Boston, was Henry Plympton, Esq. He was among the first who welcomed him to Boston in 1841, and ever remained one of his most devoted friends and benefactors. Mr. Hawkins' attachment to his friend was equally strong, and continued unabated to the close of his earthly career. The following letter from Mr. Plympton to the compiler of this memoir will be read with interest: —

BOSTON, Oct. 9, 1858.

REV. WILLIAM G. HAWKINS: *Dear Sir,* — Your kind favor of the 28th of August was received during my absence from this city; care and indisposition have prevented me from making an earlier reply. The reception of your late letter, conveying the sad intelligence of the decease of your affectionate father, gave a thrilling shock to my feelings, so much so that it required some moments to reconcile it to my mind as real. This announcement immediately carried me back to the period of 1841, when I first met him, with other friends of temperance, in Tremont Street, in a hall under the Museum. Methinks I now see him before me, depicting the haggard and emaciated form, the sufferings of the drunkard; there he stood as a monument, bearing witness to the truth of his painful description of the drunkard's life, shivering in his tattered garments, giving his experience in language as searching as the melted lava from Mt. Vesuvius; he seemed inspired for the time and occasion, and I have no doubt now, nor had I then, but he was moved by the immediate inspiration of God; and from that time to the period of his decease, he has gone forward, laboring in this noble enterprise without faltering in speech or deed; always verifying his professions by his personal example; how noble, how encouraging, it would be if all who have from time to time engaged in this great moral effort could show the same results! but it is much to be regretted that the fact is far otherwise.

Your father made the first great demonstration as the "reformed drunkard" in Faneuil Hall, in Boston, at a meeting at which the late Gen. Theodore Lyman presided, who was there at my suggestion and personal solicitation, as a member of a committee who waited upon him. I remember, too, how readily he complied with the request to preside, and remarked, "that the temperance cause must succeed; it could not fall backward; the whole country was aroused to the magnitude of its great moral bearing, and it must triumph." These are nearly his words and the sentiments he uttered. It was on this occasion that your father made the remark, and with great emphasis, "*that the appetite for strong drink never dies,*" for he had heard of instances where it had been revived by a single glass, so as to bring back the habit with all its baneful effects, after an abstinence for fifty years. This remark to me was quite original, but is the most powerful argument which can be used to the drunkard, and this remark, too, holds good with all demoralizing habits.

Please pardon this hasty sketch, and tender my best regards to your good mother, and accept for yourself and family the kindest wishes of,

Truly, your friend,
HENRY PLYMPTON.

During the months of April and May, 1844, Mr. Hawkins visited and lectured in various parts of New England. Extensive preparations were being made throughout that section of the Union, for celebrating the third anniversary of the founding of the Washington Temperance Society of Boston. The enthusiasm of the people was thoroughly aroused, and they were becoming impatient to make a demonstration that should convince the indifferent, and especially their enemies, that the cause in which they were engaged was in their estimation a most important one, and that

the evils which they were seeking to overcome were
of no insignificant character.

The 30th day of May, 1844, the anniversary referred
to, deserves long to be remembered ; other assemblings
of the temperance host had been large, but this surpassed them all.   It was emphatically a mass meeting
of the friends of temperance ; invitations, extended to
the various organizations in the neighboring States, had
been accepted, and several of the Original Six Washingtonians, from Baltimore were present.   The papers
stated that nine thousand five hundred persons came
into the city over the Eastern Railroad, and from
twenty to thirty thousand by other routes and conveyances.   The beautiful Common, furnished with its carpet
of green, spread out there by the hand of a good Providence, invited the assembling thousands to come up
and breathe the fresh air of heaven.   Long before the
hour of eleven, a dense mass of human beings was
gathered within its ample enclosure.

The Cold Water Army alone is said to have numbered ten thousand.   It was composed of children from
the Sabbath schools in Boston and vicinity, and the
children from the public schools, which were closed
upon that day.   The ordinary business of the day was
in a great measure suspended.   The American flag
was flying from the State House, from almost every
flag-staff in the city, and at the mast-head of the shipping at the wharves and in the harbor.

Says Dr. Marsh : —

At twelve the immense procession of military, his Excellency the Governor in a barouche drawn by four beautiful
white horses, together with numerous societies and fire compa-

nies from town and country, which had been admirably arranged on three sides of the Common, by S. A. Walker, Esq., Grand Marshal, moved from the State House down Beacon Street, around to Park Street, down the Mall, through two long rows of beautiful children, arranged by Deacon Grant, down Washington Street, through Milk, Kilby, and State Streets, to the North End, and back through Hanover and Tremont to the Common.

The streets through which the procession passed were magnificently decorated with flags and banners; and through their entire length, the sidewalks, balconies, and windows were filled with spectators, who, with joyful voices, and waving handkerchiefs, and delight beaming from their countenances, cheered the procession on their march. Milk and Kilby Streets were arched with flags, and from the windows of the stores rich goods of every hue were displayed.

On reaching the Common, the thousands joined in a chorus, " The Teetotallers are Coming." Prayer was offered by the venerable Dr. Pierce, of Brookline; after which his Excellency Governor Briggs, from a stand, addressed the people for about half an hour, in a strain of manly and cheering eloquence; setting forth the triumph of the temperance reformation, and its blessed tendencies and results throughout the world.

The *Mercantile Journal* reports the following remarks from Governor Briggs: —

The Governor said that that was a great day for temperance. By the blessing of heaven they had assembled under the most favorable auspices. There, on that beautiful spot, with the trees and shrubbery around clad in their most genial attractions, every thing betokened the favor of Heaven. It was, he repeated, a great day for temperance. The delegates there had come from every part of the Union, in obedience to the call of the Washingtonians of Boston, in unnumbered thousands, to express their devotion to the glorious cause of temperance. It was probably the largest convention which had ever there assembled for any purpose and on any occasion ; and could those devoted men, now in their graves, who assembled in the year 1813 to collect facts in regard to the increasing evils of intemperance, witness this result of the commencement of their labors, nothing could exceed their gratification. Could they even have seen the results which flowed from the old pledge and measures, their hearts would have been glad. Their principle of action was to train aright the rising generation, the children, leaving the confirmed drinkers to their melancholy fate. He spoke in a highly complimentary manner of the Washingtonian movement; that from small beginnings there had arisen "a mighty band of reformed men, who went abroad striving to do good;" great had been their success, the evidence of which was to be seen in the mighty host there assembled.

The banners bore numerous and tasteful devices, and attracted much notice. We refer in a note to one, which bore for its motto the words used by Mr. Hawkins in his first address in Faneuil Hall.* Several stands for speakers were erected upon the Common, and numerous addresses from each were made by distinguished friends of the cause. At stand No. 1, stirring speeches were made by Mr. F. W. Kellogg, Rev. Mr. Chapin, of Charlestown, by Dr. Charles Jewett, Mr. Hawkins,

* The Roxbury Ingrain Carpet Factory Total Abstinence Society had one of the most splendid banners, probably, ever seen in any procession, and was a beautiful specimen of home manufacture. It was woven in one of the looms of the factory, of fine material, and presented a harmonious combination of many brilliant colors. The banner was three yards and a half long by two and a half wide. It bore the name of the society on one side, and, on the other, an eagle with extended wings, holding in his beak a scroll, on which were inscribed the words : " The second Declaration of Independence ! "

and many others. Mr. Hawkins spoke also at the second stand; on each occasion, it is said, "with evident satisfaction to the people."

The temperance societies forming the procession were composed of people of all religious persuasions; a large number of Roman Catholic teetotalers from Boston and the neighboring towns, marched in the ranks. The liberal spirit which pervaded the temperance community on that day, is beautifully expressed in the following resolution, which was adopted: —

Resolved, That it is the aim of this celebration to cheer the hearts and nerve the hands of the friends of temperance ; to direct the attention of the world to the Washingtonian movement, while those results are to be seen on our right hand and on our left and in our midst, to the PIONEERS in the temperance cause — to the men who struck the first spark and created therewith a fire which can never be put out, and which will never cease to shed its greatest brightness on those who first kindled it ; to gather faith and strength from the presence and moral power of the *women* of New England ; to march shoulder to shoulder with the warm and noble-hearted countrymen of Father Matthew ; to be inspired by the beautiful and hopeful spectacle of ten thousand youthful soldiers of the Cold Water Army ; and, lastly, to mingle the Washingtonian banner with all other banners, with " THE CAUSE " for our only motto.

The fourth of July, 1844, was observed by the friends of temperance in a manner not inferior to that of former years. The meeting of large masses everywhere, and the order and quiet which characterized those meetings, was the subject of comment throughout the land. Mr. Hawkins spent the day in the village of Sherburne, Ct., where, with his rural audience and

their " homely joys," he doubtless enjoyed himself far
better than he could amid the pomp and glittering display of the city.   He was not however forgotten by his
countrymen ; in several places sentiments in praise of
his character and labors were offered. Dr. Marsh quotes
the following as worthy of a place in his *Journal.* It is
certainly highly complimentary to Mr. Hawkins.

John Hawkins and Martin Luther ; two bright luminaries
in distant eras of the world.   They cannot be forgotten ; they
must go down to the ages of eternity, the pioneers of human
liberty.

We return to the subject of Mr. Hawkins' daily la-
bors.   Previous to May 30th he visited and lectured in
the following places : — Westport, Padanaram, Hixite
Meeting-house, Westport Point, Russell Mills, Smith
Mills, New Bedford, Reading, Burlington, Dorchester,
Roxbury, Boston (Tremont Temple and Lewis wharf),
Salem, N. H., Lowell, Methuen, Pelham, Middlesex
Village, Sherburne, Old Cambridge, North Reading,
three days in Providence.   On the sixth of July he left
Boston on a tour to the Western part of the State, and
to places in New York.

On the fifteenth he wrote the following letter to his
son, at Wilbraham : —

GREAT BARRINGTON, July 15, 1844.

MY DEAR SON, — I drop you a line·according to promise.
which will inform you that I am well and having a very pleasant
tour.   I have lectured in Pittsfield twice, in Lenox, Curtis-
ville, and Great Barrington, to crowded houses.   This evening
I lecture in Sheffield ; Tuesday evening in New Marlboro' ;
Wednesday, Saundersville ; Thursday, New Boston ; Friday, at

Otis.   Saturday I return to Pittsfield, where I hope to meet your mother.   If I am disappointed I shall feel bad.   I suppose she is with you, and well I hope.   She can take the cars at 12 M. at Collins Depot, and I shall be on the look-out for her at Pittsfield at 3½ P.M.   I have good quarters for her at the Washingtonian Hotel, close by the depot, where we stay over Sabbath, and on Monday morning take our departure for Saratoga Springs, at which place I have an appointment for the same night.   I have engaged comfortable quarters for her during our short stay at the Springs.   When we meet we will talk over the whole matter of your entering college.

No more at present ; my love to you all.

J. H. W. HAWKINS.

Mr. Hawkins' visit to Berkshire County was the occasion for large gatherings of the people, and wherever he went he found the beneficial effects of the reformation.   He collected statistics, as was his constant custom in every place visited, and thus prepared himself to vindicate the cause by facts, the best of arguments. *   Says the *New-England Cataract*, an

---

* The following statistics are to the point : —

At a temperance meeting in New Haven a few evenings since, Mr. Williams gave some very important statistical accounts relative to the progress of the cause in Massachusetts, where he has been laboring for several months.   Four years ago, said he, the pauper tax of Massachusetts amounted to $200,000, and *eight-tenths* of all the pauperism was occasioned by the use of strong drink.   Two years ago this tax was reduced to $136,000 ; and last year it only amounted to $41,000.   The great reduction of the pauper tax has been brought about by the temperance reform.   There have been reformed in the State within the past four years thirty-one thousand *drunkards*.   When he, Mr. W., and Mr. Hawkins, first visited the town of Worcester, three years ago, there were *four hundred and sixty-nine* inmates of the poorhouses in *the country*, but they got almost every name to the pledge, and the last year the whole number of paupers *at Worcester* was only *eleven*.   So great had been the reduction of the pauper tax in Worcester, that the town voted an annual payment of

excellent paper established at Pittsfield: " The inhabitants of Berkshire are attending a series of mass
meetings for the county, aided by that indefatigable
laborer, John Hawkins." " Mr. Hawkins," adds Dr.
Marsh, " never stood higher than at the present time."

He concluded his rather fatiguing engagement in
Berkshire on the 21st of July. Before leaving Pittsfield he addressed the following note to his son. The
Wesleyan University is located at Middletown, Connecticut, whither his son proceeded, was examined, and
admitted.

PITTSFIELD, July 22, 1844.

MY DEAR SON, — Your mother has arrived and we leave
for Saratoga this morning, where I shall of course leave her
for a few weeks, which will, I have no doubt, improve her
health. You need not be astonished if she should remain all
the month of August, for her health must be attended to. She
tells me that it is the wish of Hannah to visit Middletown with
you, to be present at commencement. I have no objection, but
on the contrary it will give me pleasure ; and I enclose ten
dollars to bear your expenses. You shall hear from me again
shortly. I send you a *Baltimore Saturday Visitor.*

.Your father, affectionately,   J. H. W. HAWKINS.

Leaving Mrs. Hawkins at Saratoga Springs, he continued on his tour of lecturing, visiting twenty-six
towns in Massachusetts and New York, between the

——— out of the town treasury, to the Washington Society, the free use
of the large hall as a place of meeting, and also gave them lights and
fuel. One town pauper who signed the pledge at that time immediately
commenced work, his friends procuring him a yoke of oxen. Last year
he left for the Western country, with a fine span of horses, and *seven
hundred dollars* in his pocket, which he had accumulated from his own
labor, and is now settled on his farm at the West, doing a prosperous
business. — *Organ.*

22d of July and the 20th of August. After resting a few days he passed on to the neighborhood of Springfield, Mass. He reached Boston on the 21st of September, after lecturing to large audiences in twenty-five additional places.

On the 26th of September, being much worn down by his excessive labors, he left Boston, with a portion of his family, on a visit to Baltimore and places on the Chesapeake Bay, to indulge in the only recreation he allowed himself, and of which he was excessively fond. He was a most ardent disciple of Izaac Walton! His extensive travels had made him acquainted with almost every lake and bay of note in the country; he knew where to go, and when to go, and how to prepare for his favorite sport, and was noted among his friends of similar tastes for his uniform success.

Many amusing incidents are related, illustrative of his devotion to this sport. Having selected the day when he contemplated a descent upon the "finny tribe," every preparation having been made the day preceding, he arose early, and long before sunrise was on his way to the spot selected. His patience and perseverance were unsurpassed. Nothing gave him so great delight on returning home, as to share his fortune with his friends and neighbors. His sisters would sometimes ask him how he found it possible to keep his mind employed during those long days of summer sport; he would sometimes reply, that the most effective addresses he ever delivered were arranged during his fishing hours.

An instance of his fondness for angling was related to the writer a few years since. He was engaged on a lecturing tour in the State of Vermont during the "fishing season." Being in a town near to a lake, after making proper inquiry he became satisfied that sport was to be found in its crystal waters; the town next to be reached, and in which he was to lecture, was only five miles distant. He had written to the clergyman in whose church he was to lecture, several days before, that he might look for him at the time appointed. Accordingly, he sent his baggage ahead by the public conveyance, with directions to leave it at the clergyman's house, while he, having provided himself with all the apparatus necessary, proceeded to the lake. He became so absorbed in his employment that noon passed almost before he was aware of it; knowing, however, that his place of lecturing was only three miles distant, he felt in no haste to depart. Three o'clock arrived and he had not yet made his appearance at the clergyman's house. That worthy gentleman, feeling somewhat anxious, and knowing that unless the lecturer came a large audience would be disappointed, ordered his horse to be harnessed, and started along the road leading to the village where Mr. Hawkins lectured the preceding night. Inquiring by the way, he could hear nothing of him; and it was not until he reached the village that he learned that he left early in the morning. The clergyman by this time was becoming alarmed; it was growing late in the afternoon, and he was hastening homeward, when he discovered the object of his pursuit issuing from the bushes by the road side, with an ample supply of fish. It is needless to add that the discovery relieved him from his anxiety, and that his supper-table sustained no detriment from the day's labor of the *angling lecturer*.

Mr. Hawkins did not, however, spend all his vacation

in *fishing*, while he was in Maryland, as we find by con-
sulting his journal. On the 6th of October he lectured
at the Fell's Point Market, within sight of the place
where his boyhood was passed. The 21st and 22d of
October he lectured at Chestertown, on the eastern shore
of Maryland; 26th, lectured to the colored people of
Chestertown; 27th, at Quaker Neck; November 4th, at
Rock Hall; 10th, again at Quaker Neck; 16th, at
Broad Creek; 17th, at Bay Side; 24th, at St. Michaels,
famed for its fine oysters; 29th, at Easton; December
2d, he lectured before the Marion Washington Total
Abstinence Society. The pleasure of this interview
with his relatives and old friends, many of whom he
met at almost every point he visited in Maryland, was
unalloyed by a single · sorrow; he was in excellent
health, and exempt from that vicious habit which in
former days had made life almost a burden to him; he
was truly happy. On the 6th of December he wrote
to his son, then at college, of his contemplated tour
through the West and South, as follows: —

BALTIMORE, Dec. 6, 1844.

MY DEAR SON, — I suppose you feel much disappointed in
not receiving a letter from me before this. I have no apology
to offer. I have been putting it off from time to time, and am
now on the eve of departing for the West and South. I should
have been off a month ago, but have been waiting for the great
political excitement to subside.* I shall leave Baltimore on
Monday, and be in Cumberland the same night, and so on.
The *Visitor* will give you some account of my contemplated
tour. You shall hear from me by letters and papers occasionally. I shall not return till May or June.

* The Presidential canvass.

27*

Your mother I took with me to the Eastern-Shore, where she will remain during the winter with her relatives.

My dear son, I need not say to you pursue your studies with diligence, pray much in secret, "and what doth the Lord require of thee but to do justly, and to love mercy, and to walk humbly with thy God." I long to see the day, if in the provi- dence of God I should be spared, to hear you preach the ever- lasting gospel of peace to a dying world. O my dear son, live for it, pray for it, look to God constantly for it; be constant " in season and out of season "; " watch and pray," ever look- ing to that God who, " of his infinite goodness and mercy " has plucked your poor unworthy father as a " brand from the burn- ing" and placed his feet upon a rock, even the rock Christ Je- sus. Oh, for how much we have to be thankful! such kind relatives and friends, and for the great and happy change in our circumstances, which God in his goodness has so unexpect- edly brought about. Let it ever be the language of our hearts, " Bless the Lord, O my soul; and all that is within me, bless his holy name." " His mercy endureth forever."

You will see by the *Herald* I send you, that an effort is be- ing made to secure my services in this State for one year, com- mencing next spring. When I return, if my life is spared, I shall pay you a visit.

In conclusion, I wish you to write me immediately. Be particular in addressing your letters as I shall direct; the an- swer to this, direct to Pittsburg, Penn. All your friends join in love to you. I subscribe myself,

Your father, very affectionately,
J. H. W. HAWKINS.

The following letters to his son and others, contain a concise statement of his progress and labors during his tour to the South and West: —

CINCINNATI, Jan. 13, 1845.

MY DEAR SON, — Enclosed I send you a draft on New

York for seventy dollars, which is fifteen dollars more than the amount you have stated; this balance will pay your board, &c.

The papers I send you will give you some account of my travels.

I shall leave here on Wednesday next, 15th inst., for Madison, Louisville, St. Louis, &c., thence to New Orleans. You were somewhat surprised at my not being any farther on my journey; the reason was this : the political excitement raged to such a degree that it was no use for me to leave Baltimore sooner.

I enjoy most excellent health. I am at this time so much engaged that I do not feel like writing to you a very interesting letter. I shall take another opportunity, when my mind is more collected. I purchased in Baltimore a very large " life preserver " that may be of service to me. I wish you would see that Arthur does not suffer for any thing, and that he is treated kindly. Take good care of yourself. Pray much; " search the Scriptures;" pray for me, that God may keep me, and preserve my life to see you once more.

Your affectionate father,

J. H. W. HAWKINS.

MADISON, Indiana, Jan. 21, 1845.

MY DEAR MOTHER, AND ALL MY CONNECTIONS RESIDING IN THE CITY OF BALTIMORE, — I embrace this opportunity of writing to you by the bearer, Mr. Charles Shaw, a very respectable merchant of this city. I have addressed this letter, as you see, to all my connections, somewhat out of the ordinary way, supposing that all would desire the pleasure, if indeed it is a pleasure, of reading it. No doubt it will be pleasing to you all to learn that I am well, and that the cause of temperance prospers wherever I go. God indeed does continue to bless my efforts.

I held several very interesting meetings in Cumberland,

Maryland, after I left you ; a great many signed the pledge ; many of them had never signed before. From thence I went to Pittsburg, where I remained one week, addressing crowded audiences every night. Thence I took steamboat for Steuben- ville, where I remained four days, lecturing to large and respectable audiences. Thence to Wheeling, where I remained five days, lecturing to crowded houses. I then proceeded down the Ohio, by steamboat, to Cincinnati, where I was received by the friends of temperance with open arms. I remained in Cincinnati two weeks, lecturing nearly every evening to over- flowing audiences. I again took steamboat for this place, and have been lecturing here for several evenings. Sunday night last will not soon be forgotten. I lectured in the M. E. Church, filled to its utmost capacity ; there was scarcely a dry eye in the house. Last evening there was a larger meeting than that of Sunday even ; upwards of fifty came forward and signed the pledge, many of the most respectable citizens of the place, who had heretofore stood aloof, and many of them *hard cases.* I shall leave here on Thursday morning next, the 23d, for Indianapolis, the capital of the State, by special invitation, where I shall remain until about Wednesday, the 29th, by which time this letter will reach you. My course will then be to Louisville, where I shall remain a few days.

The remaining two pages of this letter contained a minute account of his numerous relatives whom he found in the West, their location having been for many years unknown to the family in Baltimore.

EVANSVILLE, Ind., April 1, 1845.

MY DEAR SON, — I fully expected a letter from you at Louisville, as I had requested you to write me at that place. I wrote for your mother to meet me at Cincinnati, which she accordingly did, on the first of March, in excellent health ; she has gained several pounds of flesh ; her cough has well nigh left her. My health is, as usual, good. We purpose returning to Baltimore about the first or middle of June. We shall not go up to St. Louis, as the season is so far advanced. We intend leaving here to-morrow, per steamboat, for New Orleans, stopping a few days at the following places; viz., Memphis, Vicksburg, and Natchez. From New Orleans we shall go to Mobile, Montgomery, and probably to Tuscaloosa, in Alabama; the latter place is the capital of the State. There the Rev. John C. Keener, son of Christian Keener, is stationed; he will be of great service to me in my work. We shall then proceed to Macon, Ga.; thence by railroad to Savannah; thence to Charleston, and home. I shall come to Middletown in a few days after my arrival in Baltimore. I feel very anxious to hear from you; how you are doing, and how you are progressing in religion. O my dear son, be watchful unto prayer, live close to the Saviour, with all your "ransomed powers." My prospect brightens before me; thanks be to God, "I know that if our earthly house of this tabernacle were dissolved, we have a building of God, an house not made with hands, eternal in the heavens." Answer immediately upon the receipt of this; direct to New Orleans, to the care of the postmaster. You will probably hear from me on my arrival in New Orleans. Your mother joins me in much love to you.

Your father, dear son, affectionately,

J. H. W. HAWKINS.

———

NEW ORLEANS, La., April 25th, 1845.

MY DEAR SON, — Your very welcome letter dated April 10th was duly received yesterday, and I now hasten to answer it. We arrived in New Orleans on Friday last, the 18th, in the steamer Paul Jones, and are putting up at a private boarding-house kept by Mr. Downer, Vice President of the Temperance Society. We met in this city with the kindest reception. In less than two hours after we landed, the keepers of the great St. Charles Hotel, Messrs. Mudge & Waterman, granted me the privilege of holding a temperance meeting in the rotunda, which will take place some day next week. The announcement of such a meeting has created great excitement amongst the people for its novelty. You may hear them everywhere in the city say, " Is it possible he is to lecture there ? Why, it is carrying the war right into *Africa.*" Only think, when I tell you that it is one of the most splendid edifices I ever beheld in my life anywhere ; the basement is the drinking place ; there is none above. I have just come from an inspection, and I suppose there were not less than three hundred there drinking at the time. The utmost good feeling prevails here in regard to me and the cause, notwithstanding. I will send you some account of the meeting when it takes place. The general opinion is that great good will result from it. I am sustained by the very best citizens of the place. I had a large number of letters to the most respectable merchants and others here, which I obtained in Boston, New York, Baltimore, Louisville, Cincinnati, and other places; these have been of great service to me. This is indeed a great city, and is destined to be the greatest in the United States, if not, in time, in the world, in commerce. I was altogether deceived in the impressions formed from what I had heard in regard to the peace and quiet of the city, for great order prevails throughout the city day and night, considering the wickedness of the place, composed as it is of a miserable fluctuating population, pouring into it from all the tributary streams that form the Ohio and Mississippi, passing down in large flat-boats with the produce of the upper countries. Besides these, it is the grand rendezvous of gamblers, pickpockets, etc., to whom the eyes of the police are constantly directed. The police of New Orleans are men who are not to be trifled with, I assure you. The Sabbath is a day little respected by the above class of men, and the rum-sellers. Of course there is a large class of highly respectable people here. Last Sunday your mother and myself took a stroll, and to our utter astonishment, ten-pin alleys, billiard tables, and card playing were to be heard and seen in every part of the city. And with all this we saw a very few persons drunk in the streets; but enough of this.

The first meeting I held was in the Rev. Mr. Clapp's church, on Sunday night; the house was crowded to excess. As this meeting was only introductory to a series of meetings, the pledge was not offered; but a collection was taken up for me, which amounted to forty-five dollars; that is a specimen of southern liberality.

We shall remain in New Orleans until about the 9th of May, and then take our departure for Mobile, where we shall spend a few days, and then proceed to Savannah, tarry there a few days, say about three or four, thence to Charleston, a few days there, thence to Baltimore, without stopping at any other place.

I shall now proceed to give you some little account of our journey after we left Evansville, Ind.; you remember it was from that place I wrote you. On the morning of Wednesday, April 2d, at eight o'clock, we took passage in the splendid steamer Harkaway, Andrews, master, for Memphis, Tenn., distance four hundred and sixty miles. It was a most pleasant and delightful passage, rapidly merging into a summer climate, which was distinctly evident to the eye and feelings. Going at the rapid rate of more than twenty miles per hour, we arrived at Memphis on Friday, April 4th, at three o'clock. In this place I delivered five addresses with much acceptance; about one hundred signed the pledge. On Thursday noon, April 10th, we took passage in the magnificent steamer Ambassador, for Vicksburg, where we arrived about seven o'clock Friday, 11th; distance four hundred miles. The passage was indeed delightful. This place, you know, has borne a most disreputable character, but within the few years past has been almost entirely regenerated, and has become a most peaceable city; seldom is a drunkard seen in the streets by night or day; a great many signed the pledge. We remained in Vicksburg until

Wednesday, April 16th, and then took passage in the steamer Paul Jones for New Orleans, and arrived here on Friday, 18th.

We are here in the very midst of a northern summer; it is rather warm, but most pleasant.· My health, which you know has always been good, remains the same, for which we have cause to be thankful, and that our late passage down the Ohio, and up its tributary streams, thence down the great Mississippi, the Father of Waters, has been attended with not the least accident, but on the contrary has been one of the most pleasant passages we have ever had. May the Lord preserve us in safety to see each other, which I hope will be about the last of June, at the farthest. I received a letter when we arrived at Natchez from your grandmother, in answer to a letter I wrote to her from Louisville. She writes that your grandfather is not in good health. The rest of the family were well. You know we are amongst something of a French people, and you would be astonished at the progress your mother makes in speaking "Parlez vous Francais."

My dear son, persevere in your studies; I will do all I can for you; you have my prayers that God may keep you. The sums I expect to receive will enable me to carry on your education independently. I forgot to mention that Gilbert Hawkins is a commission merchant in this place; he is a cousin of mine, son of Aunt Mary Hawkins. He is a true gentleman; he has treated me very kindly; we have dined with him; he lives in very elegant style. There are a great many Baltimoreans here, many of them my old acquaintances. I regret that my sheet is so small, for I have as much more that I should like to have communicated to you; but let the present suffice; you shall hear from me again. You need not answer this, as I do not know where you should direct your letter. If any thing should happen that should make it necessary for you to write, direct to Charleston.

Your father in the holy bonds of love,
JOHN H. W. HAWKINS.

The foregoing letters do not, of course, convey an adequate idea of the amount of labor performed by Mr. Hawkins in the West and South, written as they were especially for the purpose of affording pleasure to his relatives, and not with the remotest idea that they would ever meet the public eye. The extent of those labors can be in some degree ascertained by a recurrence to his journal. It is much regretted by the compiler that the files of newspapers which he once had, containing many interesting particulars connected with his father's, visits. to the different cities named, have been lost.

After leaving Baltimore on his journey, he lectured one evening in Cumberland, Md., from which place he went to Pittsburg, where, and in Alleghany City, he spent six days, lecturing to crowded houses, and obtaining a large number of pledges. At Steubenville he lectured three times in different churches; arriving in Wheeling, Va., his former place of business in 1828–29–30, he lectured in the City Hall on three occasions, arousing public feeling on the subject of temperance to an astonishing degree. He left Wheeling on the 28th of December, 1844, and reached Cincinnati on the 31st. Several days were occupied in making the necessary arrangements for his lectures in that city. He commenced his labors in the Methodist Church on Sixth Street. On the 6th of January, 1845, he lectured to a large audience in the Presbyterian Church; this was the beginning of a great work, which extended into the surrounding villages. A large amount of good, it is true, had been acomplished previous to his coming; still he succeeded in quickening the energies of the people to the accomplishment of . still more. He lectured on six occasions in the city, once at Fulton, and once at Newport and Covington. We quote from his journal: —

Left Cincinnati, January 15th, for Madison; visited Bedford, Ky., my old place of residence in 1819, 1820, and 1821. 18th, returned to Madison. Lectured in the Wesleyan Chapel; two hundred and forty-four signed. Great interest awakened among the children; one hundred and two pledged themselves to total abstinence.

Left Madison for Indianapolis. Leetured 23d, 24th, and 25th to overflowing audiences; much interest; three hundred and twenty-seven signed during my stay here.

At this stage of this memoir it will not be inappropriate to insert the following communication received by the compiler from a highly-respected gentleman now resident in Maine. It will sufficiently explain itself: —

BANGOR, Maine, Sept. 20, 1858.

REV. WM. G. HAWKINS: *Dear Sir,* — Although a stranger you will pardon this hasty note. Thirteen or fourteen years ago I was resident in Indianapolis, and had charge of the editorial columns of the *Indiana State Journal.* The Rev. Henry Ward Beeeher was then a settled minister there; from which place he was transferred to Brooklyn, New York, a few years after.

Seeing in the *Boston Journal* a day or two ago a notice of your being in that city, with a view to the publication of some memoir of your respected father, I have thought it might gratify you to know the impression made on his first visit to Indianapolis. I have been able to lay my hand on a copy of the *Indiana State Journal* of January 29th, 1845, and find the two enclosed articles on the subject; one is editorial, from my own pen, and the other, with the appended initial " B.," it will gratify you to know, was written by Mr. Beecher. It was, I have reason to know, a hearty tribute from that even then distinguished man ; it will be even more appreciated now in the fulness of his well-earned fame. * * *

Very respectfully, your friend, &c.,

GEORGE KENT.

The following are the articles referred to in the foregoing letter : —

JOHN HAWKINS IN INDIANAPOLIS. — Mr. Hawkins is now for the first time on a visit to the far West, and has lectured here several times since his arrival to thronged and deeply affected auditories. He leaves this day, we understand, for Louisville, St. Louis, New Orleans, &c. Wherever he goes, the prayers and ardent aspirations of thousands for his success will go with him. There is something in the native eloquence of this reformed inebriate which comes directly home to men's business and bosoms. Rarely have we heard an address of more power than his opening one of Saturday evening. His off-hand discourse of an hour and a half seemed to us, from its exceeding interest, of scarce half that length. If any of our friends, temperate or intemperate, want to *kill time*, let them go and hear Hawkins and Gough whenever they have opportunity. As natural seed is quickened in the earth and made fruitful only by dying — so, by thus killing of *time*, moral seed may germinate, and the fruits of " righteousness and temperance" be matured for a happy "judgment to come," and for a glorious *eternity*.

We have the pleasure and profit of a visit from John Hawkins, one of the original Baltimore Washingtonians. Mr. H. is a man naturally of sound mind, of a good heart, and fine personal bearing. If any man can hear Mr. Hawkins' "experience" with dry eyes, he must have a very dry heart. Something fastidious about such things ourselves, we, nevertheless, cried enough in one night to answer for a dozen ordinary occasions. Indeed, we were brought to a very awkward condition. We gave ourselves up entirely to our feelings, and were crying with great relish, until he came to that scene where his young daughter covered him with her little bed-clothes, one night when he was thrust into his entry dead-drunk, and put a pillow under his head and then lay down by his side. This was narrated with such simplicity and touching grace that we could only by violent effort refrain from a downright oriental lamentation. Three or four boys in the seat before us squared round, and regarding us as the more interesting spectacle of the two, leaned on their elbows and systematically watched our progress. Even this surveillance did not break the charm of this able speaker. All the temperance speeches that we ever heard (our own thrown in to boot) have not affected us so much as the opening address of Mr. Hawkins. B. .

CHAPTER XX

"He entered upon his work, in the spirit of the memorable line —
                            'Non ignara mali, miseris succurrere disco.'
If we hesitate, in regard to the inebriates whose reformation he effected,
to employ a strong Catholic expression, and say he *had the key to their
souls*,' he certainly opened their hearts by opening his own ; and led them,
by his happy example, to forsake their miserable ways."

Mr. Hawkins returned by the cars to Madison, and
proceeded thence, by the Ohio river, to Lawrenceburg,
where he lectured three successive days ; one hundred
and thirty-eight pledges were taken. On the 4th of
February he lectured at Aurora ; the next day at Rising
Sun. On the 6th he took the steamer for Louisville,
Ky., where, by special invitation, he spent five days,
lecturing on temperance at night, and visiting the unfortunate victims of intemperance during the day. On
the 14th and 15th we find him again at Cincinnati, laboring zealously in the good cause. The remainder of
the month his labors were distributed among the following places : " The Salines " at Kanawha three days ;
at Charleston, Ky., two, and several at Maysville.

On the first of March he returned to Cincinnati,
where he met Mrs. Hawkins, whom several months
before he had left in Maryland. He found her in the
care of the Hon. Thomas H. Benton, who recognized
her in the cars at Cumberland, and finding her without
an escort, very kindly volunteered his services to see
her safely on to Cincinnati. At Cumberland the party
chartered an extra stage, and proceeded to the Ohio,

where they took steamer.   Mr. Hawkins discovered
Mr. Benton on the boat before the landing was reached,
and expecting that his wife was on board, inquired of
him as soon as he could be heard, " Have you not a
live package there for me, sir ? "   Mr. Benton evaded
the question by replying, " Come aboard and we will
see."   They accordingly proceeded to the cabin, where
he introduced the parties as if they had been strangers
to each other.   Mr. Hawkins, of course, expressed himself in very grateful terms to Mr. Benton for this characteristic act of politeness.

After lecturing five days in Lexington and Frankfort, Ky., he left for Madison and Louisville, in which
places he delivered five lectures to interested congregations.   After spending two days in New Albany, he
took the steamer for Vincennes, Ind.   Lecturing there
three days to well-filled houses, he left by stage for
Evansville, where he remained, laboring with much
success, until April 2d.

His first lecture at New Orleans was delivered in
Rev. Mr. Clapp's church, on Poidras Street; on the
22d the seamen of the port were called out to hear
him in the Bethel.   We next find him at Armory Hall;
on Sunday, 27th, he lectured to the colored people; on
the 30th at Algiers.   On the first of May the interest in the city had greatly increased.   He lectured
every evening up to the 5th, either in New Orleans
or in the town of Algiers, on the opposite side of
the Mississippi; on that day he took steamer and
crossed Lake Pontchartrain to Covington, in which
place he lectured to crowded houses on two occasions.
He returned to New Orleans on the 8th.   The very
novel announcement that he was to lecture in the ro-

tunda of the great St. Charles Hotel, drew together an immense crowd. The occasion was noticed in the papers as one of great interest, which Mr. Hawkins knew well how to use for advancing the interests of temperance and humanity. Having concluded his engagement at New Orleans, he took the steamer Montezuma for Mobile, Ala., where he lectured on the 13th and 14th in the Methodist Episcopal Church ; and also upon the two following days in the Baptist Church. On the 17th he left Mobile for Montgomery, the capital of the State, where he lectured with much profit, to well-filled houses, on the 20th, 21st, and 22d. Proceeding thence by railroad and stage, he reached Charleston, S. C., on Saturday evening, May 24th.

Here he was welcomed by a host of temperance friends, whose hearts were cheered and encouraged on several public occasions, as he detailed the progress of the reform in all parts of the land. He delivered several lectures in the Temperance Hall. On the 29th he visited the barracks at Fort Moultrie, on Sullivan's Island, and addressed the officers and soldiers. On the 4th of June he left Charleston for Baltimore, and reached that place on the 6th. He delivered several addresses during his stay in Baltimore, which continued until the 30th day of July. On his way to Boston he lectured in Philadelphia, New York, Middletown, Ct., and at Wilbraham.

From Boston he went to Portland, Me., where he spent several days ; on his return he found invitations awaiting him to lecture in various parts of New England. Between the first of September and the first of November he visited and lectured with great acceptance in twenty-eight towns, closing with New Bed-

ford and Providence. On the 1st of November, being
in New York, he was called upon by the friends of
temperance from Morris County, N. J., and entered
into an engagement to *canvass every town within its
borders.* The following are among the places mentioned in his journal where large audiences were addressed and great interest awakened: Rockaway,
Dover, Berkshire Valley, Morristown, New Vernon,
Greenville, Pine Brook, Whippany, Madison, Morris
Plains, Littletown, Montville, Boonton, Newfoundland,
Snufftown, Suckasunny, Flanders, Mount Freedom,
Mendam, Chester, Schooley's Mountain, German Valley, Hanover, Parsippany, and again at Rockaway.
His visit to Morris County was spoken of many years
after as being one of great value to the cause of tem-
perance.

On the 1st of December Mr. Hawkins returned to
Boston and rested until the 8th of the month. After
spending the intermediate time in addressing good
audiences in Charlestown, Greenwich, R. I., South
Kingston, Newport, Fall River, and a number of other
places, he returned home to enjoy with his family the
Christmas holidays. The compiler of this memoir
was at home at that time, and there became acquainted
with the individual from whom he subsequently received the following letter, and whose singular history
is detailed in the letter which follows it.

It would enlarge this volume very much beyond the
limits contemplated, were we to collect the many instances of wonderful reformations that occurred during
the labors of Mr. Hawkins in various parts of the
country, comparatively few of which, indeed, have ever
found their way into the public prints. Thousands

have been blessed and saved whom the subject of this memoir has never seen on earth. Many of these now, doubtless, form jewels in the crown of his rejoicing in the sanctuary above. The reformation of Stephen R. Hunt, Esq. attracted much attention at the time; and, so far as we know, he has continued steadfast to the end. The following is the letter above referred to; it was written to the compiler soon after his return to college in February, 1846:—

(STEPHEN R. HUNT TO W. G. HAWKINS.)

Roxbury, Mass., Feb. 12, 1846.

My Dear Sir,—I ought to have written you upon my return from the Cape, but circumstances have prevented. Your father had a very gratifying time on the Cape.* I came home greatly fatigued, and have since then been to Taunton and North Brighton. At the latter place I procured forty-nine subscribers to the "cold-water petition," which at some future day we intend to present to the court at the trial of "King Alcohol;" after a little time we will have evidence enough to condemn him, at any rate before the "court of conscience."

I feel very thankful that my faculties are slowly returning. O sir, it takes a deal of time for Memory to resume her seat, and Reason to take the throne from which she has been hurled by that remorseless tyrant whose victim I have been for so

---

* In turning to Mr. Hawkins' journal we find that he visited the following places between the 10th of January and the 1st of March: Provincetown, Truro, Wellfleet, Orleans, Chatham, Harwich, South Dennis, Brewster, Yarmouth Port, Barnstable, Hyannis, Centreville, Oysterville, Marston Mills, Marshpee, East Falmouth, Falmouth, North Falmouth, Monmouth, Sandwich, Neponset, Plymouth, Wareham, West Barnstable, South and North Dennis, and Brewster. In the month of March he visited Holmes Hole, Edgartown, Woods Hole, Falmouth, Sandwich, Taunton, Stoughton, and Canton. March 31st, rest.

many years. But, thanks be to God, with his assistance I will make war against that "hydra monster, rum," until the time of my departure arrives. Whether I return to the bar or not, I am a soldier for life in that war from which I do not wish to be discharged.

Your father is now on the Cape; he will return in one week, we expect; meanwhile I am on my oars. Oh! how I do rejoice that I ever saw him in New Jersey, and that it was put into my heart to come to Massachusetts to live; for now I know something about living, when before I was dead. I believe my faculties will be again restored, and if so, I will pull all the hair from the head of "King Alcohol," as he has from mine.

* . * * I wish I had my collegiate course to go through again. I think I would redeem the time, or if I could have the same opportunity again to study my profession, I think I would improve every hour. Oh! sir, you have the opportunity; look out to be wise, and count the moments as they pass; you never again will have the same opportunity you now have.

In haste (your sister will write soon). I must be off to Dorchester. Write to me.

Yours, respectfully,

STEPHEN R. HUNT.

(JOHN H. W. HAWKINS TO MRS. SCHAEFFER.)

ROXBURY, Feb. 20th, 1846.

MY MUCH BELOVED SISTER FRANCES, — Your very welcome and gratifying letter, dated Feb. 13th, now lies before me. I have just returned from a second visit to Barnstable County, which embraces all the towns, thirteen in number, comprising that noted part of Massachusetts called Cape Cod. A more hospitable people I never travelled among. I spent the month of January, in connection with Mr. Stephen R. Hunt, of New Jersey, lecturing to them, but was prevented from filling all the appointments I had made in consequence of a most dread-

ful snow-storm and gale, which weather found me at the town
of Harwich, where I was delayed several days. I came home
for a short time, and then returned to fill the balance of my
appointments.

I have mentioned the name of Stephen R. Hunt, Esq., of
New Jersey; you may have seen his name connected with mine
in some of the papers that I sent you. It will no doubt be
interesting to you for me to give some account of him and the
circumstances of his connection with me. They are as follows: First, he is thirty-seven years of age, and has a wife and
three children in Chester, N. J. At the solicitation of the executive committee of the "County Temperance Society," I
made an appointment at Chester, his native village, where he
then resided with his family; they had been separated at one
time for nine long years; they had come together about eighteen months ago, upon the condition that he would change his
habits. Poor fellow, he tried hard, but to no purpose, for the
reason that he was surrounded with temptation, in connection
with his old bottle companions, who caused him to break all the
good resolutions which he had made to do better. He came to
the conclusion that it was of no use to try any more, and gave
himself up as lost (thank Heaven there is hope for the poor
unfortunate drunkard). The night at last arrived on which I
was to lecture in his village (Sabbath evening). I gave my
discourse a strong religious character; it had the desired effect.
At the close of the address I gave the invitation to all present,
who felt disposed, to come forward and sign the pledge. He
was the first man upon his feet. He walked up *like a man*
(for he is as fine a looking fellow as you ever saw); the vast
congregation — the house was crowded to excess — looked perfectly astonished. There seemed to be but one feeling among
the people, and *that was*, Poor fellow, *he* cannot keep the
pledge.

The next morning, early, he came to the Rev. Mr. Stowten-
burg's, with whom I was stopping, for the purpose of having

an interview with me. After having been introduced to me, we had some little conversation, when he burst into a flood of tears, and exclaimed, with uplifted hands, and in the most eloquent and feeling manner, enough to move the most obdurate heart, " Mr. Hawkins, what shall I do? I cannot stay reformed *here*, surrounded as I am with temptations and tempters on every hand, who have already declared that they will do all they can to make me break my pledge." At this moment the scene was truly distressing; the minister and his wife wept and sobbed aloud; I could not, of course, keep from joining in with them. I bade him look to God for help; to put his trust in him; he was able to save to the uttermost. After awhile he became composed, and more conversation ensued. I then proposed to take him with me to Roxbury, where he would be away from his companions, and would not be so exposed to temptation. This proposal broke in upon his mind like a sunbeam. It would have done you good to see the sudden change it wrought upon him; his keen eye flashed eloquence. " That is it, Mr. Hawkins," said he; " if you will do that, then there will be hope." He remained at home two weeks, until I had finished my engagements; he then met me, by engagement, at Rockaway, where the County Temperance Convention was being held. How changed he was! How well he looked! He had kept his pledge!

At the close of the Convention we took passage for this place. He took board with me, remaining in the family, reading and studying for six weeks, while I was lecturing in Rhode Island and in some parts of Massachusetts. During my absence he spoke several times in Roxbury and the adjacent towns, with great acceptance. William George was spending the vacation with us; he will never forget the many pleasant interviews he had with Stephen R. Hunt, for he is a perfect gentleman, now he is a sober man.

By previous arrangements with the friends of temperance I had made appointments in all the towns on the Cape. Mr.

Hunt and myself took passage in a packet for Provincetown. We arrived there January 10th, and immediately commenced our labors of lecturing, he following and lecturing every evening after me. The people were much pleased with him, he exhibiting a mind of no ordinary talent. He is certainly a *good speaker*, and a great acquisition to the cause of *humanity*, for this is the light in which *we Yankees* look upon the holy cause of temperance. He has written for his wife to come on; she will be here next week. Their children will, for the present, go to Summerville, N. J., to live with his mother-in-law, who is very wealthy and respectable, as also are the most of his relatives.

During his stay on the Cape he received very handsome contributions. I should have said before this that he had run through a large fortune, and when I met him at Chester he had not one cent. I supplied his family with money, paid his passage on here, etc., all of which he has paid back to me. My dear sister, is it not a great work thus to be engaged, in raising up fallen men, and be the humble instrument in the hands of God in doing good? God has promised a reward for such acts, yea, he has already rewarded me, and there is a greater one for me when my labor on earth is finished. When I look back on my past life my heart sickens within me, and it would stay sick were it not that I am privileged to look on a fairer picture. Oh! the change in me, in my family, in the feelings of my dear relatives toward me; yea, more, a reconciled God. My hope of heaven — this is my privilege, your privilege, the privilege of us all; let us then strive for it, my dear sister.

In one of the papers I sent you the other day you will see an interesting account of one *John Hawkins* (not John H. W.); he is doing well. He is a good-looking man; he can talk, and we think of trying to make a lecturer of him; that is the way we do here. When we find a man that has talent and moral worth, we do what we can to make him useful among his fellow-

29

men. He then answers the object for which he was created. We shall want all the laborers we can get. The great "rum case" of a Mr. Thurlow, a rum-seller, who has appealed to the Supreme Court of the United States, will be decided in favor of the good old Bay State we think, next week; then will come the "tug of war."

I will now tell you of an incident that occurred a short time since, which will no doubt be pleasing to you; it was truly so to me; it was so unexpected, and came in such good time. The circumstances are the following: The family being in need of some dry goods, I went to the wholesale store of a wealthy merchant, a well-known temperance man here, for the purpose of getting remnants, thinking they would be cheaper. This gentleman knew me, and after looking about he said he had no remnants but plenty of whole pieces. He commenced taking them down, and requested me to select for myself. I told him I did not wish to go too high. He said, in a jocose manner, "There is no danger of that, for you are a short man." I made my selection for jacket, vest, and pants for A——, and he cut them off. While doing so I discovered him eyeing my faded coat. I asked him the price of the articles. Said he, looking me in the face, "I shall charge them to temperance;" and turning round he pulled from the shelf a most beautiful piece of black cloth, proceeded to cut from it material for coat and pants, and then from a piece of black velvet a vest. "There," said he, "I make you a present of that, for it was you who brought back to me and his mother our son; and he is now a sober man;" pointing to him at the desk, he said, "he is a good boy and a pious Christian."

We are to have a great time here Tuesday, the 24th inst; that day is set apart for simultaneous meetings throughout the world. The Parent Female Total Abstinence Society of Boston, of which Mrs. John H. W. Hawkins is President, will hold a levee at Tremont Temple; it will be a grand affair. The society is supported by the most respectable females in

Boston, and they seem pleased that my wife is their chief officer, for they place much confidence in her. It may seem strange to you to hear of a female presiding at a temperance meeting; it is an ordinary thing here. How I wish you could be here on that occasion. We shall soon remove into Boston, and go to housekeeping, and I intend to have a spare bed, a plate, knife, and fork, and when I come to Baltimore I shall extend to you an invitation to return with me to Boston, by way of Middletown, Ct., and spend a few weeks here at my expense; which would be to me and mine a source of great satisfaction. I shall send you papers next week giving some account of our doings on Tuesday; shall forward you papers from time to time, when they contain matter worth reading, also packages of tracts when private opportunities offer. Excuse the length of this letter; I had so much on my mind to say, and there was no other way of communicating it but by writing. When I come to Baltimore I will give you more of my company; that is, *if the fish don't bite.*

Affectionately, your brother,   JOHN.

So incessant had been Mr. Hawkins' labors, so wide apart had been his fields of labor, and so much was his family scattered, that it was not until this period, since his reformation, that he found himself in a situation where he could gather his family around him in his own *home.* That he was not insensible to the charms of " sweet home " the following letter will disclose : —

BOSTON, March 12th, 1846.

MY DEAR SISTER FRANCES, — I sit down to write you, but not a long letter. The object of my writing at this time is to inform you and our dear friends and relatives, that we have moved into Boston, and have commenced housekeeping. We have taken a comfortable house, in a pleasant part of the city called the " North End." Immediately in the rear of the house, is Christ Church (Episcopal), whose eight bells chime most sweetly on every Sabbath morning. On last Sabbath morning and afternoon they played more sweetly than ever, if possible, more than a dozen tunes. As I sat in my room listening, every sound brought back to my mind early memories of " Old Christ Church bells " * in my own dear native city. How pleasant, and yet how painful it is, to think of the past ; especially is it sad to look back upon an ill-spent life. Yet how pleasant is the reflection that the good Providence of God has kept us through the evil as well as the good ; has spared our lives and so changed our (my) circumstances. This thought indeed brings to me a pleasure that cannot be estimated or expressed. Such joys can be felt if they cannot be expressed.

Oh, how delightful it is *in our own home* to call our family together, and around our own family altar, " under our own vine and fig-tree," worship God, — none daring to make us afraid. My dear sister, that it is indeed pleasant to live under the smiles of a reconciled God and Father, you know by experience. He has kept you in the trying hour ; he has poured into your soul the healing balm of his divine spirit. Let us strive on, ever living for, and looking to God for deliverance ; it will surely come, and if faithful we shall triumph over all, and live with him forever. All here are well and desire to be remembered to dear relatives and friends ; to all, without going to the trouble of naming them, except dear little " Jimmy " [Mr. Hawkins was always affected to tenderness towards children who had lost a parent as this child had] ; I *must* name him. I wish his name was John, but it don't make much difference ; he was named after a much better man, who no doubt lives with God in heaven.

I came near forgetting to state that I have that spare room,

---

* These were the bells that Mr. Hawkins had heard from his early youth ; they are noted for their surpassing sweetness, and have been retained in the new edifice of Christ Church parish, Baltimore.

well furnished, for you. Now, if brother William, in the dull season of summer, would take to himself a little recreation, for the benefit of his health, and bring you on to "Bosting," it would afford me the greatest pleasure. Now, I am not joking. I may be in Baltimore myself this summer; that is, if the *fish bite*, of which I think there is but little doubt. You can then return with me; I will see you safe home. I have much more I would like to write, but have not the time. I send you the *Temperance Standard.* Please have the *Baltimore Sun* sent to me regularly. No more, my dear sister, at present,

From your brother,   JOHN.

The following letter from Mr. Hawkins to his sister, giving a quite minute statement of his domestic arrangements, will be found, it is believed, highly interesting and amusing.

BOSTON, April 1st, 1846.

MY DEAR SISTER,— I have just returned *home* from a short tour of duty through Bristol and Norfolk counties, in this State, and have had great success in obtaining signatures to the pledge. The cause of temperance, morals, humanity, and religion is still progressing.

I still continue to enjoy one of the greatest blessings of God, uninterrupted health, for which I am thankful, although very unworthy of so many favors. God has done great things for me, and I have cause to be glad. We have as a family every thing to make us happy, and if we are not so it is our own fault.

I have thought it might be some little gratification to you to give you some description of our location in the city, and our "fixins" about the house, that is, furniture, etc., etc. I am prompted to do this by the fact that I have never been so comfortably situated before in all my life. I do it also because you are not here to go through the house, and say "how nicely you are fixed!" In the first place we are located in a respect-

29*

able and quiet part of the city, and oh ! those bells, how charmingly do they chime out on the holy Sabbath of our common Father and God ! Our parlor is large and airy ; as large as either of yours ; the floor is covered with a beautiful new threeply carpet, a fine rug, a new settee, a mahogany card-table, but no cards, and one dozen very handsome chairs, and other things to match ; a rather fine looking-glass, pictures, and some other "fixins."

My bedroom is well furnished. Hannah's and the children's bedroom also has every comfort. Our kitchen is a good one ; our breakfast-room exhibits some little style. We have one of the best of servants (white) I ever saw ; she came with us from Roxbury. In the cellar we have an abundance of rain-water, and in the yard a pump of as good water as I ever drank in my life. I have also a room, a nice little bedroom, *that* is also furnished, and how glad I should be if I could only have the pleasure of lighting you up to it this summer.

* * * My dear and venerable mother, remember me to her in much kindness. I hope she is happy. Dear J—— will, I know, do all in his power to make her so, and so will his good wife. I hope he will take the advice I gave him in my last letter. Do you remember it ? It seems rather strange to advise a *husband* to be obedient to his *wife ;* but without joking, if husbands would look more to their wives for advice, it would be better for them. I speak from experience, and he is a good schoolmaster. I must close.

Your affectionate brother,

JOHN.

After remaining at home a few days Mr. Hawkins proceeded to comply with invitations to lecture in the following places: Foxboro', North, South, East, and West Bridgewater, South Abington, North Dighton, South Reading, Thomaston, in Maine, where he lectured three days with great acceptance, and many

pledges were taken, Camden, West Thomaston, Warren, Wiscasset, Bath, Brunswick, and Portland. On
the 1st of May he returned to Boston, and having no
appointment on Sunday he lectured to the inmates of
the State Prison. On the 4th we find him at Fitchburg ; subsequently in Fitzwilliam, Keene, Walpole,
Bellows Falls, Rockingham, Saxton River, Chester,
Cavendish, Ludlow, and Rutland, on his way to
Canada. We find at this date the following entries : —

Left Plattsburg May 25th, 1846, for Montreal. Lectured
in that city until the 5th of June, then took passage in a steamer
for Quebec, lecturing there with great success until the 11th
day of June. On that day departed for home, stopping on the
way at Melbourne, Sherbrook, and Compton, Canada ; Burlington and many other places in Vermont. Reached home on
the 7th of July.

This tour, involving many miles of travel and great
labor, was noticed in the papers of the day, both in
Canada and Vermont, as resulting in great and lasting
benefit to the cause.

CHAPTER XXI

"On, brothers, on! though the night be gone,
    And the morning glory breaking:
Though your toils be blest, *ye may not rest,*
    For danger's ever waking.
Ye have spread your sail, ye have braved the gale,
    And a calm o'er the sea is creeping;
But I know by the sky that danger's nigh —
    There's yet no time for sleeping."

No event, perhaps, in the social life of Mr. Hawkins afforded him so great pleasure as the visit of his venerable and pious mother to his home in Boston. This visit had been long in contemplation. For over forty years he had been the subject of her daily prayers. She was a *true mother.* Even in his wildest wanderings she had been always ready to open her arms to the returning prodigal. Indeed, there was much in her that any son might love. There was a sweetness in the expression of her countenance, a gentleness in her words, and a grace in her manners, that endeared her to all who knew her. To introduce this mother to his numerous friends in Boston who loved and honored him was indeed a great pleasure. Having made every arrangement for this visit, he left for Baltimore July 14, 1846, and returned to Boston on the 30th, bringing her with him; he remained at home until the 21st of August.

His visit to Baltimore, the condition in which he found things in that city, and his present happiness in the society of his aged parent, are thus alluded to by a sympathizing friend in one of the Boston papers: —

We have had a call from our friend John Hawkins, who has just returned from Baltimore, where he says the cause of temperance is in a truly deplorable state; grog-shops are multiplying, and an entirely new set of customers frequent them; young men from eighteen to twenty years of age, who at the commencement of the Washingtonian reform in that city were mere boys. Mr. Hawkins brought with him his venerable mother, who is now at his house. She is in her seventieth year, and is, in appearance, all that she has been represented by Mr. Hawkins in his addresses. What a source of happiness must it be' to mother and son to meet under such pleasant circumstances; — she about to leave the world in peace with God and man, and he, over whom she had shed so many tears, redeemed from intemperance, and beloved by the wise and good all over the land, soothing her declining years, and making her passage to the grave a most pleasant journey. God bless them both! May they live many years to enjoy each other's society, and when the summons shall come calling her or him to go home and be here no more, may they part to meet in heaven.

Mr. Hawkins did not remain idle during the whole period of his mother's visit, but, between the 21st of August and the 20th of September, lectured in twenty-six towns in Connecticut. He returned to Boston on the 21st, and continued his labors in and about the city, lecturing once to a large audience in Faneuil Hall, until Oct. 2d; on that day he wrote thus to his sister: —

BOSTON, Oct. 2d, 1846.

MY DEAR SISTER FRANCES,—I cannot say that I am happy to inform you that mother will leave Boston on Wednesday afternoon next, October 7th, at five o'clock for *home*, for the reason that her visit has been one of uninterrupted pleasure to us. I only wish it was so that she could "always live with me;" but I cannot expect this. During her sojourn with us her health has

been good, and I have done all that I could to make her stay
happy; it has been emphatically so. We visited the great
cattle show and fair yesterday at Lynn; she was delighted.
From thence we went by railroad to Salem, took a drive
through that beautiful city, visited the East India Museum, and
returned home in the afternoon. In the evening attended a
great temperance meeting at Faneuil Hall. To-morrow, Saturday, we are to visit the Blind Asylum at South Boston; this,
too, will be a gratifying sight to her. Now in regard to her
departure, we — for I shall accompany her as far as Philadelphia — shall leave here on Wednesday afternoon, as I have
stated. I think it is likely we shall remain part of a day in
Philadelphia, so that she may see Fairmount Water-works, and
other interesting objects in the city. I need scarcely say that
somebody should meet her at the depot in Pratt Street, for I
suppose there will be a host of you there to welcome her *home*
after her long absence.

Your brother, affectionately,

J. H. W. HAWKINS.

Changing his mind, he continued his journey to
Baltimore with his mother, and returned to Boston on
the 18th of October. On the next day he wrote to his
son, remarking: —

I leave this day for a tour "down East," into the State of
Maine; the following is the list of my appointments: Portsmouth, N. H., South Berwick, Kennebunk, Kennebunk Port,
two days; Saco, Portland, Brunswick, Bath, Wiseasset, Noble-
boro', Waldoboro', Warren, Union, Prospect, Searsport, Belfast,
two days; Bath, Bowdoinham, Gardiner, Hallowell, Augusta,
Vassalboro', Waterville, Skowhegan, Norridgewock, Farmington, Livermore, Turner, Paris, Norway, Waterford, North
Bridgeton, Bridgeton, Lovell, Fryeburgh, Brownfield, Den-
mark, Hiram, East Baldwin, Standish, Buxton Centre, Lim-

erick, Waterboro Centre, Alfred, two days, and Springvale. Mr.
Hunt left here this morning for the State of New Hampshire.

He returned to Boston on the 10th of December,
where he remained until the 20th of January, 1847.
His observation of the state of things in the city had
convinced him that a more stringent enforcement of
existing laws was absolutely necessary for the protection of the unoffending people, or, if that should prove
ineffectual, that the municipal laws should be so
changed as to clothe the proper authorities with fuller
powers to suppress the iniquitous traffic. So aggrieved
was he at the increase of intemperance, that he addressed the following communication to the editor of
the *Mercantile Journal*. It was introduced by the following editorial remarks : —

We commend to the serious attention of our readers the facts
and suggestions set forth in the following communication from
Mr. Hawkins, the powerful and well-known advocate of temperance. The increase of intemperance and kindred vices in
our good city is indeed alarming, and should rouse to action the
disinterested philanthropist, and the true friends to the interests
of the city. The suggestions of Mr. Hawkins appear sound
and feasible, and we hope will be carried into operation without
delay.

BOSTON, January 4, 1847.

Mr. SLEEPER : *Dear Sir*, — The year 1846 has closed, and
1847 has come in upon us like a spring day ; it has not brought
joy to all ; we cannot say a happy new year to all.

During my stay in the city, I am in the habit of visiting
the poor, the needy, and the distressed, with which our goodly
city abounds, more than in former years. Not a day passes,
when I am at home, that I am not in the Police Court.

On the first day of the new year an unusual number of cases

of drunkenness were brought up before the Police Court. A man who keeps a notorious grog-shop opposite the National Theatre, was complained of by the City Marshal for selling three glasses of gin to two boys; one thirteen, the other fourteen years of age; both made drunk and taken to the *watch-house*. On the next day, they were brought before the Police Court, when they testified to the fact of purchasing and drinking the gin, for which the seller was justly fined sixty dollars and costs, and bound over to *keep the peace*. The two boys, for want of security to appear at the Municipal Court against him, were committed to Leverett-Street jail.

Now, sir, if the new year has thus commenced, where shall we find ourselves at its close? From the year 1830 to the close of 1839, a period of ten years, there were twenty-one thousand three hundred and fifty complaints made before the Police Court. The last six years the number is twenty thousand seven hundred and fifty-one, making the enormous sum of forty-two thousand one hundred and one. The last year the number of complaints were four thousand and ninety-three; an increase of six hundred and eighty-three over the previous year. Is not this increase fearfully alarming? Why is it that there seems to be so great an increase of drunkenness? Is it not that grog-shops have been permitted to multiply to a frightful degree? The fact of their increase is so glaring that no one will for a moment question it. Is it not in the power of our worthy mayor and aldermen, at least in some degree, to lessen their number by taking such steps as their judgment and the present condition of society demand? If it is not in their power to stop them, why in the name of humanity should not the coming Legislature so alter the present law, that the city authorities may be clothed with power so to act that the *wicked rum-seller* may feel that he shall not be permitted to grow rich upon the *poor*, and ride rough-shod over the laws of the Commonwealth.

The city, county, and State, are put to an enormous expense

by the existence of grog-shops, and humanity, bleeding at every pore, demands that something more effectual should be done. Boston, it will be acknowledged, is a great field of labor, and there are many laborers at work; and there is still room for more. I have, for several years, thought that a plan might be adopted which would lessen the sufferings of humanity, reform the intemperate, and save thousands of dollars to the city. My want of education convinces me that I am not competent to *write* out the proper and necessary suggestions. I will, however, venture to suggest a partial plan of operation; viz., appoint some suitable person who would be willing to devote his whole time in finding out and visiting the unfortunate drunkard, and endeavor so to reform him that he may be kept out of the Police Court and the House of Correction, and restored to his family, his country, and his God, and make him a useful citizen, by watching over him for good; also to visit and relieve the wants of the poor and destitute in which our city abounds. I know that the various charitable institutions have committees appointed in each ward to relieve the poor, and that the city has in each ward an overseer of the poor; but those men are generally men of business, and cannot devote their whole time to it; such an operation cannot but be productive of great good. Such an enterprise cannot be carried on without money. And how is this money to be raised? I answer, by private subscription. Several wealthy gentlemen who have conversed with me on the subject, approve the plan, and have expressed their willingness to aid the enterprise. In conclusion, I would most respectfully invite public attention to this matter, believing it to be of great importance to the welfare of the city.   Yours respectfully,

JOHN H. W. HAWKINS.

On the 20th of January he was present and spoke at the Vermont State Temperance Convention, held at Springfield. On the first of February he was again

30

invited to the State of Maine, and lectured in twenty-six towns where he had not before been, and returned to Boston on the 28th. On the 3d of March the Washington State Temperance Convention of Massachusetts assembled; a large number of delegates were present from all parts of Massachusetts, and from other New England States. Capt. W. R. Stacy was elected President; resolutions were offered and passed, expressive of devout thankfulness to God for the onward progress of the Washingtonian movement in rescuing thousands of degraded men from the evil of intemperance. A large number of effective speeches were made upon the occasion, the speakers being limited to ten minutes each.

" I fear not," briefly remarked Mr. Hawkins, " for the temperance cause. The signers of ·the pledge have stood firm to their principles, amid a thousand temptations without, and the gnawing cravings of appetite within ; and they *will* stand, despite the baneful influences around them. I feel and believe there are men around me now, who have been saved from the iron thraldom of intemperance, whom I shall yet see standing at the right hand of the throne of God. When I look at the nature of man, and consider the passions, like the flint and steel, ready to burst into flame at the slighest collision, I wonder that so many have been saved. I have now lived seven years a sober life, and enjoyed for seven years a sober sleep. There is nothing now to make me tremble. There is one sweet thought at morning and night, in summer and in winter, in sickness and in health, that my heart involuntarily and continually utters, and it is this, " *Thank God I am a sober man.*" Let us go on, brethren, nor cease our labors, until the last drunkard is saved. Never give up a man while there is life; but struggle on, and lift him up again and yet again, nor relinquish your hold upon him, until he is dead, dead, dead!" His remarks are spoken of as being highly encouraging to his co-laborers in the good cause.

On the 6th of March, 1847, a very important decision of the Supreme Court of the United States was made, recognizing the right of the several States to regulate and control the trade in intoxicating drinks within their respective limits. How this decision affected Mr. Hawkins may be learned from his remarks in a letter to his son, dated Boston, March 23d. After referring to a very successful tour in Rhode Island, where he had visited eight places in as many days, and of his intention to return and lecture there until the first of May, he proceeds : " I have nothing more of interest to write, except that the late decision of the Supreme Court has thrown the rum-sellers, all over the land, into a great state of confusion. The sentence has been pronounced; —' Othello's occupation's gone!'"

On the next day he went to Providence, R. I., which he made his head-quarters, and by the 7th of May he had canvassed the largest part of the State, lecturing in twenty-six towns.

On the 10th and 11th of April we find him again in Boston. The alarming increase of the traffic, and the distressing instances of inebriation which met his eye, called forth the following very pungent article in the *Boston Daily Chronotype*. The circumstance referred to recalled to Mr. Hawkins' mind, without doubt, a similar practice which existed at the time of his own apprenticeship, and which was the cause of so much

woe to himself, and his fellow-apprentices and workmen.

(FOR THE CHRONOTYPE.)

MASTER-MECHANICS AND LIQUORS.

I was glad to see that you noticed an editorial paragraph
that appeared in the *Bee* of the 6th inst., in which that paper
said: " *We are informed that several large master-mechanics
have put hogsheads of liquor up in their shops, and where before
they gave* $1.50 *per day, now pay* $1.44, *with the privilege of
pulling twice at the bung during the day.*"

Now, sir, I ask can it be *possible* that in the city of Boston
there is a " master-mechanic " so insensible to his interests, the
interests of his journeymen and apprentices, as to put upon tap
" hogsheads of liquor" for his men and boys? And I ask
further; can it be possible that in this age of light there can be
found journeymen mechanics who would tamely submit to so
gross an outrage as having their wages docked as above stated
for the privilege of " pulling twice at the bung during the day ? "
No, sir; I don't believe there is one word of truth in the statement. If untrue, it is a base outrage and libel upon that most
respectable class of our citizens ; if true, the *Bee* should name
them, that the parents of the apprentices, at least, may know
the temptation that is set before them. Master-mechanics
and journeymen, is the above statement of the *Bee* true or
false? What say you? are you slaves or freemen?

It appears to me that since the unparalleled outrages committed in Faneuil Hall, several of the daily papers, from
articles appearing in them, are playing second fiddle to the
rum-sellers, who have so grossly outraged the laws of this
Commonwealth. Why is this? Have they lost their independence? or have they never had any, farther than their own
interests are concerned? But I must take care how I write, or
I may bring down on my devoted head the *power* of the *press*
with all the *good moral character* of the rum-sellers of Boston.
Gracious Heavens! The good moral character of a rum-seller

of 1847! What an idea! Why, sir, you might as well talk about a pious devil, a virtuous prostitute, or an honest thief, as to talk of a rum-seller in this age of light having a "good moral character." In business matters I have not a doubt of the honesty of a large majority of them. But their business! what wretched misery has it caused in our land, and yet they are not satisfied. The cry is, give! give! Yes, they have applied to the honorable mayor and aldermen of the city of Boston for a license to continue their work of death and destruction ; and Wednesday next, the 14th day of April, at three o'clock, is set apart to hear from them, in person or through their representatives, their arguments in favor of granting them a license to *kill.* Will our honorable mayor and aldermen grant them a license? I pray God that they may not do so. They will not, unless they wish to undo all that temperance has done for the city, over which they have been called by a virtuous people to preside. I should like to be present to hear their arguments why license should be granted to them, but my engagements call me elsewhere.

I will close by entering my most solemn protest against granting any man a license to sell intoxicating liquors as a *beverage.* I care not how good a "moral character" he may bear. I solemnly protest against the sale of an agent, for the purpose of gain, which by the accordant and unanimous consent of all intelligent physiologists and physicians, carries injury and mischief to every organ, tissue, and fibre of the human body, engendering feuds and quarrels, dismembering families, and creating, wherever it comes, domestic wretchedness and anguish in their most dreadful forms ; — an agent which is the acknowledged enemy of every industrial pursuit of mankind; the deadly destroyer of industry and thrift, upon the farm, in the shop, on the ship, behind the counter, in the office, and wherever there are hands to work or work to be done ; the foe of agriculture, of manufactures, of art, and of learning ; — an agent which destroys every moral sensibility,

30*

paralyzes the conscience, and dethrones religion; the effects of which may be seen in the brutal wallowings of debased men, in the shameful spreeings of drunkenness, in the turbulence of mobs, in the abominations of the brothel; — an agent whose fell effects are to be read in the records of the hospital, in the annals of the poorhouse, house of correction, and jails, in the penitentiaries, and the gallows. And now, what shall be thought of men who, in view of these disastrous consequences of their business, will ask for a license to sell intoxicating drinks? It cannot be possible that our worthy mayor and aldermen will grant the request of the petitioners. If they do, farewell to the morals of Boston. I close by subscribing myself the uncompromising foe to the sale and use of intoxicating liquor as a beverage.

JOHN H. W. HAWKINS.

From the 17th of May until the 10th of June Mr. Hawkins confined his labors to the State of Vermont. On the 15th he was at Philadelphia, attending the celebration of the National Division of the Sons of Temperance, an order to which he belonged, and to the advancement of which he gave his hearty efforts. This benevolent society had increased in the year then past, sixty thousand; making at the date of the meeting a membership of over a hundred thousand. He remained in Philadelphia until the 19th, frequently taking a part in their deliberations. Returning to Boston, he again started for the State of Maine, and returned on the 20th of July; he speaks of the journey as "a long and laborious tour 'Down East.'"

During the month of August he canvassed a large part of Massachusetts and a portion of Connecticut; up to the 6th of September he had lectured in twenty-nine towns; during this time he spent but five days with his family. On the 6th of the above month he reached Hartford, Ct., and thus writes to his son : —

I have been well received everywhere. I held a very large meeting last evening (Sunday) in the City Hall; they have prevailed on me to remain here to-night (Monday) and give another address, consequently we (your mother is with me) shall not be in Middletown by boat to-day, as I wrote you. We now purpose leaving in the nine o'clock stage on Tuesday morning. I am to be at Haddam the same evening.

During the remaining weeks of September he delivered nineteen lectures in the same number of towns in Connecticut. He next commenced a series of lectures in all the important towns in the State of New Jersey. The impression produced in this State was scarcely less than that which had attended his first efforts. Everywhere he aroused the timid, and inspired the wavering to renewed attacks upon the foe to human happiness against which he was battling.

Completing these engagements, he returned to New York on the 20th of October. He left that city for his home on the 27th, and lectured on the way in eight towns.

The rapidity of his movements and the amount of his labors was at this period in his history truly astonishing; and the enthusiasm which he brought into the work excited the admiration of the friends of temperance everywhere. After reaching Norwich, Ct., he visited several places in the vicinity, and attended the Connecticut State Temperance Convention, held November 10th, taking an active part in its deliberations. After a rest of six days at home, we find him visiting

and lecturing in New London and several of the adjacent towns.   On the 25th of November his journal
speaks of his efforts at Plainfield, N. J., and other
places in that neighborhood.   Next we find him instructing and entertaining large audiences at Wilmington, Del.; December 1st to 6th in his native city, Baltimore, where he speaks upon frequent occasions.   After
lecturing on the 7th and 8th of December in Frederick
City, Md., he visits his mother for one day at Cherry
Grove.   On the 13th we find him again at Wilmington,
Del., from which place he went to Philadelphia; thence
to Connecticut again, where he lectured in fifteen towns,
until the 6th day of January, 1848, when, exhausted by
excessive labor, he returned to Boston to rest for a few
weeks and enjoy the society of his family.   While
there he addressed a letter to his sister, from which we
make the following.extract: —

  *   *   * I have just returned home from my tour through
the land of "steady habits."   I have held many interesting
meetings since I left Baltimore.   I have spoken in public
twenty-eight times in twenty-two days.   That much labor
would break down some of our strongest ministers, but, strange
as it may seem, it scarcely affects me; only for a little while
after I have done speaking.   What a great blessing it is to
have such uninterrupted good health of body and full flow of
spirits; not spirits of *rum*, but of a sound mind.   How much,
my dear sister, am I indebted to my heavenly Father that my
drinking habits did not break down my constitution.   *   *   *

He remained at home until the 21st of January, and
then, by invitation, lectured in Milton, South Boston,
Neponset, Cambridgeport, Raynham, Milton Mills, etc.,

and on the 30th attended a meeting at Tremont Temple. We next find him at Chelsea, West Medway, two days, Wayland, Fall River, and New York. On the 4th of February he addressed a brief note to his son, saying, —

I have in contemplation to visit the West by way of Buffalo; this I intimated to you when I saw you. If so, it is probable we shall not have the pleasure of being present in Middletown to attend the Commencement when you graduate. I shall at all events see you before we go West.

The visit of Father Mathew to this country was an event to which Mr. Hawkins looked forward with much pleasure; he longed to take by the hand and welcome the good man to this country. Letters had been received by several persons, and also by Mr. Hawkins, explaining why he was unable to leave Ireland sooner. Mr. Hawkins alludes to this expectation in a letter to his son, dated Boston, April 11, 1848. In the mean time, from February 4th, he had visited and spoken to interested audiences in forty towns in Massachusetts, Connecticut, and Rhode Island. In the letter alluded to he says : —

I had intended not to leave for the West until Father Mathew's arrival in this country, which was, you know, expected in May. A letter from him to-day informs me that he will not be in this country until the month of August or September. I have therefore made up my mind to proceed to Western New York and through Upper Canada, commencing some time in May.

He continued to lecture in and about Boston, and on the 19th of April thus writes : —

I have just this moment returned from Cape Ann, Gloucester and Rockport, and go off again this afternoon for Marblehead, Gloucester, West Parish, Saugus, Manchester, and Danvers. I shall leave Boston, positively, the providence of God permitting, on the 2d day of May, for my journey to the West and Upper Canada, sweeping round through the lakes to St. Louis, etc.

After complying with numerous invitations to lecture in various parts of New England, he went to New York, and after delivering a number of lectures there and in adjacent cities, he departed on his journey. We have not room for all the details which he recorded in his journal. In a letter to his son, dated Oswego, June 1, 1848, he says : —

I have thus far been received with marked attention, partic ularly in this place ; several interesting meetings have been held. This afternoon, at three o'clock, I address the Cadets of Temperance and the Daughters of Temperance, and at night, in one of the churches, I speak to the public. To-morrow I leave by steamer for Ogdensburg, thence I cross the St. Lawrence to Prescott, on my way through Canada West, etc.

After visiting eighteen of the principal cities in Middle and Northern New York, he passed on to the following towns in Canada : Brookville, Kingston, Montreal, Cananoque, Brockville, Belleville, Pictou, and Toronto, in each of which places he spent from one to four days. This, however, was but a small part of what he proposed to accomplish when he started on his journey. He returned to Boston on the 7th of July. The following extract from a letter to his son, under date of July 10, 1848, will account for his unexpected return ; —

It will no doubt surprise you to know that I have arrived at home. Two reasons have caused this; first, the want of support in Canada; they scarcely paid my expenses. The farther I travelled into Canada, the worse I found it; yet I hope not a little good has been accomplished; the meetings were generally well attended. The other reason — for not going into Michigan and Wisconsin — is, that the political excitement is raging in that section to such a degree that nothing can be done on the subject of temperance.

This was the canvass which resulted in the election of General Taylor. From the date of the above letter to the 26th of August, he was employed almost daily in various parts of Massachusetts, Rhode Island, and Connecticut; most of this time was spent in Bristol County.

A part of August and September he spent in the State of Maine. On the 18th, 19th, 20th, and 21st he was in Washington City, having been invited there to lecture for a few days. On the 7th of October he again returned to the State of Maine, and after lecturing in twenty-seven towns, passed into the Province of New Brunswick, speaking to interested audiences in many of its towns. His engagement closed in St. John, where he spent three days. He returned to Boston on the 16th of November, and the remainder of the year was devoted to lecturing in Barnstable county Although he had previously visited almost every town on Cape Cod, he was now invited to canvass the whole county a second time; his lectures were everywhere well received.

The cause was now making rapid advances in all parts of the State. The Parent Total Abstinence Soeiety of Boston, alone, since its formation in April, 1841, soon after Mr. Hawkins came there to lecture, had received, up to January 1848, fifty-six thousand three hundred and eighty signatures.

"But there's a fire, along whose track,
 Spring never scatters flowers in bloom,
But all is desolate and black
 As midnight in a hopeless tomb.

" Alike upon the low and high
 Falls this ' strange fire ; ' it feeds and preys
On Beauty's check, in Wisdom's eye,
 And melts down manhood in its blaze.

" Quench, mighty God ! by thine own power,
 By love and truth, with spring and well,
With stream and cistern, flood and shower,
 In mercy quench this fire of hell ! "

ALLUSION has already been made to the fact that the
subject of this memoir was in the habit of collecting,
wherever he went, statistics connected with the subject
of intemperance. These embraced reports of benevolent institutions, the condition of jails, poorhouses, etc.
The facts thus collected he was enabled to use with
great effect when the subject of prohibitory legislation
began to be agitated. Day after day, month after
month, and year after year, by personal conversation,
by public addresses, and sometimes by articles in the
newspapers, he labored to convince the public of the
wicked system under which they were living, a system
which permitted, under the sanction of law, the existence of trades which were in direct violation of the
laws of sobriety, and against the interests of human-

31   (361)

ity. In reply to the argument that the business of manufacturing and vending intoxicating drinks was sanctioned by law, he contended that the power to make laws was derived from the people, and that the wisest course to pursue was to educate the people up to the point where they would demand, through their representatives, the repeal of existing statutes and the enactment of laws which would *prohibit* the continuance of the nefarious business.

Mr. Hawkins regarded with evident pleasure the growing sentiment of the New England States against the traffic. Some of the States repealed all license laws; others began to agitate the question of making it a highly penal offence to be found engaged in the business. The period was rapidly approaching when a " Prohibitory Law " was to be the watchword of all the advocates of temperance. For the coming of that day he longed and labored. Being well acquainted with the condition of the question in all the States of the Union, his lectures wherever he went were highly appreciated, not only for the information they communicated, but for the interest in the cause which they awakened in the hearts of his hearers. To this doctrine of prohibition thousands of converts were now being made. Mr. Hawkins was acknowledged to have been no feeble instrument in the attainment of this object.

Returning to Mr. Hawkins' correspondence we find, in a letter dated at Norwich, Ct., Jan. 17, 1849, the following brief account of his visit to the " Northeast : " —

After returning to Boston for a few days, I started for the Province of New Brunswick, taking in my course the whole

coast of Maine, visiting almost every town from Boston to
Calais and many towns in the Province, including the city of
St. John. You remember I was in New Brunswick about five
years since; they were then far behind-hand in the temperance
reformation. I did not suppose that my feeble labors while
there were of any good to the people; but how mistaken we
sometimes are; we do good and don't know it. My recent
visit gave me incontestible evidence of the fact. Many came
to me and told me that they were reformed under my lecturing,
and they now have a large number of the Divisions of the Sons
of Temperance, the best conducted and attended of any that I
have visited. They were very glad to see me, and treated me
with every mark of attention. On my return, I visited every
town in Barnstable County. I then returned *home* for a few
days; then started again, visiting the following towns in New
Hampshire; viz., Nashua, Manchester, Concord, Gilmanton,
Meredith Bridge, and so on to Franklin; returned to Lowell,
and lectured there one week every night. At home one day,
thence to Clintonville, thence to this place, where I am engaged
for one week, and three weeks in the vicinity. I design to be
at Cincinnati in May, at the grand National Jubilee of the Sons
of Temperance. * * *

Between the date of the last letter and the first of
May, Mr. Hawkins visited and addressed the citizens
of fifty-five towns in various parts of New England.
Invitations poured in upon him from every quarter.
One writer says, " We want you here for the reason
that we need to have temperance truths poured upon
us *boiling hot*, until we shall be made to feel their importance." Mr. Hawkins sometimes did so, and the
result was that many individuals, not much interested
in the progress of temperance, complained bitterly of
his severity. He was an ardent opponent of the aiders

and abettors of the evil, and, therefore, it is not strange that he made some enemies.

On the 2d of May he left for Cincinnati to attend the jubilee referred to, stopping at Pittsburg, at which place there was a large assembling of the Sons of Temperance. Lecturing a few days in Newport, Ky., and Madison, Ind., he proceeded to Indianapolis, where he left Mrs. Hawkins, whose feeble health did not permit her to accompany him to the various towns where he was engaged to lecture. He visited almost every town of any importance in the State, devoting to· this work the whole month of June. The month of July he spent in Michigan, and in the northern part of Ohio. On the 4th of August he reached Kalamazoo. We make the following extracts from a letter written at this place.   •

Your very kind and prompt reply to my letter written at Ann Arbor, was duly received upon my arrival this morning in this very *beautiful* village, the most beautiful I have ever seen. From Ann Arbor we proceeded to Dexter, where we tarried two days, stopping at the mansion of Judge D——, formerly of Massachusetts. Thence to Jackson, where we sojourned in the family of a Mr. S——, secretary of the insurance company located in that place. We remained three days, and were treated in a most handsome manner. I lectured three times to houses crowded to their utmost capacity. The State Prison is located at this place. Mrs. S——, accompanied by my wife and myself, visited the prison. I spoke to the inmates and such a time of weeping I have seldom witnessed anywhere. They are mostly young men; some of them *buried* for life within these walls. One young man is sentenced for life to solitary confinement in a cell, for murder. From Jackson we proceeded to Albion; thence to Marshall, another large and beautiful village. I spoke to a crowded congregation in the Presbyterian Church at 2 P.M.; in the evening in the M. E. Church; the people could not all be seated. We next visited the villages of Cold Water, Centreville, Constantine, and Cassopolis. We shall leave this place on Monday morning for . Battle Creek, and on Monday, August 8th, go to Niles. I have changed some of my appointments from those sent you; by present appointments we proceed first to Mishawaka, thence to * * * all of which are in Indiana. We shall then cross Lake Michigan to Chicago, arriving at the latter place Monday, August 20th. From thence to Southport, Racine, and Milwaukie; thence to Mackinac; thence to Sault De Ste. Marie; at this place there is *good fishing;* they catch pike, trout, and whitefish that weigh from twenty to forty pounds. You see I must say something about fishing. * * *

Mr. Hawkins did not, after all, have the pleasure of angling in the Lakes. News reached him of the arrival in this country of Father Mathew, and after visiting a large number of places in Illinois, Wisconsin, and Michigan, he began his journey homeward, lecturing on his way in Cleveland, Erie, Penn., and Buffalo, which place he left on the 27th of September for Boston. Mr. Hawkins says in his journal, " Met Father Mathew for the first time in Taunton, Massachusetts."

The circumstances attending this their first public interview, were noticed in the papers of the day; one account thus refers to the event : —

JOHN HAWKINS AND FATHER MATHEW. — The enterprising friends of temperance at Taunton, had a magnificent demonstration on Saturday, October 6th, 1849. They met *en masse* to welcome the arrival of the far-famed philanthropist, Father Mathew. Addresses were made by Father Mathew, Rev. Mr. Brigham, John Hawkins, and G. W. Bungay. At

31*

the close of a short and spirited speech by Mr. Hawkins, he extended his hand to Father Mathew, who immediately arose and grasped it in a most hearty and affectionate manner. It was a gratifying spectacle to see those veteran heralds of temperance shaking hands and smiling benedictions on each other; as though both hearts were beating in each bosom. They are both robust-looking men, just past the prime of life, somewhat resembling each other in form, if not in feature. When Mr. Hawkins renewed the pledge he has never violated, the good friar who administered it stooped down and kissed him in a most paternal and patriarchal manner.

Before leaving the North, Mr. Hawkins addressed a letter to Father Mathew, congratulating him upon his safe arrival in this country, and expressive of an earnest desire that his days of usefulness might be many; accompanying the note was a volume of "The Reformed Drunkard." On reaching St. Louis, several months after, Mr. Hawkins received the following letter in reply: —

IRVING HOUSE, NEW YORK, November 9, 1849.

MY DEAR SIR, — Your esteemed letter has just been handed to me by my secretary, Mr. O'Meara. It affords me much pleasure to hear that you are well, and successfully engaged in the good cause. I am staying here for a few days to recruit my health, prior to my departure for the South. Next week, God willing, I purpose proceeding to Philadelphia. At present I have not decided on the period of my further appointments, but after I can arrange them, shall be happy to inform you. I take this opportunity to thank you for your interesting and valuable present of "The Reformed Drunkard." Wishing you all success, and shall always be happy to hear from you,

I am, dear Mr. Hawkins,

Yours most sincerely,

THEOBALD MATHEW.

MR. J. H. W. HAWKINS, Springfield, Ill.

Mr. Hawkins finding that the journey to the West was beneficial to his wife's health, decided to return and continue his labors in that section of the country. A letter to his son, of Dec. 17th, 1849, contains a full account of his progress as far as Springfield, Ill.; we find room for a few extracts: —

* * * On reaching Schenectady we took passage on board a packet on the "raging kanawl," for Buffalo; we were three days and four nights performing the distance, three hundred and forty-eight miles; by railroad it would have taken us only fourteen hours. On the 6th left Cleveland for Detroit. Having delivered a number of lectures in that neighborhood, I made arrangements for my visit to Illinois.

After describing a number of places through which he passed, he continues: —

This [Nov. 30th] morning at day break, we started for La Salle and Peru. One of the most lovely mornings I ever beheld; clear and mild, and we are in such good spirits; the *spirits*, too, were of the right kind. Just after breakfast we saw four beautiful full-grown deer, within twenty yards of us. It was indeed a fine sight, as, with their heads raised to their full height, they cantered away across the prairie. At noon we reached La Salle and Peru, the two villages joining each other, situated on the Illinois river, at the end of the canal, and commencement of steamboat' navigation. These two villages have a vast and fertile prairie on all sides of them, and are destined to be great places of business.

Spent two days here and lectured two evenings to well-filled houses. Monday, Dec. 3, reached Peoria, where I held three meetings; the most enthusiastic, I believe, I have ever held.

He next visited Pekin and Naples, where he met

large audiences. After speaking particularly of Springfield and Jacksonville, he concludes:—

We shall probably leave Jacksonville on Friday, for St.
Louis, by stage route, stopping at the villages of Whitehall,
Carrolton, Jerseyville, and Alton; thence by the river Missis-
sippi to St. Louis.

Among the papers left by Mr. Hawkins we find the
following testimonials of the estimation in which his
services were held in the West at the time of this visit.

JACKSONVILLE, Dec. 14, 1849.

DEAR BROTHER,—We have been directed by a resolution
of Excelsior Division, No. 25, S. T., to request you, if not
inconsistent with your other arrangements, to re-visit this
place and to deliver another address to the citizens of Jacksonville on the subject of temperance. The members of our
Division, in common with all the good and true men of our
vicinity who had the pleasure of hearing your recent lectures,
are of opinion that great good must always result from efforts
aimed as yours are, and that sure success will follow where the
weapons of the combat are as bright as those which you have
exhibited to us.

We are instructed to say to you that your charges while here
will be borne by this Division, and that they will provide for
your transportation to the next village on your route of travel.

Be pleased to advise us as soon as possible of your disposition with regard to our invitation, so that our arrangements
may be seasonably made.

Yours in love, purity, and fidelity,

JAS. BERDAN,
RICHARD YATES,   } Committee.
J. W. KING,
NAPOLEON KOSCIALOWSKI,

P. S.—Should you accept our invitation, you are most

cordially invited to make my house the home of yourself and family during your stay. J. W. KING.

BROTHER JOHN HAWKINS: *Dear Brother,* — It affords me great pleasure to forward to you the following resolution, passed unanimously by our Division.

Resolved, That the warmest thanks of the Division be tendered to Brother John Hawkins, for his *acceptable* labors in this place in the cause of temperance.

A. M. BLACKSTONE,
Acting Recording Secretary, pro. tem.

On reaching St. Louis Mr. Hawkins received pressing invitations to lecture in various parts of Missouri, a few of which he was able to accept. He proceeds with a narrative of his journey in a letter written at Louisville, February 4th, 1850, from which we make the following extracts: —

You will be somewhat surprised to hear of our making so sudden and long a jump from Nashville to this place; the reason is this. Upon my arrival at Nashville I learned that Philip S. White, of Philadelphia, was engaged to lecture in the State, and I thought it would not be right for me to be in his way. * * *

I resume my narrative at Jacksonville. I spoke a second time there to an overflowing house. The Sons met in a body at their hall, preceded by a fine band of music. We marched to the Congregational Church; the meeting was opened by prayer by the Grand Chaplain; the band then played a fine air; after which eight of the pupils from the Blind Asylum, which is located here, played most delightfully upon various instruments of music; it was indeed a beautiful scene. The exercises were concluded by vocal music, of the most affecting kind, from those blind pupils. * * * On Monday morning the friends provided us a private conveyance, at their own expense, to Jerseyville. Here we had a most delightful time. It was Christmas-eve, and there being previous knowledge of our coming, extensive arrangements had been made. The Sons took the business in hand, and it was done in handsome style. We, with a number of friends, partook of our Christmas dinner with the Rev. George C. Wook. In the evening I lectured to a crowded house. After lecture we attended a delightful entertainment at the house of a friend from our native State; our social converse was kept up till long after midnight; this you will think was a little *intemperate.* We had, however, none of the "crittur" to spoil our enjoyment, for there is not a place in this town where a glass of liquor can be bought.

Wednesday morning, 20th, the Hon. Mr. Goodrich took us in his carriage to Alton. Monday, December 31st, we took steamboat for St. Louis, and on our arrival found that our temperance friends had provided excellent accommodation for us at the best hotel in the city. * * *

On our arrival at Nashville we were met at the boat by some of the leading friends of temperance, who insisted, notwithstanding Mr. White's engagement, — he had not yet arrived from New Orleans, — that we must stay at least one week; we were provided with rooms at a good hotel. I held some very interesting meetings in the city, and at the close of a well-spent week we took passage in the steamer E. W. Edwards for this place, and arrived here on Friday morning, February 1st.

In the month of April Mr. Hawkins visited Washington, Georgetown, and Alexandria, spending one day with his son at the Theological Seminary near the latter place. He arrived at Boston, on his return, April 22d. From the 12th of May to the 4th of July he was employed almost daily in lecturing at various

places in New England.   On the 5th of July he again
left Boston on a visit to the West.   We make the following brief extract from a letter to his son, dated at
Quincy, Ill., Nov. 27, 1850 : —

    *   *   *   I have crowded and attentive audiences in almost
every place visited.   The cause has made great progress in
this country.   I have lectured two evenings in this place ; the
largest room could not hold the people.   At the close of my
second lecture, I was requested by acclamation to return from
Palmyra, a distance of twelve miles, to deliver three more addresses ; a great many have signed the pledge ; some of these
" hard cases."   After filling my engagement here, I shall return
to Baltimore by way of St. Louis, Cincinnati, etc.   I think
seriously of making Baltimore city my residence in future ; it
will be quite as central for my work as Boston.   *   *   *

Mr. Hawkins accordingly removed his family to Baltimore on the 11th day of January, 1851.   The months
of March and April following he spent in Pennsylvania, lecturing in a large number of towns in the
Eastern and middle portions of that State.   In the
months of May, June, and July, he visited and lectured
with great acceptance in every town of importance in
Virginia.   Of the numerous letters which were received from him during his sojourn in that State, we
can find room for the following only : —

RICHMOND, Va., May 27, 1851.

MY DEAR SON, — The heading of this letter may surprise
you.   It is true that I am in the " Old Dominion."   I have been
lecturing in Richmond for a week, and you may ask with
much propriety, why I did not stop to see you at Alexandria ;
or why I have not written.   Constant occupation is my only
excuse.   However, I shall do better in future.   I shall leave

here to-day for Petersburg, where I shall probably spend the remainder of the week. From the 5th to the 11th I spent with General John H. Cocke, of Fluvanna County, lecturing daily in that neighborhood. I find considerable interest in the cause in this State, and attentive audiences. Let me know the precise time when you take orders, as I wish, if possible, to be at the seminary at the time.

I am, in great haste, your father, affectionately,

J. H. W. HAWKINS.

On the 20th of August, soon after his return from his arduous labors in Virginia, he left for Portland, Me. He had been invited to canvass that State for the purpose of encouraging the people in their enforcement of the "prohibitory liquor law," which had then become a statute-law of the State. The simple principle of that statute was, to prohibit entirely the sale of intoxicating liquors as a beverage. It was subsequently materially amended in 1852, and rendered still more stringent in its provisions by the law of 1855. How this new species of legislation was regarded by Mr. Hawkins may be learned from the following communications; one of them from his friend and earnest and able co-laborer in the cause, Dr. Charles Jewett, whose name alone is a tower of strength. The first is from Mr. Hawkins to his son. It will be noticed that it was written soon after the meeting of the State Temperance Convention, which was held at Portland, on the 26th of August, and continued its session three days. Mr. Hawkins was present and participated in its deliberations.

SEBAGO, Me., Sept. 11, 1851.

MY DEAR SON, — Since I left Baltimore I have confined my labors to Maine; I hope, too, with some success. This

State now stands *first* in the cause of temperance. This you may infer from its liquor law, a copy of which I enclose in this letter; the provisions of which, if enforced in their very *spirit* and *letter*, especially in regard to the seizure and destruction of all liquors coming into the State, must *put an end to the traffic.* Thousands of gallons have already been destroyed by pouring it out upon the ground. There are now under lock and key, in various places in this State, several hundred casks, that have been seized and will be destroyed according to *law*, at the *proper time*, as you will see by its provisions. The passage of this very stringent law has surprised not only the people of the United States, but the whole civilized globe wherever the temperance question has been agitated. And what is the most astonishing part of the matter is, that the law so far has been rigidly enforced, without serious opposition on the part of the rum-sellers or their friends. Every cargo, either by steamboat, railroad, or otherwise, that has been landed or is landing at any port of entry along the coast of Maine, is closely watched and inspected by the citizens; particularly so by an order called the "Watchman's Club." There are now over one hundred of these clubs in the State, composed of thousands of its very best citizens, who have solemnly pledged themselves to enforce the law, and they will do it. Last week a young man only thirty years of age, a trader at Waterford, declared that he would sell liquor in spite of all law, and threatened death to any officer or citizen who should dare to seize any of his. Under the cover of night he started on his way to Waterford, with his team, on which he had placed two barrels of rum, that had been clandestinely secreted in a warehouse in Sebago. The next morning he was found cold and dead in the road; his wagon had upset, and the heads of both barrels burst out by the upsetting. Truly the way of the transgressor — rum-seller — is hard.

I am engaged to lecture in this State until the 8th of October. I shall then return to Boston, and on the 10th shall go

to Taunton in Massachusetts, where I am engaged to lecture
in Bristol County until the 1st of November.   *   *   *

Your father, affectionately,

J. H. W. HAWKINS.

In his journal Mr. Hawkins mentions the names of
forty-four towns which he visited, and among them
Hallowell, where the incident mentioned in the following communication from Dr. Jewett occurred.

BOSTON, January 1, 1859.

REV. WILLIAM G. HAWKINS: _Dear Sir,_ — Of the many
thousands of our countrymen whose earthly life ceased during
the year '58, it is doubtful whether a single individual left behind more sincere mourners than your father. During the
eighteen years which have passed since his reformation, no
man in the country stood upon his feet more hours in the advocacy of the temperance cause, and no one urged its claims
with more earnestness or sincerity, or gave to the world in
connection with his public labors stronger evidence of entire
devotion to the work he had taken in hand. His wonderful
success in inspiring the victims of intemperance with hope and
a belief in the possibility of their reform, and in leading them to
pronounce the important words "I will," can be attested by
hundreds of living and grateful men.

It was my good fortune to become acquainted with him when
he first visited Boston, and up to the year '52 I had frequent
intercourse with him, both on the temperance platform and in
the social and domestic circle. I have never made the acquaintance of any other man whose mind seemed so entirely absorbed
by the single question of the temperance reformation. Every
successful movement in that direction, by whomsoever made,
was to him a personal triumph, and every blow aimed at the
cause, he resented and attempted to parry as a blow aimed at
himself. While I remember any event which occurred between
the years 1843 and 1853 I shall remember the pleasure he

manifested while reciting to me the history of a transaction which took place at Hallowell, in Maine, with which we had both, at different periods, been connected as actors. I will briefly give you the history of the affair. A few weeks after the passage of the Maine Law in that State, I visited the region of the Kennebec, by invitation of my friend Neal Dow, a gentleman with whom the world has since become pretty well acquainted. I counselled the immediate and thorough enforcement of the law as the best means of securing its popularity and perpetuity. A warrant was placed in the hands of an officer to search the premises of an individual who had declared, as Madam Rumor informed us, his determination to resist to the death any legal process to deprive him of the stock of liquors in his possession. I, with another friend, volunteered to assist the officer in the discharge of his duty, and in the face of an excited rabble of " hard cases," we seized the contents of the establishment, which consisted of fourteen barrels of liquor, and despite the terrors of a broad-axe, in the hands of the excited keeper of the establishment, the liquors were taken away and safely deposited to await the decision of the legal authorities. They were subsequently condemned, and Mr. Hawkins, as he informed me, happened to reach the place just as execution was about to be done upon them. He accompanied the crowd to the place of execution, and with delight saw the blood of his old enemy flow into the gutter. As soon as the first cask was emptied he placed it on end, and mounting upon it, he addressed the crowd on the subject of temperance, while the other thirteen casks were being emptied. It was the first time he had witnessed the execution of the Maine Law, and it was to him a season of great exultation. He had often seen liquor *go* into the stomachs of men and take them with it into the gutter, and had been made sad by the spectacle ; and now, to see the liquors reach their proper destination in the ditch, *alone*, it was a scene to awaken in his breast a joy beyond the power of words to express. The full import of the great revolution

Destruction of liquors at Hallowell, Maine.

which had taken place in the opinions of the people and in the laws of the State, seemed then to flash upon his mind, and he pleaded for prohibition thereafter, no more earnestly perhaps than before, but with a stronger faith in the ultimate triumph of the cause. He has gone to his rest with a pledge unbroken and a character unstained by any act unworthy of the position he assumed in society immediately after his reformation. He has, however, left behind him an influence and a history which will fight for and with us, so long, at least, as any of *us* shall live who rejoiced in his reformation and were witnesses of his faithful labors.

CHARLES JEWETT.

32*

CHAPTER XXIII.

"There is a tide in the affairs of men,
Which, taken at the flood, leads on to fortune;
Omitted, all the voyage of their life
Is bound in shallows and in miseries;
And we must take the current when it serves,
Or lose our ventures."

THE months of February and March, 1852, were characterized by a series of mighty gatherings of the friends of temperance in the city of New York. Faith in the expediency and practicability of prohibitory legislation was extending itself everywhere over the country. The Hon. Neal Dow, and his coadjutors in Maine, had dealt the most powerful blow that had yet been inflicted upon the infamous traffic. Those who had witnessed the operation of the law in that State, were convinced that it was wise and just. The other New England States soon asked for it. New York, groaning under her miseries, demanded it.

The people were becoming aroused, and they appeared to be determined to stop at nothing short of the fullest protection, which they believed prohibition alone could secure. An alliance had been formed of the friends of temperance from all parts of the State, for the purpose of agitating the question of prohibitory legislation. The convening of a new legislature in the city of Albany was the signal to the temperance host for action. The most powerful influence against which they had to contend, was the city of New York, and it was there that they determined to concentrate their efforts.

A series of stirring meetings was accordingly held in Metropolitan Hall. The meeting on Tuesday evening, February 10th, was a large and enthusiastic one; among the speakers were the Rev. Dr. Stephen H. Tyng, Rev. Dr. Patton, Hon. E. D. Culver, Rev. Dr. Peck, Rev. E. H. Chapin, D. D., and Mr. Hawkins. Effective addresses were delivered by these speakers, pointing out the evils of the traffic and the imperative necessity for its suppression. The press lent its valuable aid in answering the arguments of the advocates of rum. The *New-York Tribune* sent forth, daily, powerful articles, which its adversaries were not able to gainsay or refute. Well-collected statistics from Maine, showing the beneficial effects of the law there, were furnished from time to time to its readers.

It was in the midst of these stirring scenes that the following letter was received, which will explain why it was that Mr. Hawkins was in New York: —

NEW YORK, February 4, 1852.

MY DEAR SON, — You must really forgive me for not answering your letter to me before leaving Baltimore. It is, however, better late than never. I left Baltimore on Tuesday, 13th January, intending to go into Rhode Island. Upon my arrival in this city, I called at the office of the Olivers & Bro. to have a chat with them in regard to the progress of temperance in this city and State, and the prospect of doing any thing during the session of the present legislature. It so happened that a committee of that efficient organization, the City Temperance Alliance, were in the office talking over matters when I entered. They at once asked me where I was from and where bound; I answered them as above. They appeared to be re-

joiced to see me, and in less than ten minutes time engaged me
to remain and speak in different parts of the city, for thirty
days.

I have now been here two weeks speaking every night to
crowded houses, on the subject of the Maine Law.   Great excitement prevails amongst the temperance party, while the
rum-sellers show evident signs of fear that their occupation is
well-nigh gone.   God speed the day when the weeping and
wailing caused by the abominable traffic shall cease.

On Tuesday, Wednesday, and Thursday, a mighty host of
temperance men and women assembled in Albany; I was there.
The object of this great demonstration, was the presenting of
a petition to the legislature, asking for a law similar to that of
Maine.   There were over one hundred thousand signers.   The
probability now is that the legislature will pass such a law.
During the above three days, immense audiences were gathered in various churches, morning, afternoon, and night.   You
may judge of the great interest felt in this subject, when I tell
you that during the three days the State Temperance Society
were holding their Convention, the State Temperance Alliance
was also in session, and both were well attended.   Western
New York poured in by hundreds, causing the rum-sellers to
tremble.   They asked, what does all this mean?   They were
answered, that the time had come to stop the rule of *rum!*
You will be surprised when I tell you that gentlemen of wealth
from Western New York who were present, announced to the
various audiences that their property to the amount of fifteen
millions of dollars was pledged by them to be taxed to any
amount necessary to carry out and enforce the law, should it be
enacted by the legislature; and that if circumstances required
that the whole should go, *let it go.*

At the close of my engagement here, which will be about
the 25th of the month, I shall return home, only for a few
days, and then return to lecture in the interior of this State;
never was there a time when the harvest was so great and the

laborers so few. I had this morning a very interesting and profitable interview with that good friend of every noble cause, the Rev. Dr. Tyng. He was somewhat surprised to learn that you was my son. * * * He said I had much to be thankful to God for; he has indeed done much for me and my family. I must now close. Remember me to my dear daughter-in-law, your wife.   Most affectionately yours,

JOHN H. W. HAWKINS.

During the time he remained on duty in New York, he addressed an immense congregation assembled in Metropolitan Hall, after effective and eloquent remarks had been made by Rev. Stephen H. Tyng, D. D., Rev. Dr. Peck, Hon. C. C. Leigh, and others. The following extracts are made from his address as reported in the papers.

The temperance cause had had its " ups and downs." Its foes were often from quarters where they were least looked for; from individuals who had not considered its *animus*. It had received more newspaper opposition than had any other enterprise in any part of the globe; more than either the missionary or Bible-circulation causes. That very fact when compared with its advance, was evidence of divine support. The ravages of intemperance were not confined to any particular class of men; no man had been placed so high in the scale of being by a giant intellect — no man had been placed so high in office by his fellow-men, but that intemperance might drag him down and offer him up as a sacrifice on the altar of Bacchus. In reference to a candidate for the Presidency, he said, if a candidate should be nominated who was opposed to temperance, and opposed to religion, when we go to the ballot-box let us deposit a ballot that will do what is *right*. There was but one office in this republic which had not been disgraced by drunkenness, and that was the Presidency. The ravages of intemperance

have run through all society. They had been told by some of
the newspapers of the city not favorable to temperance, that
their meetings had been composed of women and children; and
why so? Because they were the sufferers from the delinquencies of man. He had seen in the "Tombs" God's image
crushed and distorted by intoxicating drink. But there was a
tomb beyond the *present;* — there was a drunkard's *hell.* [The
speaker here paused for a moment, and a death-like silence
pervaded the assembly. Mr. Hawkins resumed.] There
was no child's play in this movement; no more than there
was when General Taylor, with four thousand men, scattered
a much larger force; and the cases were somewhat similar.
Some of their opponents had said that there was very little
drunkenness in this city. One paper had said that its editor
had not met a drunkard in Broadway for many years. Why,
it was only that morning that he (Mr. H.) had seen several
there; he had seen some genteel, some *scientific* drunkards.
It was a waste of time for newspapers to attack reforms of this
kind. He thought an editor should be a man of sense and a
gentleman, a man of refinement; and that when he discussed a
subject of such magnitude he should treat it in a manly and
candid way; he should not attempt to ridicule a cause of so
holy a character as this. If he (the editor) was not convinced
of the importance of the cause, they would convince him. One
newspaper in this city, in speaking of the Temperance Alliance,
had given it a name. They did not wish to assume a name,
but he did not know but what it *was* a "Holy Alliance." They
were called also a "Holy Alliance of Teetotallers," and that
it was composed of "broken-down parsons, broken-down politicians, broken-down Fourierites, broken-down fanatics, broken-
down atheists, broken-down socialists, and broken-down drunkards." Now, he had seen many a broken-*up* drunkard, but
he had never seen a "broken-*down*" one. It was clear
they had fired a shot into the enemy's camp, and that it had
taken effect. * * * Members of the same family were

frequently unaware of the existence of intemperance within its own circle, as his own experience had taught him. The extent of the evil is often unknown. And what is the remedy? " Oh, moral suasion," said one friend to him. — " What! change the heart of a rum-seller by moral suasion? Let us try," said he ; and he went to two or three dram-shops without success. At last he came to one, and said to him, " Which would you rather do; have a law passed to prevent your selling intoxicating drink, or give it up of your own accord?" — " I would rather do it of my own accord," said the rum-seller. " See," then said my friend; " did I not say that moral suasion would succeed?" But he was again asked, " Why, then, do you not give up the business?" — " Because," said the rum-seller, " it is not my interest to do so. I will not give it up until the law closes me up." Now, what becomes of your moral suasion? The States of New Hampshire, Vermont, Connecticut, and Rhode Island, had all failed, by their former legislation, to accomplish the object. Their only remedy was in a prohibitory law. In Maine the rum-seller had strutted up and down his shop with a revolver in his hand, threatening any officer who should dare to enter his establishment; but all opposition had so far been overcome. Neal Dow had begun at the right end and was determined to make thorough work of it. In describing the operations of the Maine Law, he stated that a proclamation was issued, allowing the rum-sellers to send their liquors to other States for sale. Many in this city had already begun to talk of sending their goods to another State for sale. Blood or no blood, the law once made would be enforced ; a man was not necessarily a coward because he was a temperance man; let's try him. When one Yankee dealt with another Yankee, it was " diamond cut diamond ;" but it had been found that the ingenuity of the Yankee rum-seller could not outwit the ingenuity of the temperance men. * * *

At the meeting in the Green-street Methodist church,

held in the early part of February, several addresses were made. The Hon. Thomas N. Woodruff was introduced to the audience, and in a speech of considerable length related the history of his delinquencies while a slave to intemperance, up to the time when he came forward in that church and signed the temperance pledge under the encouragement of his friend Mr. Hawkins. At the conclusion of his address, Mr. Hawkins detained the audience for more than an hour, illustrating the beneficial operations of the prohibitory law in Maine.

During the continuance of these extraordinary meetings, the *New-York Tribune* spoke thus cautiously : —

Our hopes are decidedly stronger than they were a week ago. The temperance convocations in Albany last week have exerted a decidedly wholesome influence. They went far to show that the temperance men are in earnest ; and whenever the mere politicians shall be aware that such is the fact, the Maine Law will go through. Another election may be necessary to demonstrate the truth, but we hope not. At all events the prospect has brightened.

Having completed his engagement with the " New-York City Alliance," Mr. Hawkins returned on the 24th of February to Baltimore. The month of March was spent in canvassing the principal towns in Maryland ; he delivered two effective addresses in Centreville, where his son was then settled as pastor over St. Paul's Church.

Having been solicited by the friends whom he had met in Albany in the winter to present the subject of prohibition to the people of Western New York, he left Baltimore on the 17th of April for Jefferson, Chemung County, in that State. After lecturing in thirty three towns, he proceeded on the 12th of July to Boston, where he found the people fully awake to the subject of the recent legislation in Maine. At the solicitation of his friends he remained in New England until the 16th of September, during which time he lectured in fifty-three places in Massachusetts, Connecticut, and Rhode Island. We make a few brief extracts from his letter of July 18th, written at Cambridgeport : —

On going into Boston on Tuesday morning, I received an invitation to attend the County Temperance Convention to be held the next day at Lawrence. At the convention the committee invited me to go through Essex County, which invitation I accepted. I shall commence as soon as I can get my *mouth prepared.* I have had, since my arrival here, every tooth extracted from my upper jaw ; the operation was awfully severe ; it will be some months before my *speaking powers* are in perfect condition ; at present I am compelled to use a temporary set of teeth.

This affliction did not, however, damp his ardor, for we find him on the next day addressing a large audience in Lynn, the next at Salem, and so on through different parts of the State.

The new liquor law goes into operation here on Thursday next, the 22d inst., and great and effective arrangements are on foot to enforce it. The rum-sellers begin to believe it, as they are at this moment shipping thousands of casks to distant ports ; some of the wharves are *groaning* under the weight of the *poison* upon them. Several very heavy ship-loads are soon to leave port for the Mediterranean, New York, Baltimore, Philadelphia, and the South ; in fact, for every place *except* ' Down East.''

33

On the 2d of August he writes thus from Boston:—

The "Maine Liquor Law" as passed by the last legislature of this State is strictly enforced, except in Boston. Our efforts have been forestalled by the mayor and board of aldermen in granting over six hundred licenses under the old law, and *before* the present one was enacted. It is supposed by many that these licenses will hold good, inasmuch as they paid a *price* for them.

In Rhode Island the law is generally observed, except in Newport. Providence has not *one* open grog-shop or bar-room. They have destroyed many hundred gallons seized under the law, without any opposition whatever. The traffic in Boston is doomed, for the country towns are determined to destroy, at the ballot-box, all the political and rum influence that Boston has for so many years exercised over the rest of this goodly State.

The influence here against the law is tremendous; six daily papers are using all their influence against us, besides two new papers started expressly to defend the rum interest. I have no doubt, however, of our ultimate success.

From Groveland, August 11th, he writes:—

My engagements in this State end on next Sabbath evening, August 15th, at Andover. I have a most cordial invitation to go into Rhode Island and lecture through the State. I shall begin with Providence, on Monday evening, 16th; from thence to Connecticut, where I am much wanted.

On the 8th of September, he writes, from Providence:—

I have just this moment received a letter from my good friend Mr. C. C. Leigh, President of the New-York City Alliance, inviting me to labor in that city for one or two months.

I have not accepted the offer yet, but shall decide in reference
to it when I reach New York.

Mr. Hawkins returned to Baltimore about the first
of October, to rest a few days.   Having accepted the
offer of the " Alliance," we find him in the early part
of this month, producing not a little stir among the people of New York.   October 28th, he writes : —

I am well, and holding the largest meetings in the " Tent "
I have ever addressed ; the battle waxes hotter and hotter as
the elections draw near.   B——— has acted as I expected, and
as *must* be expected of all temperance men, who love their
party more than temperance.   You will no doubt read his
leader of this week ; I have no confidence in him as an out-and-
out temperance man.   Give my *fishing respects* to brother
Martin.*

Mr. Hawkins concluded his labors in New York with
credit to himself and some profit to the cause, and went
to Connecticut.   From Hartford, Nov. 12th, he writes
thus to his son : —

Your letter to me at New York was received.   I was truly
glad at the information conveyed by your letter.   At first I felt
a *little* disappointed at the result ; *but* when you stated that you
had contemplated naming the little one after your *own* sainted
mother, oh, what a thrill it sent through my whole frame !   She
was indeed a saint on earth, and is, no doubt, a saint in heaven.   If
God in his infinite goodness spares the life of the dear one so that
I can be permitted to see it, and pronounce the name once more,
— Rachel Thompson, — how much delight it will give me. * * *
We have held, probably, the largest and most enthusiastic
State Temperance Convention ever before assembled in this

* His son, to whom this letter was addressed, was at this time residing
at Glens Falls, N. Y.   Its location on the Hudson and near Lake George,
afforded good fishing facilities.

State; it lasted two days, with meetings in the evening. The most able addresses I ever heard were here delivered, by Rev. E. H. Chapin, Rev. Mr. Wolcot, General Riley, J. B. Gough, and — John H. W. Hawkins, of Baltimore; this last named gentleman I believe you have some acquaintance with. I intend remaining in this State during most of the winter. I am to be at Middletown on Tuesday, the 23d of this month, to attend the County Convention, &c. I had a remarkable dream the other night; it may be of service to friend Martin. I dreamed that *trout* of monstrous size came up to the surface of the water, and I ran my arm down their throats and threw them out upon the banks of the river. A novel way of catching fish, *but* — it was all a dream.

Mr. Hawkins spent the remainder of 1852 in Connecticut, lecturing nearly every evening. In the month of February we find him in Montreal, having taken in his route the towns in northern New York, and returning to Boston by way of Vermont. His labors in March, April, and May, were devoted, principally, to canvassing New Hampshire and Vermont. In a letter to his son from Charlestown, New Hampshire, he says: —

I remained in Boston until the 21st of March. I was present and heard the address of the Rev. J. C. Lovejoy against the Liquor Law, and his argument for the unconditional repeal of it because it was a *violation* of the *law of God!* I suppose you have seen some extracts from it, as it has been published in the papers very extensively. I *also* heard the rejoinder of the Rev. John Pierpont; it was complete and satisfactory. * * * My meetings have been crowded thus far, and there is much healthy excitement throughout Vermont and New Hampshire upon the subject of a prohibitory liquor law.

In a letter dated Farmington, Me., August 27th, he says : —

I have been lecturing for two months past in various parts of Maine, and can give your people some idea of the practical operation of the Maine Law, and the wonders it would work if adopted in the State of New York. There is now an effort made by a fraction of one of the parties here to overthrow the law, but their defeat is certain. The election for Governor and legislature will take place on the 12th of September, and the State is now being canvassed in every nook and corner. I am lecturer at large, while county meetings are addressed by Neal Dow, Hon. Mr. Vinton, of Gray, Rev. Mr. Wheeler, of Bangor, Rev. Mr. Thompson, of Augusta, and the Rev. Mr. Peck, of Portland, and many others. * * * I shall leave this State for New York on September 5th, and after attending the World's Temperance Convention in the city of New York, which closes its deliberations on September 9th, will proceed to Glens Falls. * * *

After spending a few days in recreation at his son's house in Glens Falls, he visited his home in Baltimore, where he made arrangements for an extensive tour through the States of Indiana, Michigan, Illinois, and Wisconsin. We make brief extracts from a letter dated Milwaukie, Wis., Nov, 9th, 1853.

I have now been in this State since the 9th of October, and have had altogether a pleasant tour. I am to lecture to-night at a place called *Wau-wa-toca*, about five miles out of town. * * * Thursday, November 10th, at Racine; then at Kenosha, Chicago, and so on through the State. This accomplished, my present plan is to take the Michigan Central Railroad, commencing at Michigan City, and through to Detroit, lecturing at all the principal places. From Detroit to Toledo and Munroe, taking the back track upon the Michigan Southern and Northern Indiana Railroad, to Laporte and South Bend ; thence to Lafayette, and so on down to Madison and homeward, which will take me probably to February, 1854.

We have not space for an extended account of this interesting tour. We give his remarks on one occasion only, as reported in the *Racine Advocate* : —

The address of Mr. Hawkins at the court house on Thursday deserves more than the passing notice we gave it on Friday. He commenced his remarks by giving a history of the origin of the first temperance organization in this country, which took place in Boston in 1813, afterwards revived in 1826, under the auspices of such men as Dr. Beecher, of Boston, Rev. Dr. Perry, of Bradford, and other leading divines of Massachusetts. He attributed its success to its origin in the church, etc., etc. Some men could be found who would deny the temperance cause its paternity in this country ; but as long as the *origin* of temperance is not what we seek, but the *end of intemperance*, there is no occasion to quarrel about non-essentials. The speaker then spoke of the surprising benefits which had been conferred upon the unfortunate inebriates of the State of Maine by the prohibitory liquor law of that State. He called it emphatically " the poor man's law ; " a law which had been the means of more moral and pecuniary good to the people of that State than all the other laws upon her statute-book.

He spoke on this point not as a novice, but as an " experienced man." The great advantages of this law over the ordinary laws upon this subject, was the fact that this law removed the temptation entirely out of reach of the debased appetite of the unfortunate inebriate, who had lost all power of controlling his appetite. The glory which succeeded this enactment had given that State a preëminent name; like a star, "like a comet," she shone, and the radiance of her brilliant beams was seen across the wide Atlantic, and from England was heard the cry, "Give us the Maine Law," "Give us the reflection of this glory-beaming star." Beer-bloated and gin-guzzling England saw no relief but in the enactment of this law. The speaker was able to produce the most irrefragable testimony of those who had opportunity of knowing, that seventy-five per cent of the criminal business of the State of Maine had fallen off since the enactment of this law; that poorhouses and jails, to whose inmates he had formerly lectured, were rapidly becoming tenantless. He challenged any man to disprove by the testimony of any respectable citizen of the State of Maine, a single assertion which he had made, while, if any one doubted, he would give the names of some of the most distinguished citizens in the State in proof that his assertions were correct. These names he gave to the meeting. He had his own experience, and that of seven other men who lectured in the State last summer, to convince him of the truth of what he stated; and in a convention at Bangor, which was attended by delegates from all parts of the State, the question was put to the whole body, if any one of them knew where liquor could be obtained in an open manner; and not a man of them all could tell of such a place in any part of the State.

He asked what probability there was of the diminution of *stealing*, provided the restraint of the law should be taken from it; and said the law was just as successful for the suppression of drinking as the law against stealing was successful for its purposes.

Mr. Hawkins possesses a wonderful power over the minds of his hearers. His aptness at description, and the deep pathos of his home scenes, will start the brine from the eye before the weather-beaten face has had prognostications of a storm. We have not begun to give any thing like a sketch of what he said, nor to do him even partial justice; indeed, we have not mentioned one-fourth of the points made by him, yet our article is already too long. We are gratified in being able to say that he is expected to lecture here again on the evening of Sunday the 20th.

CHAPTER XXIV.

"From East to West resounds the story,
  'The temperance banner proudly waves;'
Maine taught the world the march of glory,
  Her gallant sons no longer slaves!
With light and love full long they pleaded;
  But when the Law in thunder spoke,
  It burst their chains with lightning stroke,
And peace and happiness succeeded."

WE have not space to give the details of Mr. Hawkins' tour through the West, in 1853–4. The enthusiasm which he enkindled spread like the prairie fire. "I have no doubt," he wrote, "but that the Maine Law will be carried in this State (Wisconsin) by not less than ten thousand majority. This city (Milwaukie), it is true, has gone by a large majority *against* the law; this was expected, owing to the corrupt German population here."

From Kalamazoo he writes, Nov. 30th: —

I have crowded houses every night. By the way, this is the last day of *grace* with the rum-sellers of Michigan. To-morrow the law goes into operation, and you may depend upon it, the temperance men of this State will make the "fur fly," and the rum too. We shall see, what we shall see. The people which sat in darkness have seen great light. I am much interested in reading Miss Bremer's work; she speaks in high terms, as she should, of the temperance reformation; I do not think it worth while to notice the mistakes she makes about myself. She is not a Trollope or a Dickens, or as other foreigners who have come to this country, and after receiving the kindest treatment

(393)

have gone home and abused our hospitality. Miss Bremer
breathes the spirit of a true Christian. Now for my appointments."

Then follow the names of twenty-five towns in Indiana, requiring a lecture every day. He continues:—

Hard work, night after night; no rest for the wicked in this
life; but, dear son, there is a rest for those who fear God
and do his will. I am thankful that my physical and mental
health enables me to hold out.

Having completed his first engagement in the West,
Mr. Hawkins returned to Baltimore late in the winter;
but so urgent was the demand for his services in that
section of the country, while the subject of a prohibitory law was in agitation, that he returned to Indiana
early in March following. He writes thus from Peru,
Indiana, March 25, 1854:—

I have had my hands full since I left home in February.
We spent four days at Pittsburg, two at Wooster, Ohio, four,
profitably I hope, in Cincinnati, thence to Madison. I lectured
two days in Lawrenceburg, and while on the steamboat to the
passengers in the cabin; from thence by railroad to Greensburgh. Here your mother has come to a dead halt, and will
remain until May; that month she expects to spend in Indianapolis, while I lecture in distant parts of the State. About
the 15th of July I shall ask leave of absence for two weeks;
that will be in the midst of harvest. I shall then go to Chicago, and thence to Sheboygan Falls. It is impossible to tell
you where a letter will reach me, as I am under the direction
of the Indiana State Temperance Committee, who send me
where they please. As regards the temperance cause in this
State, there is not a State whose prospects are better for carrying through a prohibitory law. The whole body of Methodist

clergy, with but few exceptions, — I know of none, — have or will canvass their respective districts for prohibition.   *   *   *

Just before my return to Baltimore in the winter I attended a large State Temperance Convention at Indianapolis. Twelve hundred delegates were present, from all parts of the State; great unanimity and firmness characterized their whole proceedings for two days and two evenings. Twelve thousand dollars were pledged to carry out the campaign for the present year — 1854. I am engaged by the convention, per resolution, to canvass the State. I shall probably remain until September or October. I neglected to mention that in January last I was present at another State Temperance Convention at Harrisburg, Pa.; its deliberations continued three days. Nearly one thousand delegates were present. General Cary, a good friend of mine, and Neal Dow were present.

We subjoin extracts from a few letters addressed to Mr. Hawkins, showing the demand in Indiana for his services : —

SHELBYVILLE, March 7, 1854.

*   *   *   We shall joyfully hail your visit. We are approaching a crisis of thrilling interest to our State. May the good Lord preserve your life and health for the work before you ! We have made appointments for you on Monday and Tuesday. On Tuesday there will be great numbers from all parts of the county to hear you.

GOSHEN, Ind., April 26, 1854.

*   *   *   We expect to have a large mass temperance meeting of the county on the 27th of May. It is the ardent wish of all who heard you here last winter, to have you present. We have promised the public a distinguished speaker on that occasion, and hope you will not disappoint the public expectation.

BEDFORD, Ind., May 15, 1854.

The Vigilance Committee will be pleased to have you attend our county convention on the 25th inst. We have to meet Senator —— on the 26th or 27th, to debate the temperance question. He says that to drink good liquor is a Bible doctrine ; that temperance has arisen from abolitionism, raised in corruption to overthrow this government, and take away all our liberties, &c., &c., We shall be much pleased if you can come and stay two or three days. The debate will bring out a crowd.

In July Mr. Hawkins visited Fond du Lac, Oshkosh, and other places in the neighborhood of Green Bay. After stopping a few days at Sheboygan Falls, where his daughter resided, he returned to Baltimore. Severe illness of his daughter detained him there until January, 1855.

After spending part of the winter in New Jersey, he went to New Hampshire to fill some engagements there. In the month of June he lectured in the principal towns in Tompkins County, N. Y. On the 21st of the same month he was present at the meeting of the State Temperance Convention at Albany. On the 12th of July he lectured to good audiences at Rochester, and on the 21st and 22d at Lyons, Wayne Co. The papers in that section of the State spoke of the marked attention which his addresses in behalf of prohibition commanded, and the high appreciation in which he was personally held. The *Lockport Weekly Journal* of July 18, 1855, in referring to his efforts says : " He is one of the veterans in the glorious enterprise, and has been in the field doing most effective service for fourteen years. He should meet with a warm reception everywhere."

After completing an engagement in Niagara Co., he went to Niagara and lectured to large and attentive audiences in one of the public halls of that city. He continued his labors night after night, with unabated zeal, during the oppressive heat of August.

From Lockport, August 17, he writes thus to his son : —

On the 24th of August I expect to go to Buffalo, at the solicitation of several of the most prominent citizens of that place. L am to speak in one of the halls on that night. They wish to engage my services there for awhile. After the first of September, I have about thirty appointments to fill along the line of the railroad, commencing at Batavia.

On the 26th he returned to Lockport, and addressed the children of the various Sabbath Schools in that place.

It appears from his letters to his wife, that before commencing his journey homeward he spent one week in Canada, lecturing at Hamilton, Paris, Brantford, London, St. Catharine, and Toronto. After a short visit home, in October, we find him again in the West. He thus writes, under date of Nov. 1, 1855, from Columbus, Ohio : —

I reached this city upon the very day of the session of the Grand Division of the Sons of Temperance; they voted me the privilege of sitting with them; I find here many warm friends. They welcomed me to the State, and appointments were at once made for me. I am to be at Wooster on Monday and Tuesday, Nov. 5th and 6th. * * * I commenced writing this letter in Columbus; I finish it in this place, Mansfield. You may answer this at Alliance. I send you a list of my appointments in various parts of the State.

A letter from Dayton, Ohio, dated December 4th,

34

says, "In nineteen days from this time I hope to be at home, in time to enjoy a good Christmas dinner with you all."

After a short visit home, it will be seen by the subjoined note that he returned to the West: —

FORT WAYNE, Ind., March 27, 1856.

I have passed through the most severe winter I have known for many years. I have been compelled to give up most of my appointments, in consequence of the deep snows' rendering it impossible for me to meet them; the winter has broken and I have mud instead of snow to contend with. I have appointments made up to the 11th of April. * * * I shall be at Terre Haute, Ind., about April 14th, at which place a letter will reach me.

Mr. Hawkins returned home in May, after an absence of four months on a most laborious tour, and during a season exceedingly trying to his constitution. While in Baltimore he received from an unknown friend the following note of caution in respect to his health; it was found among his papers. Its date is Baltimore, May 19th, 1856. After furnishing some facts on the subject of the adulteration of liquors, and the "deadly traffic," the writer says: —

I am thankful your life has been preserved. But I fear Satan may get the advantage of you. In extreme bad weather, or when you are sick, the people do not expect you to fill appointments; neither does God; for he will have mercy and not sacrifice. But the Devil would be glad to get you out of the way by urging you to extremes, by which your health would be injured and your constitution undermined. Self-preservation is the first law of nature. I would not have you grow weary in well doing; rather be at it and always at it.

But be discreet, be moderate, and yet energetic, earnest, and you will accomplish more in this way. By taking prudent care of yourself you may live a score of years, and do more than by filling *every* appointment, regardless of the laws of health. God help you to be wise as the serpent and harmless as the dove, both to yourself and others. Yours truly,

A STRANGER.

Mr. Hawkins was employed at intervals during the summer of 1856 in various places in New Jersey and in his native State. Nov. 8th he writes to his son from Baltimore, saying: —

The elections are now over, and the minds of the people becoming somewhat settled, and I shall proceed to the " East " to fill some field of labor.

From New York, November 25th, he writes: —

I left Baltimore on Saturday last, and shall remain in this city until December 1st, at the suggestion of many of my temperance friends, — all of them men of influence. They wish to consult in regard to the establishment of an agency whose efforts shall be directed to the reformation of drunkards. They think such an agency is needed, and that it is practicable and will result in great good ; they wish me to undertake it. They are now holding private meetings, and laying plans, etc., etc. I find in Mr. C. C. Leigh a good friend, who is ready to render me any aid in his power.

Mr. Hawkins accepted the agency, which, however, was not to go into operation until early in January, 1857. In the mean time he proceeded to Boston to fill a number of appointments in that vicinity.

From New York, January 10th, 1857, he writes: —

I reached this city on Thursday night, and last evening met the committee, and we completed the arrangements in regard to my mission in this city.

January 28th he writes: —

My health is good, and I have work enough to keep me busy day and night. I do not get to bed some nights until twelve or one o'clock. I have so little time to write during the day, that I must do it at night, when I return from the meetings or from visits to the inebriate at his home. I have been able to do some good already. I am to pay Sing Sing another visit, at the earnest solicitation of the prisoners. My hands are full of work. God is with me, and that is the best of all.

Under date of February 15th he writes: —

I have just returned from the Penitentiary on Blackwell's Island, where I addressed about one thousand convicts, male and female. It was indeed a sad sight; so many human beings incarcerated for crimes, nine-tenths at least of which have resulted, directly or indirectly, from the use of intoxicating drink. Many a tear was shed while I was speaking. I read to them the 10th Psalm, and commented upon the 7–11, 14–18 verses. * * * We are having a circular struck off, a copy of which I shall send you. *

* To the friends of Temperance and Christianity in this city and vicinity:

The New-York City Temperance Alliance, convinced of the necessity of making some extra effort to stay the tide of intemperance that threatens to overwhelm our city and ruin our families, have engaged as a City Missionary, Mr. John Hawkins, of Baltimore, one of the original Washingtonians who has labored in the temperance cause for the last sixteen years with great acceptance and success.

Mr. H.'s efforts will be mainly made for the reformation of inebriates, and the formation of Juvenile Temperance Societies, but he will lecture in various localities of the city when desired, and thus aid in the general

February 18th he writes : —

I am well, and full of work, *night* and *day*. Last night I sp ke to a grand audience in the Mariners' Church, corner of Catherine and Madison Streets; to-night a great meeting is to be held in the Tabernacle; I may have something to say there.

March 18th he writes thus : —

* * * The work of visiting the intemperate increases on my hands; I am much encouraged, as the friends of the cause are convinced that, under the blessing of God, I am doing a good work. Mr. Gray, the Superintendent of the " Tombs " — the city prison — has opened *wide* the door for my labors. The governors of the Almshouses on Blackwell's, Randall's, and Ward Islands, and the Penitentiary, have given me a hearty invitation to visit the above places as often as possible. The chaplains and keepers of the above places receive me with great kindness. Capt. Oliver Clark, who commands a nice little steamboat, in the employ of the city, which plies between there and Staten Island several times in the day, has placed his boat at my service. My friends here are *legion*. I should

work of suppressing the great and growing evils of intemperance. We commend him to your kind sympathies and generous aid.

JAMES O. BENNETT, President.

C. J. WARREN, *Secretary.*

CHAS. C. LEIGH,	
EDWARD FALCONER,	} *Finance Committee.*
NOAH WORRALL,	
J. S. FOUNTAIN,	

We, the subscribers, approve of the objects of the New-York City Temperance Alliance, as above stated, and recommend the friends of morality and virtue to aid Mr. Hawkins by their countenance, their prayers, and their pecuniary offerings.

REV. STEPHEN H. TYNG,	REV. GEORGE POTTS,
" JESSE T. PECK,	" SAMUEL OSGOOD,
" G. T. BEDELL,	" THOMAS DEWITT,
" E. H. CHAPIN,	" ISAAC FERRIS.

34*

be glad to see you here, to show you in some measure the "modus operandi" of my *hooking* the drunkards. You know I am a good fisherman, and I hope by divine assistance, following the disciples of Christ, who were made "fishers of men," that I shall not be altogether unsuccessful.

April 16. * * * I have but a moment to write; I am full of business from morning until late at night. Your mother too is very ill, and has not been out of her room for more than a week; she is now under the care of Dr. S. S. Fitch. I must close, as I have several *patients* to visit this afternoon, and a speech to make at night.

May 12. * * * We are to have a great rum-sellers' demonstration to-night in the Park. They are now putting up the stands for the speakers. It is nothing less than *treason and rebellion* against the laws of the State, passed too by their own friends; the meeting will do the cause of temperance good, as it happens during Anniversary-week.

Mr. Hawkins not receiving sufficient pecuniary support from this mission, was compelled to abandon it about the first of June, 1857. On the 2d of June he started upon a tour, visiting and lecturing in a large number of towns on Long Island, after the termination of which he went to New Hampshire and Vermont. He thus writes from Windsor, under date of September 16, 1857:—

* * * I commenced my very pleasant tour, lecturing among the granite hills of New Hampshire and the green mountains of Vermont, on the 30th of August last. I have since that time, including my lecture last evening, spoken twenty times, averaging more than once a day; my health is good, never better. * * * I wish you all to drink to my health a glass of good, pure, cold water, on *Monday morning. September the 28th;* that is my birthday, when, if I should live, I

shall be sixty years of age.   Drink it about six o'clock in the morning, as that was about the hour I came into this world of trial.   I am to speak at the following places.

Here follows a list of appointments terminating in the early part of October.   We close this chapter with the following brief and sportive note : —

BOSTON, October 3d, 1857.

MY DEAR SON, — I wrote you a very *short* letter yesterday, in a very *short* time, and on a very *short* piece of paper, saying that in a *short* time, your mother and I would be on our way to Baltimore, to pay you a *short* visit.   Your mother thinks I gave her too *short* a time for her stay in New York and Philadelphia.   Therefore, instead of meeting us at Gap Station on Wednesday, meet us on Thursday morning, Oct. 8.

In *short*, yours, most affectionately,

JOHN H. W. HAWKINS.

CHAPTER XXV.

" In all my wanderings round this world of care,
In all my griefs.— and God has given my share —
I still had hopes my latest hours to crown,
Amidst these humble bowers to lay me down ;
To husband out life's taper at the close,
And keep the flame from wasting by repose :
Around my fire an evening group to draw,
And tell of all I felt, and all I saw ;
And as a hare, whom hounds and horns pursue,
Pants to the place from whence at first she flew,
I still had hopes, my long vexations past,
Here to return — and die at home at last."

Mr. Hawkins had now passed his sixtieth year, yet his labors continued unabated. For several years he kept a memorandum of the number of miles he travelled ; up to August, 1842, it amounted to thirteen thousand one hundred and eighty-four, for a period of less than eighteen months preceding. This however, was not the most active part of his life. As the reform progressed the field of his labors widened, until it included nearly every State in the Union, and all the Canadian provinces. The number of miles which he travelled at that time may be safely estimated at ten thousand annually, or about two hundred thousand in the last eighteen years of his life. The number of his public addresses, as recorded in his journal, was more than three hundred yearly, or about five thousand four hundred in all, between the time when he commenced his labors in 1841, and the time of his decease ; and in that time he must have addressed at least a million and a half of people; and this is estimating his audiences at three hundred only; on great occasions, as upon public celebrations, anniversaries, and conventions, he often spoke to thousands at one time. The last six months of his life manifested no abatement of zeal; it rather became intensified as he drew nearer to the end of his race.

A few days before concluding his labors in New Hampshire, as recorded in the last chapter, Mr. Hawkins wrote thus to his mother, on his sixtieth birthday, from Concord: —

Never, dear mother, did the sun rise in more beauty and splendor, than on this morning, the twenty-eighth day of September [1857]. This day, sixty years ago, you bore me into this world of sorrow and of joy. How signally has our heavenly Father blessed you and yours; not one of your *own* children has he removed from you by death for fifty-five years. Taking every thing into consideration, all your children have proved a blessing to you. * * * God has been pleased to spare your life to a vigorous old age, and I hope that you are to be spared to us for some time to come. May God in his infinite mercy not allow one to be lost, but gather us all into his kingdom.

After a brief visit to Baltimore, Mr. Hawkins returned to Concord, N. H., and completed his engagements in that State. From November 1st to December 7th, he visited and lectured in thirty-six towns, to good audiences. His *Christmas* was spent in Baltimore, in the society of his mother and relatives.

In the latter part of December, Mr. Hawkins received an invitation to spend ten days in Charlestown, Mass.

There had been an increase of drunkenness in that city, and some of the ministers located there had resolved to make an effort to stay the progress of the evil. Notwithstanding the inclemency of the winter he accepted the invitation, and his labors were most signally blessed. We subjoin in a note an extract from a letter addressed to the compiler of this memoir by the Rev. O. C. Everett, giving an exceedingly interesting account of what was done, and the result.*

* CHARLESTOWN, Oct. 24, 1858.

W. G. HAWKINS : *Rev. and Dear Sir*, — * * * He [Mr. H.] commenced on Sunday evening, Jan. 3, in the First Methodist Church, and the meeting proved exceedingly interesting. The ball was now set in motion. He lectured two or three times in that week, besides addressing the children one afternoon. He visited some, but was prevented by the severity of the weather, and by a serious hoarse cold, from going about as much as he designed. I remember, at the close of his first lecture, seeing a young man come up to the platform and enter into conversation with your father in a very earnest manner. Afterwards I learned that the young man was asking his advice and assistance, how to find and reclaim a beloved, but fallen brother. That brother was found by your father at the "Home for the Fallen," and restored to those who loved him, and became, the next week, the first President of the "Bunker Hill Total Abstinence Society." Such was the first fruit, we may say, of your father's labor in this place.

These meetings, appointed in different sections of our city, were fully attended, and a general awakening of new interest was manifest. On the following Sunday evening, he lectured in the Baptist Church, and there was a perfect jam; every nook and corner was filled. These lectures were designed to prepare the way for an organization which might be effectual. The next meeting, on Monday, was appointed at the City Hall, where your father introduced Mr. S. C. Knights, who was then president of a very active and successful society lately established in Cambridgeport. Both advocated the formation of a new society in this city, which should embrace the young men, and those especially who had been reclaimed. Another meeting was appointed on the next evening in the same place, and your father had the satisfaction of seeing a new organization complete, with pledge, constitution, and officers ; and at its head, one whom he had been instrumental, under Providence, of placing in this prominent place, a leader of the new movement. From that evening to this, the

In the early part of January, 1858, Mr. Hawkins

society has maintained regular meetings, which have kept alive the interest your father awakened, and saved many from going down to a drunkard's grave.

It was about the first of May that your father and mother and sister visited our city, and were present at the dedication of a new hall devoted to temperance, and named, in honor of your father, "Hawkins Hall." It was a very interesting occasion; many expressed their gratitude to him for the impulse he had given to the cause of temperance in this city, and for the salvation he had brought to them and their families. This hall is open every evening, where the members meet for social converse, or to listen to addresses and remarks made by visitors, or by reformed men.

Your father's influence is not to be measured by the first ripple produced by his solid words in a stagnant, indifferent community; for the circle widened and continues to widen yet. Many of those first interested became members of several Divisions of Sons of Temperance in this city and in Boston. Some commenced a new Division at the north part of Boston, which has always been regarded as the hardest portion of that favored city, and were so blessed in their labors, that after seeing this new organization well established, they resolved to return to their own city, and commence another Division of the Sons of Temperance. Thus, you see, the ball continues to roll, and new places are blessed by the zeal and activity which your father's words first excited. There has not been in our city, since I took up my abode here, such interest in the cause of temperance as at the present time. There is no great excitement, no violent commotion, no loud demonstration, not much public notice, but a quiet, silent energetic influence, which is gradually making itself felt in our community.

In conclusion, I would say, that this evening (30th), I dropped in upon the society in "Hawkins Hall," and there heard the President warmly advocating a new measure, whereby the blessings of temperance might be carried to the extreme parts of our city, and urging upon his associates new activity and preparation for this winter's work. The ball is rolling —the cause is living and active; and thanks to God, that he sent to us the wise, earnest, living voice of your revered and honored father. Long may his labors be gratefully remembered.

Yours truly, in Christian fellowship,
OLIVER C. EVERETT.

HAWKINS HALL.--The following brief but interesting account of

completed his arrangement with the executive commit

Mr. Hawkins' reception at City Hall, referred to in the foregoing letter, has been kindly furnished by a friend : —

"The occasion of the public reception of Mr. Hawkins at Charlestown, on Tuesday evening, May 11th, was a most interesting one. The audience present was large. At seven o'clock, the chair was taken by T. M. Brown, Esq., President of the Bunker Hill Total Abstinence Society, who made some appropriate welcoming remarks, at the opening of the meeting, and then proceeded to read select portions of Scripture. He then invited Rev. J. S. Cushman to offer prayer, which was done in a very fervent and appropriate manner. A temperance ode was then sung, after which Mr. Hawkins was introduced, and greeted with applause. He appeared somewhat unwell, having just returned from a long and very arduous, yet most successful, temperance tour in Vermont. As he rose to speak, traces of excessive fatigue were observable, but as he proceeded, his soul all on fire with the grandeur of his theme, the physical man became endued with more than usual power. His speech was a most affecting one ; — rarely has he been more touching and effective in his appeal for that cause in behalf of which he had so long labored.

"At the conclusion of Mr. Hawkins' speech, S. B. Weston, Esq., editor of the *Boston Temperance Visitor*, was introduced. He alluded at first to the happy circumstances attending this public reception of Mr. Hawkins, and then passed to a notice of the gratifying results of his long and faithful devotion to the temperance enterprise.

"At the conclusion of these exercises at the City Hall, the audience adjourned to the hall of the Bunker Hill Society, which has been named, in honor of Mr. Hawkins, "Hawkins Hall." The hall was filled to its utmost capacity. Refreshments were provided and partaken of, after which speeches were made by Rev. Messrs. Cushman and Everett, of Charlestown, Mr. Brown, Mr. Hawkins, and others. Mr. and Mrs. Hawkins were accompanied by their 'daughter Hannah,' who received many kindly notices of regard. The following lines were sung, prepared for the occasion by the president of the society : —

> " Welcome the true and tried
> Old Washingtonian ;
> We greet him now with pride, —
> He's welcome here again ;
> While hearts made glad by temperance power,
> Rejoice in this delightful hour.
>
> " And may his lamp of life
> Long shed its cheering ray ;

tee of the Vermont State Temperance Society, to canvass that State and lecture on the subject of prohibition. Several months were to elapse before the election was to take place, and it was believed that the opponents of the existing law would exert themselves to the utmost of their power to secure its modification, or, if possible, its repeal. As the canvass went on, and the battle waxed hotter and hotter, the temperance host were led to look to Mr. Hawkins as the most effective champion who could be brought into the field to stem the mighty torrent of opposition.

"We are glad," writes the Secretary of the Executive Committee, "that you have consented to come to Vermont. Our State Temperance Convention meets at Northfield on the 19th of January, and we want you to lecture on Monday evening. During the meeting we shall want your services. This will be a good opportunity to introduce you to the State, and to arrange matters for your winter's work. Do not fail to be there."

We find by Mr. Hawkins' journal that he commenced his labors in Vermont, at Bethel, on the 10th of January, 1858, and continued them to April 19th; during this time he addressed the public on ninety-three occasions, and obtained over fourteen hundred signatures to the pledge.

> No sorrow, care, nor strife,
> Becloud his waning day;
> And when his closing hour shall come,
> May angels bear him swiftly home.

"At quite a late hour the company separated, pleased with the entertainment, and glad of the opportunity of paying their respects to one whom they loved for his faithful devotion to the great principles of temperance."

On the 22d of January he wrote to his daughter from Royalston, saying : —

We have had no very cold weather until to-day, which is very cold. I am prepared, however, for a "Polar winter." My health was never better. * * * The State Convention at Northfield have unanimously endorsed my coming into the State, &c. They make my appointments, and I have nothing to do but to fill them.

We have not space to insert the many earnest letters· received from various parts of the State, soliciting special addresses, in addition to the work laid out by the committee, and complimenting him upon the success of his labors.

April 9th he writes to his children from Rutland, saying : —

I have been unable to write you sooner, I have been so much driven in my work lately. I have spoken one hundred and seven times in succession, without one night's rest, and feel much worn down ; I am getting old and cannot stand as much as I formerly could, yet my health was never better. I have now thirteen appointments to fill, ending on the twenty-first of this month, and on the following day I hope to be with you.

Finding himself greatly· exhausted by these excessive labors, he took a rest of several weeks in April and May. He went to Baltimore, and finding his wife still in feeble health, he brought her to Massachusetts. On reaching New York, May 3d, he wrote as follows to his son, then Rector of St. John's Church, Pequea, Lancaster Co., Pa. : —

I spent the winter in Vermont as you know, and now am about to return to finish my labors in that State. I canvassed the following counties; viz., Orange, Washington, Chittenden, Franklin, Lamoille, Addison, Rutland, and Bennington. I now have the following to go through; viz., Windham, Windsor, Caledonia, Orleans, Essex, and Grand Isle, which will take me the greater part of the summer.

He reëntered upon his labors, according to his intention, on the 18th of May, and continued them without a single day's intermission, until the 3d of June, when literally broken down by excessive toil, he was compelled to relinquish any further labor. On reaching Boston he was taken sick, and confined to the house for several days.

In the latter part of the month, his son received from him the following letter:—

BOSTON, June 28, 1858.

MY DEAR SON,—I have just returned from Vermont, and *have completed my labors* for the present. My health is as usual, but somewhat worn down from constant labor. I have made up my mind not to lecture much, if any, during the summer months. I am getting advanced in years, and cannot stand the labor I once could. *Now for it!*

It is my intention, with your mother and sister Hannah, to leave here soon after the 4th of July, for "Pequea Valley." I wish you to meet us at Parksburg on the 5th; we shall have considerable *luggage*, so you will have to bring a *whole team*. What I omit in writing in this letter, we will make up in talking, if dear N—— will but give us a chance.

Great preparation was made at the parsonage for the reception and comfort of both himself and his wife, who was then in very feeble health. On his arrival at Parksburgh, he was met by his son and conveyed to his home some five miles distant, over a delightful

road, and through a scene of rural beauty, not surpassed by any in the State of Pennsylvania.

How Mr. Hawkins enjoyed himself at Pequea will
be learned, in part, from extracts from his letters.   To
a niece in Baltimore he wrote on the 14th of July,—

Your aunt has been quite ill but is now sitting up.   We
have, at the present time, the following visitors from Baltimore:
Sister Ann Hawkins, Miss Fannie Martin, Isabella and Elizabeth Courtenay ; quite a house full, but there is room for more.
We have every thing here that heart could wish for.   *   *   *
We have the greatest abundance of black and red cherries,
raspberries, &c.   *   *   *   It will be greatly to the advantage
of your aunt to spend the whole summer here.   I do not intend to lecture any until the last of October.   *   *   *   This
is indeed the most lovely country I have seen in all my
travels.   William George and myself talk of driving to Port
Deposit, which is only thirty miles distant, and proceed from
thence to Baltimore, in the cars.

How he employed himself, in part, may be learned
from the following, the last letter he ever wrote to his
mother:—

PEQUEA, July 29, 1858.

MY DEAR AND MUCH-BELOVED MOTHER,—I suppose
the girls are enjoying themselves so much here, that they have
not found time to drop a single line to *you* since coming into
this delightful valley.   This, of course, you know, is not from
any want of affection, for no mother or grandmother could be
more loved than you are.   Dear mother, could you only be
here with us, although we are all happy, how much greater
would be our joy?   We had a grand " Festival and Picnic "
yesterday in a beautiful grove near by.   I made a speech to
them upon temperance, at which all seemed pleased.   My
wife's health has improved somewhat, and she was able to ride
to the grove, and enjoyed herself much ; and so did all the

"visitors." I never in my life was spending a more agreeable time. I employ myself in the following manner; viz., I mend fences, garden a little, and look after sundry broods of chickens; but my most *useful* employment has been to paint and varnish two carriages for William George. I think I made a pretty good job of it too.

The party of visitors leave here on Monday, and you may expect us down on Tuesday; one object is to get some good fishing, of which sport you know I am a *little* fond.   *   *   *

Your son, most affectionately,

JOHN H. W. HAWKINS.

Mr. Hawkins went to Baltimore, and after a very delightful visit to his mother and other relatives, returned to Pequea. His health was apparently improving, and there was no indication of the approach of the sad event, the details of which are briefly narrated in the following communication from the writer of these pages to the Rev. Dr. Tyng, one of the editors of the *Protestant Churchman,* in which it was published, with the following introductory remarks : —

The death of this faithful man is a great public loss. Often have we read of his earnest and self-sacrificing career in the cause of temperance. Often have we met him in the course of his career with respect and delight. He served his divine Master faithfully, and he loved his fellow-men sincerely. No labors were too arduous, and no toils refused to rescue the victims of intemperance from ruin, and bring them as trophies to a Saviour's feet. We give below a very affectionate private letter from his son, the Rev. William G. Hawkins, at whose house he died.

"BOSTON, Sept. 15, 1858.

"REV. S. H. TYNG, D.D.: *Dear Brother,* — My dear father closed his earthly career, very suddenly, at my residence,

35*

in Pequea, Pa., on Thursday, the 26th of August. At his death he was sixty years, ten months, and twenty-eight days old. He came from his recent tour of lecturing in the State of Vermont, with a constitution much shattered by excessive labors; he was quite ill on reaching Boston, but soon, to all appearance, regained his usual vigor and robustness. In the spring he had intended continuing his labors until September, but in June wrote to me stating his indisposition, that he had reached an age when he found it impossible to endure the fatigue of body he once could. He announced his determination to spend the summer months at Pequea, and enjoy, in our beautiful retreat, the society of his family. He came with my mother on the first of July; the visit was a most happy one, meeting as he did a large number of his near relatives from Baltimore, of whose coming he had had no previous intimation. How much we all enjoyed his religious society, and how beautifully his Christian life seemed to shine forth towards its close! How lovingly his heart went out in prayer at our daily family altar for all his relatives, that they might be brought into the fold of Christ! His was a large heart, and no condition of man was omitted; he prayed for all. Never will his nephews and nieces forget his tender Christian sympathies, and his constant efforts to add to their happiness, during their visit to the country. How much innocent amusement did he intersperse in the exercises of each day; how often did he bring to them the basket of delicious cherries which his own hands had plucked.

"It was three weeks on Sabbath last that he addressed, in a most tender and affectionate manner, the children of my Sabbath school, and as he came from the church many of the congregation said, What a vigorous and healthy old gentleman your father is. All seemed to love and venerate him. Little did they think that they should see him no more on earth. On Tuesday, the 24th of August, he complained of slight indisposition, for the first time, but not in a manner to cause any alarm.

On the afternoon of that day we took the cars and proceeded to Philadelphia, to be present on the following day at the consecration of Bishop Bowman. In the evening he made known his intention to go in search of a poor family whom he had befriended a year previously, as he said, to see how they were getting on, promising to meet me at the church in the morning at eleven o'clock. Anticipating a crowd, services were commenced an hour sooner than the time announced; the gates were locked, and police stationed at each to prevent ingress or egress. I had no opportunity, therefore, of seeing my father, until near 3 P.M., at the railroad station. Never shall I forget the change in his features; those sunken eyes, that pallid face, and that *husky* voice. The crisis in the disease, as we now believe, had at this time *passed*. 'I found,' said he, 'that poor family, but in most happy circumstances, and they prevailed on me to spend the night with them. I did so, but,' he added, 'I have had an awful night. I have been ill all night.' I said, 'Father, why do you stand here? go and sit down.' 'Oh,' said he, 'I shall be better soon.' He thought, no doubt, by his powerful will to brave it off; he did not want to trouble us with his sickness. He busied himself in the preparations for departure; he said little, however, in the ride to Gap Station. We were met there in the carriage by Mrs. H. and his wife. I felt alarmed, and drove on as hastily as possible. He checked me, saying there was no necessity for driving so fast; that the evening was pleasant, and he enjoyed the ride much.

" He found supper ready on reaching the parsonage, but he would take nothing save a tumbler of boiled milk; he had already taken medicine prescribed in Philadelphia, and he hoped the dysentery under which he was suffering would soon be checked. He retired at 8 P.M., and we called at his room to say that if he was any worse to have us called. He would not allow his wife to arouse us, being herself feeble in health, but at one in the morning came to the door himself and called, saying, in a very calm manner, 'Go for the doctor immediately.'

In a few moments he was seized with cramp in his limbs from his knees downward. He turned to my sister, his daughter Hannah, and said, 'There is no use in doing any thing; you cannot help me now, — my case is similar to your husband's.' He had died a few years before of aggravated dysentery, being sick only a few hours. The doctor was soon by his bedside, but could do nothing beyond administering opiates and slight stimulants. At ten in the morning (Thursday) his pulse was rapidly declining. I aroused him, seeking some parting words. I said, 'Are you in any pain?' '*None* whatever.' 'Are you happy, and willing to depart?' '*Perfectly.*' I asked if he had any words to leave with his temperance friends, or relatives. 'None.' He turned to his wife and said, 'Farewell,' and gradually sank away, and without a pain passed to his blessed reward in the 'sanctuary above.'

Very affectionately yours,   W. G. H."

How the news of his decease was received by his relatives, the following letter will disclose: —

(FROM MRS. SCHAEFFER TO REV. W. G. HAWKINS.)

BALTIMORE, Sept. 3d, 1858.

MY DEAR WILLIAM, — Your letter dated 27th ult., containing the mournful particulars of your dear father's death did not reach us until Monday, September 1st. We had been anxiously looking for some tidings, and had imagined a thousand dreadful things; such as a violent death by railroad, etc. Such was the state of our minds, that when your letter reached us it was a great relief. Now we can reflect with submission, and even with joy, that he, after all his wanderings, his labors, his exposures to death in every form, should have come home to his own son's house to die in calmness and peace. I think with you, dear William, that it was God's time; that he had no further need for his services on earth, and called him up higher, to worship before his throne in heaven, where I have not the slightest doubt he is now singing the "song of Moses and the Lamb." Oh, I hope this sudden bereavement may be as a loud call to every one of us, "be ye also ready, for in such an hour as ye think not the Son of man cometh."

This unexpected blow has nearly crushed your dear grandmother. Although she sees the direct hand of God in this dispensation, her love *was strong*, her affection abiding, such as only a mother has. She regrets deeply that she has seen so little of him lately. But, she says, it will not be long before she shall meet him where parting is unknown. * * * Mr. Courtenay called to see Christian Keener yesterday, and read your letter to him; he wishes to notice your father's death in the temperance paper. * * * Is it not a mysterious providence, that mother having lost three children, should not have had the privilege of attending either of them in their dying hours? * * *

The news of Mr. Hawkins' sudden death called forth from the public press a very general expression of admiration of his services, and of the great loss the cause of temperance had sustained. Resolutions of condolence with the bereaved family were received from all parts of the country. In several places the halls of temperance were hung in mourning for thirty days. The Massachusetts State Temperance Convention met at Boston, September 14th, 1858, at which the following resolution was passed: —

Resolved, That we cherish profound respect for the memory of our late esteemed friend and fellow-worker, John H. W. Hawkins, whose sudden and unexpected demise fills us with regret for the loss of his continued labors and example. We recognize in him the truly religious spirit, the noble self-conqueror, the earnest, generous friend of the inebriate, the consistent, devoted advocate of the temperance reform in all its stages of development, and the kind, sympathizing brother ready to aid by voice and act every form of suffering humanity. We twine garlands for the victors in the field of blood; has not the day come to crown these more than martial conquerors — the moral heroes in life's great battle, achieving nobler conquests over vice and sin? In that starry roll of " names that were not born to die," we enshrine the name of John H. W. Hawkins, as that of a pioneer hero in the glorious Washingtonian reform, employing for the human brotherhood his best energies, with a brave and true heart, amid numberless discouragements, down to the lamented close of his honorable career.

The Rev. Mr. Beaman, of Salem, addressed the Convention in the following language : —

Permit me to occupy a few moments before the passage of this resolution, to express my hearty concurrence in this tribute to Mr. Hawkins. I am very glad that it is brought forward, and that the language is so expressive of the merits of our departed friend and fellow-laborer in the cause of temperance.

Those of us who remember the early days of the Washingtonian movement, bear in mind the very great enthusiasm awakened in the country by the soul-stirring addresses of Mr. Hawkins. No name stood higher at that time as a temperance lecturer, or drew together larger audiences. Wherever he went, success greeted him, and the reformations effected through his agency were truly wonderful. From that time until the day of his death, a few weeks ago, he continued to labor in the cause amid many discouragements, but keeping up his courage and hopefulness in the most desponding periods. Often straitened in his means, for, as he once told me, he never knew but one regular temperance lecturer to make money by the business, he persevered in going from place to place, animating the desponding and arousing the attention of the apathetic.

He has now closed his toils, dying, it may be said, in com parative obscurity; but not so, for angels marked the spot, and the world will take knowledge of it. Such men are the true heroes of life, far before those of the tented field, battling as they do for the best interests of man and for the welfare of the church and the world. He has gone from earth but has entered upon his rest in heaven.

We have received a communication from William B. Spooner, Esq., of Boston, speaking in highly complimentary terms of Mr. Hawkins' services; we regret that the late hour at which it was received prevents its appearance in this volume. The thrilling meetings referred to by Mr. Spooner, and the resolution offered by him in 1841, will be found in the course of the narrative. " Ever since," says Mr. S——, " the first evening at which he spoke in Boston, your father and myself have been fast friends. He possessed those natural traits of refinement, delicacy, sprightliness and sincerity, which made him a favorite wherever he was acquainted. He has frequently told me that the simple vote which I presented to the first meeting did more to give him encouragement and hope to go on with his labors, than any other circumstance. * * * I am glad you are preparing his biography; I think it will do much good, and is due to the memory of a truly good man and a great philanthropist and public benefactor."

On the 7th of November, 1858, the Parent Washington Temperance Society held a public meeting in Tremont Temple. We subjoin a brief account of the services on the occasion, extracted from the Boston *Temperance Visitor*, edited by S. B. Weston : —

On Sunday evening last, the meeting commemorative of the

services of the late John H. W. Hawkins, was held at Tremont Temple. Providence seemed to have kindly regarded the event, as in the early part of the day the storm which had prevailed during the week ceased, and the sun beamed forth from the sky above most gloriously. The muddy streets of our city were, by this means, rendered passable, very comfortably so. At a very early hour, large crowds might have been seen wending their way to the Temple. Long before the time for the services to commence, that spacious edifice was completely filled. Having been honored by the chairman of the Committee of Arrangements, William R. Stacy, Esq., with a complimentary card of invitation, we were introduced with others upon the speaker's platform. As we sat there, looking about over the large audience, we were struck with the magic loveliness of the picture presented, — the mass of living humanity, closely packed in the slips below, and rising in amphitheatre form in galleries, on either side of the house, — and we could not help thinking that the people are not forgetful or unthankful towards those who have spent their life and strength for the promotion of a great and humane cause. And then we thought that we should like to know the number in that large audience who have been directly benefited by the work of Mr. Hawkins. Could some that we saw there have spoken out the feelings of their hearts, how would they have given utterance to the warmest expressions of love and admiration for the memory of Mr. Hawkins. Could many a heart throbbing in many a female breast present have given expression to its emotions, how earnest would have been the thanksgiving ascending to heaven, for sending such a deliverer from wretchedness and woe as Mr. Hawkins. And then there were the early laborers and coadjutors in the Washingtonian reform, — men who have not only been reformed by Mr. Hawkins' labors, but have coöperated with him, — who have stayed up his hands and cheered his heart, as he has been toiling on in the great work of his life. There were Deacon

Grant, Stephen Fairbanks, Esq., Moses Mellen, Esq., Henry
Plympton, Esq., Daniel Kimball, Peter Thacher, Esqs., Hum-
phrey Chadbourne, Esq., Jacob Sleeper, Esq., and Jonathan
Preston, Esq.   Then there were the Presidents of the several
Washingtonian Societies in this city and vicinity: William R.
Stacy, Esq., of the Parent Washingtonian Society; Samuel C.
Knights, Esq., President of the Cambridgeport Temperance
Reform Association; T. M. Brown, Esq., President of the
Charlestown Temperance Society; B. W. Goodhue, of the
Roxbury Alliance, and several of the members and Directors
of these several societies.   Rev. Phineas Stowe, of the Bethel
Society, Rev. Mr. Denison, of the Neptune Temperance So-
ciety, S. A. B. Bragg, Esq., the present G. W. P. of the Sons
of Temperance, of this State, Albert Day, Esq., Superintendent
of the Home for the Fallen, William Adams, Jr., Agent for the
Home, and other firm and true friends of temperance were there.

The exercises commenced by an anthem from the choir.
The musical direction of the evening was entrusted to Mr.
E. H. Frost, and was most admirably executed.   The Tremont Musical Association performed its part in the arrangements in most admirable style, and the greatest credit is due
them.   The anthem, and the original hymn prepared for the
occasion, were all sung in a most effective manner.   Rev. Converse L. McCurdy, of this city, read selections from Scripture,
and offered prayer.   These were characterized by great appropriateness and solemnity.   The following original hymn,
written by Hodges Reed, Esq., of Taunton, was then sung:—

> There are crowns in the hall of the palace on high,
>   Laid up till the end of the days,
> For those who turn many to righteousness,
>   From their dark and dangerous ways.
>
> There's a crystal stream in the better land,
>   Which flows from the great white throne,
> Where the darkest stains are washed away,
>   When the labors of earth are done.

36

Our brother is gone for his crown on high,
    All starred with the rescued ones;
He helped them to dash the tempter's cup,
    And now they are owned as sons.

He is gone up to drink of the water of life,
    And to bathe in the crystal flood, —
He rested, while here, by Cherith's brook,
    But there, by the river of God.

Oh, come! mourn his loss, ye tempted ones!
    And catch the mantle he wore;
For he's gone to his rest, and his trumpet call,
    On the earth shall be heard no more.

The address of Joseph Story, Esq. followed. What shall we say of it? If classic beauty of diction, richness of illustration, and attractiveness of delivery, can make a good address, then was that of Mr. Story a decided success. It was attentively listened to throughout, and was evidently appreciated by those who heard it. The speaker did not seek to present any thing like a biographical sketch of Mr. Hawkins, or a statistical view of the results of the labors of the distinguished reformer, but to draw from his life the great lessons which it is calculated to enforce. He sought to catch and enforce the inspiration emanating from the Great Reformer, and to make it warm and animate the hearts of his listeners.

After the address, the following original ode, written by the Rev. Charles W. Denison for the occasion, was sung: —

Mourn we now the gallant dead?
    Weep we here the honored brave?
Freely, then, our tears we shed,
    HAWKINS fills a glorious grave!

His the grave a hero fills,
    Bravely fallen in the fray!
On the everlasting hills,
    Stands his victor-soul to-day!

Streaming from his starry brow,
  Light pours on our battle-field ;
Hark ! he calleth to us now : —
  "BROTHERS, FIGHT ! — BUT NEVER YIELD !"

By the conflicts HAWKINS wrought,
  By the victories he won !
Bravely shall our field be fought,
  Till the fight of life is done !

The benediction was then pronounced, and the company separated.

We regret that the limits of this work forbid our giving more than the few following extracts from the admirable address of Mr. Story : —

Amid the various and engrossing cares of business, there has been but little time to make a careful preparation for this occasion ; and perhaps it may be as well that our words should not be too studied or formal, but in a more social way speak forth the promptings of the heart. Let the thoughts of this hour, then, be our heart-thoughts.

But why, indeed, should I speak ? What need of words ? This which meets our sight, — this which each finds kindling within, is more eloquent far than any faltering words of mine. Surely, the whole scene within our beautiful Temple ; this great multitude of warmly beating hearts, is in itself a generous and fitting tribute to the memory of our absent brother. Brother ! — yes, for the same Being is father over us all. Absent ! — for the voyage of life is past, the bark has reached its last port, and the voyager stands on the immortal shore, whence there is no return.

It is no purpose of mine to deal in unseemly adulation, for we come not hither to pay homage to royal birth or ephemeral fame, but rather to testify our appreciation of noble purposes, faithful labors, and kindly deeds. And for those purposes, those labors, and those deeds, thousands of hearts made happy have embalmed in grateful memories the name of JOHN HAWKINS.

Let us in spirit tarry for awhile in that distant valley, amid the sturdy oaks whose summer shade he so lately enjoyed, and by the side of that spot where loving hands have laid him; around which even at this hour the autumn winds are twining chaplets of withered leaves, sad memorials of frail and fading human life. With these sweet sounds passing by us like the music of Vesper bells on the evening air, let us contemplate the character of our brother, and the genius of his labors; and while paying a fitting tribute to him, have our hearts stimulated to every noble purpose and holy work. * * *

Possessed of great energy of character, warm and tender sympathies, and a natural turn of eloquence, soul-stirring and earnest, he is called to a high and noble mission, enters with a whole heart on the work, and in coöperation with his fellow laborers inaugurates the great temperance reformation of this generation.

In cities and towns, all through the Union, the people are astonished, and throngs gather to the halls wherever this unpretending man tells of the gloom of the past and the joy of the present.

There was a mighty influence moving through the land. It was not like the spectral blazing chariot of fire, with its sweeping train rushing across the track of worlds, coming we know not whence, and flying we know not where, startling all with wonder, but bringing good to none; but it was rather like the falling dews of evening, and the gentle light of morning, covering earth with beauty and gladness, carrying blessings wherever it went. * * *

I shall never forget when this new pioneer in the noble work told us, in our own Faneuil Hall, years ago, the story of the drunkard's life, in words and looks that burned with earnest truth, the tears from many a manly eye bearing witness to the power with which he spoke.

In this great Washingtonian Reform which swept so rapidly through the land, thousands of poor degraded men were saved, and the fact demonstrated, that though cast down and nearly ruined, and though every light and hope was almost extinguished, yet beneath the black embers, and under-laying the ashes of former virtue and promise, there was still left the vital spark, which could be rekindled, into a bright flame. Shunned and neglected by others on the one hand, losing confidence and respect for himself on the other, every avenue for his escape appeared closed. In this new movement it was as when the breath passed over the slain in the valley, and the dry bones lived, and stood up on their feet, an exceeding great army. So these came forth, under the breath of the new inspiration, a mighty host, armed and panoplied for the conflicts of life, with all the nobleness of their manhood again.

To this work of love Mr. Hawkins lent his whole soul, and stood forth the leading champion of the service. It was this new principle, by deeds of love and words of tender sympathy to inspire confidence and hope in the fallen, and to cheer them on in manly trial — it was this principle that was the secret spring to that amazing success which crowned his efforts.

The power of intemperance was understood and preached as never done before; and the inner life of the inebriate was unfolded in a new light. He *was* still a man, the immortal spark not quite quenched, — a wreck fast crumbling to decay but not quite destroyed. There are throbbings there of a noble heart, crushed and lacerated though he may be. He is still a man!

> "The huge rough stones without the mines,
>   Unsightly and unfair,
>   Have veins of purest marble hid
>   Beneath the roughness there.

36*

" Few rocks so bare but to the height
  Some tiny moss-plant clings,
And round the crags most desolate,
  The sea-bird soars and sings.

" Believe me, then, that rugged souls
  Beneath their roughness hide
Much that is soft and beautiful,
  They have their angel's side."

He is an actor on the stage of life behind a mask; playing
another part, some character not his own. That trembling,
staggering body, in pains of "palsy, plague and fever and
madness all combined," that is not the man. That is the living embodiment of the curse of intemperance, stalking in human form; but hidden within is the man, bound in prison.
Search for him with an eye of pity; call to him with a voice
of love, and perchance you may give him strength to break
the bonds and shake off the prison fetters. By his faithful
labors thousands have seen that look, have heard that cheering
word the bright one spoke, "Strive and hope for better days."

Ofttimes along his dreary journey, this man of many sorrows has sighed for the former days of happiness, long passed
away, but not forgotten; in the hidden chambers of his soul,
wished he might become the child of innocence, the joyous boy
once more. Ah, those memories! floating like distant music to
his ear, but past, — all past and gone!

In a touching tradition connected with the chime of bells on
the Limerick Cathedral, it is said they were made for a convent in Italy, by an enthusiastic native, with great labor and
skill. The Italian, having afterwards acquired a competency,
fixed his house near the convent cliff, and for many years enjoyed the daily chime of his beloved bells. But in some political convulsion which followed, the monks were driven from
the monastery, the Italian exiled from his home, and the bells
were carried away to Ireland.

After a long interval, the course of his wanderings brought

him to Limerick. On a calm and beautiful summer's evening, as the vessel which bore him floated along the broad stream of the Shannon, he suddenly heard the bells (his well-remembered bells) peal forth from the Cathedral Tower. They were the long-lost treasures of his memory; — home, happiness, friends, — all early recollections were in their sound. Crossing his arms on his breast, he lay back in the boat. When the rowers looked round, they saw his face still turned towards the Cathedral, but his eyes were closed on the world.

Many of these wanderers and exiles floating on the stream of time have often had awakened early recollections of home, happiness, and friends. Yes, often have they suddenly heard the bells pealing forth from the cathedral towers of memory, and have seen "the light of other days" flash through the gloom, and then sank down to melancholy despair.

Heaven blessed Mr. Hawkins in his unceasing and laborious toil to redeem such as these; for its accomplishment, all these eighteen years, in sacrificings and journeyings, in heat and cold, by day and night, in storm and fair, his heart has never grown cold, his hands weary, or his lips silent. Upon this altar was laid his all, — time, means, and strength. My words would do injustice to the promptings of my heart, did I not pay him his just meed of praise.

Who cannot bless God that such an apostle was raised up at such a time, to carry forward so glorious a work. Bless God that he himself was lifted up, — as one has lately said: —

> " To rouse the sad inebriate, left to grope
> In midnight darkness unrelieved by hope,
> And bid him, with one last strong effort burst
> The bonds that bind him to the fiend accurst,
> For who that hears how Hawkins was made free,
> Can henceforth say, ' There is no hope for me ? ' "

Aye, bless God for this example, at once so noble, so generous, of one who loved his fellow-men. Wherein he did well, let us imitate his example, remembering that we live in a weak and erring world, — that no man liveth to himself alone. The subtle thread of sympathy runs through every heart, binding the whole family in one. Who shall wrest it from its secret hiding place? Who shall rob its pulses of their fullest circuit? Corroding riches cannot fill its place. Wealth or power cannot buy it, for it is heaven born. God plants it in the inner chamber of the heart. True love, — true charity, — it is not in the pile of gold you tender. It may be in a simple word, a look. The feeblest deed, the offering of a kindly heart, is more of love divine and charity than all the bags of mouldering gold in yonder vaults, when wrung from sordid hands. "Whoever shall give to drink unto one of these little ones a cup of cold water only, verily, I say unto you, he shall in no wise lose his reward." * * *

It is noble to crown our lives with kindly deeds. It is exalting to sow blessings around our pathway. "There is that scattereth, and yet increaseth; and there is that withholdeth more than is meet, but it tendeth to poverty." Shall we not know the happy experience that it is "blessed to give," and to do? Would we drive far hence a multitude of ills? Would we open unknown avenues of joy, and lighten many a weary care or burden? Let us give our hearts, our hands, our lips, to some good work of love, and live for others, not ourselves alone.

> "Would'st thou from sorrow find a sweet relief?
> Or is thy heart oppressed with woes untold?
> Balm would'st thou gather for corroding grief?
> Pour blessings round thee like a shower of gold."

I have not deemed it needful to enter into a detailed narrative of his various labors from place to place, or to recount all the results wrought out for the happiness and prosperity of multitudes who have been redeemed through his untiring efforts, or to speak of the great progress made in the general cause to which he was so strongly attached; that labor is already in other lands.

But I content myself within the time allotted me to dwell on the spirit and principle of the service to which his strength was first given, of the remarkable reformation with which his name is inseparably identified; which have been and shall still be the bright star of hope to many crushed and broken hearts. My heart and thoughts have clustered around the great practical truth which they developed; that a large number of those who seem to be almost hopelessly degraded by intoxication, may be reclaimed and restored to society. Yet in view of the strength and control of this unnatural appetite over its victims and slaves, I am convinced that every one who would reform (and it is often a fearful conflict), must bring into exercise the most vital energy of his own self-will, and needs to seek refuge under the hallowed influences of moral and religious principle, and above all to lay hold on the help of God, ere he can safely say, " I am forever redeemed." " Let him that thinketh he standeth, take heed lest he fall."

Thus have my words been chosen, that the lessons we draw from our contemplation on this occasion, may prompt us to those noble aspirations and holy deeds, which can make us each in our sphere a blessing to our generation.

It was appropriate at the very close of his life, that among his last acts of love should be a visit to a family where but a year before he had bestowed his blessing. It was a bright ray of light, gilding the sky of his declining day.

Death came suddenly upon him, and on the 26th of August, at the house of his son, in the midst of delightful associations, surrounded by the wife and kindred he loved, he bade the final " farewell," and like a shock of corn fully ripe for the harvest, this faithful laborer, this Christian soldier, was gathered to his rest. He has gone from among us, and who buildeth his monument?

The obelisks and pyramids of Egypt are among the grandest works of art to commemorate the deeds of her kings, but their names were stained with blood and cruelty. Wealth and

power can rear sculptured marble and costly statues to whomsoever they will, but our most expressive monuments are those
reared by ourselves, the purchase of our own lives, the work of
our own hands.

The most faithful monument to the painter, is the almost
breathing form with which he himself has clothed the canvas ;
to the sculptor, the beautiful being his own skilful fingers en-
ticed from the shapeless block of marble ; to the poet, his own
lines, the gems of poetry which make his name and fame immortal.   The noblest monument to Washington is that by which
he wins from a whole nation the endearing title, " The Father
of his Country."   Although some chiselled stone marks a
sacred spot in our own beautiful Auburn, yet the true memorials which bear a perpetual fragrance to the name of Amos
Lawrence are found in the city of the living, amid the busy
streets, in all the homes he blessed, in all the hearts he gladdened.

Whoever has passed down from St. Paul's Cathedral into
the vault below, and stood by the dust of those whose names
form a bright galaxy on the pages of English history, will well
remember the unpretending slab that marks the resting-place
of one who will never be forgotten as long as those foundation
stones endure.   In the adjoining wall is a marble slab with this
inscription : " Beneath lies Sir Christopher Wren, the builder
of this Cathedral and city, who lived for more than ninety
years, not to himself, but to the public good," and closing with
these words : " *Lector, si monumentum requiris ? Circumspice.*"
(Reader, seekest thou his monument ? Look around.)   This
vast cathedral, with all its magnificent appointments, these lofty
church towers, these public works, are all the monuments of his
mighty mind and genius.

Here, then, are the most truthful monuments to him of whom
we speak.   These happy homes, these reunited companions,
these joyful parents and children, these blessings, these kindly
deeds, scattered in cities and towns, over many a mountain and

down through many a vale, along many a river's bank, and in many a forest shade. These are the memorials which bear witness to the character of John Hawkins, and the genius of his labors.

Then, kind friends, in that distant valley, amid the sturdy oaks whose summer shade he so lately enjoyed, and by the side of that spot where loving hands have laid him, around which even at this hour the autumn winds have been twining their chaplets of withered leaves, let there be placed the appropriate inscription, —

"Lector si monumentum requiris ? Circumspice."

From the many tributes to the memory of Mr. Hawkins, received by his family, we can only select the following, from his friend and co-laborer, Wm. H. Burleigh, Esq., of New York : —

Shall we not drop a tributary tear,
O *Champion of the Fallen !* on thy bier ?
Not for *thy* sake, for thou hast found thy rest
Among the many mansions of the blessed,
Where pours no fiery, desolating flood,
Swollen with tears, incarnadined with blood ;
Nor ribald song, nor drunkard's jest profane,
Nor horrid oath, shall vex thine ear again !

Oh, who thy perfect blessedness can tell,
As lauds and hallelujahs round thee swell,
While angel hands sweep over quivering wires,
To wake the music of a thousand lyres,
And angel voices, tuned in sweet accord,
Welcome thee home, thrice blessed of the Lord !
Nay, not for *thee*, thou habitant of heaven !
But for the wine-enthralled our tears are given.

Thy pleading voice can touch their hearts no more,
Thy ministry of love for them is o'er.
Who, when the goblet tempts, shall woo them thence
With thy heart-breathed, persuasive eloquence ?

Thou, who didst once his sore temptation know,
Couldst but compassionate the drunkard's woe;
Freed from the bondage of the cup accurst,
Thou strengthenedst others from that thrall to burst
And though they stood upon the dark gulf's edge,
Saved them from ruin, through our glorious pledge!

Thou *art not dead!* for still thy name shall be
Heard in the *songs* of those thou hast made free;
The wife, whose husband thou didst toil to save,
Not vainly, from the drunkard's yawning grave,
Shall teach her little ones in coming days,
To tell thy story and to lisp thy praise;
The child, redeemed from all the shames that fill
A rum-cursed house, from woes that blight and kill,
Lisping thy name, shall link it morn and even,
With the sweet prayers that tremble up to heaven.

The ransomed drunkard, once a hopeless slave,
Snatched from a vicious life, an early grave,
Once more to friends, wife, children, home restored,
And taught the way that leadeth to the Lord, —
Shall keep thy memory treasured in his heart
Amid its holiest things, till life depart;
And bless thy name, while lip, and eye, and breast,
The strong emotions of his soul attest!

That lovely name shall be a spell of power,
To guard the feeble in temptation's hour,
And make them strong the tempter to repel,
Who binds his victims with the chains of hell;
To rouse the sad inebriate left to grope
In midnight darkness, unrelieved by hope,
And bid him, with one last, strong effort, burst
The bonds that bind him to the fiend accurst —
For who that hears how Hawkins was made free,
Can henceforth say, " *There is no hope for me.*"

And when the triumph comes — as come it will,
When baffled, flies the Demon of the still,
And heaven-born Temperance pours o'er every land,
Her richest blessings with a liberal hand;

Thy prayers and tears and toils to haste the day
Where all may join in her benignant sway,
Remembered still, shall oft recounted be,
And glad thanksgivings shall be poured for *thee*.

Farewell! in hope we leave thy hallowed dust,
To wait the resurrection of the just!
Oh, be thy faith and zeal and courage *ours*,
While called to battle with unholy powers,
And may our lives like *thine* be freely given
To bless the earth, till they exhale to heaven!

www.ingramcontent.com/pod-product-compliance
Lightning Source LLC
Chambersburg PA
CBHW031051110726
47900CB00003B/883